The Wolf Oath

TOSHA Y. MILLER

THE WOLF OATH

TOSHA Y. MILLER

THE
WOLF
OATH

TOSHA Y. MILLER

The Wolf Oath

Book and Cover design by Kreative Covers & Germancreative

ISBN:13: 9781667145624

Second Edition: June 2021

Also by Tosha Y. Miller

The Hell Dimension Series

The Dark Souls Academy

Claiming Her Mates

***

Earth and Hell Dimension Series

The Wolf Oath

The Demon Oath

The Mate Oath

(Coming Soon)

***

The Autioma Dimension (Standalone)

The Wolf Trials

***

The Lineup Series

The Mate Lineup

***

The Unnatural Series

Three Book in One

The Smokiest Grave

The Darkest Grave

The Coldest Grave

Two types of supernatural wolves:
SPOILER ALERT

Wolf shifters: They are usually people born as a human able to turn into a wolf. The stronger the wolf, the more it can talk in the human's mind. They are more stable and can live a normal life. They can shift whenever they want to. If a male is bitten, he usually becomes a wolf shifter. It is rare for a female to be a wolf shifter.

Appearance: Wolf shifter resemble wolves when transformed.

Werewolf: This is a half wolf being. Most of the time it is women who get bitten. They are controlled by the moon and their animal instincts. So, they must live in packs and have a devoted Alpha to be near them. They lose themselves during full moons and can only shift during these times.

Appearance: Werewolves resemble a half human and wolf beast. They can be stronger and deadlier that a wolf, but they are easily controlled by an Alpha.

Author's Note

This is the new edited version. This book is written a little differently than others. Yes, it's third person past tense, but **the narrator is still Piper**. She also has a voice inside of her that <u>speaks to her in first person present tense</u> since that's usually how people speak in their head. All of those incidences are italicized.

Please note this has a few triggers. There is adult language, sexual conduct, violence, demons, criminals, and investigators.

PART ONE

The change was inevitable

Chapter One

"Run! Move your sexy asses! We're almost there," her hiking buddy and old college classmate, Roger, yelled as he leaped over a massive rotten log. The wood crumbled under his muscular weight, and his body disappeared behind the broken tree. The thud and whimper from his annoying mouth had Piper Heart smirking.

Good, served him right for being a douche.

For a split second, she debated showing off and jumping over it as well. *Nope.* There was no way her unco-ordinated ass and a log that big were coming into contact. A few months ago, she could—maybe— but not now. She had an issue staying upright while walking these days —no need to tempt fate. Her new adventure would be done slowly— no falling or embarrassing herself. A broken leg or sprained ankle would be the perfect cherry on top of her shit life.

We won't even make it halfway over the log if you don't eat. Piper rolled her eyes and ignored the voice in her head.

That kind of hurt her pride, though. She ate when she was hungry. If it was only once a day, or not at all, so be it. Depression had its sharp, icy claws in her. The only thing she had going for her was her abnormal strength. Despite being a little malnourished, her strength stayed, helping soothe her ego. Otherwise, she'd have to pull a move from Nina White's book and ask the guys to carry her backpack.

Just thinking about it annoyed Piper to the bone. She needed to have a small amount of control in her dumpster-fire of a life. This was her control. Despite the ache in her back, she was going to hold her own shit.

The thing weighed as much as Nina did. Okay, so her best friend was barely over five feet tall and thin. Her hourglass shape exaggerated her hips and bubble butt, but she still didn't weigh that much. Even so, it still helped her to be proud of herself. Baby steps to being happy again, right?

Luke shuffling his feet caught her attention. "I don't know why you invited him, Nina. The dude's a jerk," Luke said ahead of them. Nina just shrugged in response.

Luke sighed. "I guess it could be worse. You could have brought Frank or Crystal." He put his hands up when Nina hissed through her teeth. "Don't get me wrong, they're cool, but we don't need a fox shifter or a witch around."

Roger grunted. "You afraid of some, what are they calling them now? Black Souls?"

Luke shook his head. "No, dumbass, Dark Souls. And those are only the supernaturals with demon blood in them. I'm talking about the Light Souls."

Roger stood up and brushed off his back. "Whatever, they're both at war with each other, so the winner will probably get to name them all. I'm just glad this place is now an English-speaking destination," Roger said as he hid behind a tree. He liked to climb trees, so when his head popped over a branch Piper wasn't surprised.

Piper wouldn't voice it, but things were changing with supernaturals. They were putting themselves in light and dark categories. But Norway was safe from that turmoil. The light had already won this territory. She was glad her; Nina, Luke, and Roger weren't accompanied by anyone else. They were all humans with no supernatural gifts, so they didn't have to worry about supernatural politics. Piper tried to stay away from that altogether.

Nina scoffed. "Luke, I didn't know you were such a bigot. And Roger you're toting a line too buddy, so don't shake your head at him." She crossed her arms. "You both know my family comes from witches, right? Besides, it doesn't matter if a person is supernatural or not, as long as they're good people who care," Nina scolded, rolling her eyes.

"Yeah, and I get it," Roger said from somewhere in the trees, probably ready and waiting to scare one of them again. The little bastard got her three times already.

She hoped the trip helped. She needed good memories.

It wasn't every day she took long hikes in the forests of Eastern Norway because talk about beautiful! The pictures she googled didn't do the place justice.

Just last month, she was sitting in her living room about ready to pull out all of her long brown hair as she went through her over-due bills. She had no one to call for help or even advice. Nina wasn't very helpful. She depended on a guy to figure that kind of stuff out. Piper was too much of a loner for that kind of life. She was too weird to let anyone get too close.

When she packed her stuff for the trip, she promised herself things would change. *No more avoiding things,* she told herself. If she got the opportunity to make friends, she would take a chance. The trip was about her transformation, and she was determined to change for the better.

She sighed as her eyes scanned her surroundings. The morning rain gave everything a sparkle, and the lake nearby shined like a flashlight running over diamonds. The tall, full, Norway Jack and Scots spruces came to a point like the perfect Christmas tree. All this place needed was some lights, and she'd feel like she was in heaven.

She grinned as she declared it The Christmas Tree Forest. Forget decorating the block and having people drive by to admire the lit-up houses. Instead, decorate the forest and have them walk the trail. Sweet Christmas dreamland!

Yeah, putting up thousands of lights might be challenging, but how cool would that be? She'd come every year to see the light show.

And the air! The crisp pine air stole her breath away, then generously filled her lungs. Each breath tasted like the cleanest water. She'd gladly fall dead here and be happy about her fate.

Piper's eyes scanned around her again; bright green moss covered everything. Her heart rate spiked in her chest. *Are we going the right way? How can Nina be sure? It all looks the same.*

Nina was quick to reassure her, reading her in a snap. "Don't worry, I know where I'm going."

You better, she thought.

Nina had been her best friend since high school, so she trusted her. She was the only person Piper trusted these days. So, when she came up with this brilliant plan to drag her through Christmas tree forest and perform a ceremony over large spiritual rocks, Piper agreed—after an hour or so of arguing, of course. She needed to say goodbye to her twin sister, Trace, and Nina promised she could if they did the ceremony.

An image of her and her sister relaxing in Trace's house library as they read smutty books flashed in her mind. The only thing Trace and Nina had in common was they liked dark smut books or shows. She loved them too, but not anymore. Even thinking about books put a sour taste in her mouth. Maybe that'd change once she did the ceremony.

Nina performed her own when her mom passed away. She found it in one of her family's old books. Since Piper refused when her own mother passed, she had to do it this time.

The images of Nina crying so hard her eyes swelled shut flashed in Piper's mind. A different person came back. Someone better, someone happier, like the sorrow and hurt just disappeared.

Ugh, that was what she needed.

I'm already about to lose my house, I lost my job, and I'm spending most of my days in bed. How much worse can things get? I want to forget. Please let these ridiculous rocks make my pain disappear too. Piper all but prayed as they continued walking.

Luke finally replied, "Yeah, you're right, sorry. But I'd rather be around my own kind, ya know? I don't hate them, just don't want to go on vacations with them. You're different, Nina."

Nina scoffed and stopped walking, making sure Piper stopped as well. Luke turned around to wait. "No, I don't want to be so close to you right now. Keep walking. Piper and I are taking a break from you guys. If Piper didn't need three other people with her for this thing tonight, it would have been just her and me anyway." She shooed him with her hand. The wrinkle on her forehead indicated her annoyance clearly.

She didn't know where she stood on the supernatural stance. Not really. She'd rather not be involved.

Her father was an investigator, so she knew exactly how evil some supernaturals could be. He'd encountered his fair share of supernaturals and demons over the years. Did that mean all supernaturals were bad...? No, but her father's cases were enough for her to keep her distance at the very least.

She met the guy they were talking about, Frank, a couple of times, but other than that, she hardly ever spent any time with them. They always seemed too cocky for her liking. Shoot, even these two guys were too much, but Nina had to have them tag along.

She glanced over at Nina as she muttered to herself. Piper didn't like seeing her upset, so she grabbed her hand to get her attention. "This feels great, Nina. Thanks for dragging my lazy butt out of bed." She jumped over a smaller, healthier log than Roger had jumped over. The dirt on the other side slid under her feet. Not enough for Piper to fall, but enough to give her a mini heart attack. She clung to the wood for support.

See! This was why she kept her adventuring to a minimum.

She breathed in through her nose and out her mouth to calm her nerves. *This is supposed to be fun and give us a new purpose. Don't go ruining it over some slippery mud.* The voice taunted her again.

Now, if only dark would come sooner. She was yearning to stargaze and to finally be able to talk to her sister...

Yep, her life had finally gone off the rockers. The new and improved Piper had done some iffy crap, but she'd try anything to get out of this slump. If new and improved can be described as heartbroken, life-throw-away-er, and chronic crier, then that's her all the way.

Nina grinned. "Hey, it's no Hogwarts adventure, but I think it'll help." Her smile warmed Piper's newly cold heart, and her eyes grew blurry, so she turned away. No crying, dammit. She was so sick of crying. She was just glad no one could read minds because if they could, she'd be labeled crazy in a heartbeat.

She shrugged. "Too bad. Maybe, if I was a witch, I could take away the pain." Piper loved Harry Potter, but she didn't even know if magical wands could help her.

Nina grabbed her hand and squeezed. She let go, knowing her affection would make Piper cry for sure. "I get it, Toots." Piper sighed at the nickname she frequently used for Nina. If Nina was using the nickname, Piper was worse off than she thought. She used the name Toots as a term of endearment, but Nina used it when things got serious.

Nina bit her plump bottom lip and tucked her dark curly hair behind her ear. Her sad hazel eyes were going to be Piper's undoing. "I love you, Toots."

Really? Two usages of her nickname in one conversation. She really was off the deep end.

Her eyes darted away from her friend. The trees needed more attention. At least they wouldn't make her cry.

No more of that. We're done crying. The voice inside her mind repeated what she'd been telling herself for months.

Yep, when she said the voice, she meant an actual Voice inside her head. It was a whole other entity inside of her, sarcastic and a pain in her ass. But most days, to her bitter dismay, the voice kept her grounded.

There was a good chance the voice could drive her insane one day, though, and she'd end up in a padded room, but for now, she needed it more than she ever had.

The supernatural world was still a mystery to her—except for what she learned from her dad—but she knew ordinary people didn't hear voices in their heads telling them what to do. Shoot, from what she knew, supernaturals didn't either. Only her sister had known about her dirty little secret. Now, no one did.

What? I'm not dirty? The voice griped at her.

It's just an expression. Remember what I said? don't talk to me while people are around. It makes me look crazy. She chastised the voice.

"Jeez, where did you go? You have a nasty look on your face like you smell poop." Nina scanned the ground. "Wait, you don't, right?"

Piper laughed, shook her head, and kicked a rock. "Just thinking... I wish I could turn off my mind. The random slaps in the face by my thoughts suck."

"Girl, I get it. Losing someone you love is the worst

heartache. I've been there." She shrugged. "My mind still is a nasty whor—"

Piper cut her off before she could cuss. "Hey, you're disturbing the animals with the potty mouth." When in doubt revert back to humor.

Nina giggled and pointed at a family of deer in the distance. They did move away, though not hastily. "Aw sorry, Bambi."

"You're so stupid," Piper said. The rare smile that stretched her lips took her by surprise, but damn, it felt good. "Be careful." Piper's hand went out to keep Nina from falling over. Only Nina would trip over every hole in the ground.

At least Piper's clumsiness was due to the months spent in bed and lack of nourishment. Nina had always been chaos prone.

Roger ran from behind a tree and yelled, "Boo!" in Luke's ear. Luke jumped and punched Roger in the stomach. Piper smirked. Luke had been wanting to do that the whole trip here. The little smirk on his face was proof of that.

Roger doubled over in pain, grunting. "Shit, man," he wheezed out.

Luke patted Roger's back. "I told you I don't react well to being scared."

"Was that necessary?" Roger grunted.

"Don't be a drama queen. I barely hit you." Luke had a smug gleam in his dark green eyes that said he enjoyed the powerful feeling.

"Barely, my ass." Roger stood but kept rubbing his belly. "That hurt like hell."

"Well, next time, you'll listen to my warning. I don't

like things jumping out at me. I've seen way too many scary movies, and the woods have me on edge. I don't want to be the next victim in some scary movie."

Roger narrowed his dark brown eyes, ready to prove him wrong. "Really, you won't die if—"

Nina cut him off. "No, Roger. I don't wanna hear about a death. Please. I'd like to be able to sleep tonight."

"Aw, no fun. But don't worry, I'll cuddle with you to keep you safe." Roger tried for the millionth time. He ran his hand through his dark hair. He still had a thing for Nina, but truth be told, he had a thing for anyone that would give him a chance.

Nina cringed, and Luke scowled. Why Nina thought going camping with her ex—Roger—and her might-be-a-new-thing—Luke—was a good idea baffled Piper.

Besides being swimmers, the guys were opposites. Roger had smooth dark skin, a bright smile, and a smug personality that Piper never liked. He was an asshole most days.

In contrast, Luke had light brown skin, bright eyes that reflected a deep green, and a caring personality. They were both into Nina, which was why she invited them. They paid for Piper's and her trip out here. Piper didn't mind their presence as long as she got to spend time with Nina and talk to her dead sister. It was nice to have some muscle with them, though, just in case, even if they were constantly bickering.

Piper took out the traveler's map. The paper was crinkled from her constant grip on it. "You better not be checking that map again. I told you I can get us there. I got you." Nina scowled at her. She didn't like Piper using a map, her controlling issues were on high. Piper couldn't trust anything right now, her anxiety rode her too hard, so she glanced at the map in secret. She was too paranoid.

Nina was focused on the guys right now, so Piper hurried. The path was marked for her, and it seemed they were on the right track. The place wasn't a tourist spot, but the local cities talked about the ancient rocks. They had to be close. The map—

Luke turned around, interrupting her. His smile bright and his shoulders sagged in relief. "We're here!"

Piper gulped and put the map away. Could someone be overwhelmed by anxiety but be excited at the same time? Because that was her.

She lifted her chin in determination. Here went nothing.

Chapter Two

The small, open campgrounds next to Nina's large rocks came into view. The four of them stood tall in a circle. It kind of creeped her out, but she'd never say that out loud. Nina wanted this to be perfect.

Piper jogged the last few feet in excitement. They had made it. Thank goodness. A pinch of her anxiety lessened.

A tear fell down her cheek. Piper swiped it away with enough strength that her skin threatened to come off. *Fucking shithole tears.* She was done crying.

Sometimes crying is okay. Our sister... Our father... the thoughts were too heavy to think.

Images flashed in Piper's mind of her dad. He had her take some online classes to be qualified, despite her age. She smirked at the thought. His thick brown hair and matching beard always made him look like Santa Claus' son. The pot belly he got over the past few years didn't help. He'd fit perfectly in the Christmas tree forest.

A wave of grief hit her in the chest. He wouldn't want

to talk to her. Sure, times were different, but bringing a kid to crime scene, even with magic to help keep the scene safe, was still frowned upon. Piper had a knack for solving cases, though. Her dad fought hard to keep her at his side, and it eventually cost him his job—the one thing that kept him sane after her mom had passed.

She mentally shook her head to clear the memories. *Now you're rambling. What's your point? I still don't want to cry.*

My point is that we may need to cry.

I'm done with that. It's not helping.

Neither is bottling it up like we do. We don't deal until it destroys us.

Piper ignored the voice. What did she know, anyway? She threw down her heavy bag. The dirt bounced in the air, congratulating her on their arrival.

"Come on, help me make dinner, Piper. I brought some good food," Nina said, pulling her along.

After the canned veggies and beans were done cooking, the moon was out. She lifted her gaze to the sky and smiled at all the twinkling stars. Stargazing was so much better away from the city.

The sound of scraping spoons picking up their last bites made Piper's gut tighten. She wasn't sure she was ready. She was supposed to say goodbye and move on, although, she wanted to hold on to her sister. But how long could she hold on without killing herself too?

They had to wait to do anything weird. Nina said something about the right time to speak to the dead or whatever. Piper didn't care. Setting up camp with tents and a fire pit took time, mainly because they had to find enough dry logs. Yet, it was spent in a daze of peaceful joy.

Nina squeezed her hand in the middle of blowing out

her fire-engulfed marshmallow. S'mores were a must on camping trips.

Roger's marshmallow caught flame. "Well, hell." He swung the ball of fire toward Luke. "Open up."

"Dude, not cool. Put that out. I'm not losing my eyebrows again because you want to play with fire."

Roger faked a pout. "Aw, come on. We had to find out what a whole can of lighter fluid would do in a barbecuer. Stop being so butt-hurt over it."

"I got called a pencil dick for half a year, dipshit."

"Well, what did you expect? Most of your hair and eyebrows were gone. You're tall and skinny. Besides, I thought it'd give you more character."

Luke blanched. His mouth opened wide as his mind worked. "You?" He blinked a few times and tackled Roger to the ground. "You gave me that name, asshole?" He yelled and smacked Roger's face several times. Not enough to do damage, but enough to be annoying.

Roger grunted as he toppled over, his stick flung into the surrounding trees behind him. *Dammit.*

Piper rolled her eyes. These idiots might kill themselves before she even got to speak with her sister. Nina needed to have a man at her side, not these children. Just as the thought was out, Nina screeched and fell backward off her log chair, startled. She couldn't help but laugh. Okay, maybe they had more in common than she thought.

Piper jogged to the small flame next to a tree trunk. Thank goodness the wood was still wet. Not enough for it to be muddy, but enough to keep the tree from catching in the blaze.

She kicked dirt over the fire. Its sticky consistency made clumps build up on her shoes instead of on the fire.

But the clusters of mud worked fine. She scooped up dirt and threw it on the flames. Stomping on fire had gotten her made fun of in high school. The whole flaming poop-in-a-bag trick was the go-to prank. She shuddered at the memory. *Never again.*

A whine from deeper into the forest caught her attention. She took a few steps forward. Then hesitated. *Am I going to be that girl who follows a weird sound into the dark?*

Yes, go. It sounds hurt.

It? The voice didn't answer. She didn't want to, but her gut said to listen.

"What are you doing, Piper?" Nina called from behind. She stayed close to the fire, but her voice quivered in fear. Nina hated the dark, and she didn't want to follow.

Piper licked her lips before speaking and turned around. "Just a second. Gotta go pee."

Nina relaxed and sat back down. Roger pushed Luke's shoulder with his and mumbled something, but at least they weren't fighting. Nina pointed a sharp finger in their direction, stopping the childish antics immediately. Her harsh whispers had Piper smiling.

Nina might not be strong or coordinated, but she played scolding mama better than her mother ever did. The words *childish* and *small dicks* were loud enough for her to hear. Piper snickered and continued.

The whining sounded again, and her father's training kicked in, so she scanned the area. He had trained her to spot danger and see things others might miss. That small yearning to be an investigator like her father had been, spiked up again. The thrill made her smile. She wished she had followed in his footsteps like her sister instead of studying psychopaths' behavior.

Images of her father pointing out all the little details on the crime scene and quizzing her about them later made her heart ache. She missed her dad. She wished they'd reconnect. But, unfortunately, it hadn't happened yet.

A sting erupted in her mind. *Ouchy.* She put her fingers to her temples, massaging them. The memory block a witch put on her, after one of her dad's bad crime scenes ended up following him home, flared to life, warning her to not go too deep into her past. She'd get that removed one day.

Another whine distracted her and made her focus again. She could deal with her issues later. Her eyes scanned the area. There were no signs of footprints or broken twigs, so the thing whining was probably an animal. She moved forward, keeping her steps quiet.

A furry head burst up from a scrub but plopped back down after two steps. She slowly walked to the animal. He needed her help.

He?

I'm just guessing. Like how I call all cars girls. It's—

I don't care. Focus. Hurt and afraid animals can be dangerous. Piper nodded her head. The voice was right.

When she came into view, the animal growled. The shadows covered him well. Was it a dog? *What is a dog doing out here?*

"I'm not going to hurt you." She put up a hand to show she meant no harm. If the dog understood that, she had no idea.

He growled again.

She moved towards him slowly. "I can help you,

sweetie. Please don't bite. I'm coming closer to see what's wrong."

The dog made a growling whine, but he didn't react when she stepped closer. Good. Did a camper lose him? This place got a lot of tourists, so maybe.

His dark gray fur was beautiful, mimicking the sky above. She winced at the bear trap attached to his blood-soaked leg.

"Ouch. I'm going to have to open that thing. I hope you can heal from this. I know nothing about dogs and their anatomy." She bit her bottom lip nervously. Her hands were shaking.

He panted harder in response. Smart dog. He must be a husky. The coat and scared honey eyes were like a huskies, but also, not. They seemed different somehow. Maybe a mixed breed?

"Please don't bite me or kill me once you're free, okay? I swear, I'm just trying to help." Her cold, shaking hands gripped each side of the trap's mouth. She took a deep breath and pulled them open.

The dog cried but didn't attack. She grunted and clenched her jaw to keep the sharp teeth from clamping back down on the dog. *Oh no, shit, shit.* She couldn't open it wide enough.

"Hurry, pull your leg out. I can't help." He didn't move. It wasn't wide enough.

Her father's voice chimed into her head. There was a case where the killer liked to use bear traps to subdue his victims. Dad taught her how to open these suckers.

"If you don't have enough strength to open the mouth, sweet bear, lean into the left side. Our right side has more strength. Use your body to get it open enough for you or another to escape."

She smiled at the memory. Her heart warmed with love, and the loneliness she felt that only a father could fill crept in. Was he doing okay? She wanted to know now more than ever.

The dog whined again, jerking her back to the present. She shook her head. "Sorry." She used her weight to open the trap wider but just barely. Her hands were now sweaty and losing grip. "Now, dammit."

The dog sprung up, taking all its limbs with him. *Thank fuck.* The trap snapped closed, scaring her into a backward stumble. That must have hurt. "That thing could take off a leg or foot."

The dog's panting caught her attention. She sucked in a sharp breath. The dog was right in front of her. He was a lot bigger than she initially thought. His sharp teeth and big feet had her heart going into hyperdrive... Not a dog. *Not. A. Dog.*

"Wolf," she whispered through her surprised breath. Dammit, she didn't want to die like this. Her body trembled at the images of sharp teeth and ripped skin.

He stared down at her. Not moving or making a sound. She gulped. "Please don't eat me, mister wolf. I don't taste that good, promise."

He closed the distance between them slowly. *Am I going to die like this?* Her mind said *run,* but her body froze.

The wolf's cold nose sniffed her. She must have smelled okay because his tongue wet her cheek. *He just licked me.*

"It's almost time. Where are you?" Nina called from their campground. Piper instinctively turned in her direction. Not smart.

She snapped her attention back to the wolf, but he was

gone. Piper stood and spun in a circle, but no animal was around.

"What the hell?" Piper squinted at every shadow. "Where the hell did it go?" Wherever he went, she hoped he'd survive. He had been scary, but he still deserved to live. Piper walked back to the campground with a pep in her step and head high. She saved that wolf. Her chest warmed with pride.

Before she left the shadows, Nina yelled, "Hey, Piper. Don't make me come in after you. You know how I hate the dark." Nina's nostrils flared in agitation, but the shakiness of her voice spoke of her worry.

"I'm coming."

She had no idea where the animal went, but she wasn't going to sit around here waiting for it to return. She ran to Nina. As her friend came into view, her nerves calmed. *Let's do this thing and go home.* One brush with death was enough.

Chapter Three

Piper fidgeted in her seat next to the fire. Its heat was aggressively pressing against her skin as she roasted a marshmallow. Sweat trickled down her flesh nearest to the flames.

Another s'more sounded like a good idea. After an unpleasant bite, her stomach protested. No more. Her rectangular-shaped body wasn't as feminine as Nina's, but maybe all the s'more would help her get bigger hips. Yeah right.

The pot hanging over the fire was so clean and shiny that Piper could see herself. Piper's ivory skin seemed to glow in the dark next to the fire. Her plump lips were missing the light brown lipstick she loved. Her high color-less cheekbones made her almond-blue eyes seem abnormally large. Even the slight indent on her chin made her sharp jaw seem darker than her cheeks.

She glanced down at her hands which just made her scowl because her fingernails were so low from her chewing them, they made her fingers stubby. She sighed.

Even her reflection hurt Piper's heart. Trace looked so much like Piper. Being twins would do that, unfortunately. Why did no one tell her how hard it'd be to have mirrors around?

Nina was doing something to her left, sprinkling stuff on the ground from her to the large rocks. The mud squished between her toes. It was freakin' cold. Focusing on the chill and Nina helped clear her mind.

Why she had to do this barefoot was beyond Piper. Nina was setting all the rules here. She was just hoping she didn't embarrass herself. All she needed was to trip or wet herself out of worry. Fear made her sloppy.

"All right, woman, we're ready." Nina shoved Luke and Roger in front of her to stand next to Piper when she reached the stones. They grumbled but let her manhandle them.

The jitters from earlier came back harder than ever, like a bat to the stomach. It took everything in her not to double over, but Piper pushed through. She'd rather feel anything that wasn't coated in fear, but she took a deep breath and walked to stand next to Nina. The salt rocks on the ground poked at her feet.

The cold air felt great on her skin, not so much on her toes and the back of her neck, but she'd deal with it. She closed her blue eyes and let the wind run over her body, giving her goosebumps. The pine and pollen in the air made her smile. She was home. This place just felt right.

She put her hand on the back of her neck to warm that spot. She needed a scarf and shoes.

We are free here. Stop complaining. The voice said. Piper grinned. Fair enough. But as soon as the good, peaceful feeling settled in her soul, something dark replaced it almost immediately. Shivers overtook her body like a dog shaking off water. *What's that?*

A sour stench stung Piper's nose.

An animalistic growl from behind her made her freeze. "Shit, shit." *Is it the wolf again?* She turned to peek over her shoulder behind her. Nina's face was calm. The lines on her face were from excitement, not fear. She was oblivious to the danger at their backs.

Double shit. Time slowed as her eyes took in one of her worst nightmares. Five giant gray wolves licked their sharp teeth as their gazes devoured her friends. *I never should have released that back-stabbing wolf. He went and got his friends.*

Piper wished she'd stayed oblivious a little longer because as soon as she spotted the danger she screamed. Her hazel eyes went wide with terror. Piper slapped her hand over Nina's mouth. Nina slowly wrapped her body around Piper's, shaking.

The wolves twitched slightly in response to Nina's scream but didn't move toward them. Instead, only their eyes raked them over, waiting.

Adrenaline spiked in Piper's jittery body. Her hands and knees shook. The largest wolf stood in the middle. He growled again; saliva dripping from his maw.

Need to leave.

Can't stay.

Leave now.

Even her brain wasn't functioning right. *Focus, Nina needs us.* The voice growled. They may be best friends and like most of the same things, but Nina didn't work out as she did. She was a girly girl, loved shopping, and got angry at breaking a nail. There was no way she could survive a wolf attack. *Shit, I can't even survive those teeth. Especially right now.*

The men, several feet in front of them, cursed and screamed when they turned around. This wasn't good.

Outrun them.

A couple of wolves snapped their massive jaws. *On my word, we run. Grab Nina and pull her as fast as we can go.* Piper's hands shook, but her fear wasn't going to cripple her. They only had one shot.

"Get back! Aaaahhh!" Luke swung his arms around. His body trembled in fear, but his face was a hard mask. The determination made his muscles flex.

Piper shook her head. *What the hell?* This was dangerous. He shouldn't be trying to be a hero right now.

"Don't," Piper whispered. That was a bad idea. Wolves didn't respond well to aggression and noise when they had a pack backing them.

A couple of the wolves snarled. Most of them focused on Luke. Dammit. Piper curled her upper lip in agitation. "Please, don't do it again." No one needed to be a hero here.

His fear sharpened into resolve. His eyes met Nina's. He locked his jaw, puffed out his chest, and stepped forward again. "Aagghh!"

There was a moment of silence. Piper sucked in air, waiting, her eyes wide and fear up to the sky. Luke yelled again. This time, his voice turned into a cry as two wolves pounced on him. *Noo! Luke!*

Now! The voice yelled.

Roger screamed. His deep voice echoed all around her.

Her heart tore into two as she watched sweet boy Luke go down in a bloody mess on the ground, wolves on top of him. But she did as the voice said and grabbed Nina.

Nina screamed, but Piper held her tighter, lifting her off the ground to run. "Goddamnit, Luke! You fucking bastard. Why?" Her voice came out in puffs.

Nina's weight was too much for her to hold for long. She hoped Nina could run by herself soon, or they weren't going to make it far.

Roger grunted next to her. Each step sounded like thunder in her ears. The pounding in her ears matched the beats of her heart. Faster... *Need to move faster*.

Twigs snapped under her bare feet. She shouldn't have listened to Nina and taken her shoes off. Her shaking arms were already crying. Instead, she put Nina's feet on the ground and pulled her along. But Nina's feet flopped around like a fish out of water.

"Come on, Nina, move." Piper's breaths came out harsh and rugged. The cold air instantly dried her throat and tongue. But Nina was a sobbing mess. She kept whispering Luke's name, not hearing Piper.

Roger let out a whine. "I'm out," he said, shaking his head and turning in a different direction. Only one of the wolves turned with him. She internally screamed. *What the hell?*

Was she just in their path? She changed her direction. Hopefully, they'd stop following her too. A sharp rock dug into her foot, threatening to stop her, but her adrenaline wouldn't allow her to.

She glanced back.

The stupid wolves had changed direction with her. No, no, no. Why?

You can question it later, move fast. They're gaining. Piper pulled her strength from her core and pushed harder. Fine. If the wolves wanted to chase her, she'd be damned if she didn't make it one hell of a chase.

Tree branches smacked into her face. She could outrun them, but not with Nina. So why didn't Roger take Nina? The bastard. She'd gladly take on the wolves alone. There was no way she'd win. No illusions there, but if Nina survived, she'd take the heat.

Dammit. We might have to leave her, hide her somewhere...

No. She wasn't losing another person. She'd rather die with her than live without her.

Chapter Four

The frigid water hit Piper's legs with urgency. The icy sting was like needles piercing her skin. The water might have slowed her down, but it'd slow the wolves down too. Her frozen fingers gripped Nina's waist as she slipped and splashed into the river. The freezing water drenched her but pushed away some of her fear.

She gasped, cried out, and instantly her teeth chattered in protest. Salty tears mixed with the river water. All she could think was *Run. Run. Run.*

Her hand shook from the cold, but her eyes narrowed in determination. These wolves could go to hell. They weren't getting them. She searched the darkness on the other side of the river. The low-hanging trees were like troll arms reaching out for her. She gulped. The growling behind her pushed her forward.

Nina's slippery wet body slid from Piper's grasp again. The wolves hadn't followed them into the water yet.

Instead, they paced on the shore. *Why the hell were they stopping? Maybe it's too cold? Or they're giving up?*

The voice growled, *maybe there's danger in the water, a bigger predator. Hurry.*

"Move your ass." Piper pulled Nina onto her noodle legs. Her fingers were numb, so they stumbled a few times. She kept repeating the same words in her head to give her strength, *we got this. We can outrun them. We can do this. Stay with me.*

The murky water tasted like a sumo wrestler's ass crack. Yuck. When their feet finally hit solid ground, the wolves howled and jumped in the water, ready to get wet if that meant getting their prey. Piper's body was heavy, and she didn't have much running left in her; the energy leaked out of her at an alarming rate. Pushing against the waves was getting too taxing, and Nina was too heavy. She'd spent all day hiking, so exhaustion weighed down her body, betraying her entirely.

Her feet were numb, but she smelled the coppery liquid pouring out from between her toes. How she could smell blood, she had no idea. Maybe her adrenaline was like nuclear waste, giving her superpowers.

Stop playing around. Get to a wall, so they can't attack us from behind... The voice paused. *To the left. Turn now!* She ran into a clearing in the forest.

The sound of splashing water behind them had stopped. The growls were louder now; the wolves were tired of playing with them. Their anger was thick in the air.

Running uphill was twice as hard, but she refused to give up. Piper's breaths came out fast and harsh. If they were going downhill, she could throw Nina down the hill. That probably wouldn't work, but going down was better than up—she didn't have the muscle to help them escape. Everything hurt, and it wouldn't be long before everything stopped working altogether.

She had to stop before she didn't have enough energy left to fight. She expected the voice to cackle in her mind, but acceptance and determination filled her instead.

So... All right, fight.

Piper pushed her hair out of her eyes and forced her legs to move faster. Her fear was drowning her, but she forced herself to stay focused. The trees cleared as a cement wall came into view a few moments later. A mixture of relief and anxiety smacked her at once. She didn't want to run anymore, but fighting off five wolves didn't sound like a good time either.

She found a nook in the wall and shoved Nina in it. She turned and screamed. Five sets of shining eyes stared back at her from the shadows. "Shit, I'm going to die," she whispered to herself. *I'm going to die in the fucking Christmas Tree Forest.*

Piper straightened her spine. Her eyes drifted to the ground by her feet, long enough to spot a large branch. She grabbed a thick wood and swung at one of the wolves charging her. The branch stayed solid and knocked the furry gray body away. He moved back to the group, shaking his head, and snapping his jaw.

Another wolf sprung from the group in retaliation. Apparently, her luck only lasted for so long. She cried out as teeth bit into her flesh, causing pain to shoot up her leg like fire. She screamed in agony, and a blinding whiteness exploded in her mind until she grew dizzy.

Fight through it. Fight.

She kept hitting and hitting as the wolf pulled and shook her. Then, by what felt like the hundredth blow, the wolf finally released her with a growl. Piper sighed in relief, tears blurring her darkening vision.

Panic sliced through her as his fangs sank into Nina's leg. She cried out in pain. Piper saw red.

"No, you piece of shit. Leave her alone!" Piper screamed, throwing all her weight into her next hit. The wolf yelped and scurried back into the group of beasts, making a laughing noise that had no right coming out of a wolf's mouth. *What the hell is happening?*

"Fuck you!" Piper spat, wobbling on her feet.

She messed up wasting her energy like that. Darkness crowded around her. She rubbed at her eyes, but her vision didn't clear.

Dammit... Her body was giving up on her. The realization of her impending doom couldn't even convince her to stay awake. *I'm going to die in the middle of nowhere. My father will never know what happened to me. He'll have nothing left.* Her eyes fluttered closed.

Red-hot agony pulled her away from the peaceful darkness as sharp teeth bit into her upper arm. She fell backward on top of Nina.

"No!" Nina yelled as Piper screamed in agony but was too weak to move or fight back. Angry blood shot out from her wound.

The salivating wolves closed in around her. She didn't have enough strength to do anything but lay there. Her eyes refused to open again.

Piper had no regrets, except for not protecting Nina. The pain of the teeth digging into her flesh numbed, and she finally let the peace in the black clouds take her. At least the pain stopped. Maybe, if luck was on her side, she could see her sister again.

Chapter Five

A noise interrupted her peaceful rest as she floated in the darkness. A bug buzzed around her, pushing her closer to insanity. *Where the hell was a fly swatter when she needed one?* The more she focused the more the sound turned urgent...

Can bugs sound urgent?

Not a bug, a voice.

"Piper..." The voice was calling her name. She sighed and focused harder, willing herself closer to the noise. This better be important.

"Piper..."

"Piper, wake up." Nina's hushed voice made her eyes pop open. Nina wasn't usually a sweet wake-up call kind of girl. She liked to jump on the bed and scream bloody murder. Something must be wrong.

Her dry lips protested, but she grunted, "What is it?"

"Where are we, Piper? Wake up. Dammit." Her small hands clung to Piper's shoulders, shaking her.

The tears sliding down her face shook Piper out of her haze. The urge to protect Nina had her waking up completely as if she was just injected with adrenaline. She sprung to her feet. The hospital gown she had on swayed, opening the back. She didn't appreciate the breeze.

Nina, in a gown as well, backed up and sat on a bed with a thin white blanket that matched hers a few feet away.

The twin beds were identical to the other four beds. The synchronicity gave her chills. Had they ended up in the clutches of a psychopath? Killer of women?

Other than the beds, the room consisted of two night-stands and a few windows. Every window and door was covered by a white cloth. The brown wooden walls were blank, except for a sign that said, *Get well soon*. They were in a hospital? *Do murderers put up signs like that?* Or had they ended up in the clutches of some insane trickster? Was Michael Myers going to pop out from around the corner?

Piper breathed heavily. The adrenaline made her para-noid and jumpy. She twitched at every sound. The wind outside, *twitch*. The tree branches hitting the roof, *twitch*. Nina's breathing, *twitch*.

Piper gulped and whispered, "I have no idea." She grabbed Nina's hand. "But let's get out of here." Piper stepped forward.

The moment her foot touched the floor again, they buckled. Her weak knees hit the ground before her arms could grab the bed to steady herself. The pain gyrated up her leg to her hips. *Ouch. Shit, do I have lead bricks attached to my knees?* Her gaze drifted down to be sure. Nothing but her trembling limbs.

Nina reached for her. "What's wrong?" she asked as she

helped Piper sit on the bed. Her small frame and muscles made leaning on her hard. *If we both go down, I'm not sure I'll get back up.*

"I have no idea," Piper repeated.

Piper moved her ankle. There was an almost healed bite mark there. *What?* She moved her ankle in circles, it stung, but not enough to make her weak. Her eyes traveled over her body. She had white bandages wrapped on her upper leg and torso. *What the hell?*

The voice in her head was oddly quiet.

She needed to clear her mind and gather her strength. She had no idea what was on the other side of these walls. Piper breathed in and out to calm the chaos brewing inside of her mind and closed her eyes.

She sucked in a sharp breath as the memory of their attack came back with a vengeance, flashes of sharp teeth and lots of blood ripped at her soul. She let out a sob.

Piper breathed out. "Wolves?" She bit her bottom lip. "Shit."

Nina's normal ebony skin was five shades paler. Her eyes widened, her pupils dilated, and she sucked in a sharp intake of air. "Did wolves attack us? I mean, what... How did we get here?"

She had no answers for her. The memories only showed her death and fear. Her heart rate and breathing increased. She closed her eyes. *No, we're okay. This is just our amygdala reacting to Nina's fear. Don't panic. So, we were attacked by wolves, and we survived. We're okay.*

Please don't say any of that out loud. It's extremely nerdy. And having a panic attack over a fictional character isn't a good look on us. At least we're a good actress.

Shut up. She told the voice, but said, "It's all fuzzy to me."

Nina grabbed her arm to get her attention and help her focus. "I thought it was just a crazy-ass dream," Nina said, blinking at Piper's wound as if she could blink it away.

A male cleared his throat behind Piper. She turned and froze. A man covered in shadows stood in the doorway, making adrenaline slam back into her chest, speeding up her heart rate. Nina moved behind her. She stood to cover Nina better, the pain in her legs forgotten.

"Whatcha doing?" She paused, so he continued. "Both of you are hurt. No one will hold you here, but I recommend you rest and get better before leaving the village. Next time, you may not be so lucky." His voice was deep and all man.

That snapped Piper out of her shock. "What? You're hurt too? Damn it, Nina, why didn't you say anything?" How didn't she spot that? That wasn't like her. She had a habit of noticing her surroundings. Her sister, Trace, used to hate playing with her as a kid because she could never trick or scare Piper.

She scanned Nina's body; on her lower arm, a white bandage was wrapped around a wound that had bled through a little.

"Yes, you both were attacked by wolves. We heard your screams and were able to stop them before things got bad." He crossed his arms and leaned against the wood door panel. "How are you ladies feeling?" His mouth opened as if to say more, but he shut it quickly.

Piper narrowed her eyes at him. She didn't trust this dude even if he was sexy. A lot of psychopaths were gorgeous.

His eyes locked onto hers. She didn't hide her skepticism well because his eyebrows smooshed together, then rose, giving her a confused once over. He locked his jaw, his eyes became unfocused, and a heat pushed into the room.

The heat hit Piper hard enough to rock her on her feet. The energy pushed against her skull, demanding entrance. Piper fought the sensation for a second, but soon the heat rubbed out her prickliness. Her spine curved and her shoulders relaxed. Maybe he wasn't a bad guy after all. How could he be, if she felt this calm around him? She trusted him.

I don't like this. I feel funny.

Oh, hush. He's a good guy. She glanced Nina's way, and she had the same trusting expression on her face. *See, it's not just me.*

Nina peaked her head out from behind Piper and smiled. She stepped to Piper's side. "We're alive, that's all that matters. So, what's your name, hero?" Nina said. Her sexy shoulder move came out twitchy with her injury. Piper put a hand over her mouth to hide a smile.

She knew she should be worried or suspicious, but she couldn't. Her brain was calm. Weird.

You go girl. She didn't blame her friend. Tall, muscular, bright smile, and almost the same ebony skin as Nina, except slightly darker.

The smiles and bashful eye drifting between those two was cute. He stood taller and shoved his hands in his pockets.

"Are you hungry, my pa—" his voice trailed off, "My fellow townspeople are about to sit for dinner."

Nina quirked an eyebrow at him. "Y'all eat together?"

He rubbed the back of his neck. "Most of the time, yeah. The village is small, and it's nice to feel like you aren't alone in the middle of nowhere. It's like we're one big family." He beamed at her when she bit her lip. Piper wanted to crawl into a hole and disappear. The heat in their gazes made her uncomfortable.

Nina must have sensed it because she dialed her hormones back. Piper's critical eye took in their hospital gowns and Nina did the same. Nope. She wasn't getting back in her hole, dirt, and blood-covered clothes again either. She shook her head. "We aren't dressed for something like that."

"Oh, that's right. I forgot." He walked to a cabinet near them. "Here are some extra clothes. Hopefully, they fit. We don't get many women here." He put a pink and black pile on the bed and left the room. Before he closed the door, he said, "I'll be right outside whenever you're finished."

They had no choice. Piper sighed and grabbed the clothes. Nina was smaller than her, so she gave her the smaller outfit and took the other for herself.

Nina scowled at a pair of bright pink pants. "What's this?"

"Clothes that don't have holes or blood on them." She sighed and shimmied into the black pants. They didn't give her any room to breathe, but at least she didn't have a muffin top. The black cotton shirt clung to her breasts and didn't cover her stomach.

Good Lord, this is uncomfortable.

"Who the heck are they getting their clothes from?" Nina whispered as she scowled at her outfit. The bright pink, sparkly shirt clung to her tiny frame. Of course. Nina could wear a brown bag and be sexy. Why not a shiny pink monstrosity?

The frown on Nina's face said she didn't agree. Piper snickered. She gestured to her outfit to distract her. "Hey, at least it fits. I feel like everything is going to burst if I breathe too hard."

"What? You look hotter than a volcano. You'll definitely make a few eruptions happen tonight. Let's switch," Nina said, lifting the hem of her shirt.

Piper had more muscle than fluff, and her curvy body caught plenty of attention. She was tall—too tall. She snickered to herself. *At least I'm above average at something.* Piper had the label average down. But she always missed the above part.

Piper narrowed her eyes. "Nina, I wouldn't wear your pink outfit even if you paid me. My legs probably couldn't even fit in those pants."

She scoffed but didn't disagree.

Piper licked her lips. "How are you doing, Toots?"

Nina sighed. "I know I should be disheveled and broken like a normal person would be but I'm not..." the last words were said in a whisper. She turned away and continued. "I feel strong and alive. I don't even know if that makes sense."

Piper didn't want her friend in pain but was it normal to not be torn up? No pun intended. But honestly, Piper felt the same way.

"I can smell the old wood on the cabin, the faint scent of sweat that doesn't smell like me or you on the bed, and the blood on the bandages. I have no idea why or if I sound crazy, but it makes me feel strong, Piper." Nina's eyes met hers, pleading for her to tell her she wasn't crazy.

Hell, to Piper, everything she just said wasn't crazy. But she knew she wasn't completely sane... Screw it. That just made them crazy together. She threw away her fear and worry. Her arms wrapped around Nina.

"I feel it too. But let's just keep all of that to ourselves for a while." Nina nodded and wiped her eyes. She opened her mouth to say something but a knock on the door stopped her.

"Hey, are you ladies ready? Dinner is being served," the guy said but didn't open the door.

Her stomach growled in response, and her fingers grazed against the soft cotton blankets as they walked. She loved the feeling of soft fabric. It calmed her and sent her back in time to when her mom made homemade blankets for her and would tuck her in after a crappy day.

She'd wake up surrounded by soft fabric. Now, certain fabrics calmed her and reminded her of better days—fresh beginnings. She sighed and followed Nina out.

As soon as they walked through the door, Nina asked, "So, what's your name?"

The guy smiled at her like a kid opening a gift on Christmas morning. Then, he bit his plump bottom lip and answered, "Oh, my manners are a little rusty. Sorry. I'm Liam."

Nina smirked. "Well, my name is Nina, and this is my best friend, Piper." She gestured towards her.

"That's your actual name. When we carried you into town, we asked for your name, but I wasn't sure because it sounded more like Pecker." Both he and Nina chuckled. Piper just frowned. *Nope, don't like the joke.*

She gave him a thin-lined smile to be polite. "Yeah, it's a weird name, but my parents must have liked it." She faked a giggle.

The explanation her parents gave popped into her head. They met in band class in high school and wanted their kid to live life to the beat of their own drum. Instead of giving her a cool, strong instrument name, they chose a flute. So, her parents named her 'flute player' in Romanian. Lame.

Ironically, she couldn't play the flute to save her life.

Nina snapped. "Hey Liam, where can a girl get makeup around here? I just saw my reflection in the window and, wow." Nina ran her fingers through her hair and pinched her cheeks. She might be acting all right, but her hands shaking and the sketchy way her eyes darted around like she expected to be attacked again spoke volume. She was using her words to distract him and herself.

Piper grabbed her hand and squeezed it to comfort her. She didn't know why, but she felt at ease here. Like she was safe. Which was ridiculous. She had no idea who these people were.

They feel like family. The voice whispered, and she had to agree. Was she drugged or something? She had no choice but to stay calm until she knew more.

Hey, where have you been? She asked the voice.

Sleeping. Healing is tiring. Piper nodded and didn't pester the voice with questions. She said they felt like family, so she'd trust these strangers. For now.

Liam laughed and shook his head as if what she said was the funniest thing. Although, Piper had to admit, the laugh lines wrinkling his eyes made him even cuter. She loved a guy that had a sense of humor.

"There aren't a lot of women around, but Doctor Patty is probably your best bet if you want makeup. She'll be here today. She's not known for having tons on hand, but she'd order you some." Liam smiled, brushing dirt off a light stuck in the ground as he passed. "But you don't need it if you ask me."

No need to glance Nina's way to know she had a huge smile on her face. Excitement vibrated off her. Good for her. So far, he seemed way better than most of the guys she dated.

The cool air felt great on her leg. She had a slight limp, but at least she could walk. The dry, dirt path made it easier, though. Several wooden cottages, a few trees, and the huge cement wall surrounding the small village had all her attention. A few farm animals were in comfortable wooden cages. She wasn't watching where she was going. In her distraction, one of the solar lights attacked her feet, tripping her. Okay, so it didn't really, but blaming her clumsiness on something else did wonders for her self-confidence.

Her face heated in embarrassment. *Ugh, I need to work on paying more attention and my graceful ballerina skills.*

The voice laughed. *Said no one ever.*

Oh, hush.

And we're never going to be a ballerina. There are too many rules.

Will you just let me dream?

Not stupid dreams that you don't want. Piper imagined slapping the voice, which had laughter floating around in her head. So annoying.

She inwardly groaned as a flashlight shined her way.

Whoever was trying to blind her needed to be slapped as well. Stupid.

A pressure built in her head until Piper was sure it was going to explode. The flashing light triggered a memory of Luke's flashlight shining in her eyes as the wolves jumped on him. Their sharp teeth dug into him.

Chapter Six

"Oh God, did you find our friends? Two guys. One was killed. The other took off. We ran —" she shook her head. "There was nothing we could do for Luke. There were too many of them to fight."

Nina's face froze, but no emotion touched it. "We ran. We should have helped but—"

Liam interrupted her. "Hey." He put his hand on her shoulder. "You did what you had to do. You wouldn't have survived a fight with a pack of wolves. Running was your only hope." He sighed. "We haven't found anyone else. We went back to your campsite, but nothing was there. All your stuff was gone as well."

Piper's insides froze. "What?"

Liam cleared his throat, uncomfortable. "We followed your and the wolves' tracks and found your camp. We can go tomorrow if you want to make sure we were in the right place. How does that sound?"

A numbness took over Piper's mind. Where had her friends gone? She didn't really care about Roger, but where was Luke's body or all their stuff? What the actual hell was going on?

Liam said something else that Piper ignored, and Nina blushed again. Although she loved Nina being happy and blushing, Piper was taken aback by how her emotional state seemed so easygoing. They were just attacked, and their friends had died. Nina liked Luke, and she was acting like he never existed. Even Piper's chest felt sore from his loss and Piper barely knew him.

People mourn in different ways. We don't know how she is feeling on the inside. You know Nina has always had trouble showing her deeper emotions.

But it doesn't seem like she is mourning at all.

We'll just be there for her when she needs us.

Fine, you're right.

Piper was still breathing heavily from the memory, but her words helped. Nina grabbed her hand. A glance her way showed the same emotionless expression staring back at her. *So, maybe Nina didn't like Luke after all... but she said she did? Oh well, she'd talk to her later.*

Before she could control her emotions, tears fell down Piper's face. She huffed and wiped them away. She was so done with tears. *Can I get my tear ducts removed? Is that a thing?*

They stopped in front of two wooden doors at the most prominent and biggest building. Liam grabbed the doorknob and opened it for them. The brightness and heat surprised Piper. She hesitated before walking in.

A female with dark red hair and brown eyes met them

at the door. "Hi there, I'm Patty, the town's doctor. Come on in. The food is hot, and the seats are uncomfortable." She led them into the room. The tension in their shoulders eased, and they chuckled. Nina went in first, then Piper followed.

Her stride stuttered at the forty or so pairs of eyes on her. Their curious faces were hungry. "Umm, hi," Nina whispered. A few guys waved in response.

Liam put his hand on Nina's lower back to keep them moving. Piper couldn't help but scan her surroundings. A dozen long tables on either side of the walkway were full of mostly men. Liam was not kidding when he said there weren't a lot of women around. She saw about ten females, but most of them were kids and the elderly.

The hungry gazes the men were giving her, and Nina had nothing to do with food. Every eye in this place was dilated and locked on them. She shivered; she didn't like it one bit.

Piper grabbed Nina's hand and glared at the guys. She wasn't interested in Nina, but they needed to stop eye-fucking her. She took a deep breath through her nose. *Control your anger, they don't feel harmful.* Hearing the voice in her head calmed her.

The only sharp, cruel scowl she got was from a dark-haired woman. Not a nice person, okay. Besides her, everyone else seemed curious or lustful.

The open walkway ended at the biggest table. It had the most food and matching wooden chairs surrounding it. A few open seats were right by a dark-haired hunk of a man sitting at the head of the table. His chair and spot spoke of importance.

His strong square jaw, Greek nose, robust body, and powerful presence gave her tingles in all the right places. Yet, the dazzling green eyes staring back at her took her breath away. They were mesmerizing against his deep sandy skin tone.

Before she could do something demeaning, like drool or fall at his feet, she turned away, focusing back on the food, but not really seeing anything. She hoped Nina would do all the talking. Her tongue went numb with nerves. He stood as they approached, but she kept her eyes off him.

Nina took her hand back and wiped the sweat off her pink pants. So, one of their hands was sweaty... It wasn't hers. Nina gave her a wrinkled brow stare, but Piper ignored her, biting her lip to stop the anxiety raging through her. *Nina had sweaty hands, dammit. I'm the calm one.*

Right.

Liam pulled out Nina's chair, and the hunk at the head of the table pulled out hers. "Hello ladies, I'm Tate. I hope you don't mind sitting with me," the guy said with a tiny accent she heard people from Norway have.

"Hi." She pointed to herself. "Piper."

Wow. When did we get so articulate? The voice taunted and snickered.

Shut up, she inwardly rolled her eyes. She didn't need crap from her own mind. She already felt silly, but something about him made her nervous... not dangerous nervous, but butterflies angrily zooming around her stomach nervous. Her hands twitched in response.

He smells good, tell him that. Or tell him, his skin looks like honey. We should taste it. It probably tastes just as sweet.

Shut up, no.

You need help. You're making us look bad. Tell him the food smells good or thank him for helping us.

"How come you don't have an accent, Liam? You can barely hear Tate's, but I don't hear it at all with you?" Nina asked.

He smiled down at her. "I didn't grow up here."

Nina put a hand on his shoulder. "Oh, that makes sense. Where are you from?"

"I'm from America. A few of us are from there," Liam explained.

"Us too," Nina said with her hand on her chest.

Piper swallowed and pushed down her nerves. "I just wanted to say thank you guys for helping us. I figured," she bit her lip, "you're the leader or whatever." What was she saying?

Nina grinned at her and shook her head.

So what? The guy was sexy as sin. His voice alone was a husky drawl. He was solid and sharp like a soldier. Liam seemed almost like a surfer boy in comparison.

Tate's green eyes never lowered to the dusty earthen floor as others did. Everything came into view at once. And his rugged presence thickened the air around her.

She focused on the room instead—anything to not drool over him. The tables were covered in delicious steaming food with every meat she could think of. Besides the food, the wooden kitchen accessories, and the blue curtains and tablecloths, the room was effortless.

She could handle simple things.

Liam moved to Tate's side to whisper in his hear. "The sheriff called. There might be a case, but he thinks he can handle it." He spoke so low; she was surprised she heard him.

"Follow up with him later," Tate whispered back.

Her mind went through his words again. *Case?* That one word made her miss her sister and father even more. She wondered if she could help them. She used to help her sister and dad. It would feel nice for some normalcy.

Ugh, what was she thinking? She shook her head. There was enough problems in her life.

"Thank you for joining us, Piper. I know it's probably not easy being here after what you two have been through," Tate said. His calloused hands touched her arm. She glanced his way. "If you need anything, please ask."

She cleared her throat and said, "Honestly, I think my mind is blocking it all right now."

"It'll probably hit us in the middle of the night or when things die down," Nina whispered, her good-natured attitude gone. She put her head on the table and fiddled with the silverware.

Piper moved to comfort her, but Liam beat her to it. He rubbed her back, and Nina leaned into him, so she didn't bother. Nina was going to deal with the trauma her way... in someone's bed.

We should do that too.

Shut up. She had no issues with sex, but she wasn't as open with new partners as Nina. She never liked Nina's way of getting over her emotions, but she loved her regardless.

"Liam said we could go back to our camping ground in the morning to hopefully recover our friend. Where do we sleep for the night?" Piper asked and grabbed a juicy steak off one of the plates before they were gone.

As soon as she reached for some food the rest followed suit. Her stomach growled, distracting her from anything else.

Tate picked up another steak and put it on her plate. "Steak doesn't last long here. Grab another just in case." He winked at her, and she almost melted all over the dining room. She was practically making love to the steak, should she have another? She might embarrass herself more. "To answer your question, you may stay wherever you want, but we have an unoccupied cabin if you'd like to use it."

We don't want to be alone. Tell him we want to go to his cabin.

No, we're strong enough to be alone. If the voice had a face, she would have seen the biggest scowl.

"That would be nice."

He would be a good addition.

Do I have to muzzle you? The voice growled but stopped talking to her in front of all these people.

"Okay, before you go there tonight, I'll make sure it is cleared, and you'll have more clothes waiting for you there." Tate attacked his meat with as much enthusiasm as she did with her food.

Nina elbowed Piper and leaned into whisper, "You're going to freak out. They have Pepsi." She grabbed the bottle and put the sweet god-sent liquid in front of Piper.

"Pepsi! Come to mama!" Piper grabbed the bottle a little too forcefully, slushing some of it on the table while pouring. "Oh, guilty pleasures." She took several long, fast drinks and filled the cup up to the brim again.

Nina tapped Piper's leg under the table to get her attention. Her eyes lifted from her drink, the whole place was silent, and everyone was watching her. Piper's face heated, and the urge to hide under the table built as the eyes never wavered from her. "What?" She shrugged.

The voice made a growling noise. *You made us look crazy*.

Nina cleared her throat. "She loves Pepsi," she said, smirking.

Tate was also smirking. "We can see that. Do you want another bottle?" Everyone tensed as if they'd all jump up and get her all the bottles they had if she said yes.

She wiped her mouth. "No, I'm okay. Sorry, it's been a while, and I needed a pick-me-up." The men around her nodded and focused back on their food. Then, the voices and noises started again.

"Was I really that crazy-looking?" she leaned in and asked Nina.

She laughed with a hand covering her mouth. "Oh, yes, but it was the funniest thing to watch. You had the spot-light for two seconds, and your face turned tomato red."

"I hate you." That just made her laugh harder. Well, she guessed it was good Nina was smiling. Even if it was at the cost of her pride.

The rest of the meal was uneventful. She ate until she was on the verge of exploding, then had two more bites. Tate escorted her to her room since Nina disappeared with Liam somewhere. Piper was secretly grateful he asked to accompany her. She didn't want to walk alone in the dark.

She nibbled at her lips. "So, how long were we out?" Piper knew that should have been the first question to ask, but she was a little afraid of the answer. Her wounds were almost healed.

Tate helped her walk without limping, so the pain was almost nonexistent. His hesitation worried her. "A couple of weeks. Just in time for the next full moon soon."

Piper froze. Her breath caught in her throat as if the H_2O solidified and got stuck. How was that possible? "What?"

"Yeah, it's not easy after bites like yours. And the magic in the air gives us extra full moon days. I'm not sure how it works." He paused and stared at her before continuing, "You know, after meeting you and seeing the way you are with Nina, I have a feeling that you could have escaped, but you chose to be loyal and stayed with your friend." He squeezed her side, where he held her, gently. "Well done, not many people would do that."

She couldn't stop the blush consuming her cheeks. "Thanks." Why did she have such a difficult time talking to him?

Their feet sounded like bombs as they stepped up on her borrowed cabin porch.

He opened the door for her but waited before walking in. "Would you like me to come in and make you some tea? You seem rattled again."

Yes! Come in us. I mean the room. The voice screamed. It took all her energy not to burst out laughing. Fucking voice. Thankfully, he couldn't read minds.

"I think I might just go to bed." Even as she spoke, she regretted the words. She didn't need sex to help her cope like Nina, but having someone to talk to would be nice.

He nodded and descended the three steps. His feet scuffed the ground and his shoulders drooped from their upright position. His face fell in disappointment, or that might have been her imagination. "Wait, I'd love the company," her voice sounded calm and collected, but she felt broken. She didn't even know what she wanted anymore.

Tate's smile made her insides heat with joy. "Perfect. I'll make you some tea, and you can talk. I'll listen?"

She shook her head. "How about I listen, and you talk?"

He blinked a few times like no one had ever asked to just listen to him. She was a great listener, and it would be way better not to focus on her bullshit life right now.

Chapter Seven

Inside, there was a door that led to a bathroom, a small kitchen, a queen-sized bed with light turquoise bedding, and one black dresser. The small space was simple but warm and comfortable.

She couldn't ask for more.

Piper took off her shoes and smiled when her feet slid on the smooth floor. The feeling reminded her of her childhood, sliding down the hall in socks.

Her smile faltered as her eyes drifted around the room. "So, where are we supposed to sit?"

Tate shrugged. "The bed?" She narrowed her eyes at the bed. Nope. She would get in all kinds of naughty trouble if she sat there. He changed his answer at her hesitation. "The ground?" His eyebrows rose in question. That was safer. Barely.

She agreed with that. "Sure." She grabbed a surprisingly soft blanket and a few pillows from the bed while Tate moved around in the kitchen, humming a song she didn't recognize.

"We're in luck, I made sure all the cabins have tea," Tate said, glancing back at Piper. "It's good for the soul." He really did care about his people. Piper didn't quite understand how they did things here, but maybe he was some kind of mayor. They were lucky to have him regardless.

The small window next to her rattled. The wind was picking up like mother nature had a whipping to dish out. She hoped she focused on the stupid wolves that attacked her. The thought made her smile.

We look crazy, staring out the window with that smile. Piper snorted. Tate's eyebrow went up in question. He smirked, shook his head, and focused back on his task.

After a few minutes, he spoke, "Being away from the outside world can be hard on people's sanity. So, I like to give the people everything they might need to keep their souls pure, and if that's some tea or yoga mats, it's a small price to pay." The kettle steamed and then screamed for attention.

Piper wasn't a yoga person, but she knew it helped people center themselves. She'd probably take up yoga in a place like this. Another smile stretched her lips as images of her twisted into a knot and getting stuck came into mind. *Maybe not.*

A rabbit darted from under a bush, running into its hole as an owl hooted in the distance. The tree branches next to her window swayed in the breeze. The movement was surprisingly hypnotic. "I love it out here, though. I feel free. Like I can breathe," Piper said as she walked to the blanket.

Tate met her there with two cups in his hands. She grabbed the black mug full of steaming green mint tea.

The soft cushion on her back and the plush blanket under her had her sighing. Perfect.

The smile he gave her made her toes curl. *Umm, hello hormones.* His gruff voice was almost inaudible. "I feel the same."

Piper didn't know what to say next. She was tongue-tied again. The tea gave her a good excuse to not stare at him. *When did I become so lame?* She blamed the trauma. That had to be it.

His knee touched hers. "Do you like the tea?" he asked, blowing away some of the steam from his cup.

The tea was too hot to drink, so she absently rubbed the blanket through her fingers, loving the silky soft feeling. "I love mint, so yeah." She still focused on the dark liquid in her cup instead of him.

"There's mint, Pepsi, and steak. What else do you like?" His voice gave her goosebumps.

For fuck's sake, if he kept this up, she'd be a puddle at his feet soon. She grabbed all her courage, and her eyes met his. "I don't know." Her shoulders lifted and dropped lamely.

He gave her a knowing smirk. "Oh, and being out here, so you like the forest."

"Yeah," her voice came out in a horrible squeak.

We sound stupid again. The voice chimed in. Her cheeks heated.

Piper wrinkled her eyebrows. *Shut up!*

Well, can we please use our words? We love to read, so we know quite a few.

Tate scanned her with an arched eyebrow. "Are you okay? Is your wound hurting?"

No, she is talking to the voice inside her head—well, arguing.

Piper held back her growl, fucking voice. *I'm going to start calling you shithead.* "No, I'm fine. Remember, the deal was you talk, so Tate, what's your full name?"

Another smirk stretched his tantalizing lips. Images of what else he could do with that mouth almost had her missing his answer. "Tate Lee Hansen."

She bit the inside of her cheek. "So, Hansen, tell me about yourself. How did you end up here, in the middle of nowhere?" Piper bit her lip to see if he'd follow the movement. Her cheeks heated when he did.

If we're not going to enjoy him, we should stop. We're only going to have a cold shower later, and I hate cold showers. She ignored the voice, focusing.

"My family has lived here for generations. We do detective work for the local town or anyone that asks for help when needed. I think my great-great-grandfather came here with a small group of people decades ago and decided to make it our home. A lot has changed since the war ended. I think the language change has been the hardest for my people, but they are finally getting used to it. We don't even have much of an accent now."

"Anyways, it was also my family's idea to start a detective team. We don't do it very often anymore, but if people ask for help, we're still here for them." He rubbed his hands on his jeans. She could tell he didn't talk about himself much.

Piper's eyebrows shot up. "Wow, I'm not sure why they changed the language, but I'm glad. But by the way, my family was in that sort of work as well, so I understand..." her voice trailed off, not wanting to get into that. "I gotta ask. You've never been anywhere else but here?" Her eyebrows shot up in shock. Had he never wanted to explore the world?

He let out a small chuckle at her reaction. "Oh, yes. I've been all over the world, but I always come home. When my father passed, I chose to stay here for good, though. As I said, I like it here." He downed his tea, so she took a few large gulps of hers. The warm mint and slight honey flavor warmed her entire body.

She sighed. This was comfortable. Even the silence didn't seem awkward like it normally did with someone she hardly knew. "So, what's your full name?" he asked. He wiped his hands on his pants. Was he as nervous as she was?

She giggled. A weird relaxing sensation fuzzed her mind. But it was probably her sleepiness creeping up on her.

"Piper Halliwell." She laughed harder. His eyebrows wrinkled in confusion.

She playfully smacked his chest. "No, I'm just kidding. That was a character's name in my favorite TV show, Charmed. She was the only Piper I ever heard of besides me, of course. My name is Piper Evergreen Heart."

His hand grazed hers and held it. "That's pretty."

She picked up one of the smaller pillows and hugged it to her chest. "Thanks. There's a story about my name. It's silly, but my mom used to love to tell it to everyone. She'd go into a crazy amount of detail, but basically, she hyphenated my dad's name when they got married. Instead of doing that to my last name, she made my middle name her family's last name." She chewed on her lip. "She was an only child and a girl, so she didn't want her family name to die with her."

Flashes of her mom battling cancer had Piper blinking away old tears. Her mom was the most caring person she ever met and strong as hell, but cancer was stronger.

Her bright smile and soothing nature poured into her. Her loving mom was strong-willed and determined to help others. She was the type of woman to check on her elderly neighbors and make sure they had enough groceries. And volunteer for Meals on Wheels. Piper lived her life to make her mother proud, but she'd never been as great as she was.

She might as well have lost both parents the day her mother passed. Her dad didn't even try once she was gone. Trace was the only reason. She knew her dad eventually got remarried but still put flowers on her mom's grave every holiday. She blinked away the tears that threatened to appear. She gripped onto her knees and ran her hands over her thighs, so she could keep herself together.

Ugh, not now, she told herself and pushed her emotions to the dark depths of her mind. She could deal with her issues another time... or never. That worked for her too.

"Do you want some more?" His voice pulled her out of her haze.

She didn't know why but her body got heavy, and her mind got a little fuzzy, but it was a good, relaxing feeling.

She leaned back on the cushion, closing her eyes. "Yes, please."

He grabbed the dishes and hurried to the small kitchen. "May I ask, why did you come out here? It's abnormally far from the camping areas."

Her tongue felt heavy, but as soon as he gave her another cup, she downed the soothing liquid. All her worries and memories seemed to disappear. He asked her again.

"I just lost my sister and wasn't doing too well, so, I..." she shook her head, "I mean, Nina, brought me out here to... I know it's gonna sound crazy, but to talk to her. At those big rocks." His confused expression made her feel silly. She was equally confused. Why did she tell him that? It was kind of embarrassing.

He tilted his head before speaking. "You mean the spiritual ground?"

She giggled. "Probably. Nina went there when she lost her mom, and it worked so well for her. She wanted me to speak to my sister too. When she spoke to her mom after her passing, Nina said all of her pain disappeared. I needed that. I had so much pain." Before the sadness could take form, she laughed again and leaned closer to him. "How horrible is it that I had to almost die to get out of my funk? I haven't even cried once for my sister. That sounds horrible."

Her mind was fuzzy now. She had no idea what she was saying anymore. She glanced Tate's way at the sound of his voice. She didn't register anything being said, though.

She hiccupped and her hand snapped to her lips, covering her mouth. "Why are you so s...pexy? Xexy?"

He chuffed out and his eyes grew softer, but with a hit of... was that guilt? "I guess that answers my big question." He put both hands on her cheeks to get her to focus. "I'm so sorry, Piper. This isn't fair to you, and I wish I could give you a choice—"

He squeezed her face more, so she made farting noises. The reasonable thing to do, right? Maybe. "I allwayss gottaa cho-choices," she slurred. Her finger pointed at his face until it went up his nose.

He batted it away. "Please try to focus. This time you don't get a choice. The bite changed you." She didn't comprehend anything else said, but she watched his lips move. *What's happening?*

Somethings wrong, I can't see, and I smell something bad. Put the drink down! At that point, most of the second cup was already gone. The voice was too late. She still threw the cup at Tate. The dark flakes at the bottom landed on his face.

"What?" Her head was beyond fuzzy. *Did he drug me?* "What was in the drink?"

He wiped himself off calmly. "Wolfsbane. That's how I check for newly bitten packmates. Only a werewolf is affected by wolfsbane. It feels like being drunk, but there are no long-term effects."

"I have no idea what you just said, but I want to kiss you." She hiccupped again, giggling at herself and getting closer to him.

No, you dumbass, he poisoned us. Kick him in the face, I would take control and do it, but I can't see. Even the voice in her head sounded small and distant. She was disconnected from the world and reality. All she could focus on was his delicious lips.

"As much as I'd love that, I'm going to put you to bed so you can sleep this off." He moved faster than she could keep up with. He had her on the bed and covered up before she took her next breath.

The sleepiness hit her then, and he walked to the door. The shadows around the room seemed to grow and take on a form. "Wait? Can you stay with me?" She rolled over. "I promise to be good. I just don't want to be alone."

He smiled and nodded. His fingers ran along the dresser. "It's not you... I'm worried about being good," he whispered, but spoke louder with his next words, "I'll stay until you fall asleep."

She sighed in blissful relief as the shadows disappeared when he moved closer. "Yes, please stay," Piper mumbled.

He walked over and sat at the foot of the bed. She felt his uneasiness in the air, but she didn't care. She was happier with him nearby. If she was going to be defenseless, at least he was there to protect her.

If he was a bad guy, he wouldn't have saved her from the wolves, and he would have taken advantage of her just now. Right?

Chapter Eight

eadache! Piper rubbed her temples. The voice didn't have to scream. Her mouth was dry as a sandy desert. *Headache!*

I get it. Stop yelling.

You can hear me?

Well, duh.

I've been screaming all night. I started screaming one word after a few hours. It was horrible. You couldn't hear me. She sounded exhausted, and like she'd been smoking five packs a day, but also a little hopeful like a child after crying and their mom reassuring them.

"What the hell happened?" No one was in her room, so no one answered. Even her voice in her mind faded in exhaustion.

She closed her eyes and let her mind work. Images of her sister Trace popped into her mind souring her mood even more. She sighed and pushed through those images. Since being here the image of her sister didn't hurt as much.

After a few seconds, flashes of Tate's face and falling asleep were all she got. She sucked in a sharp breath. *Oh, hell no.* She flung the covers off her. She was in her too-tight clothes from yesterday. She grabbed her vulva. There wasn't any soreness. That made her nerves calm slightly.

Okay, calm your tits. Maybe I just fell asleep last night? She wasn't afraid last night. The opposite actually. She wouldn't feel that way if something bad happened, right... That was good enough for her. She sighed and got up.

Piper needed to shower and put on some new clothes. She went to the dresser and almost squealed at the clothes inside the drawers. She mentally crossed her fingers as she picked a few up and inspected them. The underwear and bras were the right size and new. *No way.* Most of the clothes were dark gray and black. *Yes.*

She grabbed the first things she saw and took off to the bathroom. *Shower.* She needed one ASAP. The odor coming off her was not her favorite. It had been too long. The moment the warm water touched her skin, life was better.

She didn't have to worry about her problems or what was going on here. She knew something was off, and today she was getting answers.

"Knock, knock," Nina yelled through the door.

"I'm in the shower. What happened to you last night? Did someone get lucky?" The teasing in her voice made Nina giggle. *Awe, girl moments are wonderful for the soul.*

"Girl, let me tell you." She paused to draw out the moment. Typical dramatic Nina. Piper loved it. "He was so delicious and big."

"So, *yummy*-yummy, or just yummy?" Sometimes it

baffled her how they had their own language. That's what happened after years of friendship.

"Oh, *so* yummy, yummy, toe-curling, even." The thrill and excitement in Nina's high pitch tone was obvious. Her feet patted around like she was dancing right outside the bathroom.

She stopped washing her hair and glanced Nina's way. She was going to regret her next words. "Did he help?" The words were merely a whisper, but Nina heard her. The sound of her footsteps halted. Nina would either get mad or ignore her.

To her surprise, Nina whispered back, "Mostly. It's easier with someone I don't know because I can put on a fake smile and almost convince myself." She cleared her throat, indicating she was done. "Anyways, I'm so glad, he was yummy because my body feels like happy jelly." She wanted to ask more questions or hug her, but Piper knew Nina's limited emotion-sharing was over. At least she opened up a little.

Piper finished scrubbing the hangover scent from her skin and jumped out of the shower. "I'm happy for you, girly. Do you want to stay here for a couple of nights? Tate said we could stay as long as we needed," Piper asked as steam drifted out the slightly opened door.

Nina peeked her head into the bathroom. Piper was still dressing, but they were so close, she didn't care. They even took showers together at spas. There was no need to be shy.

"Yeah, I think that would be nice. I like it here. Maybe we can have some fun." Nina wiggled her eyebrows. "You know we both deserve to have a good time. Especially because of how this adventure started." Her eyes drifted lower and blinked rapidly like she was forcing away a memory. Piper cleared her throat, so she shook herself out of the trance.

Nina turned to the mirror to admire her dark curls. She pulled on one. Her hazel eyes shined brighter than usual like she'd been crying. Something was wrong, and she wished Nina would talk about it. Was it Luke? The attack?

Nina ignored Piper's imploring gaze and continued. Her face contorted. "But no more tea. I drank it and got sick last night, then passed out, hard. I had some crazy dreams, let me tell you."

Piper froze. "What?" Her hands froze in midair—all her attention on Nina. It happened to her too.

"Hey, is anyone awake?" Liam yelled through the slightly ajar front door. He moved to Nina with a lively smile like a bee to a flower.

Goodness, Nina, I was just naked. You should have closed the door.

She rubbed his chest and smiled up at him. "Yes, we're about ready."

He kissed her lips softly. "Lunch is about to be served. You both missed breakfast. Want to join us for lunch? By the way, we didn't know how you were feeling, so we went back to your camp sight and recorded everything. Here, if you want to look. We can still go, but hopefully, this will suffice," Liam said as he walked away from Nina and pulled a couple white candles out of his large pockets, placing them down on the dresser.

Piper sniffed. *Jasmine and mint?*

She tilted her head in confusion. They weren't lit. How could she smell them from way over here? The dresser was close to the front door; it was the furthest thing from her in the cabin. She mentally shook her head and followed the two chuckling new thing-things out the door. *There I go again, being crazy.*

He handed her a camera. Both she and Nina watched them walk around their campground. They watched them walk back to the village and nothing was there. Piper recognized everything, so she knew they went to the right spot.

Nina squeezed her hand. Nothing. One person died and another was missing. How could there be nothing?

"I'll call Roger's family later. Maybe Roger went home. Luke was a foster kid, so I'm not sure who to contact for him. But I'll figure it out. Don't worry, Piper, I'll handle this," Nina said through her tears.

As soon as her feet left the wooden steps, dust drifted from the ground. She stopped. The sun's heat, the trees, the grass, the dirt, and the food almost half a mile away from her cabin assaulted her all at once. The scents forced their way up her nostrils, stinging them. Heat flared in her stomach. She grunted and doubled over, then she plugged her nose and covered her eyes. *Shit.*

"What the hell is going on?" Her voice sounded like she was using a megaphone. The urge to scream was strong, but the worry of blowing out her eardrums stopped her.

"You okay? What's wrong?" Nina's soft hands touched her shoulders. They were shaking with worry, but Piper couldn't reassure her friend now.

The sounds were next; birds chirping, wood grunting as a person walked on it, breathing, heartbeats, little animals scampering around, making a symphony of noises.

All of it was too much for her. She opened her mouth, and a silent scream gripped her throat until she smelled blood.

Even the taste in the air made Piper want to run and hide. No, no. Stop. The overwhelming sensation bombarded her oblivious to her agony.

Chapter Nine

"Focus, Piper, calm down, breathe." She wasn't sure who spoke, but the warm essence calmed her senses. "That's right, come back to me. You're okay now." Strong hands gripped both sides of her face. "Good, show me those beautiful blues."

"Tate?"

"Yeah, I'm here." His voice was rough to her ears, but exactly what she needed. His touch was like ice being thrown into lava. Within seconds all her issues melted away into nothing.

She bent at the waist with one hand on her knee, the other in Tate's hand. "What in the actual hell was that?" She hated how shaky her voice sounded, but fuck, that hurt. On a scale from one to ten that was a hundred.

"Let's go eat, and I'll explain everything. I'm here now, it won't happen again." He waved his hand in her face until she made eye contact. "Are you listening?" She bobbed her head and walked with him. Her throat hurt and was swollen.

She gulped. As long as that didn't happen again, she would do pretty much anything. The Hokey Pokey, Simon says, twerking, it didn't matter what, she'd do it. The harsh lava coursed through her veins, still not comfortable by any means, but it faded with every step.

They walked into the dining room. The lights shining in her eyes were still agonizing, but bearable. The smells weren't too bad, but she was extremely hungry now. Every eye was on her. Her insides twisted into dozens of huge knots. The overload had stopped, but she was not comfortable and extremely confused.

Tate piled tons of different kinds of salads and sand-wiches onto her plate as Nina clung to her arm. She was grateful to have her friend, but she needed space. The touch of Nina's hot body stung her skin. *Why the hell am I so sensitive?* And if she didn't get answers soon, she was flip-ping out on everyone.

A female at the table next to hers, with sharp hazel eyes and dry black hair, scowled at her. She made relaxing even harder. Piper's face heated and the urge to rip off the woman's face snapped her out of her rage.

Whoa. What if she hurt her? Something inside of her wanted to.

Nina placed the fork in her hands. She threw the silver thing down as if it bit her and turned towards Tate. "No. No food or pleasantries. Tell me what just happened. You sounded like you knew what was going on." Her voice still sounded rough and foreign. There was so much anger inside of her.

Nina squeezed her arm for support, but Piper refused to back down. Even if Tate's stare was intense. There seemed to be waves of energy rolling off him, demanding she submits... but that was crazy. Her imagination gave Tate more power than he had.

Gasps erupted around her, but as soon as she locked eyes with the gorgeous man, something told her she couldn't break eye contact. This meant something. What? She had no fucking idea.

Liam was at her side. He leaned in, to whisper in her ear. "You need to look at me, Piper."

His calming nature eased the tension in her muscles. Staring at Tate didn't seem as important. But her instincts told her not to break eye contact. *He is disrespecting us.*

A growl vibrated her throat. She registered how weird and intense that sound was, but her brain wouldn't let her break eye contact. Her eyes were glued to Tate's, and they refused to move.

Another spicier scent approached her. "You're so beautiful and strong. Fierce and loyal. No one is trying to control you or disrespect you, lovely." A warm hand caressed her shoulder, not sexual, but submissive... *That doesn't make sense.*

I like him. Look at him. See if he is worthy of those clever words.

The spell snapped; she blinked and turned her sore eyes toward the masculine voice. The enticing gray eyes she met stared into hers for a second, then dropped his gaze to her lips. His silver hair, turned-up nose, and sharp features worked perfectly with his soft model appearance. His ivory skin tone was flawless.

He wasn't as rugged or built as Tate, but he made up for that in sheer masculine beauty. She usually didn't go for the pretty boys; her taste drifted towards the bad boys or the throw-you-around-in-bed type of guys, but she was willing to make an exception for him.

He's worthy. Touch his cheek. Piper didn't want to. She pulled on her control, but her hand slid into place.

Her heart rate increased. The voice had never taken control over her before. She needed to figure out what was happening. The delicious stranger leaned into her touch.

"I'm new here and I've met a female Alpha before. It's an honor to meet another." His voice was like syrup, sweet but a little sticky. She didn't know what the hell he was talking about, but something about him kept her calm.

She smirked. "What's your name?"

She could give him a nickname like *gray Eyes* or *sexy son of*— her thoughts were cut off when he answered, "Storm."

Ooo, I like.

Insects flipped around in her tummy. "I like that," she blurted.

"Storm, can you sit across from Piper? She seems to be calmed by your presence." Tate's voice sounded different, not like the calming and pleasant tone she knew. Her eyes drifted to him again, and he stiffened but didn't back down. Anger spiked in her again.

Piper smirked. "Yes, please. I like staring at you, Storm. He just annoys me when I stare at him." Her head indicated Tate. Which was funny, since one of her hands was still in Tate's hand.

"My pleasure. I'd do anything you need me to," Storm said, smiling wider, almost predatorily. Piper rubbed the silky blue cloth covering the table to soothe her nerves. Between that, Storm's stares, and the tranquil white long-stemmed candles in the middle of the table, her worries eased.

The smooth material let her senses reach out without her eyes following. Every table had two candles on them and a freshly washed lavender cloth as well. Past the glorious scents of meats and bread, a putrid odor made her scratch her nose. Her eyes finally drifted around; most of the people went back to eating, but a few eyes met hers and then dropped to her lips.

Fine. Move on.

She kept moving over the people until a lanky, abnormally pale man in the back came into view... *Spoiled.* A dark, dusty scent came from him as well. *Dangerous.* The growling vibration happened again.

"Whoa, she's not acting like a bitten female, she's acting like a turned male. She spotted the vampire in seconds, and he's the furthest away from her." Storm smirked at her. His chiseled form had her drooling. His warm bronzed skin was an intriguing contrast with his gray eyes.

The word he said hit her then... "What the fuck did you just say?" *Bitten? Vampire? Vampire? What game were these bastards playing?*

Tate sighed and glared at Storm, who only smirked harder. "Piper, I was hoping to do this in private and with more elegance than this. We're one of the many packs of supernaturals in the world. Since I'm the most powerful and dominant, I'm the Alpha of this pack. My job is to keep everyone safe."

Tate's eyes shifted to Liam. He straightened his fork on the side of his plate. Piper was still confused, but she had to admit, his discomfort was cute. His face screamed 'help-me'.

She bounced her leg in response. *Out with it already. Pack? Alpha? What do these words have to do with me?*

Tate continued. "The man you pointed out smells different, doesn't he?" He knew she could smell his difference. How? Could he smell it too? She pushed her questions down and nodded. She was sitting on the edge of her seat, eagerly waiting. "That's because he's different from us. The dustiness of his skin and spoiled scent indicates a vampire. That's Bobby. Don't worry, he's a friend of the pack." His tone was soft and slow. It rubbed her the wrong way. She locked her jaw and gave him the stank eye.

A throat cleared, and she was again staring at Storm. "Listen, babe, we're werewolves, and since you got bit by one on a full moon, you and your friend are wolves too... but different. Bitten females turn into half wolves."

Piper laughed. When no one else did, she asked, "What?" After a few more minutes of serious expressions and no sign of joking, Piper stood, knocking her chair over. Nina followed as she spoke, "You're all crazy." She didn't care how soothing his stare was. There was no way she'd believe his words.

No.

Sure, werewolves existed, but there was no way she was one. They were pulling one over on her. Normally, she liked pranks, but this wasn't funny.

He speaks the truth, my human. We're werewolves, creatures of the night. This is a gift.

Piper shut out her inner voice and focused on the room that spun around her. Nina was holding her chest but didn't quite know how to react.

Her mind was blank but ran faster than it ever had before. She wanted to laugh it off, but if her voice was telling her it was true, it had to be.

She ran her hands through her hair. *What they fuck does this mean? I'm a damn dog?*

No, a wolf.

Nina is too?

The pause gave her some hope, but it was ripped away when she whispered, *Yes.*

There was only so much a person could take. She just saw a friend get killed, and then, she had to fight off a pack of wolves. On top of losing her sister. This... this hand her vision blurring and her body swaying as she almost fainted.

Could it get any worse?

Chapter Ten

Tate pushed Storm out of the way, angrily whispering something to him. He bowed his head in submission.

"Piper, please breathe and listen to my voice. You're in no danger. Feel my truth in my words, hold my hand, and feel the care I have for you and your friend. I can help you. I can show you what it means to be a wolf." Tate was calm and collected, but the strain that crinkled his eyes spoke volumes. The throbbing carotid in his neck and a twitch in his left eye was the confirmation.

Tate cared, but he was worried.

She cleared her dry throat. "What are you worried about, then?"

He rubbed the back of his neck and smiled. "You really are extraordinary. Usually, it takes years of studying to identify an Alpha's emotions. I'm worried about hurting you. You're strong. If you lose control and shift, you'll hurt people." His eyes softened. "You won't mean it, but I'd have to stop you."

She knew his, *stop you*, would suck, but she didn't want to hurt anyone either. "Fine, how are you going to show me?" She needed to give him a chance. The voice had never let her down. And dammit, she wanted answers. All she got were more questions.

Tate's hand in hers was like ice-cold water in a desert. She craved more, but at the same time, she worried his kindness was a mirage. He smiled and continued. "I just have to hug you. It's Alpha magic. I'll let you see glimpses of the pack's life. My knowledge will become yours." He opened his arms but didn't move. He was waiting for her to go to him.

Smart man.

Her gut tightened as a female snarled in the distance. "How do we know she's worthy of being with our pack? I know she's female, but what if the rogue pack sent her here as a spy or something?" the brown-haired female that had glared at her earlier said. She balled her fist and continued. "It's just really convenient that two unmated females end up on our doorstep."

A couple of the other men nodded. Piper's mouth dried out completely. How the hell was she going to prove her worth? Piper had a feeling if she and Nina left, they'd be in danger.

Growls came from a few people in the back. Tate put his hand up. "Scarlett, enough. I hear your worries, but none of these accusations can be proven. Piper can also simply be telling the truth, an innocent in all of this. Everyone deserves to have a pack for love and protection. You know how scarce that is these days." The large group that was closing in on them took a few steps back. The words from their leader must've calmed their hostility.

Well, all except one. "But is it worth our safety? We should make them leave," the woman cried out. She pursed her lips until her chin sharpened. She was undoubtedly a beautiful woman. A small, thin body, short dark hair, piercing hazel eyes, and flawless skin... but the sneer on her face made her face ugly in Piper's opinion.

Not as many people agreed with her words this time. They were females and rare. But Piper didn't want to be anywhere she wasn't wanted.

She let go of Tate's hand and threw up her arms. "Fine, then, we're gone," as she said it, her heart broke. She didn't know why. She barely knew these people, but something in her gut felt connected to them.

"No," a male's growly voice startled her.

Piper spun around. A new, unfamiliar male gave her comfort. He stood tall and defensive next to her. Storm was on her left and he was on her right. She had to admit, their closeness made her feel safe.

He growled at the woman making a fuss. Piper stared up at him. When she glanced back at Scarlett, her eyes were on his feet. If she wasn't trying to get her and Nina kicked out, she'd feel sorry for her.

A guy yelled from the back of the room, "Yeah, Scarlett is just jealous. She won't be the only she-wolf in the pack anymore. I vote to let them stay."

The Egyptian god grunted and caught her attention again. His heart-shaped face, hawk nose, full lips, shoulder-length brown hair, and attire made for a motorcycle spoke to her every desire. He was the bad boy she craved. The kind of man that would ruin her in bed.

She almost purred as he stood closer. He was dominant; the vibrating wolf power pushed against her skin. If the pressure wasn't comforting, she'd be annoyed.

When he spoke, the sound waves licked across her skin. "I can vouch for her." He rubbed the back of his neck as he glanced at Tate. "I was there the night they arrived by the stones. Patrolling the area. I got distracted and ended up stepping on a bear trap."

Piper gasped and whispered, "You?"

"Piper heard my whines, and instead of running scared or killing me like most would, she helped me. Piper isn't with those mangy mutts; her heart is pure. If I knew the rogue pack was close, I would have stuck around." His eyes gazed down at her. "She deserves to be in our pack, so shut your mouths and respect her." He stood closer to her, sharing his warmth.

Her mouth opened and closed while her heart fell to the floor. The wolf she saved stood next to her as a gorgeous man. She saved his life; now he was saving her. Piper was grateful. He didn't have to stick up for her.

"What? Why didn't you tell me you got hurt?" Tate asked.

"My pride wouldn't let me, Alpha," he replied but didn't drop his eyes like most of the pack did when addressing Tate.

Tate nodded, clearly understanding his reason. He turned his mesmerizing orbs on her and smiled. "Thank you for saving my pack mate. I'd love to extend our hospitality permanently and ask you to join my pack."

She sucked in a sharp breath at his words. A warmth ignited in her chest that didn't come from her. Was it magic?

Yes.

She gulped. Being in a pack was a bigger deal than she thought. She stepped forward and approached Tate. She glanced back at the two men she stepped away from, they gave her a nod of encouragement.

Screw it, what did she have to lose? She wanted answers, and she was getting them. Nina moved when Piper did. She was acting very... submissive. There's that damn word again. Submissive and dominant. How did they become common usage for her? Did she read the words somewhere? Because that was all her mind was spitting out as people stepped closer to them. She searched the crowd, not sure what she was searching for.

When her eyes landed on Nina, she stopped. This wasn't just her life. Nina would have to stay with her, and she had a way better life than Piper. She'd be giving up a lot more to stay here.

Her best friend smiled at her and grabbed her hand. "I'm with you, whatever you decide to do." Piper smiled back at her, kissed her hand, and let go.

They were going to do this. Her stomach tightened, but the excitement had her smiling wider. She knew in her gut that this was the right choice. Besides, if they were crazy or lying to her, she'd grab Nina and run... Hopefully with weapons to kill any wolves in their way.

Chapter Eleven

Her shoes scuffed the hardwood floor as she stepped into Tate's arms. His warm embrace swallowed her up in the best way. With her tall stature, feeling small never happened, but Tate did a great job at it. She sighed into his chest; his woodsy, manly scent was like a drug. She had the urge to wrap her legs around him. *No,* she told herself.

A magical splash of hot water seared her skin as images assaulted her mind. "Just relax. It'll stop in a second," Tate reassured her.

Her skull opened, he shoved his hand inside and shook her brain. Well, that's how it felt anyway. "Ugh, why didn't you tell me it was going to hurt?"

"It wasn't supposed to." He loosened his grip, but she held onto him. "Does it hurt now?"

She squeezed him for a few more seconds. Finally, the pain lessened, and relaxation took over her muscles. "No," she nestled into his chest, "it feels good now. I could fall asleep."

"Good, close your eyes and let your body relax. The information will come soon." Tate rubbed along her scalp.

"If I start wiggling my butt or tapping my foot when someone scratches behind my ear, I'm running for the hills." There were tons around here. She'd choose one and disappear.

He chuckled, a few others did too but she stayed focused on him. "Don't worry, we aren't dogs, Piper."

She rubbed her cheek on his cotton shirt. Her eyes drifted closed, and images danced in her mind, showing her the fierce love and loyalty packs had, the beauty and strength of being a wolf.

A dark-haired little boy ran to his loving parents. When he hurt himself, the whole pack was there to help him. They shared a bond like nothing she had ever seen. So many smiling faces. Even when sad times hit, the pack was there to help and guide him through it. There was no worry of being betrayed or hurt in his pack.

Another vision of two women hit. This time the images weren't pretty. A dirt covered red-haired female with a teary gaze getting rescued from a cage. A bleeding blonde getting rescued from a malicious looking man. Both women find their mates and have children. The feeling of their happiness and freedom coursed through Piper.

More and more flooded her system. Not all the stories were good at the beginning, but once they found their actual pack—not the nightmare they were with before—their lives were filled with smiles.

She sprung a leak; her face was soaked by the time she opened her eyes again. "Was that real?"

Tate tightened his grip on her. "Yes, I can't show you anything I haven't experienced or seen."

She reluctantly let go of him and stepped away. Nina ran into his arms faster than she thought possible. "Me next. Piper hasn't looked that calm or at peace in forever." She snuggled into his lower chest due to her height. "Show me."

A low growl sounded a few feet away from her. Piper knew it was Liam. Her eyes wouldn't move from them, though. She didn't like them touching either.

Tate watched Piper but tightened his arms around Nina. A pang of jealousy spiked in her chest. She forced herself to turn away. He was not hers. She had no right to be jealous. It wouldn't be the first time Nina had gotten a guy she wanted. And that grouchy chick, Scarlett, seemed to be pining over him.

She glanced at Scarlett. Her face was tight and red. She was just as unhappy with their touching as Piper. She bit her bottom lip and glanced their way again, but immediately dropped her gaze. *Nope, can't handle it.*

Storm stepped next to her, and she relaxed in his strong embrace. He had a knack for knowing when she needed comfort. The Egyptian god stood on the other side of her, not invading her space but offering his support. A sigh of relief escaped her.

She turned to absorb their comfort. Their combined powers kept her insides from stirring. She had never been a touchy person, but that's all she wanted right now. Everyone needed to get on the floor so she could rub against all of them. *Wait, what? That sounds horrible.* Her mind knew how weird that daydream was, but her heart told it to fuck off.

It's the wolf wanting to be close to her pack. We won't rub against all of them. But we will enjoy their nearness and comfort.

Piper blinked a few times. Well, snap, she thought all her questions would be answered with Tate's hug thingy. But nope.

The Egyptian god—she needed to learn his name—leaned in closer and whispered, so only she heard. "I can tell you still have questions. Don't worry, the information will eventually come. It'll slowly trickle in. Otherwise, it'd be dangerous," his voice was a deep sexy growl that she loved. He stepped closer to her to reassure her or maybe to reassure her wolf. Whatever.

Nina stepped away from Tate. Her sobs killed Piper. She moved to go to her, but Nina ran to her and wrapped her arms around her neck before she could take a second step. Nina's short stature forced Piper to bend over to hug her back. "So beautiful," Nina whispered. She rubbed her face on Piper's chest to get rid of her tears and snot. *Ew. Thanks a lot.*

Other pack members moved in closer around them—their eagerness to comfort Nina written on their concerned faces, but Liam scooped Nina up in his arms and ran out the door. Piper pulled away from all the men now around her.

She gave them a small smile and headed toward the door to go to her friend. "Let her work through the emotions. There's something wrong with her," Tate said, gently touching her elbow to stop her.

The door swung shut. The urge to run after her friend was ginormous. Only Nina could make her want to use the word ginormous. Her curiosity won the battle, though. "What? Why? Tell me."

Tate bit his top lip. "There are two things. One, you can help her with it, and the pack will help as well. And the other is permanent. We can give our support and guidance but there's nothing anyone can do to change it." Piper's heart dropped to her feet. That sounded horrible.

She clenched her jaw tight but said nothing. Storm grabbed her hand. The tension in her shoulders eased slightly. Her imploring eyes never left Tate's.

He nodded and continued. "First, let me start with the good. Your bond with your wolf is extremely rare. You have the strength I haven't seen from a female wolf. That's unheard of. Bitten females never turn fully. When you shift, your wolf will most likely resemble an actual wolf. But Nina's wolf is going to be different." A crack sounded below her. Oops, she hoped she didn't break anything.

Piper loosened her grip on Storm's hand but refused to let go. The Egyptian god held out his hand. She snatched his limb and pulled him closer. The somersaults in her core were happening again, as anger, and a fierce protection instinct for Nina kicked in.

When she settled down, Tate continued. "Nina's wolf will look half-human. She'll not have the same strength or control that you do. The half-human wolf is common with females. Unfortunately, they can't survive without a pack and lose all memory on full moons. She'll attack anyone and everyone she smells."

"When is the next full moon?"

"Tomorrow."

She sucked in a sharp breath. It felt like poison in her throat. "Is this the thing that I can change?" She absently circled her thumbs on the hands in her grasp. The feel of them calmed her like soft fabric did.

Tate shook his head. "No, the wolf is a part of her. We cannot change or remove it. She will be forever a half-wolf, but with time she can live a normal life as long as she stays close to her Alpha."

Anguish poured into Piper's veins, like acid eating away her insides. A mournful vibration in her throat sounded, and she lifted her head, howling in agony. The pack responded, howling with her. The men around her tightened their grip and their support lifted some of the sadness.

She was howling... Howling. Her life had become mercurial in such a short time. She shook her head.

"So, what can I change?" Her voice surprised even her. Why was she so relaxed? She shouldn't be relaxed!

Her eyes drifted to Storm. "It's not going to be easy, but you have the right to know, and Nina has the right to try to get it back."

She pulled at the ends of her hair and stayed silent. Her mind was already made up. *I'm helping Nina. Of course, I am. I'd die for her if I had to.*

"The last time Nina was here, and the reason she seemed better when she went back home, was because a demon stole her mourning emotion away. Nina can no longer mourn anything. We don't even know if she can get sad or how much it took away from her. Those big rocks she put her hands on are prisons for demons."

Chapter Twelve

The dining room kept growing smaller the longer she took to absorb all the information. Faces pressed down on her like heavy weights, as if they were waiting for something from her. Any kind of sound. Their eyes left her unnerved.

Piper opened her mouth, but nothing came out at first. *Umm... Werewolves, vampires, now demons?* She spent so much time staying away from supernaturals only to be surrounded by them. It now threatened to overwhelm her. "What? How do I get it back?" The fact she spoke full sentences baffled her. Her mind was a jumbled mess.

The sympathy in Tate's blue gaze annoyed Piper, but she had to know. This wasn't the time to be sad. It was time to be angry. Angry at Nina, at the demon, and even at her sister for putting her job first and being killed.

Images of her sister's guilty voice over the phone when Piper asked to help and the worried lines that aged her face when she came over made Piper's heart hurt. If only she asked for help. Maybe we could have done something together.

Every emotion was amplified, and all her control felt fleeting. She didn't like it. She didn't like the change happening inside her.

Tate inched towards her. "First, I just want to let you know, we have a demon specialist testing her DNA from a glass she used. They'll be able to tell us more." Piper's eyes flashed with heated rage, but the air thickened and her rage dwindled.

Tate put up his hands. "I know we should have asked, but I couldn't take the chance you guys would say no. Demons are no joke. If somehow the demon is controlling her or worse, I need to know to keep my people safe." Her shoulders relaxed slightly. She didn't like the sneakiness of it, but she understood. She'd do the same for the people she loved. "Secondly, we have a small chance at getting what she lost back. I'll speak with my demon expert to be sure, but I think we would have to find the demon that stole from Nina and kill it."

Her shoulders relaxed even more. Only because there was hope. A small chance, but that was better than nothing. "Oh, so it'll be easy." She groaned sarcastically. Demons were damn near impossible to kill and even harder to find. "Wait, if it's a prison, will the demon be in there?" She stepped away from the others.

Her eyes sharpened into angry slits. She stared down everyone in the room. *Absolutely.*

The Egyptian god answered her as he rubbed her lower back, but she moved away, not wanting to be touched. "Well, it doesn't work like that. The prison is another dimension. Another world. If you somehow got access, you'd still have to find the right demon without being killed. And that's if the demon isn't released. Then, you'd have to search the Underworld."

Her knees wobbled, and the frog in her throat blocked her oxygen. *Mm... What now?* The world spun around her. There were different worlds? Different dimensions? *Holy shitballs.* Storm held her elbow to keep her from falling.

The moment his fingers made contact, silky magic wrapped her in its warmth until her worries and stress disappeared. *Whoa.* "You should bottle this shit, because wow. I can't feel my toes. You and Liam had a gift."

Tate moved his head around until they made eye contact. "Here." He handed her a glass of Pepsi. Her eyes zeroed in on the dark goodness. She greedily devoured the goddess-sent liquid. The carbonation soothed her soul.

"Before you let your rage and wolf take over, hold on for at least a couple of days. You might be strong enough to not shift during the full moon, but Nina isn't. We need to prep her for one of the worst experiences she'll ever have. Okay, Piper? Afterward, we'll do everything in our power to find the demon." Tate took her hand away from Storm. Storm didn't seem bothered. He moved to her shoulders, massaging them, while Tate's thumb circled her palm.

Every touch from these three men gave her what she needed. Tate gave her hope, Storm gave her comfort, and the Egyptian god gave her strength.

She nodded. She could do this.

Nina came first.

I'll help her through the next couple of days, then hunt down the bastard that did this to her. Nothing is stopping me from ripping his head off.

She closed her eyes, and Storm slowly eased off his calming power. Her eyes reopened to find several males crowding in on her. Anxiety grabbed her throat and squeezed. "I can't do this!" She ground her teeth and panted out, "Need space." But the men ignored her. They argued when Tate ordered everyone back.

"We have the right to comfort her."

"She's only had you three touch her so far, that's not fair."

"She could be ours."

The noise and words racketed the tension in the room. Her heart slammed against her ribcage, her pulse skittered, and her blood rushed to her muscles, causing them to twitch as she prepared to run.

And that's what she did. The crowd moved out of her way, parting in unison as she pushed by and opened the large door with a desperate breath. She needed to get away from everyone.

The cool air caressed her flesh, helping her not to self-combust. She let the sounds of the wind whistling through the top of the trees eat her claustrophobic sensation away.

Tate and a few others ran after her, bringing a cloud of dirt with them. "Piper, I'm sorry. I can't imagine what you're going through."

She turned towards Tate. The other males around her pushed at each other to be in her line of sight. "Why won't everyone just leave me alone?"

Tate glanced behind him and groaned. "I didn't think I'd have to tell you so soon."

"For fuck's sake, tell me what? Who are these guys? Why do they seem to think they have the right to be in my personal space?" One of the men stepped back, hearing the threat in her tone. Good, maybe there was hope for him. "I understand the bond with the pack, but this seems different."

Tate sighed. "Males are going to come from all over the world to try to mate with you. Your wolf calls to the unmated males. Especially, when you're upset."

Her mouth opened, making a perfect O. She rapidly blinked at him. A chuckle escaped her. A hysterical laugh threatened to take over. Her mind. Her body. Her everything. She mentally grabbed a screwdriver and tightened her brain screws. If they got loose now, she'd never recover.

Is there a point when things get to be too much? Then, your brain just explodes. She asked the voice.

Let's not find out. Just keep taking deep breaths. This is the wolf way.

She growled. "How the hell do I shut her up?"

Tate smirked. "You can't. I didn't know how strong you were before giving you the tea, or I wouldn't have given it to you. It activates your female wolf's hormones."

He bit his lip. "The only way to stop the call is to go through the trial. Once you find a mate and true pack, they'll stop coming." He stepped closer and touched her hand. The contact soothed her wolf. She was the real reason Piper was angry.

"What? So, I just found out I'm a werewolf. Now, I have to mate with someone. Why should I have sex with a stranger? Wait, do I have to have sex with everyone?"

Growls and groans sounded around her. Tate turned and growled back. He stood protectively in front of her. His hands extended with his sharp claws.

Before the tension in the air around all the men could

thicken, a man stepped away from the crowd. He put himself in between Tate and the others. "Alpha," His eyes met Tate's but lowered to his chin, "they're just feeling the same call. Let's not turn this into a fight. We're all just wanting a mate here."

Tate growled but stood taller. His claws and aggressive demeanor vanished in seconds. "You're right, Jinks. I let my primal nature take over. I ask that everyone be silent. Remember, this isn't about how strong we are, it's about Piper. Most packs don't think that way, but we're different. We won't be like other packs. We treat our women with care."

"They are precious gifts," another guy mumbled.

Piper gulped. Her eyes widened. She didn't know if his possessiveness was sexy or scary.

Tate stepped closer. "Careful, Piper, the men here are strong-willed and would never force you to do anything. But our wolves are close to the surface. So, let's keep that kind of talk to a minimum."

Yeah.

If the Alpha could barely control his urges, she had to be careful. She glanced around. The hungry, desperate gazes locked onto her. Their eyes were dilated, and they bounced on their toes. She wouldn't be surprised if they rolled over so she could rub their bellies at any moment.

She nodded.

Tate guided her to a bench nearby. "First, mating is a bond, not sex. Once you find your mate, you don't have to bond with him. Any chosen will respect your wishes. They'll just want to help and protect you."

He scratched the side of his neck before continuing, "A female can only give children to her mate, and male wolves wait their whole lives for her. You're a strong female were-wolf. So, without the trial, you're going to be hunted, but with the tea, it's overreacting." He scowled at the five men standing in front of her. "I honestly thought we'd have more time. I wish I could block the signal for you."

Piper scowled at the guys too. "Wait, it doesn't make sense. Why? Why can't I shut my wolf up?"

Tate smirked. "There is a signal of sorts an unmated female gives off. The stronger the wolf, the further the signal travels. It's to protect her from packs like the one that attacked you and Nina."

The men twitched uncomfortably, but eager, like antsy children. One played with a hanging leaf, and another kicked dirt into the air. She tightened her jaw and flared her nostrils in annoyance. "Fine, it's not like I have a choice."

THAT WAS HOW PIPER ENDED UP STANDING IN HER birthday suit in front of dozens of drooling naked men. Her only saving grace was the thin podium covering her. *Ugh.*

The large room had gold walls and plush black carpet that were stuffed with men from her pack and other nearby packs. Booths and folding chairs were everywhere with a butt in them. None from the wolves that attacked her, thank goodness. The women sat in the back. They scowled at her and glared at the men.

The voice chimed in before she could hyperventilate.

Breathe, we're okay. Don't worry about the lack of clothes, read the incantation. Let's find our mate and true pack.

What if they are not here?

The magic will bring them to us soon.

Piper rolled her eyes; this was by far the weirdest thing she had ever done. And she had done lots of weird stuff like eating pancakes with ketchup or wearing a tutu for a week to cheer her sister up.

What if he's not that attractive? I don't want to sound mean but I must be at least a little attracted to the guy I have to spend the rest of my life with. What if—

Shut up. Get on with it.

Fucking grumpy voice. Whatever.

She wished Nina was here, but Nina didn't want to face all these people after what happened. Piper didn't blame her.

And apparently, she didn't need to do this stupid ceremony for a few years. Or not at all, if she found a mate. Why was Piper so different? Did she drink extra strong tea or something? It was a bunch of bull cocky.

You're making us look bad again. Can we get on with this? Finding our mates is an honor.

She tightened her jaw and read the words on the small white paper, sitting on the dark podium. The smooth hardwood floor grounded her. "Hear my words, hear my cry, across the stormy sky, come to me and settle here, come to me without fear. I call to you, my other halves. Guide me on this new path," Piper repeated the spell seven times like instructed. Nothing happened.

How do I know it worked? Maybe it has all been a misunderstanding. The voice chuckled but didn't reply. She didn't see what was funny.

A purple light burst from her chest, leaving her, to fly around the room. The magic played ping pong with the walls. Her heart leaped in her throat as the light got closer to the men.

One guy stood up. "Pick me, please," he yelled. Piper almost burst into laughter when the magic toyed with him but didn't choose him. Even her light thing had an attitude.

The humongous floating ball split into four smaller ones. The one closest to her slammed into the wall and disappeared. *Where the hell did it go?*

The others shook violently as if about to explode. She ducked behind the podium just in case they burst into slime. They did come from her, and she'd already seen the attitude.

A powerful, sharp movement had them plunging into three chests. She still hid. The next part was going to suck. What if she hated the people or they were ugly? That made her sound shallow, but the fear was real. Although she hadn't seen any ugly people whatsoever. They were all shockingly handsome.

She braved a peek; the men were floating in the air. The same purple glow around them, coming straight for her. She bent lower and closed her eyes. *This is not happening.*

Will you stop making us look stupid? Stand and meet our new favorite people.

But what if I don't like them?

The voice sighed. The sound of feet hitting the hardwood floor in front of her made her gulp. *There are no obligations. In fact, you have the right to deny them. The power will dissolve.*

She slowly stood and opened her eyes. She prayed one last time for them not to be horrible people.

The first thing she saw was her long eyelashes, and then the world spun. Shit. The magic connected them to her. She could feel the pull to them like she wanted to smother herself in their scent.

Piper stopped breathing. Who needed air when she had them?

Chapter Thirteen

Piper's face warmed and reddened. Her mouth went dry. *What?*

A few men cried out, tucking their heads between their shoulders. The wooden chairs they sat in creaked. She rubbed the smooth wood again to center herself. *What just happened?*

We have yummy-ass men in our true pack.

Her true pack was none other than Storm, the Egyptian god, and Tate. *Mine. They are mine. Holy monkey balls.*

Piper almost snickered but couldn't find the strength between blushes.

Every time she focused on one of the men, red-hot embarrassment rocked her. A sharp pain in her lower stomach had her grinding her teeth. Ouch.

The wolf bit at her intestines in annoyance again, or at least that's what it felt like. Piper wanted to smack the furry brat. But the wolf was annoyed and had had enough of her submissive behavior.

Piper squared her shoulders and eyed her new people. When her eyes met mister unknown, he bowed his head. His hazelnut eyes and Egyptian skin struck a chord in her. His dark brown hair made his eyes appear to glow. The fierce and robust body that resembled Tate's was beautiful, but she couldn't stop gazing at his rough-hewn features.

"I'm Rockie." *Oh-my-honeysuckle-goodness.* His voice was like sex in H_2O form. The wolf that saved her, that she saved, and that she nicknamed Egyptian god was called Rockie.

"It's great to finally meet you, Rockie." Her voice was lacking in every way in comparison. *What if they don't like me? Am I forcing them into this?*

Breathe, just ask them.

Tate spoke before she could. "Piper, it's your time to choose. You need to accept us, ask for more options, or deny us. We cannot hold this much power for long." He licked his lips as he watched her.

"Am I forcing you to be with me by doing this?" Her voice was soft. The excitement hit her hard. Her hands shook, and it took a lot of control not to bounce on her feet. She wanted them, but only if they wanted her.

They all snickered.

Storm's gray eyes met hers. "Do you know how lucky we are, beautiful? We want this. If you do. We can take it as slow as you need."

Piper giggled and a small bounce escaped her hold. She covered her exposed body with the podium. "I accept you all. But I have to ask, there was a fourth ball. What happened to it?" She chewed on her cheek as the men's body glowed. They gasped as the glow sank into their skin, they panted and smiled at her.

Storm shrugged. "It looked like it exploded, didn't it?"

"Do you feel a pull to another?" Tate asked, but Piper had no idea. Ever since drinking the tea, her insides felt different. Her emotions were all over the place.

"Umm, no. But how would I know?" she asked.

"You should just feel it," Rockie said which made her shrug. She had no idea what he was talking about. What was she supposed to feel?

"Okay, so let's just say it exploded. We'll handle it if that changes," Tate said. His hand reached out for her.

She wanted to go to him but... "Umm, so, can I put on some clothes now?"

"Excuse me?" Nina moved back and forth, wearing the floor out. She stopped, bit her lip, and drummed her nails against the dresser in deep thought. "Three guys, Piper? Are they all your mates?"

Piper sat on the bed, bouncing her leg furiously. She scrunched the cotton blanket in her palm, using it as a buffer between her and the world. "Yes. I get to choose. If I don't want them all, I can deny them. But I don't know. It's all kinda weird. As I'm understanding it, everyone here is pack. They're like cousins. They're family but not household family. But a true pack is my household family. If I don't choose them all, they stay pack, but not true pack. Is it weird that I don't know if I want to choose?" Piper clutched her chest. Her heart was sore... It was weird but that was how it felt. "I don't understand it. But girl, I feel like I've known them forever. Which is ridiculous because I know nothing about them. Except that I want them around."

"But three guys? You barely tolerate one guy in your life most days." Nina had wide eyes as she bit her fingernails. She dropped her hands when Piper's gaze latched onto her destroyed manicure.

She sighed. Nina's worry and scared eyes weren't for her, not really. Nina was a sleep-with-a-person-first, then-learn-their-name kind of woman. She didn't have a problem with her three men. She was only focusing on Piper's issues because Nina had real problems. The full moon would happen tonight, and according to Tate, Nina would lose control. It sucked they'd ended up in a place magically designed to have full moons more often. Why couldn't they have gone to a part of the world that stayed daylight twenty-four-seven for months?

Piper picked at her fingernails before speaking. "Can we talk about you, Toots?" Piper's gentle voice made Nina's eyes tick.

"No. You. I can't," she whispered, continuing her pacing.

The sun drifted past the mountains and slowly disappeared. Soon, they'd be here to get Nina. She had to spend the night in a cage. Every time she imagined her friend locked in a cage; bile burned the back of her throat.

Footsteps sounded on the porch. They both stiffened and stared at the door. Whoever was outside waited patiently for the approval to enter.

"Just come in already," Nina said through a mouth full of her fingers. Her nails grew back instantly but they were a weird brown color. She stared at them and blanched.

"Are you ready, gorgeous? I have everything set up." Liam was a few shades lighter, but he forced a smile on his face.

Nina's eyes went to Liam, then her. Her face had a sickly green tint to it. "Wait, where will Piper be? I don't—"

"I'm attached to your hip, Toots. You couldn't get rid of me if you tried." Piper stood and ran to Nina. She wrapped her arms around her when tears slid down her face. "You're going to be fine. I'll be right there with you." Piper put a hand on her lower back to guide her to the door with a gentle push.

They didn't make it far out of the cabin before she stopped. "What's that smell, Piper? Is it here to hurt us?" Nina asked, but she couldn't smell anything.

"I don't smell anything. Come on."

Nina white-knuckled Piper's arm, digging in until she smelled blood, but she took the pain. If only she could take away Nina's fear.

They stepped out, and the pull of the moon's call sang to her. Its sweet melody begged for her to frolic and run on all fours. *Shift*, it whispered. *I promise it'll be the best night of your life.* She dug her nails into her palm to keep her mind focused. The urge lessened.

A few seconds later, Nina groaned. Her skin rippled like waves in the ocean and heated to the point that boils threatened to form. *Oh no.* Piper clutched Nina's bare neck like a mother would grab a cub. "Liam, we need to move faster."

His hazel eyes widened. He dashed to Nina, threw her over his shoulder, and ran. She had difficulty keeping up with him, but the sound of Nina's screams fueled her feet.

A few seconds after Liam, she rushed through the destroyed door, tripping over the large pieces of wood. Liam was having issues getting her in the cage. His fingers stumbled with the keys. The yellow lanyard had over fifteen keys on it.

"Give me the keys and tell me which one," Piper said just as Nina smacked the keys out of his hand.

Nina's eyes were wild and petrified. Her chest moved up and down in rapid succession. She clung to the cage's bars, refusing to go in. "No!" she shouted. Her voice sounded more like a growl than words.

Another male came to help Liam, but his young face pinched with worry. Liam pushed Nina back and grabbed the young man by his green shirt, forcing his eyes on him. "Go get Tate. She's too far gone and needs an Alpha to overpower her dominance. I'll try to do it, but we need him here just in case."

The blonde man scurried away.

Nina's eyes were glowing red, and her arms had slowly changed. They grew bigger, hairier, and oh so lethal. Her fingernails grew into long points. Nina slowly faded into something primal. Piper stood defeated. There was nothing she could do.

Her nose stretched until Nina's face resembled a wolf. Her muscles bulked, and white fur coated her body. Gruesome fangs elongated from Nina's mouth, dripping with saliva. All those scary pictures of human-wolf beings had nothing on the alien in front of her.

"Piper, run!" Liam shouted. Sweat covered his face as he strained to hold Nina back. She was too big. Liam was tiny next to her. Her white fur almost covered him entirely.

A crazed roar exploded out of her, and Liam flew across the room. The werewolf turned, locking red eyes on Piper. *Oh shit.*

"Nina, stay calm, sweetie. We just want to help you. I know you're still in there." Her body screamed to run. Yet, she knew running from a predator wasn't a smart move.

Nina's heavy breaths stopped, and she burst into an aggressive run, straight for Piper. Her stomach knotted as instinctively her claws drew back, ready to strike her. "Nina!"

The werewolf hesitated but threw her against the far wall. Then, with another roar, the werewolf ran straight for a large group of cabins. A male screamed, and the adrenaline hit her veins.

Nina shifted too early; everyone was still in human form and vulnerable. She growled and got up. *Where the hell is Tate?*

Ignoring her pain, she took off after her. Even if she didn't remember who she was right now, Piper couldn't leave her. She squared her shoulders and ignored the fear that made her body tremble. "Please don't eat me, Nina."

Chapter Fourteen

The frost-bitten air clung to Piper's body as she ran, following the enormous tracks Nina made in the dirt and holes in the wood cabins. *Crap, she's messing these people's homes up.* The guy that screamed earlier was crawling for cover. It was the blonde boy that was supposed to get Tate.

There goes her back up.

"I'm healing," he said, breathlessly. "Go after her!"

Another male yelled to her left. She pushed her feet on the ground and practically flew towards the sounds of pain. She moved with surprising stealth and graceful speed.

Her strong muscles and core made her more confident. Her eyes sharpened, noticing every movement and curve of her surroundings. A smudge of dirt on a cabin wall, claw marks and footprints, pointing her in the right direction.

When she cleared a few trees, the werewolf was over a bloody young boy. Two men were attempting to stop her, but she ignored them, knocking them away from her. Nina's hand lifted with her claws extended to give the killing blow. Piper didn't hesitate or think twice. She rushed to the beast and slammed into her before her arm connected.

The werewolf howled and swung at Piper furiously, shoving her away to go for the boy again. She blinked and the beast had her sharp teeth dug into the boy's shoulder. "No!" she screamed.

Something inside of Piper snapped at the thought of the young boy inches away from death. Her body heated as if flames were bursting from her pores. Her clothes ripped and shredded. Her bones snapped, and before she knew what was happening, she stood on all fours.

Nina paused and locked eyes with Piper. Tate was right, she was nothing like Nina. She could see herself in the reflection of Nina's large eyes. She was a massive red wolf.

Her teeth dislodged from the boy and stepped closer to her. Piper hoped the boy was okay, but she kept her narrowing eyes on her friend. *Shit, shit, shit. What do I do?*

Push your dominance out. That knot in your stomach, grab it, and pull. Fast! her voice shouted.

She didn't have time to freak out because Nina dove for her. She moved quicker than Piper could register. Her wolf dodged the killing blow to her neck, but Nina caught her chin. The pain was instant, but she pushed it down.

A wave of knowledge seeped into her mind seemly out of nowhere. It said go for the neck, but she'd have to kill Nina for her to submit like that; half wolves didn't respond to that kind of aggression well. *But they respond to magic.* She tried again, but nothing happened.

Dominate her now, or she'll kill you. She won't have an issue with ripping out our heart.

Piper pushed on that knot in her stomach, but Nina's massive half-human-and-wolf body slammed into her. They rolled around, fighting for dominance. Sharp fangs bit into her side. Piper yelped and kicked her off. Blood traveled down her body and onto the floor.

She wasn't going to win this. Her rapidly beating heart skipped a beat, and icy fear gripped her neck.

NO! Push out our power now. Don't you dare give up. Nina would never forgive herself if she killed us. Come on, we can do this.

She pushed past the fear and tried again. Fucking nothing.

The werewolf's large form tackled her to the ground. Her paws went up, holding her back. They were the only thing keeping Nina's sharp teeth out of her neck. Nina snapped her jaw a few times, using her massive weight to slowly get closer to Piper's flesh. Saliva dripped on her skin.

Was this how she died? Was she really going to let her friend live with the guilt of killing her? No, she fucking wasn't!

Piper roared and pulled with all her might. A powerful force expanded out from her and clung to the werewolf. Nina whined and shook her head, fighting the power. Piper grunted and pushed harder. People approached, but she ignored them and commanded Nina to obey.

A loud growl emanated from her.

Nina whimpered again and jerkily knelt at Piper's feet, turning over to expose her belly. Relief slammed into Piper. She stumbled, not sure what to do next.

Gasps and whispers of "She's really an Alpha," and "Holy hell, how?" distracted her. She locked her jaw to stay focused. Couldn't they see she needed to keep her eyes on Nina?

Tate appeared at her side, putting a hand on her back for support. "Thank god, you're okay. I got here as soon as I could. Rockie and I had to hunt down the other half-wolf." He gave her a small hug that made her focus waver. "Sorry."

He pulled away but stayed close. "Go to her and wrap your mouth around her neck. Since your power is having her submit, this will seal the bond, and her werewolf will listen to you from now on. I'd normally do this, but I'm going to be busy with the other female half-human-were, so this works out perfectly." He stroked his strong hand along her red fur, guiding her to the ground.

She wrapped her large, sharp teeth around Nina's neck. The energy and sticky force field around Nina popped. Piper could breathe again. The power ran over her body, coursing through her veins, healing her wounds and giving her strength.

As Nina got up, shaking herself off, Storm and Rockie trotted up beside Piper, showing off their dark gray wolf coats. Their wolves were beautiful, so strong and majestic, yet wild. Her wolf responded and a sudden urge to run with them that crept along her mind.

Tate shooed them away from her. "You can have fun later. We need to lead Nina to her restraints. If you are near, her beast will be calm."

Storm and Rockie puffed their wolf chests, rubbed against her, and ran deeper into the forest, nipping at each other's ankles. The smell of their manly scent, mixed with the forest pleasantries, was like heaven to her. She whined in their direction.

Tate's eyes softened. He stepped closer to her and rubbed his face against her furry one. Her wolf preened. "I'm sorry you can't run with them. We'll go for a run after the full moon, I promise. As Alphas, we don't get to enjoy the moon like the others do. We work to keep them safe. To keep Nina safe." He gestured toward the half-were, silently standing next to her.

Her eyes wandered like a child, but she didn't leave Piper's side. The sadness of not running with Storm and Rockie subsided. She could do this for her friend.

Piper turned back to Tate and her new responsibilities. She nodded in acceptance. He sighed and followed her as she led Nina away. "I meant to be here when she changed, but both of the half-weres were feeding off each other's anxiety, which had them shifting too early. Our other human-were is usually calm around me, but sensing the newcomer, she freaked out."

Piper tilted her head at Tate, and he must have understood because he continued. "Scarlett is the other human-were. She was bitten by a pack like the one that attacked you. It's hard for her to trust or listen to anyone but the Alpha. When Patty changes, I hope they can change near each other." The last part was said more to himself than her.

She wasn't listening anyway, jealousy's ugly head slammed into her. She growled and turned away from him. He couldn't help her tonight because he was with Scarlett? Nina shook her head and whimpered next to her, picking up on Piper's mood.

Piper pushed down her emotions for Nina's sake, but the green monster in her heart still festered. Which was silly because that was his job as the Alpha. It was manageable, though, and that's all that mattered. Nina calmed but seemed on edge, darting her eyes to Tate every few seconds.

Tate brushed his hand through his hair. He glanced Piper's way. "We've been broken up for about a year now, Piper. We dated for a while, but we never meshed well. I think I stayed because..." He stopped and stood in front of her. Nina growled but sunk her feet into the soft dirt, not moving. He got near her like his life source was in her chest. His hands shook slightly. If she didn't have better vision, she wouldn't have noticed.

His feet shuffled before he continued. "You weren't raised as a wolf shifter, so you don't know the pain and fear that builds up inside you from puberty. We know there is a slim chance of ever finding love because with a true mate our wolves don't connect. So, we can never truly love that person." He sighed and rubbed his face. "There's nothing going on with us anymore. If I could have another dominant be with her during the moon, I would. Especially until you and I get to know each other. I can spend the rest of my life proving my worth to you." He slowly raised his hand to her ears but didn't touch her. He waited for her to make contact.

Piper sighed, the best she could as a wolf anyway, and closed the gap. Tate's strong hands scratched and rubbed her fur. Electricity ran up and down her body, making her soul purr. How could such a simple touch be Earth-shattering?

He stroked between her eyes and down her nose. Piper about collapsed on the floor. She closed her eyes instead, pressing into his touch.

She didn't blame him for his past. And that was what

Scarlett was to him, his past. She couldn't get mad over something that already happened. She had several relationships and lovers in her past. It'd be hypocritical if she got mad at him for his.

Shoot, she stayed with men for the same reason. Loneliness was no joke. Sometimes having a body next to her was good enough.

She wasn't even mad about having to be Nina's Alpha either. Nina would never have forgiven herself if she killed that boy. She perked her ears up and stared at Tate. How could she not have asked about him before? Gosh, she was horrible. They were a pack now and needed as much saving as Nina did.

"What?" His face grew heavy with concern. Piper pointed her nose toward where they just left. He glanced that way but seemed to understand when no one was behind them. "Oh, Alan? The boy?"

She nodded.

"He'll be fine. Doctor Patty is a good healer. He would have survived even without her help, though." Tate didn't meet her eyes, so she used her snout to keep him talking. Finally, he continued. "He was one of the humans that live with us. His mother was a bitten, but she got killed by a brutal pack, so we took him in. He'll be a fine wolf for the pack."

Ugh. Why do only women turn into half-wolves? How is that fair?

She already knew the answer, but the voice spoke anyway, *most women don't accept the wolf bite like men. Maybe because they have to hold babies, who the hell knows? But unless they are extremely powerful or already have werewolves' blood, they become half-wolves, the kind from myths.*

Piper wanted to ask, or try, about Liam but he walked up, falling into step with Nina. However, Nina didn't like that, she growled and raised her claws. Piper growled back at her to keep her from attacking him. The beast snorted through her nose but calmed. Liam gave Piper a thankful nod.

Tate stopped them from walking. "Liam is going to want to be at Nina's side, so give him some of your blood and lick his neck. Because the bond is so new, this will let Nina form a bond with him as well. He'll be like a back-up Alpha, if that makes sense."

No, it didn't, but she did as he said. When Liam cut her leg and drank some of her blood, Piper gagged. Nina growled but didn't attack.

What was her life coming to?

The concern and admiration for Nina in Liam's eyes made all of this worth it. He'd stay at her side regardless. He glanced at Piper; his head dipped, almost bashful. The dude had it bad. As the Beta in the pack, second in command, she'd bet he didn't act that way often.

She smiled. Good, Nina deserved to be cherished, and she needed help protecting her. She was glad Nina had Liam.

"Thank you for stepping in. Her strength caught me off guard." That adoring gaze Liam gave Nina deepened.

Piper blew out air from her nose to hopefully say, *"My pleasure."*

They reached the cage again. This time Nina went in without a fuss. She laid down and curled into a ball. Piper stayed by her side the rest of the night, so Nina stayed calm. When the sun came up, Nina went to their cabin, locked the door, and slept the day away. Liam hardly left the porch, but Nina refused to talk to anyone.

Piper would give her space to think things over, but Piper wouldn't let her wallow for too long. Even if she had to drag her out of the cabin by her hair.

Chapter Fifteen

Piper's stomach growled again. Nina had locked her out and wouldn't talk to her. So, she sat on the porch and gazed at the door.

At least she wasn't crying anymore.

All the memories of Nina getting hurt by life flashed in her mind, making her mood worse. She had focused so much of her life on helping Nina and sometimes Trace—even though Trace was extremely independent—still Piper didn't know how to help Nina through this.

They always went out and partied to get their minds off of bad emotions. Not healthy, but after her mother died the heart to hearts stopped. Trace was even more stand offish than she was, even with her. Piper loved Trace but she never connected with her as much as she did with Nina.

Maybe that was another reason why she chose to go to school for behavior because she didn't understand it. Or how to show emotions. Maybe if she would have become an investigator like her family Trace would be alive...

Footsteps pulled her away from her thoughts. "Hey, Piper," Tate said, appearing at her side. He caught her off guard, but she didn't jump. "What are you doing? You didn't come to breakfast."

She shrugged. "I don't know. I feel hyper-focused on Nina. It's hard for me to leave her here."

He grabbed her hand. "That's the new bond and Alpha status. It's difficult to relax when someone you're supposed to take care of is hurting. But I promise she'll be fine. She just needs a little time. Her wolf senses are going haywire. Staying in the cabin is the best thing for her right now." He tugged on her hand to get her to follow him. "Come on, I have a surprise for you."

She followed but glanced back to her cabin a few times before speaking. "A surprise?"

"Yep. A thank you and an apology all in one." He smirked and winked at her.

She smiled. Tate was different today; he didn't seem so uptight. She liked it. She squeezed his hand. "What are you apologizing for? I understand why you couldn't have been there with Nina last night. You don't have to apologize for that."

"Good. But I actually want to apologize for putting the wolfsbane in your tea. I feel horrible I had to do that."

The voice squealed like a schoolgirl. *He's dreamy, and he's making an effort to treat us like equals. Alphas have a hard time with that. It goes against their nature. I'm excited to see what he has planned.*

He guided her away from the cabins to a spot in the back that was clear of trees or houses. "This is where we play sports and train."

A dark blue blanket laid on the ground with a tub next

to it. She smiled and swooned quietly. He made a picnic for her! If she didn't think she'd embarrass herself, she'd jump in place and give him a round of applause. She loved picnics.

Her family would go on a picnic every weekend when she was a kid. The memory blurred her vision. She never wanted to forget those smiling faces.

She squeezed his hand again. "This is amazing, Tate, thank you."

His smile reminded her of a boy getting an A on a test. "I'm glad you like it." He rubbed the back of his neck. "To be honest, I don't have much experience with dating. For wolves, we skip the wooing and follow our primal instincts. But I'm excited to try. I can't promise I'll be any good at it, though."

She scoffed, "You're already doing better than most of my previous relationships."

He growled. "I'm happy to hear it, but please let's not talk about old boyfriends. My willpower is only so strong."

She liked that he was jealous. It made her feel less crazy when she got jealous. They could be jealous together.

She changed the subject. "So, I'm starving. What did you pack?"

He lifted the tub and gave her a crooked grin. "All your favorites. Pepsi." She squealed, "Steak, and a mint fruit salad."

We should marry him.

She hid her lips in her mouth. He cocked an eyebrow at her. "What?"

She shook her head. "Nothing, you're just really good at this."

The way his chest puffed out at the compliment was

the most adorable thing. He made their plates and she dived in. She hadn't eaten much today because she was worried about Nina. The slight dizziness and pain between her eyes disappeared as she ate.

"I really needed that," she said, rubbing her belly.

He scooted close to her, so his chest was against her back, and his legs were on either side of her. "Is this okay?"

She nodded and leaned her head back on his chest. He wrapped his arms around her. Here in his arms the world disappeared. She felt like she had known Tate her whole life.

"I have something for you," he whispered and handed her a sparkly wrapped box.

She sat up straight and beamed at him. "What? Why?"

He shrugged. "Do I have to have a reason to give you a gift?"

She swallowed her saliva to lubricate her suddenly dry throat. "No one has ever given me a gift just because. What is it?"

"Open it up and find out."

She tore open the wrapping with a crazed gleam to her eyes. Her mouth fell open. Inside the box was a beautiful gold necklace. The chain held a thick circle pendant with a wolf and vines surrounding it.

"Oh my god, this is beautiful."

Tate picked the necklace up and put the chain around her neck. "This has belonged to the women in my family for centuries. The last person to own it was my mother. She'd want you to have it."

"I don't know. This seems really important to your family. I don't think I should..." her voice trailed off. Her heart hammered in her chest.

"I know all of this is new to you. And I'll probably never show it correctly, but you are my family now. My mate. I'll be anything you need me to be. Your teacher, friend, lover."

She leaned in and kissed his cheek. "Thank you so much."

His cheeks turned a shade darker. She rested her head back on his chest. Like before, he wrapped his strong arms around her. "So, the necklace has a few spells on it. One allows it to shift form with you. Oh, and it's also a locket. Check it out."

He lifted the gold pendant off her chest. As soon as the latch snapped open, she gasped and sat up straight. Her mouth gaping open. "Oh my... How did you get this?"

On the left side held a picture of last night. Her red wolf with Rockie's and Storm's wolf next to her and Tate on the other side of her. On the right side held a picture of her family when she was younger. Her mom, sister, and dad were smiling and tickling her. A tear slid down her cheek.

She hugged the locket to her chest as he spoke, "I looked you up and found this on your father's Facebook. I hope that's not weird. Patty said you might find it... what was the word she used... Stalker-y. I swear, I'm not. I have to do extensive research on new pack members."

He sighed and wiped her face. "I'm sorry, Piper, I didn't mean to make you cry. I shouldn't have—"

She gave him a watery smile. "No, this is amazing." She rotated, closed her eyes, and hugged him as tight as she could. The fact that he put her family and her mates in the locket was beyond amazing. The tears fell freely as her heartache for her family and her slowly developing feelings for this man entangled. They formed a beautiful warmth in her chest that had her smile growing.

She pulled back slightly, so they were only inches away. His eyes dilated, and he zoned in on her lips. Everything inside of her wanted him to move a few more inches and claim her mouth. She bet he tasted sweet just like his gift to her.

Someone cleared their throat. "Sorry, Alpha, I hate to disturb you, but one of the rogue pack members is here to see you."

Tate's eyes went wide. "Piper, go to Rockie's shop. Jinks will take you. He's my third in line and trustworthy. Please don't come out until I let you know it's safe."

He stood and she followed. "Is this the pack that attacked me and Nina? I'd like a word with them."

"No." Piper flinched at his aggressive tone.

"Yes, I'm going," she demanded.

He lowered his voice before continuing, "That's what they want, Piper. They are here for you and Nina. This is just their warning but seeing you will make them attack my pack. They don't know you're an Alpha, and we need to keep it that way." He grabbed both of her hands. "Please trust me. You'll put everyone in danger if they see you."

She sighed and locked her jaw in frustration. All she could do was nod. Words were not her friend right now. *Why in the heck does listening to him make me feel prideful?*

It's how new wolves are with their Alpha and mates. We won't want to argue or fight with them for some time. It helps build the bonds between us.

Great.

Images of stomping the rogue's face in popped in her head. They were the reason this was happening to her. A dark and selfish part of her threatened to say, 'fuck it', but she'd be putting everyone in danger. It wasn't worth it.

Jinks grabbed her upper arm and gently pulled her away from Tate. When he ran the opposite direction, Jinks let go. "Let's run there." He didn't wait to see if she'd obey.

Her nostrils flared. She followed despite her agitation. *I'm doing this to keep everyone safe.* She chanted in her head. It had better be worth it.

Chapter Sixteen

R ockie's shop was a garage filled with tons of
    different engine parts up against all four walls.
    Once Jinks said what he needed to say, Rockie
closed the big door and sprayed some woodsy concoction.

"What's that?" she asked as she sat on the table in the
middle of the room.

"It's how we hide the female scents. You smell sweet
and pretty to most males, so they can't track anyone
through this. It'll blend in your scent." He put the bottle
down and approached her. Their eyes met and he gave her
a goofy smirk. "I heard you had a date with Tate. How did
it go?"

Her eyes scanned his face but there wasn't a sign of any
jealousy. She'd be lying if she said that didn't bug her. Did
he even like her? "Yeah, I did." She bit her lip, screw it.
"That doesn't bother you?" she asked and leaned forward,
eagerly waiting for his response.

He shrugged. "If it was anyone other than him and

Storm, it would. But you have a true pack, which means they are my brothers now. I guess it kind of bugs me but only because I wasn't there." He ran his hand through his hair and groaned when he remembered they had motorcycle grease all over them. "I'm not explaining this right. I've never been good with words. We all need our alone time with you, so I get it."

She smirked and nodded. So, he did care but understood Tate was okay to go on dates with. Good. She changed the subject. "What are you working on?"

"This is my baby." He grabbed her hand and pulled her off the table to get closer. "I'm kind of the handyman for the pack. I'm not as good as a few other guys, but anything mechanical I can usually figure it out. If someone has issues with their refrigerator or TV, they come here. But I opened this shop to work on my motorcycle. Believe it or not, it was my sisters." He wiped down the black and red motorcycle in pride.

She didn't want to pry but her curiosity was a bratty whore. "Was?"

He stiffened but spoke, "Yeah, she got killed by an Alpha when she refused him too many times."

She gasped. "Rockie, I'm so sorry. I should have kept my mouth shut."

"No, you're okay. Things like that are common in most packs. Our pack puts women on pedestals, but most packs treat them like toys or breeders." He grabbed a tool off the table and knelt next to the bike to work and talk. He bit his lip as if debating on continuing. "I cried the day she was born."

"Rockie, you don't have to tell me."

"Yes, I do. You deserve to know where I come from. It's not pretty, but I want you to know. I don't want any secrets between us." He got up, approached her, and lifted her necklace. "I don't have jewelry or any fancy gifts I can give you. I only have me. All of me." He didn't make eye contact as he spoke, but his pointer finger rubbed her skin as he held the necklace. He sighed and went back to his motorcycle to focus on that.

Piper stayed silent for a few seconds. She didn't want him to think she needed those things to be happy, but that could turn into an argument. She didn't want to fight with him, she wanted to learn more about this intriguing man. So, she said, "I'd love to hear it."

He glanced her way and nodded. "I cried the day my sister was born because I knew one day, I'd lose her to something horrible. I saw how my mother got treated and didn't want that fate for her. After our parents were killed in a ranking battle, we left that pack. We searched for years to find a good pack for Natalie's sake. She was killed before we found a place."

He slammed down his tool and picked up another. "I got lost after that. I let my hunger for power take control of me. I would try to stop the numbness in women's beds, making a lot of enemies along the way. I wasn't a good person." He wouldn't meet her eyes again. "If I hadn't met Tate when I did, I would have been killed. I almost didn't take his offer to join his pack. I felt like I deserved to die. But I did, with only the clothes on my back and this bike. I vowed to clean up my act, stay as low ranking as I could, and wait for my mate. This motorcycle keeps me grounded and reminds me, every day, to live like the man Nat wanted me to be."

He met her gaze and something in her shifted. A frog clogged her throat, but she managed to speak. "I'm glad you did, Rockie."

He smiled, wiped his eyes on his arm, and glanced her way. He searched her face, maybe waiting to see disgust or something, but there was none of that. Just like she wouldn't judge Tate for his past, she wouldn't judge Rockie either.

He put out his hand for her. "Now, come down here and meet my baby." He showed her how to ride the motorcycle and a few things about fixing it, but she got lost really quickly.

After, she swung her leg over to sit on the bike again. "So, you'll have to take me on a ride for real sometime."

He smiled up at her. "I'd be honored."

She focused ahead of her and pretended to ride, making the engine sounds with her mouth. He chuckled and stood to sit behind her. He wrapped his arms around her and whispered in her ear, "You remind me of her—strong and funny, but you're more beautiful and you look good on my baby."

Her cheeks heated and her stomach fluttered. "For a guy that claims to not know how to use his words, you're doing a fantastic job at it."

He tightened his grip on her but said nothing for a few seconds while she started her fake ride again. Her lips vibrated harder as she moved faster.

"You know you'll have to sit in the back when we actually ride, right?" Rockie teased.

"No way—" A glowing light darted into the room, cutting her off. "What the..."

Rockie stood. "Don't worry, that's Ceeci." He put his

large handout, and the ball of light used it for a landing spot. The light flickered and turned into a tiny woman in a purple dress. Her matching purple hair hung short by her ears.

He moved her to his ear. "Okay, got it. Before you go, I want you to meet Piper. She's my mate. Tate's and Storm's too." She curtsied and flew off.

"Umm, what was that?" Her eyes followed the light. She went on her tippytoes as if that'd help her see the creature for longer.

"A pixie. She doesn't come out much. She's usually pretty good at being invisible, and Tate doesn't usually use her as a messenger, because she's super rare. She's not allowed to leave the village. Too many people would want to kill her."

She gasped. "Why would they do that?"

He opened the big door and turned on the hose. He pulled out a bar of soap from his pocket to wash his hands. "Pixies are messengers and can travel to the underworld—"

"The what? Wait... Are you talking about hell?"

"Yeah."

Piper about passed out. She blinked her eyes several times in a daze. The underworld... Hell. Was real. Dammit. Couldn't that one be a myth?

"Anyway, people think they're either bad or sending bad messages, so they kill them. Even though if they'd just ask, they'd learn Pixies don't go to the underworld. Demons like to eat them." He grabbed a hanging towel and locked up. "She just wanted to let us know the coast is clear, and it's dinner time. Let's go eat."

She nodded and followed him. Her mind was in a daze.

The more she learned about the supernatural world, the crueler it sounded. She was ready to relax with Nina and forget for a while.

Chapter Seventeen

Piper walked into the dining room and sat next to Storm and Tate. Rockie sat on the other side of the table. Her leg bounced when Nina didn't walk in with Liam. He sat at their table and shrugged. "She still won't come out. She doesn't want to eat."

A growl escaped her throat. Her eye twitched. That was enough. She got up from the dinner table, hitting the blue fabric because it made her feel better. "She just needs time, Piper," Tate said, standing when she did.

"No, fuck that." She pointed her finger at him. "She's eating whether she wants to or not. I'm not letting her starve." She stormed out of the dining area. Male voices hooted after her, cheering her on.

"Show her who's boss."

"You tell her."

"Yeah, bring her cute butt here."

None of their words even penetrated her mind. Her focus was on her best friend. Nina did nothing wrong, and Piper couldn't let her wallow in guilt. She stomped to their cabin, determination boiling her blood. *I'll make Nina listen even if she doesn't want to.*

When their cabin came into view her eyes narrowed. She rotated her neck, rolled her shoulders, and bounced a few times to get her blood pumping.

There was only a door in the way, and it just became fucking enemy number one. She managed to be civil and attempted to open it first, but the door wouldn't budge. She growled and adrenaline hit her. She backed up and charged, screaming. A door wasn't keeping her from her friend. The wood busted open; splinters flew all around her. *Well, hell. That was badass. Enemy terminated.*

The voice snorted. *Good for you. You killed a defenseless door.*

Shut up. That door was gangster. It had to be destroyed.

Maybe we really are crazy?

I was just kidding.

She poked her head into the room. The dresser, bed, and everything in the cabin that could be used to block the door were there. "What the hell, Nina?"

Piper hopped over the dresser and moved to the bed. She tried not to smile at all the pots and pans on it. Her foot caught on one of the bigger pots, and she tripped, landing on the floor. *Ugh, maybe I'm not such a badass after all.*

The voice chuckled in her head. *We still have a lot to learn before we can call ourselves that.*

Nina had panicked wide eyes and a trembling lower lip. "How... get out, Piper. I might hurt you!" Her voice was harsh, but it shook like she'd been crying. Nina plopped on the bed and curled her legs to her chest.

Piper sat next to her. "Girl, you only lose control like that on full moons. Tonight isn't a full moon. Besides, I let you wallow in your pain alone all day. Now, you need to get up. We're going dancing." She shimmied up the bed, so her legs weren't touching the floor.

Was it kind of stupid for the two of them to go out? Yes. Did she care? Not one bit. Piper would do anything for Nina, and nothing else would work. She knew Nina, and what she needed to get out of this depression.

Nina watched her legs sway. "W-what?" Her stutter was cute.

Nina shook her head. Piper nodded hers. "Oh yeah, and tequila. Lots and lots of tequila," she said and squeezed Nina's shoulder. She kicked out her legs like they did when it was drinking time—minor quirks that never left from when they first met.

Images of the first day she met her friend at some random bar assaulted her. Both were using fake IDs to be there. Nina had sat all alone, nursing her wounds from a bad breakup. Piper picked up on her discomfort immediately. And how couldn't she? Some sweaty guy with a huge gut and plumber's crack had his hands all over her.

After the thirtieth, "No, leave me alone" from Nina, Piper put herself between them and pulled Nina out to the dance floor. Where the guards were focused. So, they laughed and shimmied until the guy left in a huff. They celebrated their newfound friendship with shots of tequila and a leg-kicking competition.

They'd been best friends ever since.

Nina's lower lip quivered, so Piper continued. "Nina, you did nothing wrong. Both the human-weres fed off each other's anxiety, and you changed faster than expected, *but* nothing big happened."

Nina's mouth opened to argue.

Piper cut her off. "No, girl, nothing big. Everyone that got hurt healed before you were back in your holding place. And that boy you bit was planning to become a werewolf anyways. He stopped by earlier to thank you, but you didn't answer."

Nina's eyes widened in surprise. She shook her head and ran her fingers through her hair. "What happens if I do that again, Piper? I'm a menace to this place. No one wants me here." Nina grabbed a pillow and hugged the soft cushion tight.

Piper pulled on the pillow. "Don't do that, Nina. I get it, this shit sucks, but everyone in the village knew what they were getting into. They accept you." She scooted closer, tapped her shoulder with her own, and smiled. "I'm pretty sure Liam is the biggest cheerleader."

Nina snorted. "Yeah, he has been here all day. He doesn't leave for long. If I didn't feel like shit, I'd let him in." She paused, "I hurt him too?"

Piper put a hand on her trembling, clenched fist. "It was your first change. Mine or an Alpha's presence will be there next time, so you won't be as... aggressive."

Nina lowered the pillow as a tear fell down her cheek, followed by a bitter laugh that surprised Piper. "I'm not even crying because I'm sad or mourn my goddamn friend. I can't do that anymore, ugh. No, I'm feeling sorry for myself, and I'm afraid for everyone around me, Piper. I'm not right. I'm broken, that demon..." her voice trailed off. She hit the side of her head with her palm.

Piper shifted in her seat, struggling to come up with the right words. Her education was on psychopath's behavior, which wouldn't help her. Nina's lack of feeling was magical. She knew a piece of her was taken.

What do you say to something like this? That demon stole her mourning emotion and made her feel foolish and broken. Maybe Tate should have come with me? Broken people shouldn't try to fix other broken people.

Push the dancing and drinks. Her heart rate and scent have spiked. She really does want to go.

Time for the big guns. "So, how about dancing and getting white-girl-wasted?" She said the last phrase in a valley girl's voice, moving her arms like Carlton from *The Fresh Prince of Bel-Air*. Nina burst out laughing, holding her stomach as she rolled on the bed. Nina playfully elbowed her side as Piper mouthed *yes* to herself. That move always worked.

She tapped Nina's shoulder to get her attention. "Hey, on the bright side. This means Hogwarts might actually exist." She wiggled her eyebrows, causing more laughter. "But really, let's forget that stuff for now. I'm here, and I promise I'll do everything in my power to help you be whole again. I love you, Toots."

Nina wiped her face. "I love you too." She huffed when more tears fell and stood. "Okay, as long as you promise to never let me hurt someone again. Liam said I submitted to you, so you have the power to promise me."

Piper grabbed both sides of Nina's head and kissed her forehead like her mother used to do to her when she was a kid. "I promise, Toots. Now, please stop crying and eat something."

Liam came through the door smiling, with a steaming plate of food. "That's such a beautiful sound." His joy at hearing Nina's laughter warmed Piper's heart.

The coldness that had cocooned her heart when her sister died was slowly defrosting. People like Liam gave

Piper hope that there was still good in the world. He smiled at Piper and nodded his thanks. His gaze landed on Nina, and she yelled and threw herself on the floor beside the bed.

Piper rolled her eyes. Liam's panicked stare almost made her laugh. "It's a girl thing. The crying all day with no shower look is not pretty. She's not mad or anything, but we'll come out when we're ready, okay?"

He turned to leave. His shoulders slightly drooped. Poor guy didn't spend a lot of time around women.

She lifted her hand to stop him. "Tell Tate that we're going dancing tonight and having lots of tequila shots. So, I'm not sure how we'll do that, but make it happen, please."

Liam smirked, nodded, and left. If he were in wolf form, his tail would be between his legs. Piper couldn't focus on him right now. Nina was all that mattered. Her friend needed comfort and she was determined to be there for her.

She turned and put up her imaginary shot glass. "To drinking and bad decisions," shouted Piper with a wide grin. "Let's worry about all the other problems tomorrow." Nina was newly bitten, but she'd be fine with her and Liam controlling her wolf. At least they didn't have to worry about shifting. It wasn't like the movies. Shifting took a lot of power and most half-weres couldn't shift without a full moon.

Everything would be fine. Tate's, Rockie's, and Storm's claim on her should keep her safe. What could go wrong?

Chapter Eighteen

O nce she helped Nina get ready enough to see Liam again, Piper left them alone for a while. He needed some time with her, and Piper needed space to think. She couldn't bombard Nina with her problems. Anyways, Piper was a break-down-in-private kind of girl.

You know, you're never alone. It's okay to let people know you need help or just an ear to talk to. Nina can't be that ear right now, but maybe one of our mates can. They're giving us space so you can come to terms with things. But they'd be there for us in a heartbeat.

I know. But I don't want to trouble anyone. I just need a few minutes. Then, I'll be fine.

Images of her life before everything ran around in her head. She used to smile a lot more. She was a little weird. Dressing up as Pepsi for Halloween and wearing tutus to school to make others smile.

Her mother died. She was so beautiful and kind. The moment she was gone, her absence stole some of her happiness.

Once her father got fired because of her, he stopped talking to her... Well, it was more like he blamed himself for taking Piper on his cases, and she was mad he refused to remove the spell on her memories. Those two things turned into both of them not talking to each other. After that, smiling was almost impossible, but Nina helped.

When her sister was murdered nothing had worked anymore. She forgot how to function. Not even Nina could help her. How bazar that being here seemed to bring her back. These people takeaway the tar that had clogged her insides.

Yet now, she felt like a volcano that needed to burst.

All of this was too much. Even her bones hurt with tiredness. She was getting numb to everything, and Piper didn't want that. If she didn't handle her emotions, she'd lash out like she did when she was younger. Scarlett's face popped into her head. *Maybe...*

No way.

She sighed. *I was just kidding. I don't want to be mean to the woman. Jealousy just gets the best of me sometimes.*

I get it. But let's deal with what we can right now. Talking it out always helps. So, vent to me.

Instead of talking to the voice, she sent her the knowledge all at once. It was the equivalent of putting a flash drive on a computer and downloading the content. The voice already knew, but it still felt good to vent.

Tears were falling before she could stop them. She hunted for a place to cry in peace and settled for an empty cabin. She leaned against the building and looked up to the sky, heaving out the tears until the weight eased on her shoulders.

"Hey," a male voice whispered.

Piper froze. She stopped breathing. Maybe he wasn't talking to her.

"I'll go away if you want, or I can sit and cry with you. I need a good cry," Storm said. He stepped out of the shadows. His face was full of sorrow that matched her own.

The kindred spirit put her at ease and eager to hear why. Misery loves company and all. "Why do you need to cry?" she asked. She bit her lip. The only person she ever cried with was her sister. And that was after their mother died.

"My cousin was killed yesterday."

A gasp left her lips. Now she knew why their sorrow looked the same. There were only a few things that could darken a person's eye sockets and turn their face into a bunch of contorted lines, one included death of a loved one. "I'm sorry. I lost my sister recently too."

Storm sat down next to her. "It's a horrible feeling losing family." He put a hand on her knee.

"Were you two close?"

A tear fell down his cheek and he sighed. "I was in the same pack as him. The Devils Pack." He blew out a sharp breath and continued. "The name was perfect for them. They were horrible people. Like most packs these days, they're power-hungry and ruthless. They fight for status and treat the women like dogs."

She put her hand over his, and he squeezed her thigh. He continued. "When the women tried to escape, they beat them until most of their flesh was black and blue. I'm no hero, and my wolf wasn't strong enough to stop them, but I'd take the beating for them every chance I could. Only my cousin's high status in the pack kept them from killing me. But after most of the girls got away and they killed the few they managed to capture, I had enough."

Storm's eyes shined yellow; his wolf close to the surface. Piper stayed quiet. She let her tears fall. For herself, for her sister, and for Storm. It was nice to cry without feeling judged and something about Storm calmed her. She wanted to curl into him and tell him all her secrets. But he needed to talk, and she'd gladly listen. It helped her get over her shit easier.

"I left the pack. I pleaded for Brooch to come with me, but he was third in line and fought every day to keep his status. He refused. I left and came here. Brooch's brother Marcus invited me. He was a low-ranking wolf and wasn't treated like scum, so I had to check it out for myself. Most packs are cruel to weak wolves."

She wiped her nose. "But you found out this place was one of the good ones?"

He nodded. His watery eyes locked onto hers. "It's the best pack I've ever been a part of."

"But?"

"I left Brooch there. He died in one of those dominant fights. I wasn't there to help him," his words said in-between sobs.

Piper wrapped Storm into her arms. "What could you have done? I'm guessing these fights are one-on-one and your wolf wouldn't have been able to stop the fight."

He gripped her tighter. She couldn't breathe, but the contact felt perfect. By helping him, she was helping herself. Because it was true for her as well. What could she have done for her sister? She wasn't a trained fighter. She doubted she would've been able to stop Trace's death.

"You're right, I couldn't have done nothing."

"You begged for him to come, and he wouldn't listen. If you'd have stayed, all that would have done was get you killed too."

Storm sobbed harder and held her even tighter. She ran her hands through his hair. She had begged Trace to let her help her with her case or get help from another investigator, but she refused. Survivor's guilt was a mind fuck sometimes. Yeah, Storm and she weren't there when their family died, but they were alive, and their family member wasn't. It felt wrong and unfair.

She didn't know how long she cried, but holy moly, she needed a good cry. The air smelled fresher and her soul lighter. She loosened her grip on Storm and he did the same.

"Thank you. As an omega wolf, I comfort others and use my magic to help them with their emotions. It's hard for me to let out my emotions because I'm helping others with theirs. I've never cried on someone's shoulder like this." He twirled his thumbs, then made eye contact. "You have no idea what it means to me." His lips brushed hers, making her heart skipped a beat. Every nerve in her body sparked to life. The caress of his succulent lips drove Piper mad with need. It made her hungry. Not for food but for so much more than that. It took her a few seconds to remember to be normal. She was practically drooling on him. Who knew a soft and sweet kiss could melt a person's brain. She gave her a last smirk before he continued. "Do you want to talk about yours?"

She cleared her throat and shrugged. "It's kinda the same. I lost my twin sister, and the survivor's guilt is high. I wish I could have helped her and convinced her to choose differently." That was all she'd divulge, for now. She might be connecting with Storm, but she needed more time to trust him completely.

"You mean to say, there was another person that resembled your beauty? I don't believe it for a second." A chuckle slipped out. She bit her bottom lip, honestly missing his. Storm, her smooth talker seemed to always know what to say.

She leaned in, letting her lips touch his, but not quite kissing. His breath smelled like mint and whisky. Surprisingly, they mixed well on him.

He captured her lips, a sense of desperation catching her off guard, and she gasped. He took advantage and slipped his tongue in her mouth. He groaned and she matched his eagerness.

She was more of a rough, passionate kind of woman, but wow. She might need to change her mind if sensual kissing was this electrifying. When he pulled away, she missed his lips immediately.

"Ceeci?" he said. Piper's eyes shot open; her cheeks heated. The little pixie with her purple hair and dress was on his shoulder. "Wow, I'm surprised you're out and about. Piper, have you met Ceeci?"

Piper nodded. "Once, she came to Rockie's shop earlier. Hi, Ceeci. I love that shade of purple, it's beautiful on you."

The little pixie's body and light turned bright red. She went on her tiptoes to whisper in Storm's ear. "She said thank you."

Ceeci lifted in the air, her light still red. They both waved as she flew away. Once the pixie disappeared, a switch was flicked, and her body was aware of how close Storm was again.

He stared at her lips, but his eyes were filled with disappointment. "I hate to stop but the cook made you and Nina a special dish, so we better be going, or we'll have some hungry wolves hunting us down." She laughed. Storm used his shirt to clean off her wet cheeks. "I hope we can do this again sometime. I don't get to open up to people often, and I'd love to learn more about you."

She nodded. "I'd like that too."

Storm stood and helped her stand. He held her hand as they walked back to her new life. She thought she wanted a break from everyone, but she just needed someone to understand a little of what she was going through. Someone that didn't judge her or try to fix her.

Her eyes grew blurry again. But this time they were happy tears. She had people who cared for her, and she was beginning to care for them as well.

Chapter Nineteen

Piper and Nina walked out of their cabin two hours later with their hair polished and curled to perfection. Their clothes were tight, black, and slutty—precisely what they wanted for tonight. Nina had shorts, but Piper wanted to wear black skinny jeans. Their tops were the same tight, black V-neck shirts that showed of their curves.

The mascara and eyeliner from the healer, Patty, made the look come together. Patty was just as excited about going dancing. Dancing was a happy place for most women.

They laughed and shook their hips with sexy determination. Nina had the sexy part down. Piper didn't think she matched her sultriness, but she did it better than ever. Her hips moved easier, and her body swayed, mimicking Nina's natural allure.

They were meeting everyone in the dining hall and leaving. Tate arranged for everyone to go to the nearest town, a few hundred miles away, but he said they had a fast way of getting there.

Excited chills crept down her body. She was ready to dance the night away. The air was chilly, and her tiny shorts weren't even bothering her. She ran hot now. Her black shirt had thin sleeves, and the heat from the covered areas surprised her. But going naked wasn't an option, *nor would I want it to be.* The exposed tummy and cleavage made it easier to breathe, though.

Nina had to talk her into this outfit. Piper wasn't the show-all-her-assets type of person, but she felt suffocated in the other, more conservative outfits. She pulled on her shirt and shorts again.

Will you leave the clothes alone? We look great and undeniably sexy. Show confidence when we enter this room, or I swear I'll make us pee our pants.

Piper sucked in a sharp breath. *You wouldn't...*

Try me.

Piper gulped and straightened her spine. Fine, she'd rock the shit out of this outfit. No way she was humiliating herself like that in front of everyone.

Nina opened the dining door with a pep in her step. Her black short skirt and shiny halter top exposed a lot of her warm, dark skin perfectly. Piper stopped in the doorway while Nina strutted in.

Surprised male faces were crowded together, staring at them with their mouths open. They were dressed casually in comparison to them. Slacks or jeans with a variety of colored t-shirts. But damn, when did casual become sexy?

She spotted Tate in the back of the crowd. Her wolf stirred as Scarlett laughed and put her hand on his shoulder. They weren't intimately close, but her blood boiled at their nearness regardless.

Once we claim him, we won't be this jealous. Don't worry, remember what he told us. He is ours, her wolf said reassuringly, but there was still a growl in her voice.

Patty stepped in her line of sight. "You two look sexy. If I wasn't mated to my guy, I'd rip your faces off." She gave Piper a wink and a hug. "I'm so excited for tonight. Thank you for making this happen."

Patty's healing magic snaked over her body, like oily hands rubbing out all the knots in her muscles, calming her jealousy. Well, that was a neat trick. She mouthed *thank you* and stepped away from her.

Patty leaned in to whisper, "Don't worry about Scarlett. She kind of sleeps with everyone in the pack and tends to flirt with taken men. It's a challenge or something. I'm not shaming, but just know Tate only has eyes for you." She squeezed her hand. "I've never seen him look at a female the way he does you. Tate's always been over-powering, but he seems gentler with you around. If that makes sense."

She smiled, but it didn't reach her eyes. She wished Scarlett would stop because it wasn't fair to either of them. She left the girl hate fighting back in high school, and she wanted to keep it that way, but she made it difficult. Patty gave her another hug and took off to find her mate.

Piper held her head high and walked to Tate. He was already moving towards her, leaving Scarlett red-faced. His black slacks and dark shirt were simple but rugged and sexy.

Storm appeared at his side. His jeans and hunter-green shirt were equally yummy. She winked at him but had to deal with Tate first. Knowing Scarlett and him had history made her wolf want to hug him first.

As she got nearer, she sniffed. Tate's strong natural scent covered any other scents on him. Good. He smelled just like he did earlier on their date. But he didn't smell like her. She needed to change that.

She sniffed again and growled. A slight perfume drifted off Storm. It probably came from Grace. The unmated human female was standing near him when she walked in. Her green monster snarled.

She smirked at the sultry way his eyes darkened, but she was on a mission. Tate opened his mouth to speak, but Piper didn't let him. She slammed her lips onto his, silencing him.

He stiffened but deepened the kiss a moment later. Her nails scratched his neck, causing a growly moan from him. Good, he liked it. Her hands were everywhere, marking him with her scent. Yep, like a dog in heat.

Not a dog. A wolf.

Tate's rough hands dug into her hips. It was hard to pull away from him, but she had to. She was making a point. Not with just one of her men, but all of them.

Piper turned to Storm. The devilish glint in his eyes and the eagerness for his turn heated her core. Damn, maybe they didn't need to go out. Her cabin with her men sounded amazing right now.

With the same eagerness and determination, Piper devoured his lips. Their tongues stroked and caressed each other. His hands moved all over her body, matching hers. The taste of him was already familiar and addictive. Then, after the scratch to the neck, she turned.

Where's Rockie?

As if summoned, he stepped out from the male onlookers. The jeans and white shirt had a John Travolta in *Grease* feel to them, one of her favorite movies. Even the indent on his chin was a match.

She practically knocked him over as she demanded his lips. Yeah, she wasn't acting rationally, but this must be normal or at least expected from the hoops and whistles around her. Rockie gripped her hips like Tate did, but with more force. His sharp nails dug into her skin. The pain mixed with the pleasure from his mouth gave her goosebumps. After his scratch, she stepped away, smiling.

Mine. All mine. Her wolf had calmed down, but her heart still slammed against her chest. Her legs were noodles. Her guys surrounded her to keep her upright.

"Hello, beautiful," Storm said, his hand on her side. He made circles with his thumb.

Rockie leaned closer to her ear and said, "Very sexy." She giggled. His delicious growly voice pulled at her core.

Her eyes met Tate's. He was the only one that hadn't said anything. Was he mad?

His face darkened with annoyance. Piper wiggled her fingers to tell him to get his sexy butt closer to her. His smoldering gaze had her chest moving up and down quicker. The other guys turned to him and bowed their heads, moving over for him.

Piper turned to Tate when he got close, and the other guy's hands dropped from her. She growled and placed them where they were. They all closed in on her.

She put an arm around Tate's neck, the other around Storm's waist, while pressing her back and right shoulder hard on Rockie, hugging them all at once. The heat set her core on fire. *What am I doing?* Her body wasn't listening.

That strange flutter in her stomach wanted to be near all of them.

Storm gulped. "Piper, as much as I love this. It's not the place for it."

What did he mean? She wanted their touch, dammit.

A throat cleared and she came back to herself. Ice water splashed over her from the several male snickers around her. Her eyes popped open. Tate stared fiercely at the males that circled their group. Rockie's neck was tight, his jaw twitching.

Piper froze. They were in the middle of the dining room—the pack surrounding them from all sides. Images of orgies brought fear in her gut, tightening it.

This was bull shit she couldn't even control herself anymore.

It could always be worse. You could have farted in front of everyone. What if changing meant loose butt hole. Her voice chimed in not helping her mood at all.

But she was right. That would have been way worse.

Chapter Twenty

"I'm sorry. I don't know why I did that," Piper said as her cheeks heated.

Rockie grunted, "You were claiming us in front of the pack. To tell the others we're yours. There's nothing wrong with that."

She pushed against the wall of men around her, but they didn't budge. Tate and Rockie growled, gripping her tighter. Their eyes darted around them.

Storm sighed. "Don't push them away, Piper. It's a dominant thing. Let me go. I'll move the pack away. Looks like you stirred the fire up well, beautiful." He squeezed her flesh and moved away.

She let go of Storm, missing his heat immediately.

Storm gently pushed against the circle of men around them, knocking them out of whatever trance they were in. *What the hell is going on?*

The voice laughed. *The other men in the pack were getting ready to challenge our three guys. The mating and bond aren't finished yet, so other males can prove their worth by challenging them.*

Wait, what?

We're a werewolf now and an Alpha. So, we see what we want and make sure they want it too.

Piper gulped. Worry slammed into her gut and bile burned the back of her throat. *So, I forced them to kiss and touch me?*

No, no way. The pheromones only work on willing males. But unlucky for us, the whole room is full of willing males. She laughed again.

That laugh sounded a little crazy. You're enjoying this too much.

That is what we are now, primal, and perfect. All these men should bow at our feet.

Ew. No way. I only want three and no bowing.

Spoiled sport.

Piper snorted, making both Tate's and Rockie's grip tighten.

Storm yelled at the other guys again. There were a few grunts, but no one was fighting. Thank goodness. Bobby's vampire scent drifted to her, letting her know who was helping move the pack away.

Her eyes met Tate's and his grip softened. After he searched her face, so did his eyes. The other guys must be far enough away. Rockie still felt like a brick wall at her back, though. She rubbed his arm, put her head on his chest, and met his gaze.

The angle was awkward, but the movement got his attention, softening him up as well. They stepped away from her. She straightened her outfit as she pulled herself together. Her first claiming was an epic mess up.

You should tell me about these things before I make a fool out of us.

The voice huffed. *I don't know everything you're going to do. We're two separate beings. I personally thought you were going to attack Scarlett and I was all for that.*

Oh, now you want me to lash out?

Well, she deserved it this time.

No, she didn't.

The rest of the males were waiting by the door now, wanting to leave. She cleared her throat. "So, let's do this. How are we getting there?" she asked, her body jittery. She was ready to forget and dive into a bottle. Getting drunk and forgetting about her worries sounded great.

Please don't say that out loud. You make us sound damaged.

We are damaged.

Are. Not. Piper hoped the voice was right. She wasn't sure anymore. But going with the punches was better than getting punched.

"The women, including you two, are riding there. We're running," Storm said, sounding oh-so-pleased with himself as he leaned against one of the tables with his arms crossed.

Tate smiled wickedly as she opened her mouth, "What? That's going to ruin our hair." The words sounded silly even to her ears, but hell, she spent an hour on her hair.

"Actually, sweetie, we have these." Patty moved through the crowd with two large... helmets? She handed one to her and Nina, who was still chuckling at Piper's kissathon earlier. The scowl she shot her just made the laughing louder—the little brat.

Once the helmet was in her hands, she stopped. They were shaped like motorcycle helmets, but rounder and with no straps. "These babies are filled with magic. Put it on, and your hair and makeup will stay perfect."

"What? Hell yeah!" Nina put her helmet on immediately. With a loud sucking sound, then a pop, the shiny gray thing clung to her head. "This is freaking awesome." She shook her head, "I can feel a tingle on my scalp and face."

Patty smiled. "That's the magic. All right, I'll meet you there. I gotta find my mate again. He keeps running off." She nodded to Tate and left.

Scarlett sauntered up, glaring at Piper. Once Tate glanced her way, her face softened. "Who am I riding... with?" The meaning in her words was clear. "You, I hope."

Piper rolled her eyes. The wolf's jealousy wanted to emerge, but Piper fought it. She knew Scarlett was going through a lot. She lost her guy. Even if they broke up about a year ago. But there was a wolfy part of her that demanded Scarlett recognize her superiority. The two fought for dominance.

Tate gripped Piper's shoulders, massaging them. Once they relaxed, he bent to kiss her neck from behind, clearly showing Scarlett that he was hers, which calmed her wolf. "No, you're going with Seth."

She gaped at him. "But I always go with you."

Tate sighed. "Scarlett, things have changed. I'm trying to be patient with you, but you need to back off. This isn't one of your challenges. I'm Piper's—"

She cut him off. Her hands flung around with her words. "We don't know that yet. You could be incompatible. The bond isn't set—"

It was his turn to cut her off, "If Seth isn't to your

liking, there are plenty of other unmated men to choose from."

A needle pierced Piper's heart as Scarlett stomped away. She really didn't want to fight with her, but she did need to back off. She went through the ritual, and they were chosen for each other. They accepted the mating and she needed to respect that.

Piper put her helmet on. A weird buzz and tingling sensation licked along her skin. "All right, what am I riding? A horse? A motorcycle?"

Tate smirked. "Not what... *Who.*"

Chapter Twenty-One

Whoever said riding a horse was fun, never rode a werewolf. The bite of the fast wind in her face, the warm fur between her legs, the speed... the speed was her favorite part. All of it mixed like a crazy-ass hairy rollercoaster. She loved every exhilarating second.

All three of her guys wanted to be first, so they drew straws. Tate won. *I might have acted like a five-year-old and danced around a bit. But that was Nina's fault. She started it. She even made Liam pull straws with himself, so she could jump around as well. But I'll never admit to any of this.*

Tate's jet-black, massive wolf moved with stealth. Trees, bushes, logs, and buildings be damned. She had to hold on for dear life, but nothing could stand in their way. Not even water.

When a thirteen feet wide stream came into view, Piper gasped. They were moving too fast. She was going to end up in the water. She gripped Tate's fur tighter. Hopefully, the helmet protects her against water too or all her hard work on her appearance was for nothing.

Piper held her breath, waiting for Tate's legs to stiffen and push against the ground. He didn't. He sped up. Tate's agile wolf jumped on a huge rock, making Piper scream. They soared over the water as if it was a puddle. Her heart about fell out of her feet onto the ground.

Once the adrenaline rush took over the fear, she laughed and cheered Tate on. She was glad he picked the tiny straw. The others were still unbelievably big, but Tate was huge. His movements were graceful and powerful. She felt safe.

After a couple of hours, her butt went numb. After another two, she was in a lot of pain. Her bones were on the verge of breaking. Her tailbone already broke, and its pieces were bitching up a storm. At least that's how it felt.

Not soon enough, Tate stopped her other guys right next to them. The rest of the pack wasn't as fast.

"Get me off, please," she whisper-yelled to whoever would listen. Rockie was the first at her side. Storm's wolf strained and grunted next to them, pushing hard for the change. *What's wrong with him?*

His wolf isn't strong enough to fast change. The more power a wolf has, the quicker they can transform. Just consider ourself lucky, we have Alpha power. It's very painful. If she wasn't in so much pain from the ride, she'd be at his side.

Rockie's strong hands gripped her hips and lifted with ease. He sat on the ground and put her on his lap. "How are you?"

"Aah, hurting. That was painful."

He pulled off the helmet. "Maybe because you sat up the whole time. You're supposed to lay on the wolf when you get tired to give your tailbone a break," Rockie responded. His fingers ran through her hair.

Her pain made her delirious. Before her brain could work right, her mouth was opening. "I-I got too aroused... how weird would it be to come on a giant wolf." Piper put her face in her hands. She didn't mean for that to be said out loud. "Oh my... can you pretend you didn't hear that?"

Rockie chuckled. "You're so cute when you blush." He pulled at her fingers to uncover her face. "That's why only females ride, and the males run." He leaned down to whisper in her ear. "Our wolves would be honored to have your come all over us." He rubbed his prickly cheek along hers. Shivers ran down her spine, sending electricity volts to her vagina. *So, I found out something interesting, dirty talk, plus water and electricity equals body spasms. He hasn't even touched me, and I'm putty in his hands.*

Her pain spiked with her movements. She winced and closed her eyes. When she reopened them, Tate was at her side. "Are you okay? You didn't lay on me once, stubborn woman." He shook his head with a smirk on his face. "I should add stubbornness to the things you like."

She joined his smirk in between her clenched-teeth groans. Tate leaned down to kiss her cheek. "Patty should be here soon; she'll heal you quicker. Just hold on a few more minutes."

Storm finally walked over. He stood over her, breathing heavily. "I'm sorry it took me so long to shift." She reached for his hand to reassure him. Being a weaker wolf next to powerful wolves had to be difficult. Her arm extended too far, tapping something too soft to be his arm or leg.

"Whoa there."

She jerked her hand back. "Oh, fuck, did I—"

Her eyes met his wide yet amused eyes. "Just get fresh with me. Oh yeah." Rockie and Tate laughed. Now, she really did want to disappear.

"Maybe we should get dressed. I can hear the rest of the pack coming," Tate said, putting a hand on her arm and squeezing.

"I'll wait here for Patty to heal Piper," Rockie said. Tate nodded and left behind the trees. Storm followed. "You know I'm jealous now, right." He winked and pushed his wolf power at her, blocking the pain.

"Oh, how?"

"My power is just blocking your pain sensors. A little trick I learned from my mom." From what Rockie said about his past and being in bad—women abusive—packs, she knew he didn't learn the technique for a good reason, but she was grateful.

The ground vibrated and a few thuds sounded. It was either the pack or an earthquake. She didn't care. The pain wasn't that bad right now. "What happened?" Patty asked, her voice breathless.

"Piper? Are you okay?" Nina said next. Her voice was high in fear. Their faces came into view at the same time.

"Yeah, just hurting from the ride, but Rockie is helping me."

Patty cocked her head to the side. "You didn't lay down?"

"No, I thought it was bad manners." Her lower lip pouted. Now, she felt extra stupid.

Warmth covered Piper's wounds and within seconds the pain was gone. Patty's touch soothed her muscles better than a thousand-dollar masseuse. Piper smiled dreamily up at Patty. "Will you marry me?"

Patty and Nina laughed. Rockie stiffened but smirked. "Hey now, don't go taking my mate. I would miss her too much," a short man with glasses said. He reached out and helped Patty up. She kissed his thin lips and smiled back at Piper.

"I'll have to respectfully decline." Patty gripped her mate's gray jacket.

Piper snorted. "I was joking. I guess I should have just said, thank you." *Do they not understand humor?*

They understand power, and we're powerful. If we chose to take Patty, we could. Her mate is very weak.

I'd never do that!

Most wolves, especially women, have had bad experiences with powerful wolves. Patty may not be a wolf yet, but she has dealt with power-hungry wolves before. The look in her eyes gives it away. Don't take it personally. Her grip was just a gut reaction. They know you were joking. Their scent doesn't have any fear in it.

Tate reappeared at her side. "All right, everyone, be safe. If you plan on staying longer than the pack, let a higher-up know. I'll be at the club if you need me." He grabbed her hand, pulling her away from the crowd. Nina grabbed her other hand.

To her surprise and utter satisfaction, Scarlett took off with another group. Thank goodness. She didn't want any more drama tonight.

She smiled as the building with the bright flashing lights came into view. She'd bet her right boob that's where they were going. The rest of the town was dull in comparison. Most of the buildings were rusted and old. Vines and plants caressed everything around her, hugging the town in their embrace.

A few people walked along the road. There were no sidewalks, so they stayed on one side. A couple held hands, smiling, and blushing at each other. *Aw, probably their first date.*

A lone, tall male in a long black coat with flat dark hair, puffing on a cigarette, caught her attention. Visions of Jack the Ripper popped into her head, giving her goosebumps. Her hair stood at attention.

Nina let go of her hand when Tate stepped closer. "What's wrong?" He wrapped his arm around her waist.

She gave him a reassuring smile. "Nothing."

His fingers drew circles on her exposed flesh, and like a dummy, she tripped over her own feet. Tate held her in place.

Now I feel extra stupid. Who trips over nothing?

Apparently, we do, the voice groaned.

Chapter Twenty-Two

They walked through the red club door. The song *React* by the Pussycat Dolls started as they walked in.

The music gave her more confidence as dozens of eyes turned her way. She grabbed Nina's arm and dashed to the bar. She laid on the bar to get the bartender's attention. "A bottle of good tequila and two glasses, please."

The attractive male bartender with several piercings lifted an eyebrow at her. *Oh yeah, the whole bottle.*

Tate handed over the money and the bartender gave her the bottle. Piper and Nina took three quick shots and made their way to the dance floor. She waved for Storm, Tate, and Rockie to join her, but they stayed seated. Well, whatever. She'd dance with her friend then.

Only a few couples and one small group of girls were on the dance floor, so they had tons of room. Nina took another shot to get out of her head. Piper agreed and took her shot directly from the bottle.

Before the song was over, several people joined the

dance. The bottle and Nina were her dance partners until a warm presence pressed against her back. Liam took advantage and dragged Nina away.

Piper turned. A stranger's face was inches from hers. Don't get her wrong, the guy was handsome, but she wanted it to be one of her three. She narrowed her eyes in their direction and shrugged when they didn't budge from the bar. Fine. She was done caring.

She took another swig of the bottle and closed her eyes, letting the booze take away her problems. Another male approached from behind. He didn't smell like one of her guys either, so she didn't even open her eyes. The girl group moved near, and she sensed another guy coming. As much as a hot guy sandwich sounded yummy, she didn't want these guys. She spun into the middle of the girl's group.

They giggled and hollered when Piper snaked and bounced to match their movements. The guys that were dancing with her moved to one of the other girls. From their pleased faces, the arrangement was much better.

She took another swig and gave the woman to her right some without the bottle touching her mouth. Some dripped down the woman's neck. A force urged her forward, demanding she lick the alcohol off. She moved away instead.

Darn wolf was going to get her punched. She couldn't go around licking strange women's necks.

It could be fun. The voice laughed.

Just no.

Another male took advantage and pressed against her back. He wasn't hers, but man, he could dance. The way his massive hands gripped her and took over almost had her purring.

If her guys didn't want to dance with her, oh well. Another swig and her mind blurred. Only the alcohol and dancing mattered.

She drank all her problems away.

Nina pulled Liam to her, so she could dance in front of Piper. A slower song came on, *Drink Alone* by Carrie Underwood, and Piper rested her head on the guy's chest as he twisted and swayed his body to the beat. They moved to the music, drunk on the sound waves.

She opened her eyes. The guy behind her had his bright blue eyes locked on her. Oh dang, mister good dancer was sexy too. Not as ruggedly as her three, but cowboy model type of sexy. Her core tightened. It had been a long time since she had a one-night stand. Was it a bad idea? Yeah, definitely. Would it be worth it? Hopefully.

Another swig had her forgetting more. There would be no strings, no responsibilities, nothing but pleasure. She smiled and threw her arms in the air.

Her guys didn't even seem to care.

Her stomach knotted. She sighed and let the alcohol lead her actions. Her mouth moved closer to his.

Before their lips could touch, the song changed. Strong arms spun her several times until she was surrounded by brick walls of muscle. Her men. She smiled and kept dancing. Finally.

The other guy got up from the floor and took off. *When did he get down there?*

We definitely know how to push werewolves' buttons. The voice laughed in her mind.

Piper rolled her eyes and ignored her. She took another

swig of tequila. Tate took the bottle and handed it to Nina. She smiled at Piper when she reached for it. Nina laughed and took a drink. "You have had enough, Toots. Let me get on your level."

Piper nodded and pressed harder into the body behind her. Those naughty thoughts were coming back. *I'll do us a favor and make sure the pheromones don't come out.* With the voice's words, she slipped back into her happy zone and swayed her body.

Tate, Rockie, and Storm surrounded her. The mixture of their scents and heat had her body relaxing in a way no other dancer could do to her. *Mmm, sandalwood, bay rum, whiskey, and musk, such a delicious blend.*

An ancient snake possessed her and made fast S designs with her body, touching each guy. A professional belly dancer would be proud of her moves. In the middle of these guys, her confidence rose to a dangerous level.

All the other people disappeared; it was just them in the big building.

Their bodies relaxed at the same time, and their hands found her. She made sure not to show one of them too much attention. Moving around them came easier to her than she would have thought. Her wolf danced with her. Her insides felt alive.

Before she knew what she was doing, her tongue raked across Tate's neck, biting his jaw slightly when she was finished. The other two stiffened, Rockie the most. Storm whispered something in his ear, and his shoulders lowered.

She smirked. That pesky confidence reared its ugly head. Her body turned on its own accord. The air in the club turned thick as she moved—the musky male scent around her spiked as they prepared to defend her. Tate's grip on her tightened, but he didn't stop her.

Her teeth bit Rockie's neck, and her tongue licked right after. Tate was stiff but not aggressive behind her. Yet, he wouldn't relinquish any space. He stayed firmly pressed to her.

In her peripheral vision, Storm was on the outside of the group. He sighed, rubbed a hand through his hair, and backed away, probably to give them space, but she didn't want space. She could handle all three. She growled. Power rose inside of her, and he froze.

His gaze met hers, then fell to her lips. She was in front of him, with her face pressed against his neck in the next second. "Where are you going?"

Storm licked his lips before he spoke. "I didn't want to intrude. It's easier to dance with two guys. I can wait." Her teeth bit at his neck as he spoke, making his words breathy.

"You're mine, Storm. Are you going to take something of mine away?" She had no idea what she was saying, but he seemed to. His eyes dilated, his smirk came back, and primal energy came off him. He shook his head, and a shiver went down her spine.

His body pushed her back into the warmth of the other two. Their movements were no longer suitable for the public. She turned to Tate; he was the most dominant, so he had to be first. Why she cared about that now surprised her. Dominance was important to her now— perks of being a wolf, she supposed.

Her lips brushed his. He was gentle yet firm in his every move. Her toes might have curled. *Well, shit.*

She turned to Rockie next, giving Storm a wink before

pressing her lips to his. His kiss was rough and passionate, goosebumps rose across her skin. Okay, she might have made a mistake taking on all three of them. She was turning into a puddle at their feet, and she hadn't even kissed them all yet.

Storm waited patiently. The doubt in his eyes was gone. They only held hunger. Kissing Storm was different. His kisses were sweet and caring, whereas the other two were aggressive and filled with passion. She was the one who felt strong and powerful but turned on like crazy with her Storm.

She had passion, strength, and sweetness surrounding her. What else could she ask for?

Chapter Twenty-Three

The blissful moment was interrupted as a heavyweight smacked into her. Well, they hit Rockie, and he stumbled into her. Tate and Storm used their strength to keep them upright.

She turned, aiming a fiery glare for whoever interrupted their moment. Six men stood with legs spread and bent, ready to attack. Before the mating trial, the men that had come for her and the guy she danced with earlier stood together giving her men death stares. She stiffened; this did not look good.

Where was Nina? Her eyes darted around the room. But no one was there... The whole club was empty. Where had everyone gone?

"Back away from the girl. We're taking her," the tallest guy said, his goatee blowing in the wind from the club's fan.

Tate stepped forward. "That's not happening. I welcomed you into my territory because you said the mating trials would be the deciding factor. She didn't choose you. Now, leave, or I'll throw you out." Even though he wasn't directing his aggressive stare her way, she still recoiled from the power. It could charge a whole building.

"We came here for her, and we aren't leaving here without her," a shorter guy with freckles demanded.

All three of her guys growled. "Then you aren't leaving." Rockie's voice sounded like death. Shivers ran up her spine.

Storm was next. "Good thing I know a few places to bury a body."

Piper's stomach dropped. She didn't want anyone dying or fighting for her. She stepped in front of the wall of men. "Okay, okay. Let's not do anything rash here, all of you." She faced the goatee guy. "I'm sorry, but the trials and I have chosen them. Please, respect my wishes. Isn't that the wolf way? They have a claim on me."

Good, you used your words. I bet that'll help. These men didn't smell like this when they were at the trials.

Smell? What the hell does that mean?

Just wait.

"Fuck the wolf way. We deserve a mate. We can please you better than these scoundrels," the guy in the front with the freckles said.

Great, any more bright ideas?

Just wait. Their scent is changing. Piper rolled her eyes. She really hoped so.

The other guys shared a confused gaze. The warm, swarthy-skinned man turned to his companions. "I don't like this. She says no. She's not confused, man. You said that she was confused and might want us."

The freckled guy responded, "Who the fuck cares? She

hasn't finished the mating bond with them yet. When was the last time a strong female werewolf was around? I'm taking her and building my family. I'm the last goddamn person of my line, and it'll not die with me." His tone was utter insanity. Even his comrades gave him ugly glares.

That guy might be a problem. His pride and longing are turning his scent sickly. He could go either way. We need to convince him.

Piper analyzed the appalled faces around him. *Maybe I won't have to. These guys don't seem to agree with Freckles.*

The other three guys were triplets with red hair and bronzed skin. They stepped back away from the freckled guy. "Dude, I'm not forcing any woman. I said I'd fight for her but not if she doesn't want me. I'm out. She has chosen her guys," the middle of the triplets said, his brothers nodded.

They moved to Piper's side, bowing their heads. "Please forgive us. We thought we stood a chance at getting you to be our mate. You seemed confused at the mating ceremony. We see now that you know what you want. If you need us in any way, only ask, and we'll gladly be at your side," the middle triplet said as the trio walked away.

"Hey, get back here. We had a plan!" Freckles yelled as his thumb and pointer finger rubbed together. *Is he nervous or unsure?*

A dark-skinned man and her dance partner walked away as well. Before her dance partner left, he bowed. "As much as I think you're making the wrong decision, I'll respect your wishes. If you ever want a fourth, Tate knows how to get a hold of me. We could be good together."

"Don't hold your breath, Duncan," Rockie said. His

arm possessively wrapped around her hips. Duncan smiled but didn't argue. He winked and left.

Now, the fight was two to three. Piper relaxed. She had complete confidence in her men to scare these guys off and not be forced to kill them.

Wait... It's not Freckles we should be worried about. Freckles smell better, but the other wolf's scent is getting worse.

"What's it going to be, Tiran? Will you have honor like your men chose?" Tate asked.

The tall guy stepped closer to Tiran—Freckles. "Don't do it. We can still take these fuckers, and we'll share her."

"I-I don't know. I want to, but..." his voice trailed off as the other guy wrapped his strong claws around the back of Tiran's neck. Tiran winced.

"You will. Don't worry, once we're inside of her, it won't matter."

She growled with her men this time. Disgusted shivers ran down her body. Okay, that one she didn't care if he got hurt. Someone who thought like that wasn't worth her worry.

Storm scoffed, "What happened to you, Brad? Are you trying to convince him to kidnap and—"

Brad— tall guy—turned red in an instant. "You don't know me, Storm. You're friends with my cousin, nothing more. Well, since he just died with your cousin, we're not even that anymore. And you have no idea what I've been through."

Liam chose that moment to appear from the darkness. Nina tucked behind him. Her lipstick was smeared all around her mouth and her eyes were shining bright yellow. Her wolf was close to the surface.

"But I do, Brad." The way he said Brad's name made

him blanch. "I wonder what your mother will say when I tell her about this. I still keep in touch with her since, you know, I saved her from the werewolf attack that turned her," Liam said, his eyes blazed with fury Piper hadn't seen from him yet.

"Liam, I—"

Liam cut off Brad's words with a snarl. "Now, was it you or one of your comrades that hit my woman in the head while we were in the throes of passion?"

Her hackles rose, and the wolf pushed against her skin. "You hurt Nina?"

The air crackled around her. Her vision turned red. She stepped forward, but Storm put a hand on her shoulder. Her eyes snapped to his, and he quickly dropped his gaze. "Let Liam defend his female."

"But she is mine—"

Storm cut her off, "But she is not only yours, and Liam has a bigger right to defend her. Let him prove himself."

"Fine," she grumbled and crossed her arms. Her men put comforting hands on her. Their touch worked to calm her wolf.

Tiran backed away, his hands up in surrender. He knew the murderous gleam in Liam's eyes wasn't one to mess with. "I didn't want that. I just really wanted a mate. I'm sorry, I took it overboard, but I wouldn't hurt a female. They're too precious." He gave her another longing glance and stepped away, leaving his tall "friend" behind.

She leaned into Storm's warmth. He inched in and whispered, "This is a big deal in our world. Women are so rare, so hurting one and threatening to force a woman in his bed is grounds for termination."

"But I thought a lot of packs don't treat women right?" she asked as Liam stalked toward Brad.

Tate answered while Liam roughly tackled Brad to the ground. "Unfortunately, a lot of wolves think like Brad. And there isn't a lot of help for the weak, but we're hoping to change that one day. Once the magical folks finish their wars, there'll be enough manpower to focus on the little people."

The deeper she got into this world, the crazier it got. She was tired, and the buzz had turned to sleepiness. All she wanted was a bed.

She got close to Storm. "Where is the rest of the pack?"

He smiled. "They all left. They've chosen a person to be with tonight."

Her cheeks grew warm, and her mouth made a perfect circle. "Oh." Storm winked at her.

The fact that they didn't find a woman for tonight had her chest reddening. That meant more than any words they'd said so far. Actions speak louder than words, and their actions were clear. She turned away from everyone to hide her blush and went to her friend, trying to hold back her smile. It wasn't the time for smiling.

Nina ran to her, her eyes flashing yellow. *She's fighting for control of her wolf.*

Nina fell into her arms like a sack of potatoes. She squeezed her tight and growled in her ear, commanding the wolf back down. The relief in Nina's hazel eyes almost made Piper cry. Nina didn't have control. Once Liam left her side to handle Brad, she could barely stop herself.

Don't let her see the pity in our eyes. Nina's different, she'll get the hang of it sooner or later.

Piper put on a fake smile and whispered, "You okay, Toots?"

She moved closer and squeezed Piper harder before answering. "I broke the tequila bottle when I got knocked out. I'm sorry." Her soft, weak voice was said into Piper's shoulder. Anger spiked in her again. Her eyes darted around the room. She didn't relax until Liam hauled away Brad.

She pulled Nina away and gripped her chin gently. "Girl, I don't care about the bottle." Her eyebrows scrunched together. "I care about you." This self-doubting Nina was new. She had always been strong and knew her worth. "What the hell's wrong with you, Nina?"

Tears fell down her face. She wiped them away and whispered, "I almost got you violated by a demon, because of those stupid rocks. And I got you turned into a werewolf. I'm screwing everything up for you. These guys wouldn't be after you if I didn't bring you out here."

Piper's eyes blurred. How could she think this was her fault? Piper wanted to come out here. "Don't you dare blame yourself. No one forced me here, Toots. Shit happens. All that matters is we're here together." Piper hugged her tighter.

Nina pushed away and threw her arms up. "I just wished I'd suggested the Bahamas or something. What was I thinking?" Her tone was extra high.

She lightly smacked Nina's shoulder, "You were thinking about me, and how to help me. I was in a bad place, Toots, and you got me out. Yeah, this isn't exactly what we had in mind, but," she tapped her shoulder with hers, "the consolation prize," she glanced at the men, dealing with the police and brad. "It's kinda yummy."

Nina wiped at the new tears and chuckled. The stretch of her full lips had the old Nina coming out to play. She missed her flirty, confident best friend.

Storm walked to them. The smirk on his face said he heard her... Great.

As he approached, his face grew concerned. "Hey, Nina, you okay?" He touched her shoulder, and she felt the soothing energy coming from him. Nina sighed and gave him an almost drugged like smile. The sensation was familiar.

What's that?

He is an Omega. Meaning he's one of the lowest ranking wolves, which gives him soothing abilities. The dominant wolves offer protection and order. Strong submissive people like Storm offer a caring shoulder for the pack. It gives him a unique gift that lets him ease people's pain. Each pack can have a couple of Omegas, but they are rare. The voice sounded fascinated, and Piper didn't blame her. How cool was that?

Wait. I know where I remember that feeling. The brat has done it to me and to Liam... when we first met.

Liam is a special case. He was born an Omega but as he got older, his wolf grew stronger. He still has some of the Omega gifts, but not like Storm.

Nina grinned at Piper and then at Storm. Her eyes were lazy and relaxed like she was ready for a good long nap. "I'm okay. I have a bump on my head, but I'm healing."

Storm gave her his award-winning smile and nodded.

Tate approached, smiling at both of them. "Good, I'm glad to hear you're doing okay. Liam is waiting for you in the police car outside. It'll take you where you're staying tonight. Then you'll go back to the pack grounds to get a few things tomorrow. I don't know how long this case will take..." His voice trailed off when Nina's eyes drooped.

He put a hand on her arm to get her attention. "I know your instincts will tell you to stay on pack lands, but you'll have to come back. You can't be away from Piper for too long, or your wolf will get aggressive again." He gave Nina a sympathetic smile. "You and Liam will be helping on the case, but you'll be focusing on the forest. You're a bitten wolf, the closer we get to the next full moon, the more unstable you'll get. But you'll be fine if you have Piper or Liam near."

He turned to Piper. "Brad's mother will be here tomorrow evening to take him home, so he won't bother you again. He's going to be branded a disgrace. To born wolves, that's a sentence bigger than death. No pack will ever want him again." Piper nodded. She'd feel safer when he was gone.

Nina gave Piper a longing gaze as if she didn't want to leave. Her eyes flashed yellow from her emotions. Piper nodded and smiled to reassure her. The hazel orbs Piper loved came back. She couldn't stay around humans long if her emotions controlled her.

Even if the humans knew about them, seeing her eyes would scare them, and scared humans were dangerous. Nina stepped closer and gave her another hug. "Are you going to be, okay?" Nina asked.

"Don't worry about me. I'll be fine. I've got my guys to look after me. You focus on yourself. I love you, Toots." Piper rubbed Nina's back. She tugged on the knot inside of her that she felt the other night while fighting Nina. She pushed out what she hoped was calmness—or something that could help Nina. Her arms vibrated and Nina gave her a loud drawn-out sigh.

Does that mean it worked?

Yes, we took her fear away.

Like an Omega?

No, like an Alpha looking after her pack.

Whatever that meant, Piper had to figure it out later. Storm walked Nina out. So, she went to Rockie. He and Tate were huddled together, talking.

Rockie gave her a side hug and pulled her closer to him. "How's your girl?" he asked.

"She'll be fine. But I need some serious friend time." Piper bit her lip and hugged him back. "So, what're we doing?"

"Tate's callin' the pack. So, they know what's happening.

Chapter Twenty-Four

Instead of running back to the pack lands, they stayed in town. It helped Piper relax. Nina on the other hand had to go back. Her new wolf couldn't handle all the new sensations for too long. So, they left, but Liam promised she'd be back tomorrow.

It was weird, but she trusted Liam.

The yellow and brown building wasn't anything special. The few rooms and collection of cars in the parking lot she spotted gave her pause. Were there any rooms left?

Don't worry, we could always camp outside in wolf form. Watch the stars and sunrise.

It's way too cold for that. Piper ignored any response the voice had. She wasn't sleeping on the floor when she could sleep on a bed.

The clerk at the front desk frowned at his computer. His hazel eyes narrowed as he searched for vacancies. "I'm sorry, we only have one room available. Unfortunately, an event in town has our rooms booked."

Tate, Rockie, and Storm glanced Piper's way for guidance. Their eyebrows were raised in question. Her heart raced.

"Is it two beds at least?" she asked through the glass at the clerk.

He glanced at the computer. "That's a no. The only room left is the honeymoon suite. But don't worry, the Sheriff is paying for you. Besides, there's nothing extravagant in the room." He leaned closer to her side of the glass. "If you're tired of your colleagues, you can always share my room if you want." His accent made it hard to understand him, but his last sentence was unambiguous... *Ew.*

The chorus of her men growling had a smile stretching her lips. "I think we'll be fine. We'll take the room."

When did guys flock to me like this? It's getting irritating. Nina used to be the flower to the bees, not me.

Her inner voice chuckled. *What? Bees? I'm glad you didn't say that out loud. It's just the wolf. Until you learn to control it, the scent draws men to you.*

Wait, I thought that stopped after the mating trials?

It's just a scent every she-wolf has.

The clerk gulped and didn't look at her again as he grabbed the keys and their information. By the time they made it to room eight, Piper was in a werewolf sandwich. If it weren't for continuously giving Rockie a flat tire, she wouldn't mind.

Piper pushed against the wall of men. "Come on, guys, I promise I won't go to the strange, pimple-faced man's room. I do, however, need to have some personal space."

She got a couple of grunts, but they didn't listen. Not until everyone was in the room with the door locked and every inch of the space checked, did they relax. As if a switch was turned off in their brains, they sat down.

She took a deep breath to stop her anxiety that they caused. Something about them clinging onto her felt like they were protecting her, so her body was in fight mode.

She needed some more tequila.

Her eyes took in the room.

For a honeymoon room, it sucked. The television couldn't be more than thirty inches, the large bed with red silk blanket was wrinkled, the small table under where the tv was mounted on the was scratched, and the two night-stands on either side of the bed were pathetically painted.

The slightly pink walls and red curtains were the only indications that this room had anything to do with a romantic honeymoon.

Tate watched to the phone on the table. "I'll call for clean bedding and more towels. I got distracted earlier and forgot to ask."

Piper cringed. What had she done to wind these guys up so much?

The voice sighed. *It's not your fault because you didn't know, but when the clerk asked you to share his room, you blushed. You didn't stake your claim on the men. In werewolf language, that means he had a chance to ask you later.*

Her jaw locked, and she had to force her hands not to crumple the picture. *How am I supposed to know that? I was embarrassed and worried they'd punch his face in. Tate, Rockie, and Storm looked like they were going to kill him.*

They might have if he looked at you again. I'm not sure, but I think he knew about werewolves and was showing them disrespect.

Piper glanced at the guys focusing on the case notes and whispering to each other. *Should I explain or apologize?*

Good heavens, no! That's a horrible idea. Just give them time.

Okay, I'll take your word for it. I just want to hop into bed. I forgot tequila made me so sleepy if I don't consistently drink it.

Then, her eyes went to the bed again. Her nerves spiked feeling like little needles pressing into her skin. Where was everyone going to sleep? Butterflies did circles in her stomach.

Her mouth grew dry as images of her sandwiched in bed between these guy's muscular bodies flashed in her mind. Her heart palpitations went into overdrive. Is that what she wanted?

The voice purred, *Please.*

Chapter Twenty-Five

P iper's heart did a professional tap dance in her chest, mocking her as she stared at a brown spot on the pink walls. It resembled a wolf. How interesting... Okay not really. She'd find anything interesting enough to not stare at them.

Tate cleared his throat. "Piper, why are you so flushed?" when she didn't answer, he asked another question, "What are you looking at?"

"Nothing, I just..."

"What, Pipes?" Storm asked, his voice revealing his concern since she still didn't want to meet their gazes.

Will you stop making us look ridiculous? We do not have to sleep with them. But it would be so much fun.

"Shut up."

Storm's face dropped. "What? We just want to know if you're okay."

"Oh, I didn't mean to say that out loud." That didn't help him feel better, as he flinched slightly. "No, really, I wasn't talking to you guys."

Shit...

All three of their intense eyes focused on her, confused and curious. Finally, Rockie was the one that asked, "Then who were you talking to?"

Damn it on toast.

You already said it, spill the beans. They will understand. Her inner voice said with a little chuckle.

Yeah. I'm going to end up in a padded room.

Piper licked her lips. "Well, um, I kinda have a voice in my head... It's not scary or creepy, though. It's more like intuition."

"Wait, so is it an actual voice or intuition?" Storm asked.

She was biting her lip now. "I have never told anyone this, but," she scuffed her foot on the floor, "it's more like a person speaking to me."

Tate's green eyes widened. "Does she know a lot about your werewolf side?"

The question took Piper by surprise. Where was the laughter or screaming that she was crazy? She squirmed under his stare.

She scuffed her foot on the crappy carpet. Why did she feel like a child in trouble? "I—yes. She said the knowledge exchange thing gave her the information she needed."

More silence and gaping mouths. "What?"

Tate shook his head. "I'm sorry for my reaction. What you're describing sounds a lot like your wolf."

"What? That can't be. I've always had her in my mind. Well, as long as I can remember anyway." Piper needed to sit down. She stumbled over to the head of the bed, grabbed a pillow, and hugged it to her chest. *That couldn't be right.*

"That's a trait of a full-blood werewolf. My voice started after puberty. He's like another person inside of me, telling me what to do and butting into everything. He has his own opinion and thinks he knows it all." He thumped his temples and smiled. "Oh, he didn't like that."

Piper couldn't help but smile back. "That sounds a lot like my voice."

Hey! Not funny.

You know it is a little. The voice grunted her dislike. *Is what they are saying true? Are you my wolf?*

Yes.

So, I've had a wolf this whole time? Why didn't you ever say anything?

The voice...um... wolf was silent.

"Are you speaking to her?" Rockie asked. Now all three of them were sitting on the bed. Storm put his hand on her knee, giving her comfort.

"Yes, I'm trying to see if she has any answers."

It's nice to be a part of a conversation and for people to know I'm here.

Are you going to answer me?

The voice sighed. *I couldn't come out before the bite. Your parents used a witch to suppress me. I could only communicate with you, but I wasn't able to tell you the truth unless you figured it out on your own. The bite set me free.*

Piper's mouth fell open. Her heart may have stopped beating but she was in shock. She had no idea how long she froze for. The guy's touch broke her out of her trance. "Um, she says the witch that put a block on my memory also stopped me from becoming a wolf, and the bite brought her out. But why?"

Tate scooted closer. "That makes a lot of sense. Being a

half-wolf is the typical female reaction to the bite. The question is, why would your parents do that?"

"Yeah, if it was even her parents. The main thing I learned about witches is they always have a high price and tend to be tricksters," Rockie chimed in.

Piper watched her clammy, shaking hands. They moved in sync with her heart. "So, I'm a born wolf? I thought you said I just had wolf blood in me. What's the difference?"

I'm sorry I was never able to tell you. You already thought you were crazy; I didn't want to add anything else. Besides, we're extremely rare. A sure thing for pups which means packs like the rogue pack would hunt us down and kill anyone in their path to get us. We're more powerful than any changed female.

Her men slowly scooted closer, and the heat lessened her anxiety. They each put a hand on her leg. Rockie whispered, "Did she tell you?"

Piper nodded. She growled her frustration, pushing her body's reaction down as best she could. She took deep breaths, not knowing if she wanted to scream or cry. How was this happening?

Her parents knew... They hid that from her. Why the hell would they do that? And hell, she was putting her men and pack in danger by being with them.

"It's okay, Pipes, we're going to figure this out. We won't stop until we get answers," Storm's soothing voice said. He moved to her side and gestured for her to lay next to him. The shock still clung to her, and as she laid down, the men found a spot around her. They made sure each guy had a piece of her and fed her comfort through their touch.

Piper was numb. If they weren't holding her in place,

she'd have floated away by now. But Storm was right, she was not going to stop until she got her answers.

Her to-do list kept getting more massive by the day.

Her parents had to have done this to her for a reason, right? They wouldn't just make her feel like she was crazy her whole life for no reason. Right? Right...

PART TWO

Wolf shifter can be investigators too

Chapter Twenty-Six

Staying here another day was just what Piper Heart needed. When she started this journey, she wanted to change herself for the better. As she woke up covered in warm arms, she could gladly say she found it.

She had a long way to go, but this was a great start.

The jingle from Tate's phone on the bedside had everyone jerking awake. Rockie pulled Piper closer to him and put his nose in the crook of her neck. Her cheeks heated, but she didn't move away. His warm motor oil scent was soothing.

"You smell amazing in the morning," his rough voice purred in her ear.

She gulped. *Good lort.* Her mind couldn't even say words correctly as her panties were destroyed.

Storm was above her head. He turned away from them and snored louder. The guy had some pipes on him.

"What's up?" Tate grumbled into the phone.

She could hear one of his pack mates on the other end. Probably Liam. "A pipe burst and destroyed a lot of food.

I'm going to have to stay behind in order to get all of this situated." There was a pause. "Nina is doing okay. She struggles mostly at night, but one more without her Alpha will be okay. We'll meet you back in town tomorrow. If you plan on staying longer that is."

Okay, definitely Liam. He glanced her way to ask her which had a smile stretching her face. "Staying would be nice, but if it gets too difficult for Nina have him call. We'll go home."

Home?

Shoot, she totally said home.

They noticed. Rockie tightened his grip on her, and Tate matched her wide smile. These men were cute.

"Just keep me updated," Tate said and hung up. "So, what do you want to do today?"

Her eyes drifted to the snoring Storm. Sleeping at the head of the bead had probably kept him up last night. "Let's get food and talk. I want to let him sleep."

Tate smiled and nodded. He grabbed jacket off the table. They all decided to sleep in their clothes. Except Rockie, he gave Piper his shirt, so she was more comfortable.

She tiptoed to the bathroom to change. The skinny black jeans felt like sandpaper on her skin this morning, but she ignored it. After twisting her hair into a high bun, wiping under eyes to get rid of the extra makeup, and using the mouth wash the hotel provided, she was ready.

Rockie was leaning against the wall when she walked out. His confidence and swagger spoke of a man with lots of experience with women. Piper didn't like thinking about the other women, but she was eager to see those talents in action.

"Let's go," he whispered. "I wrote a note for sleepy head, so he'll let us know when he's awake."

She nodded and took his offered hand. They got in the now warmed up car, thanks to Tate. "Where to, love?" Tate asked as she closed the door.

"Um, food?" She shrugged. "Wherever."

Rockie Perked up. "There's this mom and pa kind of diner by the sheriff's office. I haven't been there in a while."

Tate nodded and took off, knowing exactly where to go. The small town had several shops and offices. They were all crammed together on one road. Surrounding it was houses and hotels. Not every road had cement or a sidewalk, but it was still a cute place to live.

There was even a massage parlor that she wanted to check out. Maybe another day, though, when she knew the guys better. Could they do a couples massage? Her cheeks heated just thinking about it.

The woods surrounding the town was thick, but oddly calming. The plant life gave the place some color and had the air fresh.

Breakfast was good. The guys ate differently from each other. Tate ate like a man being watched and that didn't want to make a mess. Whereas Rockie ate like a man in prison. Fast and sloppy.

She couldn't blame him. Her waffles, eggs, and bacon practically melted in her mouth. She ate so much her stomach stuck out a little by the time they left.

Rockie put an arm around her shoulders while Tate held her hand. "We haven't heard from Storm."

Tate nodded. "Yeah, he hasn't been sleeping well since losing his family member." She nodded. The fact that the demons still practically run the place is hard on him as well. He knew something like this was going to happen, but I told him what can you do?" That part was said to Rockie who nodded with sympathy.

She didn't know about the demon part, but it was Storm's story to tell, so she didn't ask any questions. Once they were back in the car Rockie leaned forward in the back seat. "Let's take our little wolf to the heated springs. We don't have to go in today, but it's a beautiful place."

She perked up. "Heck yes!"

Rockie kissed her cheek and sat back. Tate drove in silence until they were almost there. "Most people don't know about this place. Not even the locals."

"How come?" She asked. Her eyes drifted from the woods around them to Tate. His strong jaw and sharp features were hard to take her eyes off of. He was like a statue every woman wanted to hug.

"During the war here, things got bad for the humans if they went into the woods. So, not many venture out of the town. Some still call our pack to help if they have to."

She nodded. "So, you have a good relationship with everyone?"

They parked next to a huge tree. The air was hotter over here. A little humid as well.

He turned off the car. "We try to. My team, which is pretty much our true pack, me, Rockie, Storm, and Liam do investigative work for the sheriff sometimes."

"Fun. Lot of my family went into that line of work as well, so I understand needing to make nice with the people. It's easier for you to get answers from them in the future," she said as she got out and closed the door.

Behind the huge tree was where all the beauty was

held. She smiled as the fresh sent of rain and dirt in the air.

There was a small dirt trail that led to two boulders that were steaming. "Come on." Rockie pulled her along while Tate followed. "If you climb on this rock you get to see the inside is hollowed out and full of hot water." He helped her up, Tate close behind her just in case she fell. "We don't know if it's magic made or natural, but it's awesome."

The rock dug into her flesh. Not hard enough to break the skin, though. It was warm to the touch, but not hot. Rockie peeked over, his hair swinging forward to cover his face from her. She tucked the curtain behind his ear, so she could see his smile.

When he directed it her way, she malfunctioned and glanced away. The water was the perfect escape. It was clear and slightly bubbly.

"It's beautiful, huh?" Rockie asked. His excitement was contagious.

"It really is. We could come back her with Storm and relax. I bet it feels great." Her fingers played in the smooth water for a second. Her other arm stung with overuse, so she climbed back down. Tate held her hips most of the way. "Thanks."

Rockie jumped down. He didn't land right and rolled into a crouch. "Smooth," Tate said. His hands hadn't moved from her hips which meant they were close. His body heat soaked into her.

Now we're getting somewhere. I kept quiet out of boredom. So, bend over and present for him. Let's spice things up. Piper laughed at her wolf. She had read enough romance books with werewolves to know what she meant.

Humans down bend over and show off their vaginas. She snarked back.

Well, aren't you glad you're a shifter?

Still not doing it.

Tate's phone stopped any argument that her wolf wanted. He answered with a, "We're heading your way now."

"The sheriff is here, so you better make it fast," Storm's groggy voice said on the other end of the phone.

They sped walked to the car. "Okay, but we'll be like fifteen minutes."

"Got it. I'll keep him occupied." Then, he hung up.

"What's going on?" Piper asked as they started the car. Way would the police be at their hotel room.

Tate bit his lip. "We might have a job." He glanced her way. "Rockie could take you back to the pack. We don't know how long it's going to be or what it even is yet."

She shook her head. "No. I've helped on cases before, I want to with you guys. Besides, it'll be another way for us to bond, right?"

He grabbed her hand and kissed it as he drove. "Okay, love."

The fact he didn't argue or force her to leave gave him a lot of brownie points in her book. She took a big gulp of air. She really hoped she could do this.

Chapter Twenty-Seven

A man with a Sheriff's uniform was sitting in the only chair in the hotel room tabbing his fingers. Storm was talking way too fast for it to feel natural. His breaths were heavy as he got up. He lost his footing and stumbled to Tate. Tate grabbed onto him to keep him from falling. The sheriff bent over and put his hands on his knees, exposing skin on his beer gut between the buttons.

His brown eyes were wide as he spoke, "Tate, I need your assistance, your private investigator assistance. A third group of people was just found murdered in the forest. The only survivors are badly injured, and another child is missing. I-I..." His accent made the words drawn out, and like his tongue was too big for his mouth, so she found herself focusing on the pronunciation, not his words. Tate didn't have that issue.

Tate put a hand on the Sheriff's shoulder to calm him. They guy's hands were shaking. "I'm here. Don't worry, my people will look into it."

The Sheriff's eyes grew shiny. "Thank God. I don't know how to handle this, Tate. This guy is brutal. We sent everything to forensics, but it'll be weeks before we get answers from them. Our department didn't have enough money to keep our guy. And the kids and more dead—"

Tate's jaw twitched. "Sheriff Willy, breath with me." He mimicked Tate's deep breathing until his shoulders dropped and his face got more color to it. "I wish you'd have asked for help when you called to inform us about the case. Two groups of people dying, and a child kidnapped is good enough for me to get involved."

The Sheriff rubbed his face. His eyes darted too the floor to his left away from Tate's gaze. "I thought I could handle it. I wanted to prove that I could..." his voice trailed off. He cleared his throat to continue, "But I know I'm way out of my league."

Tate growled. "Well, you have help now."

Remember the map we kept holding on the hike? The quote about this place being a neutral ground. Well, that means Norway has magical protection. A lot of the human government wasn't happy about it. Then... She asked her wolf, so she didn't upset the guy.

Where's the magical protection then? Her wolf filled in the blank. *They're dealing with another problem. From what I know from Tate's memories and from what he just told us, they're fighting a war in Australia. Supernaturals are divided into dark and light, and humans are teaming up with the light. Tate doesn't know a lot about the war. So, unless it's important and has to do with supernaturals, they aren't going to help.*

Well, shit. This sounded important to her. The bastards. *You just can't trust any form of Government these days.* She left it at that. There was nothing she could do to help with that issue, but she could with this case.

Her heart was pounding in her chest. She never let the thought form, but she had wanted to follow in her sister's footsteps to become an investigator. Maybe even figure out who killed her. This could be her way into that life. Yeah, there'd be more schooling in her future, but what would Trace do?

She crossed her arms in front of her chest. Trace was stubborn and would have never given up.

THE RIDE TO THE CRIME SCENE WAS SILENT AND HEAVY. Piper was exhausted, but she wouldn't complain and hold the guys back.

The yellow tape that wrapped around the trees and boxed the scene in, had her flashing back to her father's games. Well, she thought they were games. It wasn't until later that she realized how serious playing was to others.

The bitter copper scent permeated the air. The wind somehow constantly blew in her face despite where she stood as if the air didn't want her there. The body was covered with some type of blanket, but a gray-blue hand or foot stuck out.

Her dad wouldn't let her see the body, but he would test her on the crime scene. What she saw, and what conclusions she drew from the scene. At first, she loved the game. She was good at finding the answers the grown-ups overlooked.

But as her answers became different from the other officers, the visits were more of a burden than anything. They'd say suicide, but the distance from the window that the body had fallen from said otherwise. When they were proven wrong, they became hostile.

An officer cornered her in the break-room and threatened her father's life. She refused to go with him as often to keep him safe. She didn't want her daddy hurt. He got suspended for the first time shortly after, putting an end to their game anyway.

He'd try showing her pictures and videos, but the game was never the same. Soon, he lost his job completely, she lost her memory by a witch, and her mom died, so there were no more games or even smiling after that.

As she stepped under the yellow tape, grabbing a few rubber gloves an officer offered, her anxiety picked up. She knew her dad or those crooked cops weren't here, but she was triggered nonetheless. Storm gripped her hand, giving her worried eyes. She gave him a thin smile.

It's okay; no one can hurt you while all of us are here. You are safe. The voice was like the warm hug she would never admit she needed.

Her eyes focused from her panicked haze. Her surroundings didn't help... at all. Blood dripped from trees and tents. A couple of body parts were staged next to a notebook with writing on it.

Her heartbeat pounded in her eardrums, blocking out any other noise. The guys' mouths moved, but she didn't hear them. Her sister's murder and cold dead eyes kept flashing in her mind. *Why the hell did I agree to come again?*

She took a deep breath and focused on her breathing.

Leaves fell from the trees around her. She closed her eyes and pushed her fear and anxiety into a little box in the back of her mind. Her heart rate slowed, and her muscles relaxed. Her eyes darted around, reading the area.

The other officers stood on the sidelines, giving them control and keeping the scene untarnished with too many footprints.

Rockie examined a large tree, hopped on the trunk with his claws extended, and climbed until he was more than halfway up. His eyes scanned over the scene. He laid out what the ground told him.

"It looks like the campers were gathered by the campfire. The attacker came from the East. The campers ran to their car, but something stopped them. It looks like they all fell to the ground. What the hell can do that?"

Tate grimaced and swore. "Magic," he sighed. "I was hoping it'd be the local rogue pack, but they don't have the power to do magic like that."

Storm cut in. "So, what? We're looking for a witch?"

Tate rubbed his hands through his hair, thinking. "I don't know. Witches tend to leave a doll. Almost like a voodoo doll type of thing. I've had tons of experience with witch victims, and this doesn't look like witches."

Images of her father's photos of magical cases popped into her mind. Aggression, magic, and murders...

"What if—" Piper's voice trailed off. Her pointer finger tapped on her thumb as she let her mind work. Could it be? The sting from the block in her mind flared again. She ignored it and focused on keeping herself from wincing.

"No, go on, Pipes," Storm said. She smiled. The nickname was cute.

She licked her lips before speaking. "What if it's a demon?"

The others glanced at each other before Tate responded. "I don't know much about demons, only that they are rare and cannot physically be in our world. They'd have to possess a body or be extremely powerful."

Piper glanced his way. "That's a myth. Most can come to Earth, but they don't because they can't blend in.

Powerful and half demons can." She paused for a second. "My sister even said things were changing with them. The Earth counsel is giving them different names and trying to send them back to Hell. The only other thing I remember about them is their markings. They love bragging about their kills, so their marks are high up."

Tate narrowed his gaze and scanned the area. His eyes grew wide. "Like on a tree?"

Piper blew out a sharp breath. *Exactly.* "I think that'd be the best place. It's tough to notice unless someone is looking for it."

"Like this?" Rockie said, still in the tree. He had his face almost pressed against the rough wood of the tree he stood on. "It looks like a goddamn smiley face."

Piper's whole body froze over. Her heart stopped, her breathing stopped, her fucking existence stopped at that moment. "A what?" Tate stepped closer to her, probably sensing her emotions.

Rockie faced away and didn't register her mood change. "Yeah, a smiley face." He snickered.

Tate squeezed her shoulder, and her body restarted itself. Her heart mimicked a woodpecker's tap, and her pores leaked out sweat to cool her overheated body. She took a gulp of air. "With a wink?" Her words were harsh and growly. *Please say no.*

All eyes drifted to her. Rockie jumped down, but Tate was the one who spoke, "How did you know that, Piper? You didn't look at the mark."

Her nails dug into her thighs. If she was right, this just got a whole lot bigger. "Because that's the mark that was carved onto my sister's dead body."

Chapter Twenty-Eight

A loud bang made Piper jump. Wood shot all around them. She glanced up to see Rockie beating a tree trunk. Tate ordered him to stop, but he punched the trunk one more time.

Storm stepped into her line of sight. His eyes dilated in fear. "Excuse me? What the hell did you just say? A demon killed your sister?" All three of the men were at her side in the next intake of breath. Their scent made her nerves settle.

She cleared her throat before speaking. But the pain made it difficult. Her whole body hurt, her throat, her stomach, her fucking soul. "The reason I came here with Nina was to help get me over my sister's murder. A smiley face with a wink was carved into her belly." Piper's eyes darted everywhere until she was dizzy. Her stomach turned, threatening to spill out its contents all over the evidence.

No, we need to inform them. Hold on. Her wolf—or what felt like it—massaged her insides and pushed soothing waves of energy to the rest of her body. The voice was right, but she didn't want to relive her shit. She tightened her jaw until it was sore. She could do this.

Her throat pain subsided slightly. But she still needed a bucket of water to drink. "I don't know where to start."

"Start from the beginning," Tate rumbled.

"My dad was an investigator that always seemed to get the weird cases that no one wanted. He knew all about the supernaturals, so he could solve them, and he was good at it too." She bit her lower lip. This was a sensitive subject. Every time she spoke of her dad, the ache to talk to him was strong. She hoped he was okay. His daughter's death had to have been hard on him. Her throat grew tight as if swelling up on her. Ugh, she hated crying.

Storm took her hand in his and squeezed, pulling her out of her downhill spiral. "Keep going, beautiful. Remember what I told you, I'm here for you, and so are your other mates. We care for you and want to know."

She nodded. His words helped ease some of the tension. "The job destroyed my family. For my dad, it wasn't until the cases started following him home that it became a problem. I don't remember much because he had a witch block my memories after my family was attacked. He didn't want me to remember any of it, which is why I don't know a whole lot about supernaturals. He used to take me to crime scenes and teach me everything he knew, but only the work part of his teachings stuck with me." She rested her hand on her forehead. "I'm rambling."

Rockie pulled her into a hug.

Speaking was more effortless in the burrito of men she was now in. "Well, a few months ago, my sister, who decided to follow in my father's footsteps, got killed investigating several weird murders." She buried her face in the crook of Rockie's neck. "Ever since the memory wiping, I don't see my father much. He's distant, and so am I. My sister was the only connection we had. So, when I lost her, it was like losing the whole family. A family I keep forgetting shit about." *Well, that didn't quite make sense, did it?*

It's okay, I'm sure they got it.

"We won't let you forget from now on," Storm said, rubbing her back.

Tate got them back on track. "Do you remember anything about her case?" Tate asked.

Piper shrugged and rubbed her hand on Rockie's shirt. The cotton wasn't as soothing as silk, but it helped. "Only that she thought he was a preferential offender, but his last two victims took that off the table. They were women in their early and late twenties. Whereas before, he only liked younger kids, and he'd leave them alive." Piper gave up on the shirt and ran her hands through her hair. "I knew she was afraid, but I never knew how dangerous the case was. Or I would have helped or forced her to stop. I may only be a few minutes older than her, but she listened like a younger sister." She let out one huff of a laugh. Trace listened but it took a long time to get her there.

Piper licked her lips and continued. "It wasn't until the day before her murder, she opened up. After the perp changed his MO, he became violent, way too violent for a new killer. People don't just wake up and start being that aggressive. It was like he was a different person. That's when she thought of possession. She called me to tell me there was a break in the case and wanted to come over to discuss them. She loved running her ideas by me because of my psychology and behavioral background. The next day she was murdered with those markings on her."

Piper's face was hot and wet with tears. She was so tired of this crap. So tired of demons. "I only knew about the demon because I saw her body and heard the whispers of demon marks."

The Sheriff walked over to them. His hands were in his pockets and his face was grim, but hope shined in his eyes. "Everything okay?"

"Yes, Sheriff. Everything's fine," Tate said, stepping away from the huddle.

He nodded. "Okay, I figured I'll give you the case files and tell you what we found since some of the scenes have been disrupted." He turned and pointed east. "Tons of branches are broken, and the same footprints are all scattered about in one spot as if a person stood there for hours. After attacking the person, he used a pillow to silence his shots. Which doesn't make a lot of sense because he used a lot of overkill, mutilating everyone's genitals."

The Sheriff took his hat off and ran his hands through his blond hair. "One of the women had signs of rape, and the M.O. matches a rapist we have been trying to catch, but nothing else does. He wraps their t-shirt around their necks. I didn't only see one step of footprints for this guy. I'd say it was a team."

Tate glanced at Piper. *Yeah, the demon theory is probably correct. But a team?* the voice said. *And how did the demon get here? Norway isn't a super touristy spot. Could it be here because of us?* She locked that thought away. Because the two options dancing around in her head were too terrifying.

Either it had been following her... or Nina. And that

meant she or Nina had accidentally gotten people killed. She rubbed her face. But that didn't explain her sister. Dammit.

Could there be two demons with the same mark?

No, demons are very territorial. I think they use magic in the mark to get them street credibility in the underworld.

She pushed the voice away and focused back on her surroundings. The scuffle on the ground was inches away from the camper's blue van. These people were inches away from safety.

Something silver caught her eye by the front tire. She walked away from the group.

Storm followed while the others listened to the sheriff. "If you need to go, I'll take—"

She cut him off, "It's not that, look." She grabbed gloves from her pocket and put them on. She picked up the silver device that was mostly buried in the dirt. "It's a phone."

She tried to turn it on, but it was dead. Storm called the guys over, placed it in a bag, and handed it over to Tate. Tate turned to speak with the Sheriff. "If you don't mind, Sheriff, I'm going to take this and return it tomorrow. You know from our previous investigation assistance that we'll take care of it. We won't taint the evidence. But we'll have to charge the phone."

The Sheriff's jaw tightened. His eyes narrowed at Tate, but after a few seconds, he sighed. "Let my boys take it first, to dust it for fingerprints. They'll deliver it to your hotel room after. Along with pictures of the note too and information on any other evidence we have. It should only take a few minutes. But it needs to be in evidence by tomorrow." He took his sheriff hat off and scratched his balding head before continuing, "If it wasn't for the missing kids, and the great detective work that you've done for me, I wouldn't let you take the phone, but you're the kids' only hope." He rubbed his face. "I can only hide the fact you have evidence for a short time. If higher-ups get involved and you get caught, I'll deny this conversation ever happened. Don't make me regret this. Just find those kids."

Tate inclined his head to the Sheriff. "We'll do our best to find them."

The hope in the Sheriff's and deputy's eyes pushed her forward. Despite all the questions and shit happening to her, she'd put it all on hold to help those kids. There was no hope without them. There was no pack taking care of them. No outside help was coming. If they didn't figure out where they were, they'd be lost forever.

Damn... No pressure.

Chapter Twenty-Nine

Once they were back at the hotel, they all conversed about a plan of action and supplies they'd need while waiting for the Sheriff's guy to show up.

When the knock finally came, she was about to pee her pants with excitement. Her hands twitched in eagerness as she ignored the dancing pops of graphology information that swirled in her mind.

She waited a full minute before asking, "Hey, can I see the note that was left?"

Tate's shocked face took a second to clear. Maybe he thought she wasn't interested in helping? Tate nodded and pulled it out. "Yeah, here."

The irritation crinkling his eyes took a second for her to notice. They all had that same darkened expression. *What's up their butts?*

She took the note to the small table. Besides the TV, large bed, and nightstands on both sides of the bed, the room was empty. The slightly pink walls and red curtains were the only indications that this room had anything to do with a romantic honeymoon.

She nodded and focused on the handwritten note. The words had her throat closing as she read. *"Too bad they weren't strong enough to protect themselves or their young. The question is, are you strong enough to stop me?"*

She bit her lip and let out her breath. The note wasn't directed at her. It was just a crazy person taunting the authorities. The best thing was to focus and get as many answers as she could.

"Whatcha doin'?" Storm said teasingly. He was always the icebreaker, for which she was extremely thankful.

She smiled. "I'm using my education." She wiggled her eyebrows. "I've studied human behavior, and I love getting inside of murderers' brains. Even the tiny things, like penmanship, tells a lot about a person. If this guy was intelligent, they'd have typed the note."

Storm smirked. "So, you're even awesomer than we thought?"

"I'm pretty sure awesomer isn't a word," Rockie retorted with a soft chuckle. Their banter was cute, but she focused on the note.

Gotcha. Her smile widened. "Interesting... he uses small print, which means methodical and non-social. His narrow spacing means irritability. He probably has a low-level job and is overlooked. He wants recognition for his work and probably flips out when he doesn't get it."

"How do you know that?" Storm asked, startling her. Oops, she said that out loud?

She shook her head. "Sorry, I was just thinking, apparently out loud."

"But how do you know those things about him?"

Rockie came to sit across from her. His footsteps were soft against the worn-out tan carpet.

"My dad's specialty was behavior. I'm not a professional, but the small print and narrow spacing tell me a lot about him."

"So, how accurate is your skill? I have a friend from college that specializes in graphology. I was going to send the information to him," Tate said, hovering over her.

She nodded. One of her father's cases popped into her head. She knew how to catch this guy. "Well, you might want to send it off. I'm rusty and not specialized in graphology," she said in a daze as her mind worked in over time.

She put her pointer finger up like Velma in Scooby-doo as she solved the case. Might as well have fun with this. "But I've seen this type of killer before. He'd be pretty painless to trick. His menial existence can be used against him. If we bring the wrong person in, indicating we solved the case, he'll be so enraged, he'll make a mistake or come after us himself."

Snapping his fingers and pointing at her, Storm said, "That's not a bad idea," He stayed on the bed but gave her a suggestive smile. "Great work, beautiful."

Tate squeezed her shoulder and walked back to the bed. "If we control the spread of the media, we can control what the people hear. So, if we suggest that we have a man in custody, the killer will hear it."

She rubbed the brown table's soft surface. "But I want to make this very clear. I think you know this, but there is a chance the killer will murder again in spite." Piper's stomach turned. They'd have to wait for another murder to catch him.

Dread twisted her gut into a massive ball, and her lunch once again threatened to come up. *It's the name of the game, sweetie. We need to catch this guy, but we have to do it the human way without magic. Werewolves are powerful, but we aren't witches.*

That's it!

Tate was going to say something, but Piper stood quickly and paced the floor as her mind worked, biting her nails. "Do we have a witch nearby, perhaps?"

Everyone gave her a puzzled stare; their foreheads were so wrinkled Piper almost laughed. Rockie was the first to recover. "Yes, I know the local witch, but I'm not sure she's going to help."

Her head tilted in confusion. Was this witch evil or something? "Why?"

He couldn't meet her eyes, but he kept glancing at his pack mates. "Because she is my ex, and we didn't end it well." He wouldn't meet her eyes as he went over the criminal's note like it was the most interesting thing in the world.

Piper's fist became tight white balls of fury. Why couldn't she have been evil? Ugh.

A green giant crawled out of her chest and snapped his head off... Well, in her imagination, it did. She was glad her skin didn't turn green as the heated rage of jealousy spiked in her.

I have no right to be mad at him for the past. It's none of my business who he was with before. I'm not jealous, just mad we can't get the witch's help.

Right...

I wish I could smack you. She told the voice.

"We still need to try," Tate said, packing up everything

and hiding it in the air vent. Piper lifted a curious eyebrow at him. He smiled. "We need to make sure the evidence is hidden while we go talk to the witch."

"What? Tonight? It's like one-thirty in the morning. I don't think she will be very receptive if we wake her up in the middle of the night," Storm said, his eyes pleading with Tate to reconsider. Storm knew women, and he was right. Piper agreed with him. An angry woman wasn't helping anyone.

Rockie nodded. "I think tomorrow morning is best. She's a morning person, so we'll go bright and early."

The bratty green monster came out and chomped off his arm this time. Piper cleared her head with a slight shake. *Stop that.*

"Fine. We'll go at 6 a.m." Tate declared. His eye was twitching with agitation.

The lack of sleep was going to suck.

Chapter Thirty

Piper closed her heavy eyes, and a second later, Tate was waking her so they could go meet the witch. Well, that's how it felt, at least. Did she even sleep?

"Come on, beautiful, I'll get you a huge coffee with as many shots as you want." Storm rubbed her hair as he spoke.

"Oooh. I love it when you talk dirty." Piper managed a small smile. Everything inside her said roll over and go back to sleep. She was surprised she could even be sarcastic this early.

It might have taken her several minutes, but she rolled over and stared up at him. Ugh, she knew it. He looked at her differently now. The lines around his eyes weren't there yesterday. Was that pity?

Smell him. He is not pitying us. He's worried his wolf won't be enough for us. And if we didn't have the other two, he'd be right. But his wolf levels us all out.

Her wolf... *Wolf? Stop barking. We aren't dogs.* The voice laughed at her joke.

Piper smirked, but the emotion quickly turned into something nastier.

She didn't want to be awake. She didn't want to think about her parents lying to her. The stress building inside of her was too much. *Let's see, hmm, I'm adopted, or do I just have a bunch of backstabbers for parents?*

She didn't want to see the concerned faces of the guys. She didn't want to go meet the witch. Her right eye twitched as she thought. She wished Nina was there, so she could talk to her. But she couldn't even do that anymore. Nina had too many issues of her own to help deal with Piper's.

"Are you okay?" Tate asked. Clearly, she wasn't hiding her emotions very well.

She ran her hands through her hair. "I'm fine. I just feel like I'm going to burst. I'm so mad at my parents and shit, even the world. I don't know why, though. I usually can brush things off and focus on them later."

"That's your wolf. You didn't get a good change during the full moon; it wants to be out. So, it makes everything exaggerated." Tate put a hand on her shoulder. "Tonight, we'll take you out for a wolf run. Try to hold on until then. If it gets unbearable, let me know. I can help you contain her for a little longer."

She nodded.

Her voice...wolf scoffed, *How rude. It's not my fault. It's the wolf magic. It wants to be free, so I can take over.*

She grumpily stomped around the hotel, got ready, and left. Rockie sat in the back with her. His eyes kept wandering to hers. She didn't glance his way. She was too busy convincing herself that today was going to be a good day.

No one said anything on the short drive there. When they arrived at a big sign that had a palm on it, she almost growled. Her wolf was jealous and biting at her insides to be set free. Piper's human instincts brushed off the fact that the witch was Rockie's past girlfriend. There was no reason to be mad. She'd judge her when she met her. She fought with her instincts. Maybe a little too good. Her mind was numb. One second, she was in the car, and the next she was on the porch. "Hello, Miss Carmel, this is Investigator Tate. I need to talk to you. Please open up." He lightly tapped on the door, and Rockie stayed in the car with a very uncomfortable slouch, assuring she'd be more helpful if he wasn't around.

Piper couldn't lie to herself; she liked that he wasn't going to be anywhere near her. It let her wolf relax. Her wolf wanted to chomp on every female's neck until their blood was seeping into her mouth, and she didn't like that feeling.

The door opened, and a tall blonde woman with angelic features stepped onto the porch. *Oh my god, she's beautiful.*

She smiled at Piper.

"I'm only out here because of her. I can feel the pull of her magic. I'm intrigued." Her dark brown eyes raked over Piper.

"Carmel, that's fine. We're here about the murders and missing kids. We need your assistance." The woman's intense stare was interrupted by Tate.

Her gaze met his. "I can help you find the kids but nothing else, and only if I get to read her." Her eyes drifted to the car and narrowed. "And I get to kick Rockie in the nuts."

Rockie's head popped up from the back seat and Piper almost burst out laughing. Knowing she didn't want him back made being around her easier. She just smirked and waved Rockie over.

He approached with a wounded dog kind of look. Her and her wolf loved it. She didn't know why. Was it jealousy? And he was getting his punishment?

No. She didn't want him punished.

She wanted him... *that's it.* Her wolf added.

This was a goodbye for them. Yeah, not a typical one, but after she kicked him, Rockie would be Piper's. She couldn't help but smile.

Was that vindictive of her? Maybe. Did she care? Not so much.

"All right, one good kick and a reading, then you help us," Tate said when Rockie gave him an approving nod.

"Puurrffect," Carmel said and winked. Her smile reminded Piper of the cat in *Alice and Wonderland*.

She lifted her bare foot and hit Rockie right between his legs. The smack of her foot hitting, and the slight squishing noise made Piper cringe.

Aww, the sweet sound of goodbye. The wolf had Piper laughing. Which was the wrong reaction for the moaning pains that Rockie made.

"I'm so glad this was entertaining for you," Rockie said with the scowl on his face. She knelt and kissed him on the cheek.

Storm was not at all sorry for his laughter. Carmel perked up; her shoulders did a happy shrug dance. When she turned around to walk back into her house, her blonde hair almost hit Tate's face.

She knew what these guys were, and yet her attitude didn't falter. The chick was badass. Piper kinda liked her. As long as she stayed away from her Rockie.

Carmel pulled on Piper's arm to gesture towards her house, silently inviting her in. "Everyone else stays outside."

Piper glanced at the guys. Their worried faces didn't give her confidence. Regardless, she followed the spunky witch in her home. "Okay, sugar, sit your cute butt down on the couch." Carmel shimmied around the small living room that reminded her of a health center waiting room mixed with a house from Halloween Town.

The furniture coloring and placement were made for lots of company. Lots of sitting areas, bland grays and tan that were too simple to be homey, and a line of magazines on the coffee table. All painfully normal.

The decor, however, was nothing close to normal. Several skulls were around the room. Pictures of bats, cauldrons, and fake spider webs covered the full bookshelves. If Carmel pulled out a fog machine, Piper wouldn't be surprised.

Carmel walked toward the hallway, away from her. Piper stood to follow but she stopped her with an outstretched hand. "I'll be right back. My crystals are put away. Stay in the living room. Some of the rooms have curses on them, and I'd feel horrible if you ruined that pretty face."

Piper coughed and nodded. She had no desire to tangle with defensive magic, so she gladly stayed put like a good girl.

She leaned back on the couch to wait for the witch. She wished the guys were with her. Soon, her leg began to bounce uncontrollably, and her heart matched each frantic movement. Finally, she sighed and moved towards the door to check on the guys.

She heard grumbling and agitated sounds coming from them, but their voices sounded far away and underwater. Regardless, if she just saw them, she'd feel better.

A few steps away from the couch, the air changed around her. It crackled with static electricity. The hair on the back of her neck stood to attention in response. "What the?"

A sparkly blue light appeared in front of her before she could reach the door. At first, she wondered if the witch had a pixie. But the light got bigger. A small blonde with a cute blunt bob haircut and delicate features popped into her path. She smiled with bright enthusiasm. Piper relaxed; no one with a smile as sweet as that could do her harm, right?

The blonde scanned the room, and her smile fell. She waved her hand, mimicking the shape of a rainbow. Piper opened her mouth to let her know Carmel was getting crystals, when fear and rage blazed into the woman's sparkling hazel eyes.

Her small hand flew up, and a gust of wind slammed into Piper. Piper screamed out and flew across the room, smacking into a hard bookshelf.

"Goddammit," she cried out into the crook of her arm. This sucked. The muffled sound of her guys skyrocketed outside. Then, a banging started that echoed around the room.

She opened her eyes and scooted closer to the floor as

the woman hovered over her. "Where's Carmel? What have you done with her, Dog? If you have hurt her, I'll—"

Carmel came out of nowhere. "Sarah, what the hell?" She ran to Piper's side to check on her. Piper groaned when her hand hit a sore spot. Carmel's palms heated and most of the pain disappeared.

She let out a grateful sigh but kept still. Her gaze stayed away from them. She wasn't sure she could control her wolf if she made eye contact.

Damn fucking right! How dare she attack us without cause. Kill her. The anger rolling off her crashed into her heart. She did her best to calm and sent soothing waves to her wolf. They needed the witches' help. She had to stay calm.

Piper kept them in her peripheral vision, but she focused on easing the rest of her pain and her sore muscles. She never thought she'd wish for a flimsy Walmart bookshelf in her life, but flimsy sounded good right now.

The shouting and banging from outside increased again. Carmel glanced towards her door. "She's fine. Calm the hell down before you break my house."

The banging had stopped, but the growls increased. Worried. Demanding answers.

Sarah crossed her arms defiantly. "You hate wolves after that ex of yours. Why is she here?"

"I'm doing a scan on her and helping her with an investigation." Carmel stood and narrowed her gaze at Sarah. "You didn't need to attack her."

That appeared to clear Sarah's rage. Piper stood as well. "I'm fine," she called out to the guys. She might have a few bruises, but she'd be fine. Piper brushed the small wood chips off her clothes. Her eyes never left Sarah's, watching her every movement to make sure she didn't attack again.

Sarah noticed and glared at Piper. "Sorry, I just overreacted. I got attacked a few months ago. I'm not handling it well."

Piper sighed and nodded. The constant adrenaline spikes and overacting behavior were common. She took a deep breath to restart.

Then something occurred to her. She shuffled her feet before speaking, "I don't want to be rude, but can I ask... were you assaulted by a man?"

Carmel cleared her throat. "Yes, I'm helping her to learn how to defend herself. The spell she used on you was one we learned last week, in fact." She moved towards the couch to redirect them to a less cluttered area.

Piper smiled. "She must be a good student."

Carmel sat down on the couch, rubbed her small hands against the fabric, and locked her gaze on Piper's. "I know where your questioning is going. The answer is yes. The same guy that you're looking for is the one that attacked Sarah. She refused to go to the station when asked. She didn't want to relive that crappy night over again. That's why I am helping you if you prove to be a worthy person."

Piper joined Carmel on the couch. Her back was stiff as a board. "I get that you don't want to talk about it, but I am trying to find this guy. Is there anything that you can remember about his appearance?"

Sarah's face fell. Her shoes became the most fascinating thing in the room. Her eyes glistened with the trauma of her past. Piper felt like crap, but if it helped get the guy off the streets and save the kids, she'd deal with it.

Carmel gestured for Sarah to come to her. Sarah practically ran into her open arms and sat on her lap. Carmel whispered in Sarah's ear. Piper looked away, wanting to give them some privacy.

Their movements became intimate, touching soft, and alluring, with their eyes devouring each other. Piper shifted in her seat uncomfortably.

That caught Sarah's attention. Her eyes snapped to Piper. "I didn't get a good look at him. He had me on my stomach most of the time. All I remember was his white skin, dark hair, and horrible voice. It sounded high-pitched and phlegmy like he drank a lot of milk. I know this doesn't help, which is why I didn't want to talk to anyone about it."

Piper's eyes softened. She wanted to hug Sarah or put a hand on her shoulder to let her know that it was okay. She was grateful that Carmel did just that, comforting her.

Sarah abruptly stood; her cheeks were redder than a baboon's behind. Piper smirked. That was a feeling she knew all too well with her men.

"I'm going to go now and let you guys continue. I am sorry that I overreacted and that I can't give you more information." Before Piper could respond, Sarah disappeared in another swirl of blue lights and sparkles.

"So, how does this reading work?" Piper asked, observing the colorful vials on the table. *Bat blood?* She wasn't going to ask a question she didn't want to know the answer to.

The witch gave her a devilish smile. "It'll be fun and sweet. We're going to have sex."

Chapter Thirty-One

Piper shot from her seat as adrenaline slammed into her, knocking the glass vials over with her shins. "What?" The guys were outside, and she sat alone with a woman that had magical powers. She didn't like this.

Her heart pounded against its restraints. There was no way she'd have sex with Carmel. It wasn't happening. *Not even for the missing kids.*

Her wolf needed to stop the guilt trip because, just, no. The avalanche of guilt tore at her heart. Dammit! Was she really going to let those kids die or be hurt, when there was a way to save them?

She groaned and sat back down. Had the guys known what Carmel was offering before this? Betrayal stung worse than the nails digging into her palms.

She was going to have sex with a woman. The color drained from her face. She didn't have anything against same-sex interactions, but she never thought she'd be in one.

"Oh my God, breathe. I was just kidding. It's just going to involve me touching your hand and a little blood." She laughed as she gathered her supplies. Piper's mortification was on a level higher than the ceiling. "You totally would have done it too. I saw it on your face. Good job. Many people would have said hell no and forgotten about the kids."

Relief wasn't even close to the emotions cleansing her body. That was cruel, but Piper laughed anyway. "You're wicked. I just had a mild heart attack."

"Hey, babe, don't knock it unless you try it," she said as she moved to sit down next to her. Her hands were full of crystals and herbs. The sharp, swirling knife in her hand gave Piper pause.

Her teeth clenched together to keep her face as neutral as possible. She wasn't in the mood. "No thanks."

"All right, I had enough fun for the day. Here's what's going to happen. First, I'm going to take some of your blood and put it on the crystals. The herbs will focus the power. Then, I'm going to mix our blood to draw sigils on our foreheads. It may sting if you are very powerful. Then, we'll finish by touching foreheads, so I can read you."

Piper rubbed the cushion beneath her. "What does that mean? Read me."

The crystals moved in her palm, making a figure eight without any assistance from her hand. Piper gulped. Carmel chuckled. "I knew you were new. Females around here tend to be backstabbing assholes. Well, the men are too. I don't know if it's the weather or all the outdoor space, but I make sure to check the females before letting them get their claws into anyone."

Piper hissed when the blade cut her thumb. "So, how

much of that was true, and how much of it was about Rockie?"

Ugh. Did I just say that?

HA! Yes.

Carmel chuckled and shook her head. "I don't like him like that anymore. Not after he broke my heart. But he'll always have a place in my heart. Even if I tried to get rid of it," she said as she worked.

She cut their thumbs again and smeared the crimson liquids together. *Before you embarrass us, we are supernaturals. We cannot get diseases like this.* Her voice comforted her. The mark on her forehead was some type of flower.

Carmel grabbed the back of Piper's head and brought the two symbols together. The instant they touched; heat shot from her head down to her toes. That, she could handle. The twisting, however, was painful. She felt like a noodle in a spaghetti bowl, twisting around the fork and getting pulled away from her bowl.

Her breathing came out fast, and strained sounds escaped her lips. She kept her eyes closed as she rode out the pain. *Sting my ass. Is she ripping out my soul?*

Carmel flung herself away from Piper with a nasty pop. "Holy hairy butt, that was some crazy shit." Her eyes snapped to Piper, her breath coming in big, pleasured gulps as if they *did* have sex. "That was delicious. Don't ever let a witch do that to you again. If I didn't have crazy self-control, I would have killed you."

Loud thuds turned into banging once her ears popped. Her men were pounding on the door, walls, and windows. "I'm okay," the sound of her voice slowed the franticness of their fists on the house, but they didn't stop.

"Let us in or get your ass out here," Tate yelled. The freaked-out tone in his voice bit at her heart.

"We're coming out. Chill, I told you I was just doing a reading, and your kind is not allowed in my house."

They stood. Piper licked her lips and pushed down her anxiety before asking, "But I'm his kind?"

She smirked before answering, "No, sugar, you're definitely higher class and much more delicious."

Piper's leg bounced even as she tried to stop the damn thing. "I don't understand. He's a wolf. So am I." Piper didn't know if she really wanted the answer, but it was better to know. This chick could be a bad enemy.

Carmel's eyes brightened. "It has nothing to do with them being wolves and everything to do with them being men. I refuse to let another man into my house, my heart, and especially my pants." Her jaw twitched as she glanced towards the closed door and the men on the other side.

"Rockie was a good wake-up call. I won't let another guy hurt me again." When Piper gave her a wide-eyed worried stare, she put her hand on her knee. "Don't worry, he was a good man and boyfriend, but his wolf didn't like me, so he ended it. Too bad for me, I was already in love with him."

Piper had no idea how to act. Her gut twisted hearing about how she loved her mate, but hell, she sympathized with her. How horrible. It wasn't either of their faults. If his wolf didn't choose her, they could only be together for so long.

Piper put her hand over hers. "I'm sorry, know that he didn't mean to hurt you."

Carmel smirked and whipped at the edge of her eyes.

"I know. That's the only reason my heart hasn't turned to ice, and I didn't kill him. It just wasn't meant to be."

Piper smiled and moved to leave.

Carmel stopped her. "Piper," she turned and met Carmel's intense glare, "if something happens to me, the spell will fade."

She nodded. "Okay, so don't let anything happen to you." That earned her a smirk.

"See ya, sugar. The spell that's going to help you find those kids will be waiting for you outside."

Piper's forehead wrinkled in confusion. But she let it slide. It was time to leave, but maybe she'd hang out with Carmel when the case was all over. She seemed like fun. Even if she did like to give her mini heart attacks.

Tate, Storm, and Rockie pushed against the force field a few inches away from the porch. Carmel must have extended the protective magic. Smart woman.

"Come to us now," Rockie said. His worried eyes made her run to them. But, good lord, they really were concerned. Jumping into the middle of their warmth had every fiber in her body pulling in three different ways.

I love this moment. It feels like heaven, her wolf said, a purring in her throat catching her off guard. She didn't know wolves purred. *We do for our mates.*

Chapter Thirty-Two

They walked back to the car. A blue vial with a note sat underneath the glass waiting for them. The witch gave Piper a way to track the kids using nature. Things like the wind, shadows, plants, and maybe even the weather will guide her.

She gulped the potion quickly. Yuck! It was disgusting. She imagined horse poop and dirty socks tasted about the same. But the witch said the magic would only work on a female, so she got stuck with the job.

Piper looked out the window as the car zoomed past the nature outside. She looked at every tree and plant, but nothing was acting weird. So, how the hell does this work?

"All right, I drank that potion, but nothing is happening," Piper said on the drive to the station.

Storm sat next to her in the car, rubbing his temples. The poor guy looked exhausted. "You won't see anything for a few hours. These types of potions take a long time to activate and work. You won't be able to find them with ease. It's going to suck trying to find clues that are real.

I've used one before. The question will be, if a shadow moves, is it a sign or a trick of the light? We could end up chasing nothing."

Well, that was encouraging. She rubbed her hands along her jeans, fidgeting with the fabric. "Okay, well, at least we have something. So, what's the plan for today?" She needed to change the subject. The more she talked about the bad things, the more self-doubt would grow. She didn't need more doubt, more confusion.

She needed hope.

Tate's eyes met hers through the rearview mirror and smiled. "We're going to question the survivor. Rockie and Storm will be leading a group of humans to search the forest while we wait for my pack to get here. A few have come but we'll need more. If they're in a fifty-mile radius, the pack will find them, but that's not for a couple of hours. So, we'll go back to the room, eat, and get ready for the day."

Storm handed Piper the kids' files, but she held the folder like it was a bomb. She deliberately didn't go through them last night, but he was right, she needed to. She had taken the potion that made it her job to find them. Glancing through the tan file will have to do for now. Nothing magical was happening outside the window.

Her heart couldn't take much more. She needed a little break... and a two liter of Pepsi. If that made her weak, so be it.

ROCKIE AND STORM DROPPED TATE AND HER OFF FIRST
because her bladder was a crying brat and needed release.
They refused to let her stay alone, so the big strong men
did rock-paper-scissors to decide who was staying... No lie.

The satisfaction in Tate's green eyes would forever
warm her heart. He puffed out his chest and gave her a
wink. As they left the car, she glanced back at her other
guys, all sporting a pout.

She couldn't help but laugh. These guys were big
babies. But damn, their boyish actions made her want to
fold them up and stick them in her pocket.

As soon as the door was open, she darted to the
restroom. There was nothing compared to relieving a full
bladder. Washing her hands felt like washing the rest of
the morning and duties away. Right now, she didn't have to
find the kids or hold that responsibility. That could be
future Piper's worry.

Tate's shoulders relaxed when the bathroom door shut
behind her. His un-breachable demeanor flicked off like a
light switch. His tense jaw relaxed, and his eyes softened.
A vulnerable, worried man sat in his place, like there was a
rain cloud over his head.

Piper didn't recognize him. The invisible weight on his
shoulders did something to her. She moved to his side and
wrapped her hands around his shoulders before she knew
what her intentions were.

He stiffened for a heartbeat, but then relaxed at her
touch. "You know you can't control everything, right? Let
your pack hold some of this weight."

He squeezed her tighter and tucked his face into the
crook of her neck. He breathed in deeply. "Being respon-
sible for others and now this, knowing the town is

depending on me to find these kids—" He sighed. There was no need for words, she had the same desire to help and sense of responsibility for the kids. "When did you turn into such a smart cookie?"

She laughed. "I know a thing or two about guilt and responsibility, but I don't know if I'm a smart cookie. You're pretty smart."

He pulled away from her to gaze into her eyes. "You're smart as hell, Pipes. Please don't sell yourself short."

She bit her lip and nodded. "Promise. I'm here, and I'm also pretty strong. I'll hold some of your stress." That earned her a chuckle.

He squeezed her for a second and loosened his grip. Piper preferred the tight grip if she was honest. "Thank you for letting me relax. It's not often I have the luxury of showing emotions. I just needed a break."

Tate rolled his neck, and his shoulders lifted again. His airy, calm power rolled over him. He smiled, but the smile didn't reach his eyes.

She knew her other two men were coming, but she had to ask. "What's with you being weird about your emotions? A demon didn't take them away, did they?"

Too soon, Piper, too soon.

He rubs the back of his neck. "The pack could perceive doubt as weakness. If they can't have full confidence in their Alpha, chaos happens. The dominant wolves will try to challenge me because they worry about the submissive. I just can't appear to be weak." His hands moved to her hips. "I'd love another date with you when this is all over. It was the best time I've had in a long time. Maybe next time we'll hike to this beautiful waterfall. Would you like that?"

She bit her lip again and nodded. Images of their date flashed in her mind. Their lips grazed, their wolf powers mingled, and their comfortability with each other was addictive. Something inside her flipped, and Piper didn't want the blocked emotionless Tate next to her. She wanted his green eyes to darken in lust. She wanted him to lose control with her. Her wolf demanded it. Before she could overthink her actions, Piper straddled Tate and claimed his mouth. Whoa.

Their soft tongues danced in the perfect waltz. The guy had mad tongue skills. Her toes curled, and she moaned into his mouth.

"So. Fucking. Delicious," Tate whispered against her mouth. He moved to the crook of her neck and kissed her overheated flesh. "Can I touch you, my sweet Piper?"

His strong, calloused hands traveled to her pants button. She knew what he meant, and goodness, she wanted his hands there. She nodded and let out a breathy, "Yes."

He claimed her mouth again as his hands opened her pants. He moved slowly down her belly, causing goosebumps to ripple over her skin and finding her wetness. He sucked in a sharp breath. "You're so wet for me, love. Do you have any idea how sexy that is?" he said while kissing her hard enough to fuzzy her mind.

Words? What were words?

She was so close as soon as his fingers circled her swollen clit, she shattered into a million pieces. Her screams were so loud, that not even Tate's kisses could silence them.

The door unlocked and opened. Tate stiffened underneath her, but his smirk and hungry eyes weren't worried or regretful.

Rockie walked in and stopped at the door entrance. She slowly slid off Tate's lap, he gripped her tighter at first but eventually let her go. Her cheeks were red and on fire in embarrassment like a kid getting caught with their hand in the forbidden cookie jar. Not regretful though.

Rockie's nose flared, his jaw tightened, and his eyes shined with his wolf. Piper's heated face turned cold and sickly. Did she do something wrong?

No. But Rockie is a dominant wolf. His instincts are telling him to attack Tate for touching his mate. Until we seal the bond between us four, their wolves will worry. We could still deny him, or he could lose us in a challenge. He'll be fine. Her wolf's words made her feel a little better, but her stomach still was in knots.

She hoped they weren't going to fight. Her eyes kept moving back and forth between the two unblinking men. *Please be okay.*

Storm walked in, sliding past Rockie. The smile on his face almost hurt her eyes. He was bright and loving. Her shoulders relaxed in response. He walked to her and kissed her swollen lips. "I always miss the good stuff." He winked and handed over a bag of food. *Mmm, Chinese.*

Rockie closed the door, his previous mood still on his face, but he seemed to be less aggressive. He kissed her and pressed his forehead to hers. She smiled at him, letting her happiness show on her face.

He took a step away and stopped. He growled, sat next to Piper, and put her in his lap. He handed her a cold drink. "Sorry, Piper, they didn't have Pepsi." She thanked both of them. Her stomach unknotted and rumbled in anticipation. That seemed to lighten the air in the room. All the men relaxed and smiled at her while she dug into her bag.

Ooo, eggrolls.

Rockie moved her to one side of his lap and his food to the other. Storm shot from his sitting position near her feet to grab the remote. "Let's watch a movie." He scanned the tv with more enthusiasm than she could manage.

"Hey, *Twilight*. Remember when this first came out how so many people wanted to be us? Team werewolf." Storm grinned at her.

Rockie growled. A simple "No," was his answer.

Storm laughed and kept scrolling. "*V for Vendetta.*"

"Remember, remember the fifth of November," both her and Storm said at the same time. Then, their eyes met and they burst into laughter.

He sat on the bed and captured her lips, but then pulled away too quickly for her liking. He picked another movie.

She hadn't seen what movie he chose, so as she waited, her leg bounced, anxious for something fun. Fun would distract her.

A picture of two of her favorite actors staring at each other came up. She let out a squeal. "*Blended?*" A playful smile spread across her lips. Perfect.

Storm gave her a wink and sat back at her feet. "Hey, it's a fun movie." Rockie gripped her hip as he stuffed his face with rice. She glanced over at Tate, but he had moved to the small table. His face was in a case note and his pen scribbling furiously. She wished he'd come to snuggle, but she understood. She even appreciated his constant work ethic. It made it easier on her guilt for needing a small break.

Rockie nodded sagely and grunted his approval. She smiled even wider. Yeah, this would help her mood. Some normalcy and her men.

Chapter Thirty-Three

S torm and Rockie got out a block away from the station. As they walked to the crowd of people, Piper's stomach turned. She didn't like not being near them. What if they ran into trouble?

"It's okay, Piper, the guys are strong, and they have backup and weapons with them. They'll be okay," Tate said as he gripped her hand to reassure her. That, and the vibrations from the car engine helped her worry. The cold leather seats weren't as comfortable as she'd like, though.

Piper nodded. This was the first time she'd be away from them for long and it didn't feel right. She sighed and focused on what mattered. "Can I call Nina?"

"Yeah, I called earlier. They're going to go out into the forest to search for the kids, but you can probably catch them. They planned to shift and leave at ten."

Piper didn't want to disturb them. All that mattered was Nina's safety. *She isn't far, smell out the window. We can possibly catch her scent.* Piper listened and the new wolf jasmine and spice scent of her best friend smacked her in the face.

They parked the car in the sheriff's spot. She definitely missed her friend now. As soon as they got back, she was—

"Are you okay? Do you need me?" A voice interrupted her thoughts.

Piper jerked away, letting out a little squeal. Nina was poking her head through her window. "Where the hell did you come from?"

Nina rubbed at her chest. "I felt your longing for me. I'm about to hop on Liam's back to search for the kids, but I wanted to make sure you were okay."

Piper got out and hugged Nina. "I'm fine, just missing your face."

Nina gripped her tighter, and Piper could smell Liam jogging toward them. "I missed you too."

"Jesus, we are ridiculous. It's not like we didn't just see each other last night." Piper laughed but squeezed her again.

Tate rubbed Piper's lower back as Liam stepped next to Nina. "It's the bond you created. Piper is essentially your Alpha and true pack member, so, distance, even for a short period, can be hard for the first year."

"I know, I almost cried last night. I thought I was going crazy. I love my girl, but shit. Liam explained it to me and was dominant enough to keep me calm," Nina said as she snuggled into Liam's embrace.

"Always. But next time you need to run to Piper, let me know. I turned around for two-seconds, and you were a block away," Liam spoke in her hair as his arms squeezed her.

So, she wasn't the only one being overprotective. That

made her feel better—for Nina and her sanity. Liam seemed to like Nina.

"Is Liam your—" Piper's eyes bulged, and she shut her mouth before she could stick her foot down her throat. Shit. Nina had commitment issues, and she was about to use a lifelong commitment word, *mate*.

Nina flinched slightly, but Liam seemed to calm her. His hand rubbed her back, and he kissed her temple. "Anyway, thank you so much for coming to me, girl. I love that, but I didn't mean to take you away from the search. Finding the kids is important."

"That's okay. We were waiting for a few stragglers anyway. Well, I love ya, Toots." Liam and Nina ran back to the others. Her heartstrings were sore. Nina was still her best friend, but every day she seemed to become more animalistic.

Nina hated running before, and now she ducked and dodged Liam's playful attacks at a crazy speed. A bright smile was on her face. She was happy that Nina was happy but sad that her old friend wasn't the same.

"It's okay. Nina is strong." Tate's constant circling hand on her lower back kept her grounded. The annoyance she once felt wasn't there anymore.

"I know." Piper walked to the station door. A small greeting sign made her smile. '*We protect our town's people because they're our chosen home.*'

Home? Is this home now?

"We're here to ask the guy questions about the attack, but I need you to focus on keeping him calm. The Sheriff said he was a ladies' man."

She bunched her forehead together. "What?" Pictures of a guy in a dress popped into her mind.

"A male that prefers to be around women. Men tend to irritate him." Tate opened the door for her.

"Okay, gotcha."

They were in the room in seconds, to her surprise. She had been dreading the long wait or briefing she expected. But, instead, they ushered them in like they were the honored guests of a ball. Her dad never received that kind of welcome.

The man in his mid-thirties sitting on the other side of the table was not what she expected. To have survived a demon attack, one needed to be extremely big and strong or small and not worth the demon's time. Yet, this guy was neither. If the dictionary used pictures, his would be under ordinary.

His round face, straight nose, brown eyes, and average build were the definition of forgettable. If his name was John Smith, she was going to break his nose. Only to help him out. At least that'd be something interesting to look at.

"Hello. Your name is Sam Gunther correct?" He nodded. "Good. Thank you for coming in. This is my partner, Piper, and my name is Tate. I'm new to the case. May I ask you a few questions?" He sat down and put his light brown files down on the metal table.

Sam agreed, so he continued. "I need you to walk me through the night of the attack."

"I already told the police everything I know," Sam said. His voice was rough like he had been screaming a lit. Since he was one of the victims, he probably did do a lot of screaming.

His head twitched slightly. I wonder if he was on drugs.

Her wolf wasn't a fan of him either way. He was a coward in her eyes.

His hands twitched, but he put them under the table before the movement was detectable. His jaw tightened and his micro-expressions were frowning. He didn't like this.

Her wolf bristled. *Who does he think...* Tate's large hand wrapped around her knee, so she shook her head to clear it... *Oh right, be professional, Piper.*

We don't like him. He makes us want to wrap our mouth around his neck. He should have fought—

We need to stay focused, so get it together. Tate said I had to do the talking. The way Sam is scowling at Tate, he needs me to help.

Of course, he doesn't like men. He's not one.

Shut up. He was attacked as well. It doesn't matter if he's a druggy or coward. Now hush. The wolf made a chuffing sound but listened.

She cleared her throat and focused. "It's okay, Sam, we just want to hear your story from you. Sometimes a new pair of eyes and ears can find new things. Can you tell me, please?" Piper said.

His eyes softened, and his cheek twitched, but Piper focused on him, not his body language. Her wolf was on edge.

"Okay, honey, just for you. Like I told the others, me and my number one girl were hanging out in our tent when we heard screams. I went—half naked—to go check on everyone and this big, huge dude charges me." He paused. "I'm not sure what shit he was into, but lights and sparks and heat were all around me. It happened so fast." He cleared his throat probably worried we wouldn't believe him. Several years ago, he would have been thrown in a psych ward. Now, most people knew better.

He didn't have the local accent, only a few words sounded Norwegian. *So, he didn't grow up here, but he's been here long enough to pick up a slight accent.*

He scratched the table with his thumbnail. "He seemed to focus on the women more. Then, something hot hit my back, then several stinging burns. The doctor said I was stabbed. Don't ask me how I survived that, but after a few seconds, I could move again. So, I took off into the woods." His hands went through his greasy dark hair. "I only got away because he was still focusing on the girl. She was fighting him or something. I don't know." His face reddened in what she assumed was shame.

"It's okay, Mister Gunther, we understand. No one is blaming you for this. You did what you had to do to survive." Tate was nicer than she would have been. He truly was a coward.

Calm down. She had no right to judge him for surviving. Her heart hurt for the woman, though. She needed to stay neutral. She couldn't protect any of the victims by scorning a survivor. If he were a woman, she probably wouldn't have been as mad. That wasn't right.

Her pep talk helped. She gave him a half-smile when his eyes drifted back to her. "No one knows what they will do in a situation like that. You had the right idea."

He nodded and covered his face. "I ran until someone found me."

"So, what were the injuries you obtained?" Tate asked. His green eyes drifted to Piper. Yeah, this was a sensitive subject. A blonde female opened the door, setting down a pitcher of water and a paper cup.

"Four stabs, golf ball-sized burns on my lower back, a cracked rib, and I lost a lot of blood. I almost died. Today is my first day out of the hospital." Sam poured himself some water.

Tate finished scribbling on his notepad. "Do you remember anything else about your attacker?"

Sam ran a hand over his face. "No. I only saw him for a second. He was big and muscular, with white and dark hair, I believe. I'm sorry."

"Not your fault. Well, Sam, I'd like for you to see the town counselor. She might be able to help you remember more. Please fill out this paper." Tate pulled out an information sheet from the folder and put it in front of him with a pen. "The form just gives us more information to keep you safe."

Sam glanced up from the paper. "So, knowing if I'm a supernatural and what stores I shop at will help keep me safe?"

Tate nodded. "We don't know what is relevant right now. This could be a supernatural hate crime or an angry co-worker. The second is unlikely, but having all the facts helps us narrow down a suspect."

Sam nodded his agreement and filled out the paper. He handed it to Piper. *So, he works at a grocery store and isn't supernatural. He hasn't left the state or country in years, and besides his dad, he has no family.*

Tate asked him a few more questions and walked Sam out. As she left the building, she requested Sam's medical chart. The plump receptionist shrugged. "I'll put in the request, but it may take a while."

"No worries. Thanks." Her stomach growled to the

point of making her frown. She didn't need food right now, she needed answers.

Tate chuckled. "Let's go eat. They have a great local sandwich shop."

"Yeah, if I don't eat something my stomach might attack." As they left the station, Piper glanced at the clock on the wall. It was already eleven.

Tate grabbed her hand and pushed comfort into her. "Let's take a break and eat. We'll focus on the case after."

Ugh, she was so glad she did. The delicious salami sandwich might as well have been sex in her mouth, because *wow*. Nothing had tasted this good in a long while. *We were hungry. It takes a lot of strength to hold me in.*

"Don't worry, once we go for a run tonight, the hunger won't be so aggressive," Tate said and put another sandwich in front of her.

Oh my gosh, we should hump his face.

"Ha!" Piper choked on the piece of sandwich in her mouth. She banged on her chest while Tate hit her back. Thankfully, the terror of not being able to breathe only lasted a few seconds.

"I'm okay," she said through coughs.

"What happened?" Tate asked.

Her cheeks flushed. "My wolf is just a dirty bitch."

He smirked. "What'd she say?"

Her face heated and was probably bright red. "I don't want to say."

Tate bumped her shoulder. "Oh, come on. I deserve a good laugh."

Piper groaned. Anxiety, fear, and a crazy amount of urgency to run came over her. Yet, her mouth opened and granted his wish. "When you brought me the second sandwich, she said," she paused, "I should hump your face."

He let out a surprised chuckle as well, green eyes glowing. "That could be arranged, if you'd like."

See, he's perfect.

Great, now her face was on actual fire. She glanced away as heat pulled at her core. "Maybe, another time. I don't know if the sandwich shop is ready for that."

A choked laugh in the back of his throat told her he wasn't expecting that answer. "Yeah, they probably aren't."

Chapter Thirty-Four

"All right, beautiful, we're going to go for a run and join the search party. Then, you can run and let your wolf out while using the spell. What do you think? Sound good?" Storm asked.

There was a small trail, but it ended. They needed more searchers, even the human variety. The forest was too big.

His exposed glistening chest made it hard for Piper to concentrate. Storm was the smallest of the three, but, whoa, he was still all muscle. His light skin and gray eyes made him mesmerizing. But she wished he would have put on a shirt because her lady bits were trying to take over.

Her face heated as he caught her ogling him. "Don't look at me like that, beautiful. Or we won't go anywhere except the bedroom."

The thought gave her goosebumps. That's what she wanted. Her wolf was chomping at the bits, demanding her attention.

"It's okay, Pipes, I get it. Your wolf is forcing her way

out. She'll want sex and to be free. You can let her out. It'll be easier to handle her. The sensations won't be as bad."

Tate stepped out of the sheriff's office. His face grim. They didn't have any leads and a popular festival happened in a couple of days, so tons of tourists were in town.

"What'd they say?" Storm asked, his hand holding Piper's. His thumb made little circles that relaxed her.

"They are useless. I need more free-range with the investigation, but they're only bringing in witnesses that agree to come in and a small number of suspects," Tate explained. The muscles in his jaw were throbbing in agitation.

He rubbed at his face. "The DNA on the murdered females matched a recent rapist they have been searching for. But no one can tell us anything, and some of the victims refuse to talk to us. And none of the tests will be done for at least a week."

Piper closed the distance and wrapped her arms around him. "Well, I didn't tell you but one of the victims was at the witch's house. She said she didn't know anything. Maybe that's why they're refusing to help, they're ashamed. Anyway, we still have the spell and the media presence. Once we say we got the perp, either the demon or psychopath he's in will be furious. He'll make a mistake." She rubbed his arm.

"Yeah, Alpha, then we can catch this fucker." Storm put a strong hand on his Alpha's shoulder. He straightened back up when Tate nodded at him. "So, let me get this straight, are we saying this rapist is possessed by the demon? Like a demon is in his body?"

Piper shook her head. "Demons make deals, not possessions. Usually, anyway. From what I can remember, my dad said only weak humans get possessed, and they don't live more than a few days. Their skin deteriorates. But demons can kill without possessing or being in people. But it's easier for them to have a body. Makes it so no one can track them by their demon magic."

Storm nodded, but she didn't miss the whitening of his face. "I hate demons."

Yeah... demons sucked. She never hung out with a vampire or ghoul, so she didn't know if they were as dangerous, but she'd rather be hunting them, though. A sense of dread hovered over her, and her shoulders couldn't relax.

Tate rubbed his face when Piper pulled away. "All right, I'll get my head out of my ass. Let's join the search for the kids." He kissed Piper's head, grabbed her hand, and walked towards the tall trees.

Piper's anxiety spiked as she got closer to her release. Would she be able to shift on command? Will she turn into a wolf and hurt someone? Will she be able to find the kids? Why the hell did the witch make the potion for female use only? Tate would have been way better at it. But, shoot, Storm seemed to know a lot about potions. He'd find the kids. Could she?

"Don't worry, beautiful, we'll get through this. It's unnerving to shift without the moon's call, but you can do this. She'll follow our lead," Storm reassured her. He grabbed her other hand.

When the trees and the strong scent of bark, leaves, and fresh dirt surrounded them, her wolf relaxed. "All right, take off your clothes, so you don't rip them. If you're embarrassed, you can hide behind a tree, but I promise we won't look." The way Tate and Storm turned to take their clothes off helped her insides from going haywire.

Except her heart was missing a piece... *Where's Rockie? He has been running off.* What the hell was he doing? He'd been spending a lot of time on his phone. Old worries of cheating men crept back in her like a slimy slug. Her jaw clenched at the thought.

Mated wolves are different. He'd never do anything like that to hurt us. He's with the other wolves since he's more dominant than Storm.

Piper shook her head and took off her shirt. Her wolf was right. As she unbuttoned her jeans, the feel of comfort surprised her. As if she'd gotten naked for them millions of times before. Weird.

It's okay, we're safe with them. I'll make this easy for you. I'll follow their lead. Do not fret.

Did her wolf have everything under control? She had no clue, but she had faith in her. All three were naked. The men faced away with their backs to her still, and wow, the view was breathtaking.

Ugh, she needed to show them as much respect as they showed her. Her fingernails were the next best thing. *Don't look, don't look.*

They don't care if you do. Besides, you need to look to change. I have to see what they do.

Her eyes went to the men's backs. Their skin was smooth with a few scars, but that just made them even yummier. Tate had a few slices and claw marks. Storm had teeth and claw marks. Both told a powerful story of their strength.

"Okay, love, watch us change. I will go slow, but Storm can't. Your wolf will follow. It's hard to know which person the wolf will follow if we can't see you. I'll be listening to your grunts as judgment. So, don't hold back," Tate said, his eyes still focused on a tree.

Piper lifted her shoulders higher before speaking, "You can look. I want this to be as easy and fast as possible. Both of you can look."

Storm jerked to stop himself from changing. He pivoted her way slightly. His eyes were darkened in lust at her words. "Are you sure?"

She had to remind herself to breathe. "Yes."

They both turned in slow motion, giving her time to change her mind. She struggled to not cover herself, but honestly, it wasn't as difficult as she thought. Instead, her focus was on the firm disappearing butt and dreamy strong bodies they were showing off.

Tate was large with muscles *everywhere*. Storm's body was pure fluidity as if he had the power to control water and mimicked its fluid nature. They had different skin shades, hair colors, and eye colors. Yet, her heart ached for both the same.

They were magnificent and mouthwatering.

It took every ounce of her self-control to not openly leer between their legs. She would wait until they were in bed together. If they kept staring at her with hunger in their mesmerizing gaze, that would be sooner than they wanted. But this wasn't about them. It was about the kids and solving the murders. So, when their bodies cracked and morphed, she was happy for the distraction.

A different kind of pressure grew.

Her body blazed with heat. Pain covered every inch of her, but it didn't last long. Soon, she was on all fours, the forest around her, hugging her like a mother's loving touch.

The urge to run was intense.

The need to run was unforgiving.

The wind whistled through the treetops, intriguing her wolf's senses. Her feet hit the forest floor hard and kept going, moving faster and faster to follow the scent. Tate's wolf followed, like feathers thrown at a ball covered in honey. There was no space. *Find, find, find.*

Piper pushed through the desire to let her wolf take total control and searched for signs. But, what would be considered a sign? She watched the shadows and plants, but nothing seemed abnormal.

The wind picked up, and she focused on the gust of air... The wind was invisible, dammit, how was she supposed to be led by something she couldn't see? The scent of candy and feathers grew stronger.

Left.

She didn't know if someone said that or if she did. All three of them turned at the same time. The scent grew even stronger. Hope spiked in her chest.

The green bush raddled around her, egging her on. She pushed against the wind, leaves, and dirt flying in her face. Nothing else mattered; the odor was getting close. *The kids...*

She ran faster until she was in the lead. Tate nipped at her ankles, but she kept moving. Storm made a barking sound on the other side of her, but she was too focused and in the zone to pay them any mind. *Stupid guys, don't they feel and smell the kids nearby?*

Yellow moss gleamed in front of her. Her paws felt like

they were floating over the ground she was moving so fast. Every fiber of her fur tingled.

Her mind was examining her new sensations and noticed the change in the air. Or the thin wire, she just broke. Sharp dark stakes rose from the ground with a snap.

She yelped, turned her body, and fell to her belly. Tate was there, gripping the nape of her neck to pull her away. Her tongue hung out as she panted, and her heart palpitations twisted in her chest. Somehow, she managed to go under the long spikes.

"It's okay, beautiful, we got you," Storm said in his naked human form. Tate gripped her and pulled her away. She ground her teeth and pushed through the pain.

When she was far enough away from the stakes, her body shifted back, and she heard the cracking of bones telling her Tate was doing the same.

Big arms and warmth wrapped around her. "It's okay, love, we got you," Tate whispered.

Piper shook in their arms. A cold chill sunk into her bones. Her skin was sensitive. The cold wind made her chilliness worse.

"What happened?" She glanced at the row of sharp, pointy sticks directed at her.

Tate rubbed the back of his neck. "The demon set a trap. If you hadn't gotten in front of me, I probably would have died. I'm a lot bigger than you. I wouldn't have been able to fit under those," Tate said and pointed at the stakes. He rubbed her arms to soothe her shivers.

"We can shift and go back. If there are traps out here, we need to inform the others." Storm's body pressed against her back. The skin-on-skin contact kept her sane.

Piper nodded. "We need to scout this area. There's a reason he set a trap here, maybe we're getting close."

"True, but we need more people and better light to survive these traps," Tate said, his green eyes lined in worry.

She grabbed his hand. "I'm okay. Let's get back up."

They got up and changed back into their wolves. She didn't even blink at the nakedness this time. Well, not as much. Her pink cheeks and fluttering stomach still were there.

They were getting close to finding the kids. They'd rest for the night. In the morning, she was saving those kids even if it was the last thing she did.

Chapter Thirty-Five

By the time Piper got back into the hotel room, it was dark, and she was ready for bed—ready for the day to be over. The parking lot was empty, so they had the hotel to themselves. Not even the front desk clerk was there.

She hung out with Nina for a while as Tate and Rockie questioned a few more people. Piper got to watch the recording, but nothing pointed them in the right direction.

After losing another game of rock-paper-scissors, Rockie and Storm went to get food and supplies. She was starving. She also needed deodorant, a toothbrush kit, and a hairbrush. Bad.

"Ugh, I feel like a failure, Tate. I didn't see any signs," Piper sighed out her words, flopping on the bed and hugging a pillow. "My dad never took this long to solve a case. He was so good."

Tate sat on the bed and rubbed her back. "Pipes, don't do that to yourself. We're getting close to finding the kids.

The demon put up traps to stop us. He probably has them in a cave. Caves have a natural temperature and heating source. So, that's the best place to hide."

She ran a hand through her hair and pulled. "But how did we find a scent and the others didn't?"

Tate hesitated before answering, "I think the scent was planted, but I watched the elements fight against you as you ran ahead. I think you will find them tomorrow."

It's standard protocol to work nonstop for the first 24 hours after a child abduction because that's the typical lifespan of kidnapped kids. Hopefully, the fact that he was a demon and inside an adult preferential rapist's body, the time frame didn't matter.

Piper closed her eyes. Tate's touch reassured the wave of emotions slamming into her. "I hope you're right, and I hope the 24-hour thing isn't relevant here. It's with a demon, so he might want them for something else."

The pressure of finding the kids made it hard to breathe. So many worries raced through her mind. She feared for the kids' lives. What if she couldn't find them? She feared what the demon might do. Even thoughts of her sister's violent death kept drifting in her mind, panic threatening to overtake her. If the guys weren't there for her, she'd have broken down by now.

He wrapped his arms around her. "Me too, Love."

Tate moved on the bed to get closer to her, grabbing her hands. "Can I give you a massage?" Worry and guilt were written in his eyes. She shook her head and squeezed his hand.

She appreciated the offer, but she didn't want to be touched right now. Her skin was too sensitive. She just wanted to focus on the case to get her mind off everything.

She wished she had her cell phone so she could call Nina. She needed her friend's time... Wait—the phone.

Piper ran to the side of the bed. She opened the drawer and grabbed the silver phone, still in the evidence bag next to a bible. They must've forgotten about the victim's phone.

Her whole body relaxed as the screen turned on. "It works. There has to be something on here."

Tate joined her and scanned the evidence through the bag, so they didn't damage the evidence. They weren't taking any chances. If the murderer got away—after they caught him, of course—because they contaminated the evidence, she'd kill herself.

Tate had to help her switch the phone to English and read the stuff that wouldn't change. So, she was glad he was there. She scrolled through her photos, and when the pictures changed to the victim in a city and lingerie, she stopped. Especially with Tate watching.

She checked the search history. But that was about makeup, sex, and how to kill bugs while camping. Nothing. She did, however, figure out that lavender candles and mint spray kept spiders away. She needed to remember that shit. *I hate spiders.*

Text messages were next. There were four numbers with texts: Mom, Best Bitch, Work, and Good Dick. She checked the contacts. There were only five phone numbers... and one was her brother, who was murdered alongside her. *Well, shitballs. We only have four phone numbers. What are the chances one of these phone numbers will help?*

Piper groaned. "Well, that isn't helpful. Why couldn't it just have their actual names?"

Mom had nothing but worried texts and demanded she come home. Best Bitch spoke about her new guy and going to a club when they got back into town. Work fired her when she didn't show up this morning. *Rude.* Good Dick said he couldn't wait to see her and sent her a phone number on the day of the murder. Nothing else after from him.

Piper put the phone back on the table by the bed. "Dammit, not even Good Dick could fix this."

Storm snickered as he walked into the hotel room, the bagged food in his hands. "Then, it's not doing it right. Don't worry, I'll show you. Good dick can fix anything." He wiggled his eyebrows at her.

She guffawed but smirked. "I bet you practiced that line in the mirror."

The other guys snickered. Storm didn't seem fazed. "The only person I gaze at for a long time is you, beautiful." He dropped the bags on the table and kissed her on her head.

Piper changed the subject. The blush heating her face was telling enough. "The phone is charged, but nothing points to anyone."

Rockie smirked as he sat down at the table, pulling food out of the bag. "Were you expecting a collage of photos with the title *he's the killer*?"

Piper snickered. "No, but I was hoping for something." Her face heated in embarrassment. This better not be a dead end. Her heart couldn't take it—she needed to find the fucker.

"Try calling the numbers. Maybe we can get somewhere with that?" Rockie suggested, putting his hand on her shoulder for support.

She glanced at his hand. The feeling of his warmth on her felt right. Yet, out of all her men, he was the most confusing. Did he even want her? At least he didn't have the phone in his hands.

She shook off those feelings—it was time to focus on the case.

They called every number. But none gave them anything. Her mother cried for twenty minutes but knew nothing. Best Bitch was also one of the victims, and her family called but knew nothing. All they knew was that they went on a camping trip with their friends.

Good Dick's phone was disconnected. The other number was a dead end as well. His mother answered and informed us that he had been in the hospital all week, thousands of miles away. Tate checked and she told the truth.

The soft blanket crumpled under her fingers. She tightened her grip on the phone as well. She growled and chuckled the damn thing at the wall. Before it could smash into exquisite little pieces, Storm caught the silver monstrosity. She narrowed her eyes at him.

He gave her a small smile. "Sorry, beautiful, we need to return this. We're already going to get chewed out because it wasn't back today." He placed the item near Rockie on the table.

"They'll have to deal with it. I'll return it early in the morning. I'm going to have my friend scan the phone just in case. Thankfully, he can do it remotely," Tate said, his eyes narrowing, as if begging for someone to challenge his decision. He was on edge. He wanted answers as well. They all did.

Storm was the only one with a reassuring smile. That was his omega nature shining through. She hoped he wasn't holding everything in again. Their connection blossomed through heartache and tears, and her shoulders were always there for him to cry on. Was it weird she liked when a man trusted her enough to cry? Oh, well.

"Okay. How about we relax, and watch a movie together? Our wolves are on edge and we're no good if the wolves fight against us," Storm said and climbed on the bed. "You can use my stomach as a pillow, Pipes." He patted himself.

Her wolf's anger and agitation disappeared. Goodness, she needed a good cuddle, her body vibrated with anticipation. That's what her wolf needed, but her mind wouldn't let her relax. "What about the kids? Or the next victim? I can't just relax when they're out there." She rubbed at her face and let her fingers travel through her hair. *How did my father and sister do this kind of work, I feel like I'm going to explode?*

Rockie knelt in front of her. His strong hands were on her knees. "Don't feel guilty for enjoying your life. That's how you survive in a world like this, my warrior. You've been through a lot lately. Sometimes it's okay to let go of your worries."

She bit her lip, tears threatening to fall down her face. Tate crowded her space.

He's right. I'm tired. With the attack and losing my friend, the change, the mating, the poor kids, the demon being connected to my sister's death, the demon's magical traps, and the dead victims haunting me, I'm close to insanity. I feel like I'm getting pulled in different directions and I'm about to be ripped in half. Not even my wolf senses can help here.

Her wolf sighed. She pushed calming energy in her, but Piper barely felt it. *We need to rest our mind. Let our mates help with holding the burden. It's not all on us.*

Strong hands from all sides massaged her body. Her eyes stayed shut but her body slowly relaxed with each circle and grip from them. Finally, she took a deep breath and let herself drift off to sleep.

A deep voice whispered in her ear, "It's okay, love. Let go, we got you."

She wasn't sure who said that, but her body floated on a cloud, so she didn't care. Her headache that she didn't even know she had lifted. Her wolf settled in like a dog on its favorite bed.

The darkness pulled her away as sleep overtook her body. They were right. She would get rest and find her mark tomorrow with a clear head.

Chapter Thirty-Six

The heat surrounded her like a cocoon. The sweat covering her back didn't help cool her. Her arms stretched but didn't make it very far. Two large bodies clung to both of her arms.

Fear spiked, but Tate's handsome face deep in sleep calmed her. Rockie's disheveled hair made her want to run her fingers through his dark locks. Instead, she used Storm as a pillow, the back of her neck just as hot and sweaty.

She needed a shower.

So, climb over them, stupid.

She rolled her eyes at her wolf. The bratty wolf had a mouth on her. She pulled her arms out of their grips, she swung her leg over Rockie's body.

Shower, then wake them up.

Warm, strong hands rested on her hips. She froze. "This is how I wish to be woken up from now on," Rockie's husky voice had her chest heating. Good lord, how did a sentence make her insides go haywire?

She smiled. "I didn't mean to wake you. I just needed a shower."

He gripped her hips tight, then rubbed his thumb in circles to soothe his intense grip. He might as well have dipped her lower half in water; she flooded her undies. Sexual energy zinged through her. Her skin flushed with desire. The heat way more intense than the warmth that woke her.

Rockie's nostrils flared, and his wolf showed itself. His hungry eyes glowed, and his groan sounded more like a growl. It was one of the sexiest things she had ever heard. She ran her hands over his chest, under his shirt. His warm skin was firm and smooth under her palms.

He lifted off the bed slightly to put his face in the crook of her neck. His lips grazed her as he licked her sensitive skin and sniffed. "You're so beautiful."

As soon as he laid back down, she bent to claim his lips. The pressure in her core built as she glided up and down the impressive bulge in Rockie's pants. *Goddammit, wow.*

Another growl, not from under her, had both of them freezing. She knew that growl and the power level that came with it. Tate...

Piper sucked in a sharp breath. They turned toward the man slowly. This was the first time any of them had gotten this intimate with all of them in the room, and she wasn't sure how he'd react.

His eyes were shining bright, and his body was still as a statue. No one moved, the tension between the two dominants thick in the air.

Piper held her breath. Rockie growled back.

A hand landed on her lower back, rubbing. "Mmm, is

there room for more?" Storm's sleep-filled voice sounded amazing, so wistful and husky at the same time. She released her breath.

She didn't feel the bed move, but he was at her side, slowly peeling her off Rockie. He gripped her hips once, but Tate growled louder, so Rockie let her go.

Storm leaned in, licking her neck. "I love that you were enjoying yourself, beautiful, but there is a hierarchy you must follow. Rockie is dominant, but Tate is superior. By touching you with all of us in the room, he's challenging Tate for his Alpha role in this true pack. They'll fight if we don't make it right."

She gulped, but a thrill went up her spine. "How do we do that?"

He bit her ear. "I know this might be a lot to handle." He put his hand under her chin to gaze into her eyes. "You can say no, and they'll just fight it out. There's no pressure here."

She slightly shook her head. "I don't want them to fight. It was my fault. I didn't know."

Thanks for that.

Hey, I thought you were going to get off him. You've been running away whenever things get interesting like a little pup, how was I to know you'd finally grow some tits?

"Well, then we'll have to finish what you started. I'm going to get you hot and bothered and enjoy every moment. Tate will challenge me, but since I'm not a dominant, he'll merely push me out of the way. Once you have come for him, Rockie will be allowed to make you come as well. Don't worry, this time will be all about you and your pleasure. We're not having a full-on orgy today." He smirked and moved closer. The heat from his body cocooned her as he continued. "Is that okay, beautiful?"

YES! You better say fucking yes!

Shut up!

They need this. We cannot deny them the hierarchy. If you want a chance with all of them, this is how it has to be.

I know, geez.

She licked her lips. The moisture in her pants increased, making the men groan in response.

Storm kissed the crook of her neck. "If this is too much or too fast, just say the word, and we will work our shit out a different way. We don't want to force you into anything." He slowly rotated his hips against her core. A pitiful noise escaped her lips. He smiled. "But I can smell your desire, beautiful, and we'd want nothing more than to quench that desire for you."

She nodded, but when he kept staring at her, she used her words. "Yes," her voice came out in a husky whisper.

He kissed her lips gently. His kisses traveled down her body. "Are you sure, beautiful? You have full control here. Say the word, and this ends," Storm said as he rubbed his cheeks across her stomach.

Good lord, how did something so simple feel so electric? She couldn't speak again. The heat in her core was up to her throat now, choking her with need. Picturing their hands and mouths on her gave her chills. Were lady boners a thing? Because if so, she had one.

This time, he accepted her nod and traveled lower. The anticipation and other males' intense stares almost had her coming then. This was the craziest thing she had ever done sexually, but holy monkey balls, this was good, and nothing had happened yet.

Storm pulled off her pajama pants, leaving her in her undies. He snapped the string of her gray thong, kissed her inner thighs, and yanked her undies down.

On instinct, she closed her legs. Storm's firm, rough hands gripped her thighs. "No beautiful, no hiding from us. Never from us." He slowly opened her legs, not forcing her, just encouraging them with kisses and massages on her thighs. As soon as they opened, his gaze grew intense. "You're already soaked for us. So fucking beautiful," Storm said, his breath teasing her wetness.

She squirmed, needing his mouth already. The need was turning into an excruciating ache. She whimpered, and Tate and Rockie moved closer, but they growled and snarled at each other.

Storm had to put their focus back on Piper, so he dove into her heat like he was diving face-first into his last meal. He tongued her hole, using his nose to stimulate her bundle of nerves. "Holy shit fuck, Storm." His laugh was the perfect amount of vibration she needed.

His tongue and face knew exactly what they were doing. Her body tensed and her mouth opened, making a perfect O shape. She lifted her shirt, grabbed Tate's and Rockie's hands, and put them on each of her boobs. But they couldn't look at her. Their staring match was hot, and the fact they didn't ignore her made it even hotter. Both men pinched and rubbed her nipples. *Fuck!*

She growled. "Storm, I'm close." He couldn't be the one to make her come, though.

Tate moved, pushing Storm out of the way. Piper could tell he was using his Alpha powers to push against the others. His animal was in charge. There was no hesitation.

He took control. His warm mouth found her clit in a frenzy. Her whole body lifted off the bed.

Skilled fucking mouths. They all must have taken classes in pleasuring a woman. Holy hell. She moaned louder with each tongue stroke. She tended to be a quiet lover, breathy but quiet.

Movement caught her attention. Storm held Rockie back, promising his turn was coming. Still, he fought, but not at full force. Piper could tell he held back.

Her mind could barely register what was happening. The pleasure climbed up that hill of satisfaction. Her toes curled, her hands gripped Tate's soft hair, and a black rose attached to sparklers bloomed in her vision.

She screamed her release. Her eyes might have crossed, but who the fuck knew. Her shockwaves rippled with each breathy pant.

Storm was at her side, stroking her hair and kissing her sweaty forehead. "That was the sexiest thing I have ever seen. Are you okay to continue?"

Tate was on her other side, running his strong fingers up and down her arm. Even that small touch sent sparks zapping her. Tate brought his lips to her ear. "You tasted like the sweetest wine. I could get drunk off you, my love." He kissed her hard. The taste of herself still clung to his lips and she moaned. Fucking dirty monkey balls, they were going to turn her into a crazy sex addict. There was no way she'd ever get tired of them. "Next time, we won't have to do this. We're stating our place now, so no more fighting over who goes first." He devoured her lips again. "Thank you for letting us pleasure you."

Piper gazed into those sweet green eyes. The hardness

of his face had softened for her. She smiled and linked hands with him. There were no real complaints on her end. It had been a long time since another person had given her an orgasm, and he might have broken her, but she didn't care.

Rockie snarled and broke their connection. Storm purred as he rubbed his face along her bare breast. When the hell did her shirt get ripped open? Oh well. "Rockie needs his turn, beautiful. Are you ready?"

Her confidence rose with all her men staring at her with such hunger and love in their eyes. Her legs were spread wide, and Rockie scanned her opening as if calculating a plan of attack.

"God yes!" she gasped. Her voice was so eager and demanding. All her men smiled such devilish smiles. Her toes curled.

Tate and Storm devoured her nipples, swirling each one with their soft, wet tongues. Her whole body burned in excitement. She wouldn't last very long once Rockie started.

Rockie's growl sounded more like a groan. Then he dove into her cream. His face smeared its way through her folds as if she were the tasty fruit in a melon-eating contest.

Yes, eat it all up, her wolf purred.

The scorching flames of her desire rose again, fast and hard. He was oh so delicious. His mouth took turns devouring her clit, then tonguing her hole. Over and over in the perfect rhythm. She couldn't take his movements anymore, so the men held her legs open.

Her toes curled and her body tensed up. "Holy shit. I'm gonna—"

Tate whispered in her ear. "Yes, come for us, my love."

That's all she needed to have her orgasm explode out of her. Her back arched off the bed, and she gripped Rockie's face between her legs.

Tate's mouth was rough and hot as he stole the screams from her mouth. Storm's mouth was soft and warm, circling her nipples. He kept blowing on her nipple, making it cold. Fire and ice. Rockie's mouth was a whirlwind of goodness, keeping her on her cloud of ecstasy.

Storm came to her ear. "I can't wait for my turn, beautiful. But we've run out of time. I loved every minute of watching you and tasting you." His mouth devoured hers, promising what was to come next time.

She couldn't wait either. These sexy men just blew her mind. She wasn't sure she'd survive the next time. But what a way to go.

Chapter Thirty-Seven

After her much-needed shower, she called Nina to check on her. When all was good with them, she sat and studied the case notes more. There had to be something else.

She didn't know how much time had passed, but when Tate touched her shoulder to get her attention, her eyes were red and hurting. Her brain was fried.

"You look like a coked-out college student studying for a test. Take a break, love," Tate said and ran his finger between her shoulder blades, but her brain was too gone to register his touch.

She rubbed her face. "Well, that's rude."

He smirked. "You know I'm just kidding. But seriously, I know this is stressful, but these ten pages of notes aren't helping you. Get up and move around, get the blood flowing to your brain." He rubbed her shoulders and her annoyance with him vanished. "Rockie's outside working on the car. It needed an oil change and other things. He refuses to take it into a shop. Maybe go talk to him. I'll take over here."

She damn near cried, and she had no reason to. She was just so frustrated with herself. *Ugh, such a horrible feeling.*

She nodded and got to her feet. Her butt was numb from sitting for so long. She rubbed the poor abused muscle.

Tate leaned in, "I could do that for you if you want?" He got closer, "With my tongue even. If you ask nicely enough."

Synapsis sparked and came alive in her brain finally. Her core reaction washed over her body from her toes to her head. Mother nature must have been playing a dirty trick because she wasn't ready, and her brain malfunctioned. She might have turned into a statue for a few seconds as her panties melted off her... Could panties melt?

Ask him to check for us. Her wolf chimed in.

Storm laughed. "Tate, you broke our girl." He came over and kissed her neck. "Go check on Rockie before you pass out. Are you even breathing?"

She smiled and smacked his arm. Tate winked and sat in her chair to go over her notes. She sighed and went outside. Her guilt lessened knowing Tate was still working.

She opened the door to Rockie's sexy ass in the air and his head in the car. His hand worked a tool as he spoke to the car. "Come on, baby girl, work for daddy. Don't be stubborn."

She leaned against the wall and crossed her arms. "I think I'm getting jealous of the car."

Rockie jerked up... Too bad for him he was under a hood. His head smacked into it. "Aah, shit."

She ran to him.

"Dammit, I'm sorry. I thought you knew I was here. I didn't mean to startle you." She rubbed the back of his head.

He frowned down at her. "Well, you did," he said and ran his finger over her nose. His engine oil-covered finger.

Her mouth gaped open, and her eyes went wide. Her face heated. *No, he didn't...*

Her brain sparked to life, and no longer hung somewhere near her ass. She wiped at her nose but the heavy oil scent clinging to her skin told her he did smear it on her face.

In one quick movement, he kissed her cheek and ran away. He laughed and playfully howled. Her wolf-chasing instincts kicked in.

Before she could reach him, she slipped on ice. Her already sore ass smacked the ground. "Shit. Ouch," she said and groaned as the painful shockwaves up her spine eased.

Tate and Storm came out. Their eyes darted everywhere, searching for the danger. When they didn't spot any danger, their eyes drift to her sprawled out on the floor.

The glint in Tate's eyes had her jaw ticking. As if planned, they all burst into laughter but moved closer to help her. Tate was the first to recover. "Are you okay?" he asked between chuckles. He raised his hand in surrender at her glare. "I'm sorry. I shouldn't have laughed."

She growled. "Want to make it up to me? Hold Rockie down, so I can tickle him."

Tate's wicked grin shot to Rockie, and he gulped in response. "Shit," Rockie said and took off.

Tate's eyes lit up. "Storm, get his legs," he ordered. Storm's predatory glint matched Tate's, and he took off behind his Alpha. Their wolves howled as they swiftly moved into the forest.

She wanted in on the action, so she got up and followed. Her wolf connected with her human form, making it easier for her to maneuver between the trees. She wasn't slipping this time.

Her legs pumped faster than they ever had in this form. The chilly air didn't fight against her but helped her. She pushed past the scent of the forest and zeroed in on their manly aroma. Within seconds, she caught up.

Tate and Storm were close to Rockie, but he kept changing his direction to throw them off. She pulled more of her wolf out. Determination fueled her revenge. She was nearly on top of Storm, so she moved to the left... just as Rockie moved... to the left.

Yes! He's ours.

Storm wasn't fast enough to grab him, but she could. When he sensed her about to pounce on him, he moved back the other way, right into Tate and Storm. Storm slammed into his legs while Tate pushed his upper body to the ground.

"Got him, Pipes, attack!" Tate yelled as he held Rockie's arms. Storm laid on his legs as he kicked to get him off.

She jumped on top of him. He squirmed but her hand came up slowly, exaggerating every move. Her fingers explored his sides, armpits, and knees, searching for his spot. When she did find it, she attacked without mercy.

Rockie bucked and laughed but was no match for all

three of them. "Aah, I give up! Piper, I'm sorry," he said through fits of laughter.

She finally relented and let her wolf go, then him. They all laid on the cold ground, lightly panting. Storm's eyes met hers. Like magnets, their lips clashed.

She kissed Tate next, loving the sensation of his Alpha pride buzzing through the air. She hesitated before kissing Rockie. "Hey, I said I was sorry. Want me to take off my shirt to clean your nose?"

She chuckled. The smile on her face lightened her soul. These men were slowly becoming hers. Soon, she'd be too attached to ever let them go, and that was the scariest feeling of all.

After everyone relaxed and settled down, they got up and walked back to the room. Tate had a hand on her hip while the others held one of her hands.

All four were connected. They slowly were becoming exactly what the other needed. A family. A pack.

Piper waited on the hotel bed about forty-five minutes later. Tate and Storm had gone to get everyone food. Her leg bounced and her stomach growled. Where were they?

Rockie was bent over, studying the case notes and crime scene photos, mumbling to himself. Every time he glanced her way, she blushed like a lobster. He'd just smirk and go back to his work. The chip on his shoulder was well deserved. They all blew her mind in bed and captured her heart outside.

Her constant stomach flutters were annoying, but she could get used to it. Their relationship was no longer just their wolves pulling for them to mate. Her heart was getting involved.

Fear, guilt, and excitement crashed around inside of her. She feared getting too close because she wouldn't survive if she lost them. She held so much guilt at enjoying her life while two kids were out there scared, that the excitement of her new relationship tasted sour in her mouth.

She dropped her gaze as guilt curled her hungry stomach. The morning's escapades were life-changing, but she kept thinking about the kids and the victims. Was it fair that she enjoyed herself while they couldn't?

We can't stop living because we're helping people.

I know but...

No buts unless it's one of our mates' butts. We can't change the past, but we can make a difference in the future. Yet, how great will the future be if we don't enjoy the present?

Wow, what self-help book are you quoting?

Her wolf chuckled. *None but it would totally be an awesome book. I'll call it sex and murders.*

Piper snorted. *I'm not sure that screams self-help.*

Tate walked through the door. The sun shining around him like a food-delivering angel. The steamy yummy of goodness stopped her conversation and might have made her drool. She wiped her mouth just in case.

Storm came in after him, snorting at her reaction to the food. She was so glad the Chinese place here opened early. Some people did breakfast for dinner, well, she did dinner for breakfast. The guys didn't complain either.

Tate gave her a bright smile that made her blush. "Hungry, love?" she nodded. He leaned forward to capture her lips and put her food on the table next to her. "They didn't have Pepsi, but they had that corn chicken soup you wanted."

Next, he moved to Rockie, who, like Tate, had a huge bag. He might have drooled too, but she didn't focus on him long enough to see. She grabbed her spoon and dove into her food like a starved maniac.

Her wolf snuggled into her. All she needed was her drink. She had no idea what Tate got but it wasn't Pepsi, so she didn't want it. Screw it. She'd go get one herself. Maybe they had one outside? She untangled her legs and stood.

"I'm going to get a drink from the vending machine," she told them over her shoulder with her hand already on the knob.

She needed a break, anyway. Reading the case notes put her in a horrible mood. All the death and pain the demon caused. She needed to step away from it all for a moment.

"I'll go," Storm said, his hand gently grabbing her wrist.

She turned. "I've got this. It's right outside. Okay?" Storm nodded and pressed a kiss to her cheek.

As soon as the chilly air kissed her skin, and the beautiful pinks and yellows of the sun came into view, she felt better. She took a deep breath of air. Freedom.

Snow scattered the ground. The weather channel said that in two weeks the area would be covered in snow. But right now, the white beauty just speckled the ground, marking its territory.

Even though she didn't feel trapped with her men, occasionally, she'd have to be alone. There was only so much she could take.

She turned towards the forest behind the vending machine on the side of the hotel, careful to not fall. Their car parked in front of the door still had warmth coming off the engine. She pulled her navy sweater closer to her body as a chill overtook her.

The words Brus Drikke in big, bold letters shined on the machine. She assumed that meant drink or soda. She recognized the different colors of the sodas, but the names were different. She had no idea what kokosnottvann in Norwegian was, though.

Her phone with the translation app on it was left in the room. So, after putting money into the machine, she picked the drink with the darkest color and pressed the button. Fingers crossed.

Chirping laughter sounded behind her. Adrenaline spiked in her veins. She spun around, but no one was there. Soft fur rubbed on her ankles, almost giving her a heart attack.

She might have squeaked, but she wasn't going to admit it. Nobody was around to catch her, which meant it didn't happen. No judging, it's true.

The wolf in her grumbled in irritation. *I don't like foxes,* she complained. The white and silver foxes that sat at her feet were adorable. They almost blended in the snow. "Aww."

What are they doing here? Their kind don't usually live

around here. They must be evil, kick them, the wolf said and growled.

No. Bad wolf. Sit.

I'm not a dog.

She ignored her wolf and knelt. "Don't listen to the cranky wolf inside me. You two are the cutest things." They continued the fast-cooing noises that sounded like laughter as they showed her their tummies and rubbed their backs on the dirt.

She ran their fluffy fur through her fingers. The huge smiles on their faces and gekkering noises were kind of creepy, but they were too cute.

No, ew. Don't touch them.

Hush. That earned her a huff.

"You guys really are so cute." Her fingers brushed through their soft fur. The feel of the silkiness put a smile on her face.

"Hey, sugar. Definitely not a sight you see every day, huh?" A familiar woman's voice startled Piper. She shot up from her crouching position.

Her wolf shined through her eyes. The faint yellow glow on the witch's face told her so. "What the hell are you doing here?"

"Hey." She put her hands up. "I'm sorry, I didn't mean to startle you. I was on a walk with Minx and Trix. They took off, and I followed them here."

Piper narrowed her eyes but didn't say anything.

Carmel tugged at her dark shirt. "I really am sorry. I never expected them to get anywhere near a wolf. Wolves usually scare them. I didn't even recognize you until I got closer."

Carmel sighed and pulled at the edges of her hair

before she continued. "But I'm glad I ran into you. I had a vision. It wasn't clear, but the meaning was. Something bad is going to happen." She tugged on her sleeves. "I have no idea what, but the feeling of dread won't leave me."

Carmel did seem disheveled. The bags under her eyes, the dirty, wrinkled clothes, and pale skin weren't a good sign. Piper bit her lip, letting her mind work. "Maybe you should take a vacation? Travel somewhere nice."

Carmel snorted. "I wish, sugar. But the vision may not even be about me. It could be about you or the case. All I saw was the case files, brown hair, tears, and I heard screams. It's mostly the feeling of doom that worries me."

Piper's hands twitched as her adrenaline left her. "Well, thanks for letting me know," her tone was soft. She knew her vision had some merit, but whatever she did wasn't going to help. Not unless she got in the car with her mates and zoomed far away.

Carmel gave her a sharp nod. Her eyes darting to the ground. "Welcome. So, will you let my pets up?"

Piper glanced towards the ground. The foxes were laying on their backs, showing their stomachs still. Their wiggles were the cutest thing. Piper shrugged. "I'm not holding them."

The witch rolled her eyes and popped her hip to the side. "They're submitting to you, so you need to let them know it's okay to get up."

Her wolf mentally nodded her head. *She's right. Make a clicking sound. That'll let them know they can move without getting hurt.*

When were you going to tell me that?

Her wolf did the equivalent of a shrug. The mental gestures of her wolf were a weird feeling. Piper clicked her tongue. The foxes danced around her feet before going to the witch.

They twirled around her feet and darted back into the forest. The witch gave Piper a nod and a smile before she left with the foxes.

Fucking foxes ruin everything, her wolf said. She bet if her wolf was out right now, she'd turn around and show the foxes her butthole like a damn cat. Her fluffy tail up in the air and all.

The wolf gasped in horror. *Take that back.*

Piper chuckled, grabbed her blue soda can that thankfully had Pepsi in it, and walked back to the room. That was weird.

She opened the door and had to slam her hands over her ears. Tate's obnoxious horn ringtone might as well be a dog whistle. The sound went deep into her ear drums, shaking shit around. Tate gave her an apologetic glance and answered the phone.

But the pain was worth it. Tate hung up with a smile. "They found more witnesses. Several campers that were nearby. Let's go; they're down at the station," Tate demanded. They were ready. Ready for the day and ready to kick this case's ass.

Chapter Thirty-Eight

T he road zoomed by quickly as they drove. Piper still didn't understand what signs to search for. But she kept her eyes wandering, just in case.

We can do this. Stop doubting yourself.

Why can't it be a literal sign and say something like, "Hey, bitch, this way?" Or even an arrow pointing in the right direction.

Because the world and magic are not that easy. We just need to learn how to find the answers. The signs will come, just don't second guess yourself.

Tate parked, and they all filed into the police station, ready to find answers. These men were connected to the case somehow, and she was eager to find out how.

Rockie was the first to speak. "Okay, let's split up. Piper and I will speak with Richard and you two with Harold. Then, we'll switch if there are any suspicions."

He grabbed Piper's hand and gently guided her away from the others to a pale off-white door. Tate wasn't happy. His face had angry lines and strain all over it. Storm playfully grabbed his hand. "It's okay. I'll hold your hand, boss."

Tate laughed and pushed him away. Storm had such a difficult job, keeping all the dominant wolves from lashing out at each other, and she was extremely thankful.

The interrogation room was exactly like all the television shows. Bare tan walls, a big one-way mirror, and a dark brown table with black chairs squished into a tiny room.

"Hello, Richard. My name is Rockie, and my associate here is Piper. We're here to ask you a few questions," Rockie said, his hand guiding her to the seat next to his. She placed the case files on the deceased and the missing kids, to be prepared if they needed them. She ran her hands over the edge of the folders.

The dark-haired male with a square jaw and dark eyes stood, knocking his chair over. His fingers drummed against the table impatiently. "I didn't do anything!" the man yelled. His beady brown eyes were wide. They darted around as if he expected someone else to pop out of nowhere.

Piper put her hands out to show she meant no harm. "That's fine. We aren't accusing you of anything. We simply want to know what happened on November twenty-first. Can you please recap your night?" Piper asked, her voice seeming to calm him slightly. His eyes stopped moving, and he focused on her.

He sat and continued drumming his fingers along the table. "Okay, okay. I went camping that day, ya see. I love to camp but don't get to go very often. I'm a security guard down at the warehouse. Two-Step, but myself and one other work there, so it's lots of work. They are—"

Rockie had a small notepad that he kept writing in. He stopped and glanced up. "Richard, I'm sure the job is great, but we need to focus on that night. What happened? What did you see or hear?" Rockie redirected the information coming out of his mouth.

Richard's jaw tightened. "Sorry. I was making beans for dinner when I heard screams. The... almost an explosion or fire moving." He grabbed his head in frustration. "I know that sounds weird, but it's what I heard. I checked on the noise, but the sound of people crying out had me cowering like a little bitch. I took off." Richard's hands shook, and his leg bounced in sharp, fast movements.

Her training went into hyperdrive. Her eyes became a weapon as she scanned everything about the guy. His forehead vein pulsed in irritation, his upper lip grew wet with sweat, and his thumbs were bouncing off each other. Perfect. He unintentionally gave her what she needed. His tell.

Piper narrowed her eyes. "Did you hear anything else?" There was something off with him, but it could be just the stress of being around death.

He turned away and bit his lip. "I don't know. Those sounds freaked me out. So, I tried to ignore them." Thumb, thumb hit again.

Piper's gaze drifted to her folder again. "Were you able to eat dinner?"

Richard was caught off guard by her question. His mouth opened and his eyes dropped to his fingers. "No. The sounds came before it was ready." No thumbs.

"So, you took off and left everything behind?" She inquired. Her gaze drifted to his hands as he spoke. She made sure he didn't catch her by picking up the folder.

That way she appeared to be focused on her paperwork, not his movements.

"Yeah." Thumb, thumb hit again. "I hopped in my truck and called 911." No thumb.

Piper smiled to reassure him. He wasn't telling the whole truth, dammit. Everyone had certain *tells,* when they were lying or being deceitful. His thumbs didn't move when he was telling the truth. She needed more from him. "I get it, don't worry. What I need from you is to close your eyes."

His legs bounced faster. "Why?"

Piper shrugged. "Please just do it. Take a deep breath." When he did, she continued. "Focus on the smells around you. Only smells. How do the beans smell?" Piper asked, her voice low and soothing.

He sniffed the air. "Like Worcestershire sauce. I love putting that in my beans. It gives it good flavor, ye see."

She toyed with the folders in front of her again. "Good, what else? Just focus on the smells around you."

Richard's thumbs swirled around each other but didn't touch. "Dirt and beer. I had a few to relax... And nothing, never mind."

She squeezed the edge of the file, intrigued. "No, go on."

He sighed. "Sulphur? I think. Or maybe it was just burning coals."

She nodded, even though he couldn't see her. His eyes remained closed. "Okay, expand to sight. What do you see?"

His eyes moved around under his lids. "My camp and the fire with the beans cooking. The bag where I put the bottles in. Dirt was all around me, and trees, but further away. I stared at the stars too."

Piper was probably jumping the gun, but she had to get him while his guard was down. "When did you hurt your hand?"

Richard's face paled, and he leaned back in his chair, opening his eyes. "I-I did that at work." Thumb, thumb tap again. "It wasn't there. Anyways, that's all I got. Can I go? Or do I need a lawyer?"

Rockie and Piper glanced at each other. Dude was lying, but they couldn't hold him. They would have to find out through his work and approach him then.

"Yes, thank you for your time. Please stay in town," Rockie said and walked him out. She walked to Tate and Storm, who were eating in the back room.

Her wolf sensed where they were.

"How'd it go?" Tate asked. There was no worry or anger on his face. Piper sighed in relief.

She sat down next to him. "Richard was lying. I noticed his right hand was hurt and when I asked, he was spooked and said he hurt it at work. But his heart sped up and his sweat glands were hyperactive. If he didn't demand to leave, he would have been soaked in seconds. He also seemed to tap his thumbs together every time he lied. He wasn't telling us the whole truth."

"You think it's him?" Storm asked, putting down his donut.

"I don't know. Something was off about him, though." She walked away as Rockie came back to grab a donut of his own, his phone surgically attached to his hand.

Ooo, sugar donut! Her wolf practically jumped out of her skin. Her body jerked forward.

Fine, calm down.

Don't be mad. We got something. Just follow this through. I have a feeling it'll work out.

She grabbed a coffee and sat to eat. She needed to keep up her energy. She sat at an empty table to focus and write everything down.

The men quickly joined her, squeezing close. The space she thought she wanted wasn't what she needed; her men were. The moment their bodies pressed close to hers, her mind settled, and her thoughts moved more smoothly.

They had a place to start. That was more than what they had earlier.

Chapter Thirty-Nine

Piper was jittery and eager to get answers. The car ride was silent, everyone's minds working overtime. Rockie broke the silence first. "All right, the Two Steps building is open for another couple of hours. But he isn't on duty today." His arms brushed hers as the car jostled them around. Small towns equal tons of potholes.

"That's okay, we don't need him to be—" Tate stopped talking at the angrily vibrating phone on his dashboard. He picked it up, "Hello, this is—" Again, he didn't finish his sentence, probably getting cut off. He grunted and gave a couple of "Got it," answers, and hung up.

Tate sighed. His jaw ticked and glanced at her in the rearview mirror. "That was the Sheriff. There was a body found. He said it looks like it's connected to our case." He flipped the car around, then continued. "He sent the address to my number. Storm, can you—"

"On it." He grabbed the phone, and within seconds, he was guiding Tate.

"What about Richard?" Piper asked. She didn't trust him and knew he was hiding something. But ugh, she didn't even understand why.

Tate shook his head and gripped the steering wheel tighter. "If we had a second car, I'd say let's split up. But we have no idea what we're dealing with here. We have no idea of his power level, so, for now, we'll have a look at the body. Then we'll get Richard. If he's behind this, the fucker's going down."

Rockie and Storm grunted their approval. "Yeah, this could be his retaliation for getting the wrong guy like you said, little warrior. We gotta take a look," Rockie said, his face in the fucking phone. If it wasn't for his cute nickname, she'd had snapped the thing in half right now.

He glanced her way and apparently her annoyance showed on her face. "It's the pack. Since I'm fourth in line, Tate is on a case, and the pack has issues with Jinks because he likes to make the subs do his laundry and other menial shit, they contact me. Most of it is stupid questions, but if there are real issues, I need to be available for them. I promise I'm not ignoring you." He grabbed her hand and squeezed.

She smiled. "What are you dealing with now?" she asked as Tate's phone rang again.

Rockie groaned and leaned to whisper to Piper. "A pipe busted in the kitchen. They lost a lot of food. But they cleaned everything up and there wasn't a whole lot of damage. So, I'm arranging for Marcus, Storm's cousin, to order new stuff. It's a lot of telephoning for them, but it's not too difficult. Just wish Jinks would get his shit together."

Tate covered the speaker on his phone. "I'll have a talk

with him when this is over. Thank you, Rockie," he said and continued on the phone. Then he hung up and addressed everyone in the car. "The Sheriff just said he's holding everyone off, so we can get the first look at the body. Just in case it's one of his people, and they tamper with evidence."

"I doubt it," Piper whispered to herself. Werewolf hearing, though.

"What do you mean? Scumbags like this love uniforms. Anything to feel powerful," Storm said, turning around in his seat. Rockie bumped her shoulder with his after a few seconds of silence.

She rubbed her hands over her jeans. "Nothing, it's just, this is too small a place for someone like the Sheriff. He would see a big difference in his officers. But who knows? All I know is having a demon inside me for too long, even with a deal exchange, would be hard to cover up for long." She shrugged. "It's better to be safe than sorry, though."

They all nodded their heads in agreement. The air in the car darkened with their moods. This was one part she hated about this line of work—dead bodies.

The GPS stopped by a store with the windows boarded up. Several cop cars were parked around the entrance of the alley next to the empty store. Newspapers were stuck on the walls and a few windows.

The map said they were at the place, and the police cars confirmed it. They got out, and the difference in the air out there sucked. The sickly decaying scent in the air was too thick around her. And something vaguely familiar. She'd take the anger and worried static-filled air back in the car anytime.

"I'm sorry, but this area is closed off," an officer said when they approached.

The Sheriff walked up then. "That's all right, Trent, these are the guests of honor." His tone was that of a defeated man. The urge to wrap him in a bear hug was strong. Poor guy.

Bending under the yellow caution tape brought flashbacks of her and her dad going to crime scenes. His husky voice and cigarette smoke scent filled her senses. The thought comforted her, and she needed it.

The cold, eerie alley got worse as they walked in deeper. The heaviness in the air threatened to suffocate her. *Who in their right mind would come down here?* Her warning sensors were going haywire.

The Sheriff walked with them as he spoke. "Since you're here, three other officers will join you. The forensic team got here about five minutes ago, but only the photographer was let through. I'll stay here to help keep everyone back, especially my men. They're not happy about being on the sidelines."

"I'll help," said Rockie. He gave her a nod and turned around.

There was nothing down the alley except a big garbage can and dirty crates. She ignored the rats moving around. Her nerves could not handle them at the moment. *Nasty fuckers.*

The pee and mold filling the air distracted her perfectly. A combination that she never wanted to smell. She rubbed at her nose.

The air was heavy and almost oily. It clung to her flesh. It was suffocating. Evil. That was the only word that came to mind. Goosebumps rippled across her skin in a warning, confirming her thoughts. Her steps faltered. Her hands shook with fear.

She tightened her fists and pushed through. Nothing was going to happen; she had her men with her. That eased the tension that held her brain hostage. She could think again.

Her brow pinched together. There was no way someone would go down the alley unless forced to. Either by a job or by brute strength.

She cursed under her breath as a woman's ashen gray, lifeless body came into view. Wasn't it a woman's number one rule to not go down dark, creepy alleys? What was she thinking?

Her mousy brown hair was scattered everywhere. The killer had ripped it out. Probably in some attempt to control her. But the amount indicated he wanted to cause her pain as well. Why would he do that, though?

Anger? *At us or her?* His M.O. was genital mutilation. He hated the women because of their gender. This didn't match.

She scanned the area for a weapon nearby. Nothing shined like a blade or scissors. So, her attention went back to the female.

The body laid there crumpled up like someone's garbage—a gray blanket covering her face from the others on the street. Her black pants were torn, but not in the crotch. Her gray long-sleeved shirt was destroyed with blood and stab wounds. The slash and stab wounds were everywhere.

The killer knew the woman... Her heart rate spiked. A sharp unexpected stabbing sensation hit her through the haze. The sympathetic pain that she got when near a dead body. It had been so long; she had forgotten about it.

Hate like this wasn't meant for a stranger.

The scent made it difficult to speak, but she covered her nose and pushed through. The guy must be a local. She'd bet the girl was too. The brutality here was personal.

The note on her stomach just said, *Too bad, so sad.* In the same handwriting. The same personality shined through. Except for the heaviness of the writing. That was anger. So, this kill was for them too, dammit.

Piper cleared her throat and spoke. "This seems different from the other cases. He didn't annihilate the genitals for one but decided to torture her instead. He was angry, not because she was a woman like the others, but because he knew her. And maybe, a little because of us. Regardless, from what I see from his behavior, he doesn't have a spouse or any responsibilities like kids. The kills are not organized or thought out. They're impulsive, like an experienced bachelor trying to find a woman." She grabbed the rubber gloves one of the officers handed her as she told them about her theories with the note.

She moved the note from her breast area and put it in an evidence bag, while Tate scanned the lower part of the body. Not a lot of marks were by her breast either.

"Her shoes are expensive. He didn't even take her wallet. It's still in her pocket. So, she wasn't a random homeless person, and I'll bet she wasn't a tourist either. Most tourists come here to hike and explore the forest. I agree with your analysis, Pipes," Tate added.

Another officer next to the nearest cart kicked garbage out of the way to search behind the crates. Storm growled and stomped toward him. His voice was low, warning him to not compromise the scene. Who knew what evidence he could be kicking?

The forensic photographer took pictures of the deceased's head. The snaps of her camera made Piper's eye twitch. They were fast and almost aggressive, like a paparazzi.

Tate waited a few minutes before distracting the forensic lady. "Can you show me the face please?"

"Yes, I've taken enough pictures." She shook her head, and her face fell. "All of your theories seem to be accurate, from what I can tell anyway. Miss Carmel should have known better. You think a witch would have more common sense."

Piper's body tensed up like a board. *What? The witch?* Panic sensors flared to life inside her, clouting the synapses in her brain. That was the familiar scent. Oh no. She glanced Rockie's way.

Rockie gasped at the name, his nostrils flared, and the others went stiff. *Oh goodness, this better not be who I think it is.* As the blanket lifted, the air chilled around her. The pale, lifeless features of the once beautiful witch stared back.

The woman knelt to the body. "There was no rape, but the death was slow. The killer knew how to cause extreme pain and keep her alive. The approximate time for death is about four hours."

Her stomach threatened to relieve itself all over the ground. She took a few breaths through her mouth, trying not to breathe through her nose. The smell seemed to intensify. The killer knew she helped them.

"This was payback," she said.

Tate nodded, agreeing with her. He took her hand in his, giving her comfort, squeezed, and let go.

"Not just that. Spells don't work after the witch is dead. So, we have a few hours and that spell you have is useless." He ran his hand through his hair. "The rest of the pack isn't here yet, but we might have to do without them."

After a few more clicks of her camera, the woman spoke up again. "I agree as well."

Piper glanced her way. "Anything different with this body? Except for the multiple stab wounds?"

She nodded. "The victim had her eyes forcefully shut postmortem."

Piper's mind moved faster than she could keep up. *What does this mean? How does this change things? Who's the killer? Was that the human or the demon side? Why would they do that? They'd never done this before.*

Time seemed to slow as she thought, and let her schooling take over. She rocked her head from side to side, thinking about it. "The way he closed her eyes shows his insecurities. I once sat in an eight-hour-long class that studied the reason psychopaths close their victims' eyes. It takes a lot of thought to pull themselves out of their killing high to fiddle with the body. Well, unless it becomes a ritual. But the other bodies didn't have it, so I'm inclined to believe that's not the case."

"Do you think it's remorse then?" Storm asked as he stepped closer to her—his warmth giving her comfort to keep going.

She bit her lip and shook her head. "No, he was too brutal with the killing to have remorse, too angry. He didn't want her to see him. And the blitz attack means he doesn't have the skills or attractiveness to get his victims any other way. He lacks the smoothness that puts people at ease, which is why he's angry." She paused, tapping her thumb to her lips. "Yeah, this is a jab to us, but in the processes it became personal. I bet she didn't find him attractive, so he got offended."

Storm slid his fingers across her lower back. "Damn, beautiful, you're even sexier as a badass investigator," he whispered in her ear. The sickly turn of her stomach and heart disappeared.

The wink he gave her spoke of his intention. He knew she was about to jump off the ledge into the deep end of depression. And her old friend would have gladly welcomed her back. Since starting this new adventure as a wolf, her depression levels have been almost nonexistent. She didn't want to go back.

We like him. He needs to lick us again. He deserves a face full of cum. Her wolf mumbled.

Piper burst out laughing like a crazy person and focused back on Storm. Her ears were hot with arousal and embarrassment. Glances from everyone around her made her anxiety spike. Damn, wolf. *For someone that complains about me making us look crazy, you do a splendid job of helping that image.*

I guess that's why we're perfect for each other.

She smiled. Her degree and father's experience had never made her as proud as right now. But it was squashed quickly. The sadness of Carmel's death came back. Slamming into her wave after wave. Ugh, she wished the witch would have taken her advice and left. No one deserved to die like this.

The media had said they had someone in custody this

morning, and the killer took his revenge on her. He must have used the demon's magic to help fight her off. So, they were in an agreement... where the human could use a little of the demon's magic? Well, shit.

Piper gulped. Her anxiety spiked. What the hell would he do next?

Chapter Forty

She and her men had had enough of this brutal crime scene. All the smells, colors, and objects were too much. It was one thing to deal with a dead body, but another if the dead body was a friend. Her emotions ran around her like headless monkeys trying to climb a tree. She went from being on the verge of tears to wanting to punch something every few seconds.

Carmel knew something bad was going to happen, what was she doing going in the alley? Piper's throat grew tight and swollen. Why didn't the witch take her advice and leave when she could?

Piper stiffened. She ground her teeth to keep from punching the wall and messing up the crime scene. "Let's get out to Richard's workplace. There's something about him. I know he's connected to this somehow." Piper touched Rockie's shoulder. He hadn't blinked since the blanket had been removed.

"Shit," Storm said as he put his phone back in his pocket. "The pack still won't be here for an hour, and a storm is about to hit. Sniffing out scents is gonna be damn near impossible."

Tate put his hands in his pockets. "We've got what we needed here. The others could give us more later if we missed anything. I have a bad feeling about Richard too," Tate said, standing. He moved to where the Sheriff stood, speaking to onlookers behind the tape.

"Let's fucking go. She didn't deserve to die like this. She was good people," Rockie said, still not blinking. His body and aura around him were calm. She didn't believe his calmness, but she matched his facade as they left.

Their steps were heavy and fast, but the anger on their shoulders had everyone getting out of their way. Smart people. She wouldn't want to be tangled with their group right now. But they had some aggression to get out, and they'd gladly take it out on an easy target if given a chance.

The time for being subtle had gone. It was time for action. The screeching of the tires on the wet ground both scared and pleased Piper. The drive there was a blur of spinning tires. Thank goodness she wasn't driving. They'd end up in a building.

Faster than she thought possible, the car pulled into the parking lot at the Two Step Company. The snowflakes smacked her in the face as she hopped out of the car. The weather got here before the pack did. *Hurry, please, wolves.*

Richard's workplace at the storehouse was humungous —at least five stories, but not every floor had windows. A shiver ranked down her spine at the thought of being on a floor with no windows. She bet the doors locked from the outside too.

Apparently, Two Steps was famous for being able to buy stuff in two simple steps. Storm checked their information and background on the car ride here. They were legit. But expensive.

She went through their website too. They sold everything a person needed. Food, clothes, furniture, accessories, and car parts. Everything.

A leather jacket costs over three hundred dollars. Piper's heart broke at the price. She wanted a good leather jacket, but there was no way she'd fork over a heavy amount of cash for it. Her parents taught her never to spend too much on material things. She'd rather spend it on good times and great memories.

The dark brown square building resembled a prison. The place seemed locked down too. The bars on the windows and the dark gloominess of every window creeped her out. The thick, impenetrable brick walls were intimidating. Even the grass had a sickly yellowness to it.

Her lower belly tightened, and her skin threatened to run for it, leaving her behind. The creepy factor was hardcore here. They must get a lot of attention on Halloween.

Piper sniffed the air. The snow masked most of the senses around her. She just better not smell like a wet dog after this, or she'd be pissed off. She hated the wet dog smell.

The door swung open, and a smiling blonde waved them forward. Her face seemed kind, but something about her eyebrows made her appear odd. They moved too much, and every time her group stopped, they narrowed. At first sight, she had appeared soft, but as she got closer, her features grew harsh and sharp.

"Hello, nice to meet you, detectives. Please come in." Her voice was just as soft as her face tried to portray.

Piper didn't like this one bit. The hairs on the back of

her neck moved. Something wasn't right. She didn't know if it was with the female or the whole building.

She glanced at the men, but they weren't tense or worried, so Piper took a deep breath to calm down. Her mind was not her friend right now. It needed to stop.

I think we are right about her. Something is off.

But the guys aren't?

We have always been able to sense things differently, haven't we? Why would we question those instincts now? They have always gotten us out of a bind.

Her shoes squeaked on the tile floor, even though she dried them on the carpet at the door. The inside of Two Steps resembled an insane asylum.

The interior included a combo that she was not a fan of. Bare walls and pictures covered by clear plastic. Also, the plain furniture was almost hidden in all the white. They needed some color in their life.

Nope, I'm out. She took a step back, but her wolf took over her legs and halted her movements.

We don't run from such things. I will take over if you take one more step backward. We're not cowards. If these people mean us or ours harm, we will rip their throats out. The promise of her brutality helped.

Images of the bloody mess that could happen had Piper shivering. She hurried to catch up with the men. The scowls on their faces now mimicked hers, which didn't help her nerves.

Tate slowed his strides to grab her hand. His hand was like honey, sweet and sticky, which captured all her bad feelings in its stickiness and pulled them out of her, helping her sanity and calming her nerves. Her shoulders lost their tension, and her breaths came easier.

Her hand tightened around his to show her apprecia-
tion. He gave her a warm smile, then focused back on the
woman. Another female opened one of the many doors in
the back of the building. The clickety-clack of heavy feet
walked towards them. Whoever it was, loved pink.

Once she got closer, Piper's eyes widened. *No way.* Tate
flashed his credentials while Piper had a small mind fuck.
Her palms grew wet, and the heat suffocated her—not in
terror but in what-the-fuckery.

The woman in a familiar pink skirt suit had her mind
going haywire. *No way, she's the evil happy bitch from Harry
Potter!* The dark shadows over her face were totally
Slytherin.

Her wolf snapped like an angry mother snapping at a
misbehaving child. She flinched. *Control yourself. Harry
Potter isn't real.*

*That's what people said about werewolves a few years ago.
And look at us now. If she pulls out a wand, I'm tackling her.* Her
eyes darted around for an exit.

Laughter echoed in her mind, bouncing off her skull.
Ouch. She was so glad her anxiety attack amused her wolf.

The woman's curly brown hair and sparkling hazel eyes
told her what she needed to know. She wasn't a shifter;
they tend to have light-colored eyes. She focused on her
eyes. They at least seemed nice. People actually wore these
suits in real life?

*We need to monitor your intake of movies if this is how you're
going to behave. Ridiculous.*

Shut. Up.

Heat slithered on her open side. She glanced over
without moving her head. Storm. He touched her hip,
letting his fingers glide across her jeans.

He leaned in. "She looks like that crazy chick from that wizard movie, right? I only saw it once, but wow." He lowered his voice even deeper. "She's probably crazy." His wink made her insides twirl in a professional pirouette, soothing the anxiety.

SEE! I'm not the only one.

He squeezed her flesh. He was the cutest guy in the world.

"Hey, I'm here to help you in any way I can, but I already told you, mister—"

Tate interrupted her. "Yes, we know he's not here. Please let my associate, Storm, have access to your database. We can get most of our answers there. We're all in a hurry. I know you ladies would like to go home as well. So, the faster we get this done, the faster we can leave." He paused but continued when she hesitated. "We could always get a warrant, but I'd wait here until the judge approved it, and that'd look bad on the company. Your choice." He shrugged like either way he knew he'd get his answers.

The pink-suited woman's jaw tightened several times, and the whole villain aspect came into quick view again. Her suspected guilt was showing, but the woman knew if she denied them, that would prove it. Her thin-lined smile and jerky nod to the blonde were not happy.

Piper held in her smirk. *Yeah. Slytherin never wins!* Her wolf rolled her eyes. At least that's what her reaction felt like.

She straightened her suit. "Cherry, please show him to the control room."

Cherry? Really?

The blonde's eyebrows narrowed but moved again,

softening her appearance. She hid her anger behind a bright, toothy smile. Ew, these women were creepy. Evil eyebrows and evil suits were too much.

Cold chills ran up Piper's spine. Tate took over the questioning with the suited woman, but Piper ignored them, focusing on her surroundings. When she moved away, Rockie followed.

The waiting room around the quarter had more life to it, thank goodness. The magazines on the coffee table and the one dark green couch made all the difference. It was not as bad.

"This place is weird," Rockie said, brushing her lower back with his fingers.

She smiled and nodded. "I know, it's not a good place."

She felt his gaze on her. Her face heated in response.

He cleared his throat. "I'm sorry, Pipes."

The nickname they all used made her want to dance in delight. But she had no idea why he was apologizing.

"What for?"

He licked his lips and glanced away, which she knew was difficult for him. *Dang.* Dominant males never liked breaking eye contact first. Submitting went against their nature.

"I made our first time together difficult when it was supposed to be magical." He bit his lip even harder, his gaze never meeting hers.

He thought their first time wasn't magical?

She turned to face him—her body inches from his. Her hand grazed his cheek. "Rockie, this morning was beyond amazing. Yes, it was different, but there's nothing to apologize for. I enjoyed myself. I'm sorry it wasn't as good for you, though—"

He cut her off with a deep chuckle. "Do you really think that wasn't a life-changing moment for me, Pipes? I know you don't understand wolves' customs or wolves in general, which is why no one is holding you to anything. But what we did this morning was the biggest moment of our lives." He shrugged and smirked. "The fact most of us are dominants is outrageous. I expected you to tell us to fuck off this morning."

She opened and closed her mouth, but she didn't know what to say. Was everyone being high-level wolves bad? Would they rather be with a submissive wolf?

He cupped her face to get her to focus again. "You're our mate. Yes, my wolf wanted to be the first and the most dominant, but not enough to lose you. I don't want to scare you off. Yet, you need to know, this is what every wolf searches for their whole life. Please don't worry about us, we want and need to be here in this true pack. I personally never felt so alive. I told you about my past, so you should know that's a big thing for me. I haven't played as we did earlier since I was a child."

Whoa...

He kissed her soft enough that she barely felt his lips, and the thrilling shivers still went down to her toes. *Well, damn.*

Her mind was spinning. She ignored most of the words and focused on the beautiful desperation, his sensual voice, and the fact they had a good time. The other stuff she could come back to later when she felt more prepared.

Chicken.

She ignored that too. She needed time. All she did was nod and smile. Worst fucking response ever, but shoot, she couldn't function right now.

Rockie stiffened. "Hey, what's he doing here?" he said, walking away. She followed. Her mind was still in a blended mess, so she blinked rapidly to focus.

Her eyes widened at Sam mopping the hallway. The victim that ran away when his friends got murdered. Her forehead went into a tightly strained crinkle. Piper got the tingling sensation on the back of her neck again, like someone was watching her.

Rockie stormed away, so Piper followed. "Hey, Sam, what are you doing here?" Piper's mind flashed back to when she asked Sam questions at the police station. He seemed nervous, but not too guilty. Right? Or did he? She needed to go over her notes.

His eyes widened. "I work here?" His gray shirt and black pants were disheveled. He rubbed his hands along his pants.

"Oh, I must have forgotten that. I don't remember you saying you worked here," Rockie mumbled. His face curled in confusion.

Where was that stupid paper when she needed it? What had he written down? She mentally shook her head. *I don't remember, do you?*

No.

"What are you guys doing here?" His eyes went side to side, probably worried he'd get caught slacking off.

"We're checking up on things. No need to concern yourself." Rockie turned to leave.

"Hey, how are things going? Any closer to finding the bastard?" Sam's voice sounded desperate. His hands kept clenching. He was mopping but his name tag said security. *So why would he be cleaning up instead of guarding?*

Rockie's voice became stoic. "Nothing I can talk about,

unfortunately, I'm sorry. But as soon as we have something solid, I'll let you know." They both turned away.

Sam grabbed Piper's arm, and she didn't like the feel of him. An uncomfortable vibe was cloaking him, just like Richard.

"I heard there's a search happening. Can I help? I'd like to get this jerk. The screams haunt me." He stepped closer, as if to go with them to the search right then.

Rockie removed Sam's hand from her. He was less forceful than she would have been, so she was grateful. "We appreciate that, but not at this time. Maybe if there's another one." This time, Rockie guided her away with his hand on her lower back. Even after Sam kept talking.

"Please let me know," was heard all around the building.

Another female with freckles and a plump body walked towards them. "Oh, I'm so sorry, but we are closed. But our website is always working."

Piper gave her a polite smile. "We're here with the detectives, actually."

She blinked at them as if wanting to push them away with her lashes. "I'm sorry, I thought you were someone else. Can I help you with anything?"

Before Piper could say anything, Tate walked over. "No, thank you. We got all we needed. We'll be going, now," he said and guided her toward the door, replacing Rockie's hand.

His body was tense.

"What's wrong?" she asked in a low whisper, squeezing his hand behind her.

Storm jogged up next to her, handing her a paper. The

words on them almost had her wolf slamming out of her skin.

They sell supernatural organs here.

Her heart dropped. Supernaturals don't donate organs. Most of them are immortal and only die in fights. If they had organs, then they were getting them by force.

"We don't have the manpower to deal with it right now, and the Sheriff can't handle a supernatural problem. We got Richard's and Sam's info because apparently, he works here too. We'll focus on this case, then come back to this. The kids need our full attention. We're running out of time."

She completely agreed, but they were definitely coming back to figure this shit out. And was the demon connected to this somehow? It couldn't be a coincidence. It didn't matter. She'd stop these bitches even if she didn't have the manpower. But the kids came first.

Chapter Forty-One

The cold wind felt mocking. All they were doing was getting more things to do. She wanted answers, not—

Richard's head popped out of a bush. His eyes darted around before tiptoeing out. His belt had some shiny detailing on it, so he wasn't hard to miss.

"No, fucking way." Piper smacked Tate's arm. Richard glanced back, his eyes widened, and he ran away from the Two-Step building. "Hey, stop!" she yelled.

"Shit," Tate said as he took off after him. Rockie followed.

Storm took Piper's hand and sped to the car. "We're going to cut him off."

The jerk of the car had her neck hurting, but her adrenaline kicked in, stopping the pain.

Storm hadn't driven since having the car, and she was glad. He drove like a maniac. Curbs and traffic signs were apparently invisible because he ignored them. She grabbed the *oh shit* handle, which earned her a glare from Storm.

What? Drive better, and I wouldn't be holding on for dear life.

Storm rolled down the window and sniffed the air. He gripped the steering wheel tighter and made a fast, neck-breaking right turn. Piper smacked into his body with a grunt. Her hand landed between his legs.

"I know you want me, but this is not the time." He chuckled and winked at her.

She laughed and smacked his shoulder. "You wish."

"Yes, yes, yes, definitely. I definitely wish," Storm's desired-filled voice had her face heating. She twirled her hair absently as her mind wondered. Goodness...

This isn't the time to get hot and bothered.

Piper groaned; she knew that.

Storm glanced her way. A smug smirk on his face. "You're killing me, Pipes."

Great, he could sense her need. *Fine, stop the car and climb on his lap.* Her wolf suggested.

What? No... She stammered.

Then focus on this. I can sense the scoundrel is near... Alley!

Piper stiffened and pointed. "Go down the alley."

Storm gripped the wheel tighter. "You sure?"

She rolled her eyes. "Yes, my wolf says so."

That seemed to be enough for him. Then, the car made a hard left, smacking her head into the window. *I think next time Storm drives, we wear a seatbelt.*

Good idea.

She quickly clicked it into place. Kinda stupid since she'd probably need to take the belt right off, but only if she made it alive. With Storm's driving, that wasn't guaranteed.

Halfway through the alley, a body slammed into the car,

denting the hood. Both Piper and Storm jumped. She might have screamed, but she ignored that sound. Hopefully, Storm did as well.

Storm was quick to open his door, but Tate was laying the man on the ground before either of them made it there. Especially her because she had to fight with her seat belt.

Tate grumbled, flipping him on his stomach. Her brain knew moving him might not be the best option because he could have a broken back or something, but she didn't care. If this was the killer, he deserved the pain. Flashes of the women's destroyed bodies he killed shaped in her mind. Please let this be him.

Rockie stood next to them. He mumbled under his breath, "You cheated." Piper couldn't help but smirk. But, of course, they'd make this a challenge.

Her smile vanished when Richard yelled, "I didn't do anything!" His face smashed on the alley's cold ground. This one had garbage all around but didn't feel as heavy as the other one.

"Then why run?" she asked and stood by Rockie's heated body. The anger rolling off him was dangerous. The power nipped at her for being so close, but she stayed put.

"He'll kill me. I can't say anything," Richard's words came out breathy. None of the men except Richard were winded.

"Who? We can protect you," Rockie said, but that just made Richard laugh.

"No one can protect me against him. The evil, the almighty. I saw his face that night and he haunts me every moment. He says if I need help to say this incantation."

Another crazed laugh escaped, making blood shoot out of his mouth.

"Wait, don't," Piper yelled. Demons don't help. It had to be a trick. "Cover his mouth." But by the time she spoke, he had finished his curse.

"Et datum est illi quae potest auxilium reddere pretium," Richard's speedy words ended in a scream. The air thickened and turned black. His body thrashed on the ground, like a shark out of water. Everyone backed away quickly until they were out of reach of the dark air.

Storm took a step towards Richard, but Piper stopped him. "Don't. He cursed himself. He thought it would help him, but it only helped the demon, so we wouldn't figure out his identity."

"Shit! I'm tired of this fucking demon," Rockie yelled, clenching his upper body into a ball as if forcing all his rage out.

Piper put her hands on his shoulders, but his body didn't relax. She was just glad he didn't pull away from her.

"We're going to get this asshole. I promise." Piper took a deep breath. Then, as he finally relaxed against her touch, she sent up a prayer for help. Because right now, they needed it.

Chapter Forty-Two

Tate opened the pink door of the posh cafe that Piper had to visit before the day ended. The light gray walls with yellow and turquoise accents gave her a sense of peace. An image of her sitting while reading and drinking Pepsi without a care in the world popped into her mind.

She smiled. Maybe someday.

Piper clung to her warm panini sandwich. With her luck, the food might run away if her fingers eased up on her grip. She moaned in satisfaction. She needed this after losing their only real lead.

A pink-nosed little girl walked through the door. She had a blonde ponytail on top of her head and pretty blue eyes. Her face twisted as she met Piper's gaze. The look said, *mommy, this woman is weird.*

She shrugged. No little girl was standing in her way of a good meal.

She gave the girl an open-mouth smile, full of yummy food, which earned her a smile in return. Good.

"You okay?" Tate asked. His large hand rubbed her lower back to comfort her. Goosebumps traveled up her spine, spreading to her fingers and toes in response. The bell on the door jingled at their departure. The sound made her feel at home. Her favorite store back home had the same bell.

"I'm okay, just hungry. So freakin' hungry. I don't understand." Her growly words made his smile grow wider.

She needed to focus on the little things because the big picture kinda sucked. Going through the case notes and all the crime scene photos wasn't helping. It messed with her mind. The victims' faces kept flashing in her mind.

Piper needed to find her happy place. Since tequila wasn't an option, she had to go to her favorite, Pepsi. And food. Her stomach had become a needy part of her.

The cute pink door slowly closed behind them, and the cold swirled around her. The strange feeling clung to her heart and put a smile on her face. Joy? Maybe her heart was already defrosted?

Tears almost welled up in her eyes. It had been a while since she was joyful, not since her sister's death, that was for sure. Yet, every other emotion didn't have a problem consuming her whenever the moment happened.

"The wolf demands more food intake, but it should subside after a while, or you just get used to eating more. After the last shift, it should have helped, but maybe your wolf will need more nutrients for longer than most female wolves because of your high-power level. I've never met an Alpha female, so your guess is as good as mine." He locked his fingers in hers as he pulled away from the parking spot in front of the cafe.

She dived back into her sandwich and took a big gulp

of carbonated drink. *This is heaven*. She did a little happy dance in her seat.

Another flash happened and the cold eyes of a woman that was brutally murdered came into her mind. Her good mood vanished.

She tucked her now unappetizing meal away, her stomach no longer growling. "Ugh, I just need to have a long, dreamless sleep. I feel like I'm a horrible person for not finding the kids yet and enjoying my time while people are dying and suffering." The words hurt to say, but she needed to get those words out.

Tate squeezed her hand as he turned a corner. They needed to pick up Storm and Rockie from the sheriff's station.

"Please don't. You're not doing anything wrong by enjoying the small things. That's how we survive a life like this. We take our happiness where we can get it." His thumb made small circles on her palm. "Even if it's one laugh or a relaxing night. We can't live for the job, or we'd go crazy. Believe me, it won't end well. So, you just focus your all when it's time to work."

A massive explosion rocked the car. Piper's heart dropped as the car swerved. Several cars braked and loud crashes had Piper hyper-focused.

"What was that?"

The thick smoke wafted in the sky, darkening the once beautiful day behind them. Tate flipped the car around, cursing. A powerful clawed hand gripped her heart, pouring adrenaline into her. What did the demon do now?

They turned the corner, and Piper gasped. The cafe they were just at was up in flames. The roof was destroyed, and the fire slowly overcame its way down the walls.

There were people inside.

As soon as the car stopped, she jumped out and ran to the building. Tate yelled behind her, but she didn't stop. The picture of the little girl in trouble kept playing in her head.

"Piper, you need to wait. We can do this together, but we need to make sure the others don't come in. It might be a magical fire; humans can't come near it. This town is small, they don't have firemen, only townspeople volunteers," Tate said, grabbing her arm.

"Then do that. I need to help them!" They were already in the damn building for crying out loud.

"We're here. We can do that, Tate, save these people," Rockie said from outside. They must have run over here. Perfect. She'd give them a big fucking kiss after this.

Tate let her go. "Please stay close." He moved to help a few people that hovered in the corner.

She focused on finding the girl. Something told Piper that she needed her. *Where is she?* She asked her wolf.

To your right, I smell blood. Her mom might be hurt.

Piper ran in that direction. Tate swore behind her but didn't follow. There were other people he needed to help first. The place she once thought was calming was now covered in ash and burnt furniture. Flames still licked the walls, and smoke threatened to attack her lungs. She needed to hurry.

"Mommy, please wake up. It's so hot here. Mommy," the tiny form shook an ash-covered body while whispering to her mom.

Piper moved a hot-as-hell table out of the way and ran to the voice. "Hey, I'm here to help, sweetie. We'll get you and your mommy out, okay?" Piper made her voice as sweet and caring as possible. The smoke around them made acting normal difficult.

Get low, smoke rises.

She nodded and knelt by the girl. "Can you crawl?"

The girl blinked a few times and wiped her face, making more ash cover her skin. "Like a baby?"

Piper smiled and nodded. "Yes, we can't stand. The smoke will hurt us, okay?" She didn't have the heart to voice that the smoke was going to hurt them regardless of if they stood. She needed a wet cloth to cover their nose and mouth, but the kitchen was too far away.

The little girl nodded. Her body shook in fear. She didn't move as Piper pulled her mom's body away.

Piper crawled back. The growing flames behind the girl made her adrenaline-induced heart increase even faster. "Hey, what's your name?" She focused on keeping her voice soft to not scare her.

She let out a little whimper and wiped her sweaty face. "Lilly."

Piper rubbed her back. "That's a beautiful name, Lilly. I'm Piper. Do you want to get on my back, sweetie? I know it's scary, but we need to get out of here." Flames grew bigger in outrage.

"Like a horsey?" Her voice squeaked. Piper nodded. Lilly chewed her lip, then nodded. "I like playing horsey with my daddy."

Piper had to hold back from grabbing the girl forcefully and running away. Lilly's mom needed her too, and if the girl ran off, Piper couldn't help them both. "Good, sweetheart. Let's play, so we can go see your daddy, okay? Get on my back and hold on tight."

The girl climbed on. Her arms wrapped around her

neck. The death grip made it hard to breathe but reassured her. She could do good here. She needed to.

Pulling the mom was a lot harder with the girl on her back. Not being able to breathe well and not being able to stand up didn't help. She was going too slow. Fire licked at her feet. Piper bit her lip to keep from screaming. Shit, she wasn't going to make it...

Piper pushed harder. *Let the mom go. The fire is magical, we can't make it out at this speed.*

No. I might have not been able to save those murdered victims, but I can save these people. Her wolf whimpered in response. Fire blistered her skin. Piper couldn't help but cry out. Lilly cried harder on her back yelling for her daddy.

"Piper, where are you?" Tate yelled.

"Over here!" She croaked back in relief. *Thank fuck, Tate can help.*

She spotted him hunched over, moving big objects out of the way. His eyes widened as they found her. "Shit, Pipes."

She put up her hand to stop his search for her. "I'm fine. Get the woman out. I can't pull her fast enough."

He gave her a defiant calculated glare. Her vision went red. "Don't you dare pick me over them. Get her out of here. Don't you fucking dare. I'm coming, dammit." The tenebrosity that surrounded him matched his glare. He would... He'd sacrifice them for her. If he did, she'd never forgive him. Mate be damned. He clenched his jaw but nodded.

She almost handed him the girl too, but she gripped on tighter and whispered, "No go with scary man."

Tate growled but obeyed. He knelt and swung the mother over his shoulder. "You better hurry." Her body was weak, but her wolf healed her as the fire did every-thing in its power to devour her. Pieces of the roof fell, but Piper dodged them.

Dammit, maybe he should have taken the girl despite her fear.

No, we got this. Move our ass. This place is coming down.

The little girl gripped her neck tighter and coughed in her ear before talking. "Come on, horsey, we need to follow my Mommy." She tightened her legs around Piper as if she was a real mare.

The sound of the little girl's voice was what she needed to keep going. She smiled and moved quicker. She may not have saved the kidnapped kids yet, but she was saving this little girl.

Cracking sounded above her. Shit. The smoke increased around her. She sensed Tate and Rockie coming near. Her wolf called out to them.

"Piper, the roof! Run!" Tate cried out.

She tapped into her wolf more and stood. Her hand supported the little girl, so she didn't fall. But, the magical fire wounds weren't healed yet, so she cried out and crashed to the floor. Their footsteps grew louder, and she used all her strength to keep moving.

"Piper!" Rockie yelled.

Her eyes snapped to the ceiling. Piper grabbed the girl as wood broke and covered Lilly with her body. The screams and shouts all drifted away as the heat and dark-ness enveloped her.

Chapter Forty-Three

Mumbles tickled Piper's eardrums like an annoying fly. Ugh.

She groaned but focused on the words being said. "She's waking up." Storm's voice pulled her out of the darkness that drowned her a second ago. Piper laid in his lap while he brushed through her hair with his fingers.

"What happened?" she asked, holding her head. *Why does it feel like a hammer hit my head?*

"A damn building collapsed on you. You promised me you'd get out, and you lied. I knew I should have grabbed you," Tate said.

He turned the corner sharply. Storm's head hit the window. Everyone complained.

The memories of the fire and the girl came rushing back in. "Where's the girl? How are they?"

Storm put a hand on Piper's chest when she moved to get up. "They are okay, Pipes. You saved them. The mom still needs surgery, but the doctor said she'll be fine."

"You, however, almost fucking died, and if you were human, you would have," Tate grumbled.

Rockie cursed as his arm hit the car door. "Slow the fuck down, or I'm driving," shouted Rockie from the passenger seat.

Piper covered her face as her stupidity hit her. "I'm sorry, guys. I don't know what happened. I was so focused on that little girl, I didn't think."

Storm smiled, but it didn't reach his eyes. He pulled her hands away from her face and brushed her hair behind her ears. "Blame your wolf. It's her fault. You found your mates and as a female wolf, you connected to the child. It's an instinct a mama wolf has, to help protect her cubs. It usually doesn't happen until you're pregnant, but since you're a born wolf, it might be different."

"Yes, Tate knows this, but he is still being an ass," Rockie grumbled from the front seat.

"She almost died," was Tate's defense as he white-knuckled the steering wheel.

Rockie punched Tate's arm. His scornful gaze did most of the beating. "You know damn well if you let those two die and dragged her out, she'd have never forgiven you. She would have broken the bond unintentionally. So, you did the only thing you could, and it turned out okay."

Tate's grip on the steering wheel tightened even more. His fingers might turn the wheel to dust soon. When it made a cracking sound, he loosened his grip. She knew it.

He growled out, "Fucking barely." Her heart tightened at the truth in his words.

Piper gazed up at Storm, who was still admiring her. There was something else that was bugging her. "What does he mean the bond would have broken? I thought wolves mate for life?"

Storm nodded. "We do, but we haven't finished the mating bond. So, it's not completed yet."

"What makes the bond whole then?"

"A ritual and sex," Storm's blunt answer caught her off guard.

She bit her lip and focused on Storm. Her body grew heavy again. "So, without those two, we aren't mated?"

Both men from the front seats growled. Storm just smiled wider. "We're yours regardless. The ritual and sex are you saying that you're ours too and helps you smell more like a mated female. It locks the magic in place. But there's no pressure here. We're enjoying this time to get to know you. Even if you scared the crap out of us by almost dying."

"You don't seem very mad about that?" A small sliver of doubt crept into her mind. *Did he not care as much as Tate did?*

Don't be absurd. He's a sub. His reactions are different than a Dom or Alpha. Doms want to protect, and their first instinct is to make sure their mate comes to no harm. Subs want to protect their mate but know they also need protection.

"Of course, I'm a little mad, but the love and pride overshadow the anger. You're going to be a fierce momma wolf. No one could ever hurt our pups or pack, Pipes. Not with you around. Now that's something to be rejoiced, not scorned."

Another growl came from Tate. "Fucking subs and their logic."

Piper couldn't help but smile. Yeah, the whole almost

dying for a stranger's kid was a little concerning, but what Storm said filled her with so much pride. Her wolf was prancing with her head held high inside of her.

Chapter Forty-Four

Piper and her men let out a huff as they walked into their hotel room. The messy bed gave her tingles in her core, but she pushed them away. So not the time.

They all took turns taking a shower to wash the burnt building off them. When she was clean and dressed, she focused back on the case. Burning that building was the last straw. It was time to swallow her pride and ask for help.

She was lost and needed a new person to bounce ideas off or just talk about the case. Someone that knew her and how she thought. The men would get there but they weren't there yet.

She'd call her sister, she wished, but that wasn't an option anymore. There was only one more person that could help. Fuck.

"I'm going to make a phone call. I'll be right outside," she told the guys. The concerned lines on their faces and stiff bodies were almost comical.

They didn't want to let her out of their sight, especially since she apparently almost died earlier. Tate and Rockie glanced at each other. Storm narrowed his eyes at them. She smirked.

Being a sub was way more responsibility than she thought. He was the oil that made this train run. He winked at her, and the heat crept up her neck.

"Don't go far, please," Tate said, his tone stiff.

She nodded and went back outside. The cold, damp air felt good. She needed to be as comfortable as she could be to make this phone call. *How long has it been since we talked to Dad?*

Ages. A bit of anger found its way into her gut. He lied to her all her life. Never telling her that she was a were-wolf... Or maybe he didn't know? Was she adopted? *No, don't call him in a bad mood. Let that go. We can find out what happened later. For all we know, it was Mom who lied. Maybe she was a wolf or cheated on Dad.*

You're right. Piper took a deep breath and let the anger go. She needed to be clear-headed to speak to her father.

She sat on the trunk of the car. The forest rustled all around, and the vending machine's bright light lit up the area. She laid back and stared up at the sky. The stars twinkled at her.

"Here goes nothing." She pulled out her phone and dialed the only number she knew by heart. He made her memorize it growing up.

The phone rang several times. Piper's shoulders drooped. He wasn't going to answer. He was still mad at her. Finally, a click on the other end of the phone had her holding her breath. She wasn't ready for him to answer.

"Sweet Bear?" Her dad's voice sounded groggy. Shit, she probably woke him up.

How did he know it was her? She bit her lower lip. The use of her old nickname blurred her vision. Her voice wouldn't come out.

"Are you there?" More silence from her.

Come on, talk. Her wolf demanded, but she couldn't. Her voice was caught in her throat.

"Please don't hang up. I've been trying to get a hold of you. But since..." his voice trailed off. She knew what he was going to say, 'since your sister died.' She was the glue to the family. The only reason Piper still got a gift and an invite to the holidays.

But Trace was gone. Her sister was gone. Could her dad still want her around? *Give him a chance.*

She bit her lip before speaking. "Hi, Dad."

A long sigh happened on the other side of the phone. "Oh, Sweet Bear, there you are. Thank goodness it's you. I'm so sorry for the way I've treated you. I thought my job was my life, but in old age, my mind has cleared. You, my family, are my life. We lost so much, sweetie, I can't bear to lose you too."

Good lord, he wasn't holding back. A tear escaped its confinement. *Dammit, one falls, and they all do.*

Suck it up. It's okay to cry. Her wolf poked her in the ribs.

I've done enough crying, wolf.

Aww, we're young, and we have a lot more tears to shed in our lifetime. Enjoy this moment with him.

"I love you too, Dad. And I forgive you. I forgave you a long time ago. I get it." A lump in her throat threatened to render her speechless again.

Without warning, pain blasted into her mind until

there was nothing but white all around. Flashes of what happened to get her father fired had her gasping for air. What? No.

The attack at their home remained blurry, but one incident was very clear. Blood, tears, and angry faces bombarded her. Why had the blocking spell on her memories stopped? She sucked in a sharp breath. It tore into her lungs.

Her father's downfall was her fault. That damn block on her memories gave her a false truth. "Oh no," she whined. She covered her mouth.

"No, no, Sweet Bear, dammit, I was afraid my voice would open up your memories." She let out another whine. "Please don't cry, those people's deaths are on me, not you. You were a child, and I shouldn't have burdened you with my work. I was young and foolish. You told a family that they were in danger because no one else would. That took courage."

She scoffed, "I got them killed. I didn't understand the killer was waiting for them to leave. I'm so sorry." The blasted tears ran freely now. She scuffed the ground.

He sniffled. "Hey, we're both sorry. How 'bout that?" He cleared his throat. "I've done some horrible things to you, sweetie, and all I can do is try to make up for it. I can get the mind block removed if you want. But I hope you won't. There's no reason to relive the attack and stupid mistakes I made. All I want to do is be in your life, though, Sweet Bear. Whatever it takes."

She let out a quick laugh. The "how 'bout that" statement was how he used to solve all the fights between her and her sister growing up. And it worked every time.

It didn't matter what they fought or argued about. The

we-were-both-sorry bit worked with toys, boys, and lies. Then he made cookies and talked to them about what happened.

Talking with her father again brought back the scent of fresh cookies swirling in the air. The urge to feel that fatherly embrace was strong. She sighed. That and his heartwarming words made another piece of her frozen, broken heart heal itself.

"So, Sweet Bear, I have a feeling there was a reason you were calling?" The sound of his feet tapping on the hardwood floor at his house made her homesick. She even missed the cold-ass floor.

She wiped her face on her shirt, flashing anyone nearby. Oh well. They could just deal with it.

"Yeah, I'm assisting with a case. I know you don't work anymore, and you may not like me doing it, but I need your help. These murders are brutal, there are missing kids, and it might even be tied to Trace's death. I'm not sure, but I think I found the demon that killed her."

Her father sighed. "I was afraid of that. There's no point in me telling you to stop your search, is there?" She didn't respond, which was enough of an answer for him, "Your mother always said you took after me, and if I wasn't so old, I'd be out there hunting as well."

She kicked a rock on the ground. "Thank you."

Movement on the other end of the phone had her ears getting bigger. She could picture him grabbing his small notepad to write everything down—old habits. "So, lay it on me. Demons possess people, but they don't live long. If the human made a deal with the demon, the demon typically follows the human's desires for the most part, and

I'm assuming you know a lot about the human but can't find him."

She smiled. Her dad was smart. "Yes. Several are dead, and two kids were taken."

"Fucking psychopaths, I miss bringing those bastards down." He growled out. It just made her smile more.

"Okay, this is what I got. He's a white male in his late thirties to late forties. He didn't cover the bodies afterward, so there's no sign of remorse. The high violence in the crimes indicates this wasn't his first crime. Probably a buildup, theft, or hurting animals. Now, he likes to mutilate genitals. Which shows his hate of both sexes? He probably has been humiliated by both genders somehow. Either by family members or growing up."

He grunted, the sound of a pen scratching on paper sounded before he spoke. "Well done, your behavior background is perfect for jobs like this. I could have used those skills back in my hay day. Have you checked anyone's background?"

"Yes, but nothing popped up. A few women have been raped that follow the killer's style, choking them with cloth, but he was never caught. Most of the women were tourists and left quickly after. Or they just don't remember enough about him to help."

"Understandable. Where are you, by the way?"

"Norway."

"Shit. I have no allies way over there. Okay, continue."

"He's someone that blends in. Very average looking with an average job. He doesn't have the confidence to approach the women. He blitz attacks every time, which means he isn't attractive enough or smart enough to get these women otherwise."

Her father grunted again. "Those are usually the worst kind. They turn into murderers quicker."

She sighed before continuing, "He probably has a low-level authority job like a probation officer. These types of guys love uniforms, but the town is too small for them to be police officers. The Sheriff would have noticed his strange behavior by now. He won't have enough skill to pass as normal in any high-level position of authority. But that's all for the human, not the demon. The demon made a deal with the human and lent him some of his magical abilities. He's the one that went after the children and is unpredictable. He has that same smiley face mark. He is high level, covering up his scent and using magic, but that's it."

He drummed his fingers as he thought. "Try not to focus on the demon's wants and abilities until you get closer. With the counsel using new technology to track demons down, they might be following the human's orders, depending on the terms of their deal. Focus on the human, and you'll find the demon. Anything else?"

She lifted her shoulder to shrug but stopped. "As for evidence, we had a survivor, but he couldn't tell us much. Only that the demon threw fireballs. He ran when the demon focused on the females."

"Fucking coward." He grumbled and took a deep breath. "Anything else?"

She curled her fists into tight balls. "I thought we caught the guy today, but he was just a scared witness that killed himself by trusting the demon." She snapped her finger. "Also, we're searching an area in the forest that has a trap, so we're hoping to find the kids soon. I took a spell that's supposed to help me search using the elements, but

I haven't found anything." She may not have enough time to use it, but if he had any answers maybe he could help.

The sound of rummaging through papers and opening and closing doors came from the other side of the phone. Tate's head popped out from behind the curtain. As soon as they made eye contact, he closed them.

Piper smiled.

His senses told him she was okay; he probably needed his eyes to be on board. Being outside was silly, but the illusion of privacy helped. *We're okay. They understand.*

"Ah ha."

She leaned against their car. "What is it?"

He laughed before answering, "The spell you have, I've had it before. It's a high-velocity spell, witches never tell you the whole story. They just assume you already know the answers. You need to be running at a powerful speed to get the signs."

Piper moved away from the car. Her feet moved back and forward on an invisible line. No wonder it hadn't worked.

Her dad continued. "I had to ask local shifters to help me on that case. They only agreed to help because our family had wolf shifters in our bloodline. But I guess it skips generations or something. Who knows?" He chuckled and his voice grew deeper as he remembered. "Actually, they wouldn't help at first despite our family line. But once he met you, with your cute face and cute Halloween detective uniform on, he agreed."

"Wow, I don't remember that." She glanced up at her hotel window. No one was watching her. Just as the thought developed, the curtains moved.

Storm appeared in the window but closed the curtains

with a smirk. She wasn't going to tell her dad over the phone, but she was glad he was her actual father. And it didn't sound like he lied to her. He just didn't know anything. She smiled and let out a quiet sigh.

"Anyway, anything else?" He coughed, so she waited. She hoped he wasn't smoking anymore.

"Not really. We used the news to provoke him, but instead of targeting us, he targeted the witch that helped us. Proving my weak and lacking confidence theory. I wish—"

"Don't do that."

Piper's head tilted to the side. "Do what?"

"Blame yourself and hold all the burden. I used to do it too. It was so hard for me to enjoy life at first because I felt guilty. I can hear it in your voice. The witch chose to help. You did nothing wrong."

Piper smiled. How did her father know her so well? Even after all this time? *We're a lot like him. I come from his side of the family after all.*

She stayed quiet for too long, so he continued. "Don't worry, Sweet Bear, you'll find him. You were the one I always thought would follow in my footsteps. Is that all?" The sound of liquid pouring into a cup had her thirsty too.

"Just a stupid phone with nothing on it but a few phone numbers. We looked into all of them and came back with nothing. One of the guys had the number in the text traced but nothing there too. The guy lived on the other side of the world and has been in the hospital for weeks. Tate is having his analyst friend look into anyone who fits my description. But because Norway is no longer connected to the human government, records are limited."

The sound of a glass slamming down on a hard surface

on the other end of the phone made her jump. "Wait, you sure the number that was texted is a phone number? Have you tried putting them in as longitude and latitude? I had that happen to me on a case. They tend to be ten numbers or more, but I thought the one was part of the number in the beginning. Fucker was slick, but I got him that way. It led to their hiding place."

She smiled and let out a little squeal. "Dad, you're amazing. I'm going to do that right now. I love you."

"I love you too, Sweet Bear. Please be careful. Demons aren't things to mess with. Do you need me to go to Norway?"

She walked back to the room with a pep in her step. "No, Dad, I have three guys on the case with me. I promise, I'll be safe."

"Good, I don't want to lose my Sweet Bear."

Tears slid down her face again. Damn bleeding heart. Why weren't they all dried up by now?

"Then you won't, Dad." She bit her lip and nervously continued. "How's Beka doing?" Their relationship might be shitty, but she'd be willing to make an effort to fix it. Even if shit like this made her awkwardness shine bright.

She couldn't see her dad, but she could feel his pleased smile through the phone. Her father had managed to find a woman to spend his older age with, and Piper had never warmed up to her, even though Piper could tell he never forgot about her mom. He still put flowers on her grave every holiday.

"She's doing well. Still working at the hospital. We're enjoying my retirement. She's been thinking about going on vacation. Maybe you could join us."

She rubbed her face. "Maybe. I'm happy for you, Dad."

Goodness, this was awkward, but she had to show him she wanted a relationship with him again. But she wasn't ready to go on a vacation with him and his new wife, but maybe someday.

"Me too, sweetie. Please keep me updated. I'll worry if I don't hear back from you."

"I definitely will. Bye, love you." She hung up the phone.

She swung open the door. Storm was on the computer, typing away. He glanced up with a bright smile as she walked into the room.

"Your father is one smart man. Those numbers weren't phone numbers. They were the exact location of the campground. So, whoever the disconnected phone number belonged to is the killer."

Chapter Forty-Five

They went to the sheriff's station and all the leads beside the number were cold. They had no more answers for them or witnesses. They just had to wait... Wait for the pack, wait for Tate's connections to find out who the number belonged to, and wait for the plan. They wanted to track with the pack for backup. The human could use demon magic, so it was dangerous going on their own.

Storm straightened his back as if he were ready to run a marathon, but his voice was laced with what sounded like exhaustion. "All right, we'll go back to the room to change. Then you and Rockie can go have lunch with Nina and Liam. She needs you. Tate and I will keep working on the case. Maybe revisit the crime scenes or question the witnesses further. We're missing something. The pack should be here soon."

"But shouldn't we go with you?" Piper asked. She wanted to see Nina, but the case was important.

"No. You need to help Nina. You're her Alpha,

remember? She needs you around. Although, Liam says she's doing way better than a new were-shifter should. So, enjoy your time with her. Then, we will go on the hunt."

"What about her lack of mourning? Do we know anything more about that?" she asked.

He shook his head. "I have someone looking into it. There might be away to get inside the prison, but we need a way to find the demon. Sorry."

Piper nodded. "It's okay. Thank you for continuing to try."

"Always. Now go help Nina."

She nodded again in her agreement. She wished all her men would relax and enjoy lunch with them, but the children deserved their attention more than she did.

"I'm going to get a soda. I need a pick-me-up before we leave," Piper said as they pulled into the parking lot at the hotel.

She could do coffee, but that tended to rumble her tummy all the wrong ways. Pepsi was her safety blanket. She needed that right now.

Tate smirked, Storm winked, and Rockie gave her an amused shake of his head. *Hey, I don't drink soda that much...* With quick steps, they disappeared into the room. She pulled some money out of her pocket as she walked to the machine. *Ugh, I so need this.*

An ankle brush and quick sounds like laughter had Piper smiling. The foxes. *Ugh, not again. Kick them.* Her wolf grumbled.

Be nice.

"Hey, Trix and Minx." A tear fell when the witch's stiff dead body popped into her mind. They had lost their owner, and if they were domesticated, they wouldn't survive long on their own.

"I'm so sorry, sweetie," she told the white fox. The silver fox ran out of the tree line and twirled around her legs. Instead of that semi-creepy smile, his mouth was full of some type of glass bottle.

She leaned closer. "Whatcha got there, sweetie? Let me see." With her luck, it'd be a bomb.

A glass vial she recognized fell into her hand. A white rolled-up paper tied with a red string attached to the glass. *Wait, is that...*

Unrolling the paper, she read: *Hey Piper, if you're reading this, my vision was about me. I'm either dead or in a coma. Either way, the magic in that spell I made for you will disappear. Take this one a few minutes before you run. However, because the potion is from a dead witch, there'll be long-term consequences. You'll be linked to my foxes because they're my familiars.*

You'll also have the effects of the spell for the rest of your life. Which means, every time you run fast, nature will guide you to your destination. Don't tell anyone about this or you'll have magical beings hunting you down to steal it. If you choose not to take it, please destroy the potion. This in the wrong hands will get a lot of people killed. Please don't let that be the legacy I leave behind. I wish you the best. Never let this cold world tarnish your spirit.

She hugged the note to her chest as she blinked to clear her blurry vision. The witch didn't deserve to die. Even though the potion could put her life in danger, Piper was thankful. Now, that she knew how to use it, she could find the kids. The price she had to pay was worth it.

"All right, Trix and Minx, you're going to stay in my room while I get some lunch and hunt down the fucker for your owner. Sound like a deal?" Their creepy sounds grew louder.

PIPER'S SHOULDERS BECAME LIQUID HEAT AS NINA CAME into view. Her light brown skin and bright smile were exactly what she needed.

The three men that were with her blurred as she zeroed in on her best friend, her soul sister. Nina's face grew frantic, and her feet pushed against the ground before she could stop herself.

They ran into each other's arms with a hard, bruising smack. Her new heavy vanilla scent surrounded Piper.

"I know, I had to get a body wash from the store here. It was either vanilla or flowers," she said against her shoulder.

"I've missed you. I know it hasn't been long but—"

Nina cut her off, "Liam says it's the bond we created with our wolves. Normally, we would have to stay close together for a few weeks, but as long as I'm not too far away we're okay."

Piper brushed her hand through Nina's curly hair to comfort herself. She pulled away knowing they attracted the attention of everyone around. Small towns probably don't see many same-sex relationships, so the analyzing stares made sense.

She wasn't with Nina, but no stares were going to stop her from showing her love. "You're the bear."

Nina smiled. "You're the stuffing."

Their inside joke felt good on her lips. Flashes of her going to Nina's house for the first time and being bombarded with her love for stuffed bears came to mind. So, she made a joke and they laughed for a good long time. At the end of the night, Nina mumbled, "Thank you for being so great. You're the bear."

It might have been a sleepy mix-up, but Piper just smiled and whispered, "Well, you're the stuffing." They loved that saying ever since. But they hadn't used it in years.

The endearment was exactly what her heart needed. They linked their arms and walked to the cafe. Liam stood on Nina's other side. "Hey, Piper. How are your guys?" They walked onto the town's main street, passing by the only grocery store in town. The potted plants overflowing with pink petunias that had flickers of snow on them guided the way.

She squeezed Nina's arm. "They're good. Rockie is holding the table, but Storm and Tate are working on the case. Storm is working with Tate's contacts to get info, and Tate is meeting the pack. They should be in town any minute."

Piper grabbed a magenta petunia from one of the potted plants and placed it in her hair. "Yeah, they said more bad weather is coming. I'm just glad it isn't snowing right now."

"Me too, you know how my hair gets in the wet weather. I might have to shave it all off if we live here." Nina's spirits drooped. She loved her hair, but moisture in the air wasn't good for it. It turned into a hot mess.

Liam touched her shoulder with his. She met his stare. "You will look gorgeous no matter what."

Her smile went back to the bright-natured one Piper loved seeing on her friend. Liam was a good man. She hoped they'd work out.

Liam kissed her cheek and walked to grasp forearms with Rockie at the table. Nina's blushing face turned to Piper. "Isn't he adorable? I'm usually an asshole kind of girl but his sweetness is really doing it for me."

Piper smiled and they did a little dance with their arms still connected. "I'm so fucking happy for you, Toots."

"What about you and your orgy fest?" She puckered her full lips and gave her a knowing stare.

Piper's face heated this time. They were getting close to the guys, so she mouthed, "Oh my god, so good." Piper almost squealed.

"Good, good, or yummy?" Nina asked and bit her lip.

"Way beyond yummy. Mind-blowing." The smile on Nina's face took ten years off her age.

Nina glanced around to make sure everyone's focus was elsewhere. "All of them? At once?"

"It was a ritual thing or something but," she opened her mouth in a big O. "I'm ruined for life, and it was only their tongues."

Nina squealed, and that got everyone's attention. She awkwardly waved at all the men around them. "We're so talking about this later, bitch."

"Only if there is alcohol."

She shook her head and chuckled. "Deal." Nina bit her lip again, but this time worry colored her face.

"Hey, what is it?" Piper asked, squeezing her shoulder.

"I didn't want to ruin anything or make you lose focus on finding the kids, but when I went back to the pack grounds..." her voice trailed off, and she pulled out her phone. "Here, let me just show you." She searched through her messages. "Patty records every time the Rogue pack attacks. She doesn't use the camera, that's just a jumbled mess, but it's good for voice recording.

She pressed play. The video was pointed at the sky. It moved around, getting shaky trees as Patty ran. Piper put her ear to the phone.

Sounds of bones breaking were loud and clear. "Please don't shift, Nina. Your Alpha isn't here, and you're too new to have control. Please. Take deep breaths," Patty pleaded. Piper glanced Nina's way and she winced.

The video cleared for a second. A small group of females waited outside one of the cabins that had tons of colorful flowers around it.

A hole in the ground opened as Patty approached. She was out of breath, and the panic in her voice was evident. "Get in, everyone. Be quiet."

An explosion burst from the speakers. Piper jumped but focused back on the recording when male voices began to yell. "We want our two women! We bit them. They're ours!"

"Yeah, Nina, Piper? Where are you?" Piper froze at the sinister tone of a voice she recognized. She took a sharp gulp of air.

Everything stopped. Smells, noises, and even her sight blurred. No. No.

But he left.

The noise came flooding back in at his sinister tone. "Come out, come out wherever you are. I can make you feel good again, Nina. Just come to me. I promise no one will hurt you."

She didn't want to believe it.

Roger? No.

Dammit, was Luke with him? No, she saw him get mauled.

"Freaking A, get the hell in, Nina," Patty whispered. Her voice was full of panic. The image cleared as she sprayed something in the air. Then, the video ended.

Piper's poor lips were going to be raw with how she nibbled on them. "I can't believe this. Are we sure it was Roger? Maybe—"

Nina cut her off, "Liam described him perfectly. It was him. The bastard. I can't believe I dated him."

Piper's wolf pushed calm waves of energy into her and Nina. That cleared her mind. She relaxed. They had a pack to help them now. They could get through this. *Wait...* "Is everyone okay?"

Nina nodded. "The pack is fine, and no one was hurt, except on their side, but Roger knew shit about us, Piper. What if..." her voice trailed off.

She didn't need to finish that sentence. Piper knew. It was bad. Like, go home and hurt their family bad.

We don't know that for sure. So, we focus on the kids because we must, dammit. Then deal with that spineless weasel.

Piper nodded to herself. "Okay, this is what we're doing. First, we find the kids, deal with the demon, then deal with that asshole. I know our list is getting long, but now we have a pack backing us. Okay," her voice held authority. Piper knew Nina needed her Alpha right now, not her friend.

Nina's lip shook but she nodded in agreement. Liam whispered in Nina's ear. Her shoulders drooped, and she took a deep breath.

Rockie took her hand and led her to the table. He

winked at her when their eyes met. Good, she did the right thing.

THEY ORDERED AND ATE WHILE TALKING ABOUT anything that wasn't connected to the case. The normalcy recharged her. Life could still be filled with good, even if it were surrounded by bad.

Rockie squeezed her hand, letting her know their short break was over. It was time for the heavy again. Tate and Storm were ready.

A jingle had Piper searching for Rockie's phone. Storm's name flashed at her. She answered it, worry creeping along her spine. Something didn't feel right.

"Hey, Stor—"

Storm cut her off, "Piper, it's Sam Gunther. I just got the results back from our connections and the report you requested from the doctor. He didn't have any wounds on his feet. So, there was no way he ran through the forest to escape. And get this: the numbers that pointed right to the camping grounds were sent from Sam's old goddamn phone. We're at his house, but nothing." The sound of doors slamming made her wince. "We're going to try his family's house next, be careful, beautiful." Piper held her breath immediately at the screeching tires.

He didn't continue. She called his name to make sure he was okay. "Storm?"

No answer.

"Shit! Tate, they have us surrounded. Shift and call for the others. They aren't that far away," Storm whispered.

Glass shattered and the line went dead. Everyone at their table stood. If they didn't hear her conversation, they definitely heard the massive howl that sounded a few miles away. The urgency in it pulled her center to the right. Adrenaline smacked her in the face.

They all turned the same way and moved. Their Alpha and pack members needed them. Her wolf demanded to be released.

BOOM!

A massive force lifted Piper in the air and flung her into a nearby wall. The impact was hard enough to have black dots taking over her vision. The shouts and cries twisted her gut.

"Piper, Liam, help!" Nina's scared voice had her springing to her feet. She wobbled, but that wasn't going to stop her.

"Nina." Everything was gray, and the random swirl of colors scattered around her were confusing. She wiped at her eyes.

"Let me go! Piper!" Nina's raspy, shrill tone sent a chill down Piper's spine.

"Help!" Piper yelled and struggled through the gray fog covering her vision.

"Stupid bitch bit me. Keep the fucking crystal on her, or she'll shift," a rough female voice said. Piper moved towards the sounds.

"Fight, Nina, tell me where you are," Piper pleaded. The sound of a struggle had her moving faster. Her legs and arms hurt like hell, but she couldn't think about that now.

"Piper, watch out!" a male voice yelled, but her voice was muffled as she focused her everything on Nina. She needed to save her. "Piper!"

She ducked and rolled on instinct. Another explosion pushed her forward but didn't hurt her. The noise took the last of her hearing. "Nina!" Her voice was muffled like she was being smothered.

"Piper!" someone yelled, but the deafness, dizziness, and pain won. She kept moving in the direction she thought Nina was, but a warm body stopped her.

Tate?

His masculine scent was strong. He gripped her cheeks, and cold liquid fell over her face. Drowning her...

She fought against the embrace.

It couldn't be Tate. He would never hurt her. Another bucket of chilly liquid poured against her face. Water went into her mouth and nose. Her heart hammered against her chest.

Help!

It's okay, I think they are helping us.

Another drowning sensation had her coughing and collapsing on the ground, strong arms wrapped around her stomach. She sat on their lap while the hands on her cheeks stayed strong.

"One more, my love. I'm so sorry."

The devouring sensation was the worst kind of torture. She couldn't move or think. Her body just gave up.

"That's it, cough it out. The poison in the bomb should clear soon. Just keep breathing," Tate said, his hands clung to her cheeks, making tender circles. He pushed his calming energy into her.

"We got you, Pipes." Storm rubbed the same circles on her back.

The crying that shook her body sounded pathetic to her ears. But as the pain and weight of everything came crashing down on her, she couldn't stop them.

"Nina?" She cried out, knowing she wouldn't answer.

"We'll get her back."

Chapter Forty-Six

Piper's ears rang, and the broken clutter all around her made her want to punch someone. How the hell did this happen?

She took a deep breath and screamed. "He fucking took Nina! I can't believe Sam is the damn demon. It doesn't make sense. Wouldn't we have sensed him?" Her hands gripped her head. Her brain hurt. "No, possession wouldn't let us sense him." Her fists balled into tight balls. "If he hurts her, I'll rip him into pieces," Piper kicked broken furniture and building parts that lay around her. She slammed her fist onto the only table still upright.

The anger had her change coming without her permission. Fur rose on her skin, her bones popped, and her eyes shined with her wolf.

No.

I'll find that fucker. You're too weak.

No, dammit. We need to have a plan and backup. Please don't change.

Rockie tightly wrapped her in his arms. His dominant

wolf power and strength pushed hers down, forcing the change back. She took a deep breath and focused on control. *Fine, I won't change yet, but I won't be stopped for long. Let me out or I'll take control. We're her Alpha, Nina won't be hurt on my watch.*

The sweet restaurant where they enjoyed a small moment of peace was destroyed. Dishes, food, and broken furniture scattered the floor. A few people were injured, but nobody was dead, thank goodness. The demon had a thing for destroying places... Or was that Sam's thing?

Rockie loosened his grip as he spoke. "They said Sam killed his father. I didn't know the guy, but anyone that could do that deserves to die."

Liam yelled, swinging his arms around. "He killed his own father? Who the hell does that, man? He has my Nina!" Shock and fear darkened the edge of his eyes and created worry lines on his face.

He wanted to be strong, but the strength it took to hold back his wolf had his hands shaking. Her Alpha wolf sensed these things, even when she wasn't entirely confident in the innate feelings that overcame her. All she knew was she wanted to help him.

Her wolf growled. *If you won't give me control to go after this fucker, let me do this and help him. I have the power to soothe his wolf. Put our hands on his shoulders. I'll do the rest.* As they waited for the others, she could do that for him. She stepped away from Rockie's comfortable embrace.

Nina and Liam had gotten close, so she could imagine what his wolf was going through. She already almost lost control and her wolf was close to taking over.

She spread her fingers wide and placed them on his shoulders. Her skin met his warm flesh through the holes in his shirt. Liam stiffened when her hands touched him. Her hands were cold, she should have rubbed them together to warm them first. Within seconds they grew warm, though. Really warm...

The heat that came off her palms surprised her. The sensation was like hot water traveling down her arm, but without the wetness. After a few deep breaths, Liam's shoulders sagged. His head drooped as tears fell down his face.

She squeezed him through his clothes to show her support. Thankfully, no one was watching them, her men probably wouldn't have appreciated that, but they were amongst the chaos of werewolves organizing and planning the search.

Liam's rich chocolate eyes were dilated enough to appear entirely black. He glanced up at her. "Thanks. I didn't know you were that level of an Alpha. Only Tate can do that, as far as I know." He turned around and hugged her so tight that her back popped.

She squeezed him back. Their shared pain leaked from their embrace. "We'll get our girl back, I promise," Piper said, letting him go before she cried.

Someone cleared their throat. When did it get quiet? The stark silence spoke volumes. Whatever happened was enough to stop the chaos and noise. *Oh, snap.* Everyone's wide eyes were on her. *What's happening?*

You said we couldn't go after Nina without backup, so I didn't just help Liam. I helped the whole pack. I calmed them through the link in the pack so their nerves wouldn't get the best of them to let them think properly. Her wolf sounded prideful.

Well, that would definitely be why they are staring at me like I'm crazy.

Let them know we'll protect them, and if we work together as a pack, we can get our people back. You weren't paying attention, but they're scared and worried. None of them have gone up against a demon. Piper wanted to laugh the situation off and go hide behind one of her mates. But she wasn't that person anymore. There would be no hiding. This was her pack and they needed her.

She nodded and stood next to her men. The shocked faces and the animated glow of the wolf's eyes soured her tummy. She wrapped Tate's arms around her waist and held the others' hands in hers to show the pack their union.

She took a deep breath and spoke, "I'm not going to pretend to have all the answers. But I know we can do this. Demons might be scary as shit, but the demon doesn't have what we have. Each other. And together we can defeat anything. I'll fight with you, and so will my mates. Together, we can stop this bastard, and keep this pack and the town safe. We can do this."

The following shouts were a perfect boost to her confidence.

"Yeah!"

"Hell, yeah!"

"Damn straight!"

"My mate helped us focus to think clearly on our hunt. Everyone has their locations and the meeting spot. If you find anything, howl," Tate said, holding Piper tighter.

When he let her go, Storm and Rockie took turns hugging her just as tight. Separating from them sucked, but they had to go with their group. She was with Tate and Liam. They would leave from exactly where they found the first trap. The three highest-ranking wolves had to go from there since more traps were guaranteed.

Piper hid behind a thick tree to disrobe and secretly take the extra potion before shifting. She rubbed her hands together to keep her mind from wandering. Her stomach was knotted at the thought of leading the group again. She'd have to take control of her group's speed if she was going to activate the spell. The last time she did that, she almost died.

Don't worry. I got us. That won't happen again. Her wolf insured her.

The determined expressions on everyone as they changed and shifted gave Piper more hope. She sensed their peace. Her wolf was proud and content but still on edge. But she listened and didn't take control. *We are using your body and senses now, show me how it's done.* Her wolf grinned with excitement. Probably was creepy as hell.

Tate's large dark wolf and Liam's gray wolf nodded at each other and then at her. Contrary to popular belief, wolves didn't share thoughts. They projected feelings, and maybe even intentions. But thoughts... that would have been chaos. *Twenty or more people in my head at once, no thanks.*

Together they took off, every group going a different way. The small snowflakes made smelling difficult but that wouldn't stop her. She needed speed. The men on either side of her kept pace with her increasing speed as she took the lead. Tate nipped at her ankles to tell her to slow down, but she couldn't.

Now, it was just her and the forest. No one could distract her. Not even with his nipping and whining. Her wolf was on a mission, and she wouldn't stop for anything.

The heavy wind blurred her vision. The smells were almost overwhelming, but she focused on the senses that could help guide her.

Fast. She needed to go fast.

Shadows to the left moved without cause. She turned, following her instincts. The pathway was wider this way. Her wolf bristled; openings weren't good. There was more room for traps. She picked up the pace even more.

A movement to their left almost made her hesitate, but she pushed through, following her body's natural directions. Shit. She whined a warning as she spotted a massive boulder in a tree ahead. *I'll bet a million dollars that as soon as we get closer, the thing will try to squish us.*

Shit. Shit. It wouldn't be an issue if they were going fast enough that it'd miss them. She picked up her speed again.

A cracking sound came from the trap. She held her breath as the boulder fell. She zoomed past unharmed but glanced back to check on the others. Liam just barely passed the danger. He tucked his furry black legs in to not get hit but he made it through. She let out a small howl in glee. Not enough to alert the others but enough to pump Tate and Liam up. *We got this.*

The memory of Roger wanting her to jump over a huge log when she first arrived here popped into her mind. She was scared and knew she couldn't do it, now she could jump over ten of them stacked on top of each other if she wanted to, proving how much she had changed. Her muscles worked better than they ever had. Pride coursed through her.

A small patch of flowers shifted to the right, catching her attention, but a forceful gust of wind pulled her left.

She guided the trio in the direction of the wind. A sharp scent of stone and smoke drifted through her. A cave?

Her ears perked up. That was where Tate said he would be. A damn cave!

She couldn't slow down now. Her wolf locked into her hyper-focus and wouldn't let go. She turned back at her pack-mates again to make sure they were okay. Her human side seeped in. That fucking boulder was inches away from hurting one of her pack. *Maybe we should slow down.*

No.

Wolf, be reasonable. We're not thinking like a human. We're thinking like an animal. An animal can't defeat a demon.

She growled and turned back again. *You're right. Liam could have gotten hurt.* Her wolf's voice was harsh but defeated. *We'll slow down.*

Tate made a barking noise that prompted her to focus straight ahead again. The scene in front of her shimmered. The way was no longer clear.

Shit! A patch of familiar heavy leaves was in view. Her heart sped up. Fake leaves...

Another fucking hole trap? Stop! Her wolf's paws dug into the wet dirt. There wasn't enough traction. She couldn't stop. The ground disappeared underneath her. Adrenaline slammed into her as if a needle pierced her heart, forcing her brain to kick into gear.

Piper spun around and dug her claws into the mud. The damn thing was too slippery; she was going to fall in. She whimpered. The sharp tip of one of the stakes in the trap dug into her back paw.

Tate whined above her. His claws pierced into her front legs. She hissed but didn't fight against his sharp claws digging into her flesh, staining her fur red. Tate licked her face, letting out small whimpers before he gripped the back of her neck with his teeth. He pulled her up, enough to grab onto a strong branch sticking out of the ground. Her sharp teeth latched onto the wood. Splinters poked her gums and blood swelled in her mouth. She ignored the pain and pulled herself up out of the hole.

If she could shift back, using her hands would work better, but the wolf wouldn't relinquish control. She was too scared.

A panicked yelp froze her. Liam? Her head snapped up. His wide eyes focused on her. He was trying to stop himself from running but he only slid forward in the mud. He couldn't stop.

Tate turned as Liam's heavy form slammed into him, knocking them both over the edge.

"No!" Piper screamed. Powerful energy took over her body and gave her strength. She pulled herself up the rest of the way until she stood again.

Piper turned, whimpering. The area in front of her was covered in trapholes. A few other pack mates must have gotten stuck as well from the sound of their whimpers in the distance. She'd howl for help, but that could ruin the mission. They were only supposed to howl when they found the kids. If she drew everyone there, it might be the wrong place. That could cost the kids their lives.

She focused back down the hole, Liam had one of those sharp wooden edges stuck in his wolf foot. His cries hurt her soul, but he'd survive. Tate stood in his human form as well, moving to help Liam.

"He's okay, Pipes. Please don't make those noises, my love. I can't bear it. We're okay, I promise." Tate's pleading green eyes helped clear her mind.

Her wolf finally settled down and gave her the chance to shift back. Her bones popped into place. The breaking and snapping felt better this time. The shift wasn't as painful.

That was close.

No shit.

The guilt hit her like a hammer to the temple. Black roses bloomed in her vision. The darkness threatened to take her. She couldn't breathe.

"Piper! Come on. Piper, breathe. We're okay. This wasn't your fault," Tate said. He threw small rocks at her to make her focus. The air she let into her lungs stung. She deserved it.

She didn't pay attention to where she ran, concentrating too much on the signs instead of their well-being. If Tate were leading the group, Liam wouldn't be hurt.

Tate grunted. He pulled the stick out of Liam's foot and spoke, "He covered these traps with an allusion. It doesn't matter who was in front, they wouldn't have seen these traps, Pipes. Just find something that can help us get out. You were close, I smelled Nina's perfume."

Piper scanned the area. Her body trembled. She was naked in the middle of nowhere and fucking freezing. "I don't see—"

"No, leave us alone. Mama, Daddy, please!" A child's tiny voice cried out in pain in the distance. Piper snapped to the left. She took a step forward.

"No, Piper. Let me go with you," Tate distracted her. She nodded and turned back to him. She'd get him out, then go help them.

"Aahh!" a woman screamed in pain. *Nina.*

"No!" Tate called after her, but she didn't listen this

time. She couldn't when Nina was in trouble. "Piper!" Tate's voice was lost to her as she ran toward the screams. There was no way she could wait.

A wolf's howl followed by others in the distance gave her chills. *Perfect. I'll distract him, and they can kill him when they get here.*

She knew she couldn't beat a powerful demon, but she was going to try. And who knew, maybe luck would be on her side, for once.

Chapter Forty-Seven

The cries of the young girl and boy got louder as Piper entered the cave. Their moans made her skin bristle in anger, and her vision burned red.

She knew she should wait for the guys, but as she stepped into the cave, the image of the children and her best friend trapped in a cage, not even big enough to stand in, pushed her over the edge. There was no waiting.

The entrance was long and shadowed. Perfect for her to hide in. Most of the opening to the cave was to the right, hidden from the outside. So much so, that the light couldn't be seen. The dirt floor wasn't even, and the stone walls were jagged.

Other than that, the room was large wasn't much to look at, but it was boxed in. There was nowhere for him to run.

I'll help you kill this demon. Shift, and we have a fighting chance.

I agree, together we are stronger. Her wolf preened in pride. She loved the praise.

Her blood boiled. Sam stepped into view with keys in hand, and Piper crouched down. Once he opened the cage, she would attack. His back was to her, so this was her chance. Just one chance, right now.

Waiting for the sound of keys turning and unlocking was the longest wait of her life. The demon must have been in slow-motion because she swore ten minutes had passed. Finally, when the pop and rattling of the lock opening happened, she was practically foaming at the mouth.

She sprang into action. Her body shifted as she moved towards him. Her bones cracked and morphed into her beast.

The surprised yelp under her egged her on—her teeth sunk into flesh. The blood tasted like overcooked marsh-mallows. Ew.

"You bitch." The demon shook Piper off, her teeth shredding the human's flesh. She knew what the human did to the poor women he came across, so the sound didn't even turn her stomach. She reveled in it.

The demon slammed the cage door shut, and appar-ently, that meant the prisoners couldn't get out because Nina slammed into the door as Piper charged him again.

Her teeth sunk into his calf before a huge fist slammed into her head. Well, shit. A house falling on her head would have felt better than that.

The world spun. A large hand gripped her neck. "What do we have here? A nice new plaything?" The scent of his rotten breath curled her stomach.

Piper squirmed and warm liquid seeped from her head onto her chest. Well, double shit, he hit her harder than she thought. She was in trouble.

Why aren't we healing?

It's the demon. I'm not sure, but he must have magic-suppressing abilities.

Fuck, that's how he killed the witch.

We need to leave. I can't help you.

She shifted back into her human self. In front of a rapist... Great.

"What? Why the hell not?" He scoffed. "The demon doesn't want me playing with you. He doesn't want me killing the kids either. Too bad. I'm in charge. I made a deal with a demon. Get him to Norway and I get to kill and do the ritual. He's inside my body, the fucker needs to stop telling me what to do. I don't understand what the demon's problem is. You'd think he'd be happy to kill or bring his kind to Earth." He scratched his head as his eye twitched. "I need to finish the ritual. I have to kill me some kids and a half bitch. Then the demons will walk the Earth and this ass wipe can get out of me."

He brushed the hair out of her face before continuing, "I don't mind the power boost, but this demon has more morals than I do. I can't even play without feeling disgusted. It's horrible."

"Aw, poor you. You feel bad for raping and killing people." Piper knew she shouldn't poke the bear, but damn, her mouth was a stupid thing sometimes.

"Oh, don't worry. Lucky for you, I have the willpower of a god. I'll be back. Don't die, kay? I do want to play." He patted her on the head and dropped her on a large rock. The skip back to the cage was a little much, but psychopaths did weird shit.

I'm not going to make it if I keep bleeding out like this.

Crawl to the entrance. The wolf's voice was fragile. Not good.

Piper clawed at the ground, pulling on large rocks that were too stuck to be moved. She watched the dirt as her arms did the work. The wound bled down her cheeks. How deep was it?

She didn't feel that much pain... was that a good thing? Sure, it was there, but Piper always thought a killing blow would hurt more. The only thing that was concerning was the blood and the cold. She shivered hard enough to make it a dance. Fast, full-body shimmies. *Broadway, eat your heart out.*

Nina's cries made her move faster. She needed to heal and help her. There was no way she was losing another sister. She grunted her way through the rocks digging through her skin.

One of the children cried out in pain. No. She army-crawled faster. *Fuck, fuck. No, please.*

As soon as her head touched the opening of the cave, her body shifted and began to heal. *Thank goodness.*

The other kid cried out in pain. *No.* She turned around, tears welling up in her eyes. Her battered and not yet healed body protested as she rose.

Wolf huffs sounded behind her. Piper turned back around. The several shining wolf eyes staring at her at the entrance were like hot chocolate on a snowy day. *Yes, her pack was here. Wait...* The sense of relief was gone instantly. Something was wrong. They couldn't come into the cave.

The pack slammed their bodies against an invisible barrier. She sighed and turned away from them. *I guess I'm on my own.* She needed to get to the kids and Nina. She'd worry about the pack later.

"Wait," she smiled and turned to the sound of Rockie's voice. "Are you okay?" he asked and wrapped her up in his arms. She nodded, even if it wasn't true. She felt like shit. "Only Tate, Storm, and I can make it through the barrier. I'll shift back, then we'll go in together. You focus on getting everyone out. We'll distract the demon." He kissed the top of her head before shifting back. She shifted with him.

Growls had the demon freezing. A sharp knife dripping with blood hung above his head. He gripped the knife tighter.

"You can't stop this. The kids are dead. Now all I have to do is kill this little half bitch to open the door to hell. I'll be rich and powerful like I always should have been," Sam said, turning to face them.

They all charged at the same time. Storm was flung away as Rockie clamped onto the demon's ankle. He let out a pained cry and tossed Rockie away.

Both wolves stood and moved to help Tate. First, she needed to get Nina. Once she was safe, Piper could join the fight and bring the fucker down.

The three wolves worked well together, moving him away from the victims by nipping and pouncing him to the right. Nina called out for her. Her arms and legs were bound, so she couldn't move.

The kids laid next to her. One was still blinking, and the other was too pale. The stab wounds in their chests were fatal. There wasn't much time. Piper shifted back to human. She wouldn't be able to become a wolf again until she got back to the entrance.

Piper sliced Nina's restraints with the knife Sam dropped. She scooped Nina up, placed her on the floor, and set the kids on top of her. She'd have to drag them out.

The sting from the cold turned into a burn as she tugged on Nina's shirt. They both groaned together with each pull. "We got this. We're almost there."

Tate's large body flew through the air. Piper held her breath as she watched. She couldn't leave Nina alone, but her gut twisted. She wanted to run to him. He didn't land on his feet this time. Instead, his head smacked into a boulder.

Piper screamed. Dammit. She pulled on Nina harder. She needed to get to Tate.

"Where do you think you're going?" Sam's voice rang out. She kept her focus on Nina.

Big mistake.

"Watch out!" Nina yelled. Storm's face was the last thing she saw before a heavy mass slammed into her, and she blacked out.

HER EYES BLINKED OPEN. A SCREAM WOKE HER FROM A deep slumber. "What's going on?" Her head hurt like nobody's business.

She focused on the screams. "Piper, help!"

The demon dragged Nina away by her hair. Her small body kicked and scratched at him. The beast didn't even bat an eye in her direction. His movements were on autopilot, jerky and robotic.

"No! Let her go." She was too dizzy to stand or fight. Even her words sounded weak.

He laughed, turning back to her. "No, not happening, I need her. The demon is tired of doing the underworld's dirty work. So, I'm going to open hell, so demons can do their damn work."

This guy was crazy. Where were the rest of her men?

Her eyes darted around. Nausea made the room spin. No, no, no. She had to be hallucinating. Three large bodies lay on the floor, bloody and broken, their chests not moving. The two children next to her legs were forgotten at the sight of her mate's bodies. "Aaahh! No!" she cried out. Her heart exploded and fell to her feet. She didn't need that bitch anyways. The ache was unbearable.

She covered her face. *This can't be happening.*

"Yes, they're dead. I did you a favor. These wolves would have never chosen to stay with only one woman. I— Ow. You bitch." He punched Nina in the face and pulled his bloody finger out of her mouth.

She slumped on the ground, unconscious. Then, the tears that had threatened to spill out of her soul the past few days were let loose. Piper screamed.

The pounding from the pack on the outside of the barrier grew louder. There was nothing they could do now. Her mates were dead. Who cared if she died?

But Nina... Her wolf whimpered.

Fine, let's fight to get Nina out. But after, I'm done. I give up.

"Let my friend go. I'll take her place," her words were but a whisper, but the demon heard her just fine.

The thin, pale body shook. His narrowed face contorted in pain. Piper leaned away from him. Images of him exploding were halted as red glowing eyes met hers.

The human was no longer in control. Those eyes belonged to the demon. She gulped.

He tapped on his lips, thinking. "Humm. You caught me. With no training, only instincts. Not even your sister could do that. She had to make a deal with another demon to even get close to me. Interesting..." his words trailed off as if he spoke to himself, not her.

His red gaze snapped to hers. "Do you know how upsetting that was for me? My brother almost killed me over the deal. Which was stupid because I wasn't the demon that did the crimes she was investigating. I had to kill her to break the curse on me. I even had to kill my brother. He might have been stupid, but he was still blood. I'm not sure making a deal with you would be smart on my part. She was your twin after all."

Her growl rumbled the ground under her. "I don't believe you. She'd never work with a filthy demon."

The smirk on his ugly face twisted her insides. *No. There was no way. The demon is lying.*

"I know that look. You're trying to talk your way through my words. I promise you, all I said is the truth. I might be a demon, but my word is my bond."

"A bond of a demon isn't worth shit to me," Piper spat out. She shook her head, hoping to shake off the dizziness. She needed to think straight and be able to fight, dammit, but she wasn't healing.

He put up a finger and gave her a smirk. "On the contrary, if I break my word, I have to free all the souls that I've bargained for."

Piper's confusion wasn't easy to hide. She kept her mouth shut, but he gave her a slight bow and continued. "I'm a soul demon and an assassin by birth." He flicked his fingers as if flicking the word assassin away. "Any soul demon that breaks a deal or their word will lose power, status, and of course, all their souls."

The red haze blurred her vision. "Why the hell are you telling me this? So, you killed my men and decide you want to fucking chat? Screw you. Just kill me already, and let my friend go, stop gloating." Piper's words came out tough, but her heart ached for her men. They didn't deserve to die.

The ice that had been chipping away in her heart solidified again. She clung to her chest. The pain threatened to break her. She focused on her rage to keep from breaking.

The demon's Cheshire cat smile had her scooting away until her back pressed against the cold cave wall. The pain in her head stung with each move.

"Very well. I'll let you take her place. I'm tired of one of my jobs but can't resign. When you're born into a job, there is no quitting. That's where you come in. I tried it with this guy," he gestured to his body, "but he's cruel and disgusting. Might as well be a demon, and I need someone that is stealthier. Your skills with little training have me curious about what you could be. Bringing the demons here wouldn't be ideal for anybody. There are already tons of half-breeds and demons hiding from the *Light Soul* counsel causing issues." He used air quotes for the counsel's new titles. "Could you imagine what would happen if thousands were set loose at once? However, that was one of the pesky human's requests." He brushed his hands together. "Thankfully, the agreement was voided when a better alternative came up." He rubbed his hands together while his eyes drifted up and to the right.

What the hell was he thinking? She wanted to get this

over with. The pain in her chest threatened to overwhelm her. There would be no saving for Nina if she let fear and pain take over.

He leaned against the wall and crossed his left leg over his right as if chatting with an old friend. After a few seconds, his gaze met hers again. "I'll make you a deal. I'll bring back your mates if you become my assassin and assistant. Although, that means leaving all you love behind. I'll take you to the underworld to train for a few years. After that, you can come back to earth, but you'll always be my assassin and do the jobs I tell you to." His posh tone got on her nerves, but could he do that? Would her men come back?

No, we're not slaves. Don't do this. We can still take care of the pack.

I won't survive without them. Can't you feel it? I'm dying. My broken heart is poison.

Her wolf replied, but she ignored her. She didn't understand.

He laughed at whatever joke was going on in his head, "Both of the words have ass in them." His beady eyes ranked over Piper's body. The lust in them made her sick.

Bile rose in her throat. *Ew.*

She pushed the rest of her willpower to her voice and mind. She needed to think clearly for five minutes. Her wolf obliged, and waves of heat traveled to her mind, clearing the fog.

"I'll do it, but how I see it is that you need me. I want them all to come back, kids included, and be released. My friend included. You or anyone connected to you will never harm them or seek them out."

The demon growled. "Very well, except for the little

boy. He has been dead for too long. If I bring him back, he'll be a zombie."

Her jaw tightened. Poor boy. His parents were going to be wrecked.

She hit the wall to keep herself from crying. "Fine. But I kill only the guilty and no kids. Never someone I know, and no torture." She pursed her lips. "Oh, no sexual stuff either."

His fingers drummed on the table Nina was bound to earlier. "I'll give you everything except the last one. That'll be up for negotiation. With me anyways. But, I will promise to never force you. I'm nothing like this human I made a deal with." He ran his hands over his dirty clothes. "I'll make sure he has a special owner in the underworld. One that treats him the way he treated women."

Piper rolled her eyes. She didn't believe for one second that a demon cared. He was just acting, but it didn't matter, she had no choice. "Deal, I'll take all of them to the pack outside and—"

He cut her off. His nostrils flared in agitation. "We leave immediately. The men won't wake for a few hours, and we'll be nowhere near them when they wake up. So, hurry or I'll let them rot in this cave, alive of course. I am a man of my word after all."

She bit her lip and closed her eyes. She snapped out her response, "Fine." Dammit. She wanted to say goodbye and help them understand she wasn't abandoning them.

He walked to her and grasped her forearm. "The deal is binding."

Flames dug into her flesh. Her vision went white as agony took over her mind. Piper screamed, but no sound came out.

The pain didn't stop until the demon stepped away. She panted and whimpered. "What the fuck? I said no torturing." She watched as markings decorated her arm like a tattoo.

"First, I had to mark you. You wouldn't make it very long in the underworld without my mark. You'd be raped and tortured for sure. Second, that sealed the deal we made. And third, that wasn't torture. That was necessary pain. Torture is different for demons. You should have been more specific."

Piper narrowed her eyes at him but said nothing. The asshole demon. *Still worth it if he brings them back.*

The demon pranced to the dead, said a few words in a language she didn't understand, and a bright light snapped from his fingers to the men and little girl. When he was done, he pointed to the boy.

His eyes brightened, and he clapped his hands together like a crazy person. "Can I keep him? My uncle eats kids and—"

She snapped her response with force and determination. "No! He gets to go home and have a proper burial."

He sighed. "Very well. Hurry along. Take everyone to the dogs outside and come back. If you run, they all die. I'll make sure their souls end up in hell as well."

She nodded her head and somehow felt her heart was already dead inside. "I won't run."

Chapter Forty-Eight

He did it! He fucking did it! The heartbeats thumping all around her blurred her vision. Everyone except that little boy was breathing and alive. *Our mates. We can't leave them.*

We must. I already made the deal.

Can't we...

No. Piper squared her shoulders and pushed all her emotions down. They couldn't help her now.

Piper grabbed Tate first. Hopefully, seeing their Alpha unconscious would distract them long enough for her to get the others and slip away with the demon. *Fat chance.*

She grunted while attempting to lift him. *Geez, he weighs as much as a car.*

"We don't have all day... Here." The demon put his hand on her forehead as he did with the others. The words still sounded like nonsense to her ears. "Now, you have some of my strength and will heal faster. Get this over with."

She scowled at him but listened. Anything to get her

people to safety. She didn't want to risk him finding another loophole to hurt them again.

The second time she lifted Tate, he felt more like a heavy ass sack of potatoes than a car. *Cool.* She could get used to the strength.

As she got closer, the pack stopped banging on the barrier. Fuck. They were bloody from slamming their bodies against the wall to get in.

Liam stood in front of her as she walked out. "Tate will be fine. He'll need a couple of hours to rest, that's all," she said.

"What happened? Is the demon dead? Is Nina okay? We've been trying to break this fucking magic, but it didn't even budge a little."

The worry and torment on his face were replaced with hope. She handed over Tate. Two other wolves had to help him. That earned her more surprised glares.

She went back for her other two mates. Those were done in a blur. After asking hundreds of questions and not saying anything, the pack stopped asking and helped her as she brought out the people.

Storm felt like a few pillows in comparison to the other two. She went back in for the children, and her heart hurt for the boy she couldn't save.

Walking out of the cave this time, no one moved to help. They could smell the death. "I couldn't save the boy, but I wanted to make sure his body got back to his parents."

Tears flowed down her face freely. She didn't need to be strong right now. She needed to mourn a beautiful life snuffed out too soon. She wasn't going to make it to the funeral, so this was her send-off to him.

Liam was the only person to move. She handed him the girl first, who snored in his arms. She handed him the boy as well. "I'm so sorry."

She turned back to the dark cave. One more person and she'd be a slave for a demon. The demon that killed her sister.

Piper wiped her eyes. Nina didn't feel heavy in her arms anymore. To think, if she had this strength when the wolves attacked a few days ago, she'd have saved them from this fate.

She cradled her like a baby and brushed the hair out of her face. "I'm so sorry, I got you into this. The demon won't ever hurt you again. Please forgive me."

She kissed the top of Nina's head. Her steps were slower than before. She wasn't ready to leave. But Nina's breathing and alive solidified her resolve. She'd gladly sacrifice herself for these people to live.

Who knows, maybe I'll kill the demon and come back to you guys. She smiled. That seemed unlikely, but she'd use that as her focus to keep going. And she'd never stop trying.

"Nina! Tell me she's okay, Piper," Liam wailed across the barrier. She gave him a nod but couldn't speak.

This time only half her body went across the magic. She gave Liam Nina and stepped back behind the barrier.

As if Nina could sense what was about to happen, she woke up. She screamed and fought until her eyes locked on Piper's. Her screams turned to sobs.

Piper stepped into the shadows. If they focused on Nina, she wouldn't have to explain anything. Her mates and friend didn't need to hold the guilt she knew they'd have.

"Where's Piper? Piper, no!" Nina cried out. The waves

of sorrow were like a tsunami against her skin. It hurt and killed her instantly.

Well, so much for a quiet getaway. She wasn't completely out of sight yet. She knew she should ignore her, but she couldn't.

Damn, my heart.

Nina smacked into the barrier. "I heard you, Piper. I know what you did. Please don't. Please don't leave me. Not like this." The tears soaking her face matched Piper's.

So much for not letting them know she sacrificed herself for them. The clever little minx.

Liam's eyes darted between them. "What's going on? Piper, why are you still in the cave? We need to get out of here."

Nina slammed into the barrier again. Her small body barely had any impact on the magic. "She made a deal with the demon. Her mates were dead. Shit, everyone was dead. The demon had me, and she was too hurt to fight. He brought them back and released all of us because Piper gave herself to him. You bitch."

She continued to throw herself at the magical wall. "I won't let you do this, Piper. You hear me? Get your ass over here right now."

"It's already done, Toots," Piper's voice broke. Dammit, she wanted to be strong for them. "I have to go now."

Liam and other shifters joined Nina and threw their bodies at the magical wall. "Please don't. Your mates can't live without you. This pack needs you."

"Piper, I swear I'll drag your ass out of hell. Don't go, please. Don't leave me. Not like this, not like this," Nina cried out, but Piper shut her friend out. She had to.

Everyone was safe that's all that mattered. It was time to go. She was being selfish by standing here.

The demon stood behind Piper and slipped his hand around her neck as if he owned her. "On the contrary, my deal with Piper means the men can live and even take a new mate after some time. Mate bonds aren't easy to break, but they did not consummate the bond, so no worries, dog boy. She made sure you and the world are safe. Now come, I've grown bored of this world."

Nina's knees collapsed. "Take me instead. I—"

The demon stopped Nina from continuing, "I don't want you. I want her. You are all safe and alive because of her. Don't try to find her or me. That'll be foolish and will end in your deaths. Come now, my queen, it's time for us to go home." He stepped away from her. His hand did a little dance, and everything went silent.

Piper's gaze drifted to her pack. Their mouths moved, but no sound came out. The demon sighed. "Don't worry, as soon as we're gone, their voices will come back. There are only so many pleas I can take before the soul demon part of me gets greedy. This way, I won't break our deal. Come."

Piper stepped into his open arms. He turned her around. Her pack still fought with all they had to break the magical wall.

She turned away, but a strong masculine figure stopped her. "No," she whispered.

Our mate is strong. Go to him. He can protect us from the demon. Her wolf pleaded, but Piper knew better. Going to him would mean his and the others' deaths. She couldn't handle that.

Tate stood naked, a few feet away from the barrier. He

screamed. The sound he made would forever haunt her dreams. He ran to her. The anger and pleading in his eyes hurt her soul. *Fuck.* "Fight him, Piper. Fight. Don't leave me."

She had no idea how to explain or what to say. What could she say? She leaned forward away from the demon. She was okay with her choice, and she had to let him know that at least. "It's okay, Tate. This wasn't your fault. Be free and move on." She smiled and blew him a kiss.

He crossed the wall of magic just as easily as last time, but her body was already fading into the black smoke the demon produced. It was too late for her. She saved them. That's all that mattered.

Before Tate could reach her, she disappeared. Her old life was gone. Nothing left but darkness and a demon at her back.

Chapter Forty-Nine

*S*hitballs-on-dry-toast, did I just make a deal with a demon? Leaving her mates and soul-sister was the hardest thing she had ever done, but they were alive. That's what mattered.

The demon left the human he possessed behind. The man that stood in front of Piper wasn't a scrawny nobody like the human.

His skin was tan and flawless. His eyes were the color of bright clouds with a dark blue outer edge. Scientists would probably do studies on his eyes.

His body was the perfect swimmer's body as if he swam against the Mississippi River twenty-four seven. Not bulky, but dangerously toned.

Every inch of his bare body was a pain in her eyes. Why was evil so attractive? The stupid demon had to appear naked for their first day in hell. *I wonder if I can castrate him?*

Her wolf snickered. *We can try. I don't like it down here... I can't breathe.* Her wolf sounded weak. She didn't like it.

He moved when her eyes did. He was determined for her to keep looking at him. She fought her instinct to glance below the belt line and scowled at him. He wouldn't rattle her.

Besides the two horns on his head, he was practically human and resembled a model. She wondered if he was a fallen angel. *I guess the saying 'sexy as sin' is a real thing.*

She amped up her anger when he began posing. She had her men, and he wasn't one of them.

"Welcome to my home." He purred and flexed his arms, moving his pecks. "Care to negotiate about the not having sex rule yet?" His knowing smirk had her fist balling.

Her fist connected with his hard-ass face the next instant. Pain shot up her arm. *Ow!*

He stepped back, holding his cheek and chuckling. "You do know that's like foreplay for demons, right? For future reference, if the answer is no, cower a little and maybe even say 'please no,' that is an extreme turn-off." He shivered in disgust. "You have no idea how difficult it was in that human's body. It wasn't even worth his soul."

He pulled his hand away from his cheek to check for blood before continuing, "But there aren't many evil bastards traveling these days. They have the internet." His face scrunched up. "Pitiful."

"Whatever, the sex thing is still a no," Piper snapped back. The pain in her hand kept her from saying more. His face was hard as... hell. That was a horrible saying now.

He nodded. "Very well." He turned and walked towards what she assumed was the kitchen. It had a fire and a pot over the flames, a few storage cabinets, and a place to get water, like a medieval fountain.

A glowing ball appeared in his palm. "Put this away," he said to the wall and the light disappeared in it. What the?

She ignored that and glanced around. Was this a house? The furniture was familiar. A gray couch, a blue blanket, a few black bookshelves, and black tables were the only thing she recognized. Instead of carpet, a squishy moss lit up under their feet.

There were no walls, just shimmery blocks that prevented access. The demon touched it, and it turned into a lit turquoise solidification. She touched the soft surface but couldn't push through.

"There are a few rules. The house will not let anyone in or out without my acceptance. She is very sensitive, so play nice—"

Her teeth clenched as she grabbed the blanket off the couch. She was done being naked in front of the demon. "What do you mean she?"

"The house. It's different than in the human world. She's alive. If you need food or anything, let her know. If you anger her, she'll make your life horrible. Please learn to respect her. I don't care about many things, but she and my gargoyle are the exceptions."

She gulped. The house was alive. What? She couldn't even comprehend that right now. "Gargoyle?" was the only thing that would come out.

His eyes met hers. "Yes, he's very protective and likes to bite, so I recommend staying away from him."

She nodded. "Kay."

Was this her life now? Trapped in hell with a naked demon, his alive house, and crazy bite-happy gargoyle? And she thought she was crazy before because she had a voice in her head. Now, maybe, she was crazy.

Piper squared her shoulders and took a deep breath. Yeah, she was in the underworld. But that wasn't going to stop her. She was going to survive and figure out how to kill the fucking demon. For her sister, for her mates, and for herself.

After all, the agreement said nothing about her not killing him.

I Hope You Enjoyed Reading The Wolf Oath

Leave me a review on Amazon to help out future readers and the author. You have no idea how much every review helps.

If you want to continue diving into The Wolf Oath World, read on with <u>The Demon Oath in Hell.</u>

Acknowledgments

I can't believe it. I'm beginning a whole new world, and I'm so freakin excited. This book series is going to be the tits. I hope everyone loves them some werewolves.

I want to thank all my beta readers: Mary, Chris, Sceenic, Jfel30, and all the rest. Also to my friends, and family that supported me. You all helped make The Wolf Oath possible.

A special thanks to my editors for helping me on this bumpy journey, Isabel Barbi and Erin Bledsoe. With your help, I had the courage to finish and publish my book baby.

You are all awesome, thank you so much. I couldn't have done it without all of you. This world is just beginning, and I hope all of you enjoy the brain candy I provided.

Thank you!

About the Author

In addition to her writing career, Tosha Y. Miller is a behavioral technician. Helping people enjoy their lives is important to Tosha. She enjoys every minute of communicating with her readers and working with her clients. They are what makes her world go around.

She's pretty sure all her clients are of the human variety. Or at least, she thinks they are. But anything is possible.

To learn more or talk to the author, visit her website. www.toshaymiller.com

Also, visit her on any other social media, including her YouTube Channel, Twitter, Instagram, Tiktok, and Facebook.

Just search for Tosha Y. Miller and she'll be there.

Praise for Tosha Y. Miller

Tosha Y. Miller has truly exceptional taste in fantasy worlds.

— THAT GUY WHO'S ALWAYS AT
STARBUCKS

A voice for a new generation.

— LONGTIME READER

Once every so often the world hears a new voice. Tosha Y. Miller is the person to whom that voice belongs.

— VELLUM REVIEWER